P9-DNE-384

DAVID WEBER
HEIRS OF EMPIRE

BAEN

HEIRS OF EMPIRE

Copyright © 1996 by David M. Weber

A Baen Books Original

Baen Publishing Enterprises
P.O. Box 1403
Riverdale, NY 10471

ISBN: 0-671-87707-0

Cover art by David Mattingly

First printing, March 1996

Distributed by Simon & Schuster
1230 Avenue of the Americas
New York, NY 10020

Typeset by Windhaven Press, Auburn, NH
Printed in the United States of America

Slower Than a Speeding Bullet

Harriet was less than a kilometer from the cutter when her eyes widened and she slithered to a halt in the darkness.

Her head whipped around and she went active with every implant, probing the night. People! At least a *dozen* of them! Her implants should have picked them up sooner, and she cursed herself for not paying more attention to her surroundings and less to the pleasure of running. But even as she raged at her foolishness her mind whirred with questions. She hadn't looked for them, but, damn it, what were they *doing* out here in the middle of the night without even a torch?

Questions could wait. She turned back the way she'd come, but a voice shouted, loud and harsh with command. Crap! She'd been seen!

She abandoned her attempt to sneak away for a blinding pace no unenhanced human could have matched, and her thoughts flashed. They'd agreed not to use their coms in case they were picked up, but if there were people *here*, there might be more of them. The others had to be warned, and—

Light glared and thunder barked behind her. Something whizzed past her ear, and something else slammed into her left shoulder blade. She staggered and snatched for her grav gun, spun to the side by the brutal impact, and the beginning of pain exploded up her nerves. A second fiery hammer hit her in the side, throwing the grav gun from her hand, but before it really registered there was another flash, and a sixty-gram lead ball smashed her right temple.

BAEN BOOKS by DAVID WEBER

Mutineers' Moon
The Armageddon Inheritance
Heirs of Empire

Honor Harrington:
On Basilisk Station
The Honor of the Queen
The Short Victorious War
Field of Dishonor
Flag in Exile
Honor Among Enemies (*forthcoming*)

Path of the Fury
Oath of Swords

with Steve White:
Insurrection
Crusade

To Jane's Friends

COLIN I—Also styled "the Great" and "the Rebuilder." Born Colin Francis MacIntyre (q.v.) April 21, 2004 (old-style), Colorado, U.S.A., Earth; Lieutenant Commander, USN; NASA astronaut; founder MacIntyre Dynasty; crowned July 7, Year One of the Fifth Imperium.

This Emperor's ascension to the Throne ended the Interregnum resulting from accidental release of the Umak Weapon (q.v., see also Umak, Director Imperial Bio-Research), thus initiating the Fifth Imperium. As Warlord, he utilized the reactivated Imperial Guard Flotilla to crush the first Achuultani Incursion (see Aku'Ultan, Nest of; and Zeta Trianguli Campaign) ever defeated.

Following repulse of the Achuultani, His Majesty began the task of civil reconstruction and the military buildup to accomplish the ultimate defeat of the Achuultani. As Emperor of the Fifth Imperium, he and his consort, Empress Jiltanith (q.v.), set about their task, unaware that . . .

—*Encyclopedia Galactica*, Vol. 6,
12th edition, University of Birhat Press, 598 YFI.

Heirs of Empire

NORTH HYLAR

Valley of the Damned

Cragsend

Shalakar Mtns.

Israel landing site

Cherist Mtns.

Thirgan Gap

Keldark Valley

Malgos

Camathan

Cherist

Thirgan

Malagor

Keldark

Showmah

Kyhra

Vral

Santu

Walak

Tormahk

Doras

Sardua

Old Aris
The Temple

Eswyn

Mahska

Telis

Tarnahk

Manikor

Alwa

Seliwyn

Morkahn

Salith

Tesnia

Sorfah

New
Aris

Sehwan

Seku

Chelis

Darvan

Arwah

Asfar

Qwelth

Qwelth Gap

Selthis

Boram

Segwyn

Anorahk

Manak

SOUTH HYLAR

Talth

Vorwal

Tresha

Artan

Sanaka

N

800 km

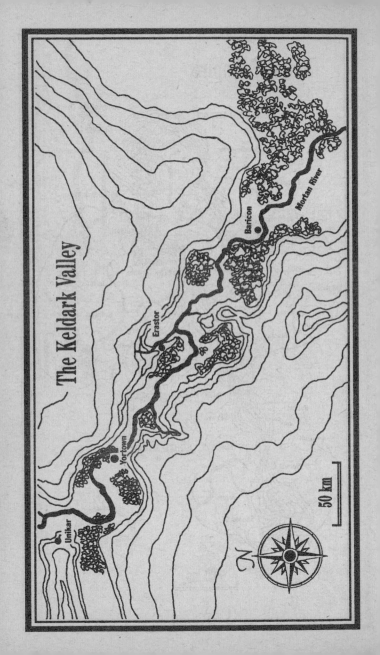

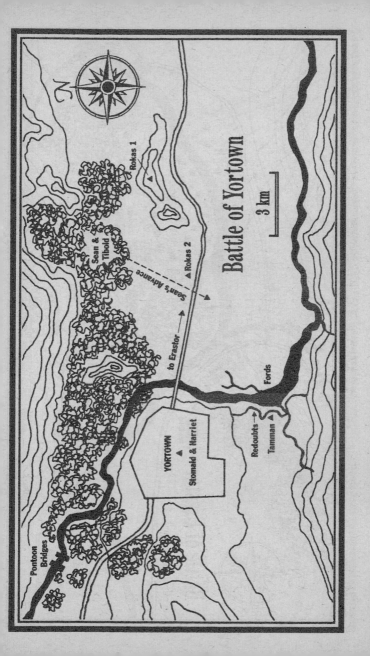

Battle of Yortown

3 km

Rokas 1

Sean & Tibold

Rokas 2

Sean's Advance

to Erastor

Pontoon Bridges

YORTOWN

Stomald & Harriet

Fords

Redoubts

Tamman

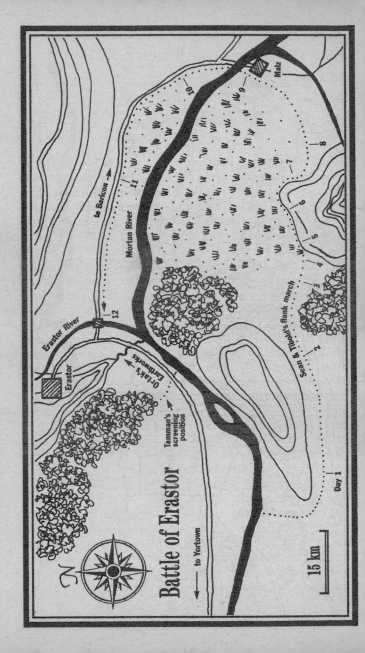

Chapter One

Sean MacIntyre skittered out of the transit shaft and adjusted his hearing as he dashed down the passage. He shouldn't need to listen until he was on the other side of the hatch, but he still had more trouble with his ears' bio-enhancement than with his eyes for some reason, and he preferred to get set early.

He covered the last hundred meters, slid to a halt, and pressed his back against the bulkhead. The wide, silent passage vanished into a gleaming dot in either direction, and he raked a hand through sweaty black hair as his enhanced ears picked the pulsing sounds of environmental equipment and the soft hum of the now-distant transit shaft from the slowing thunder of his pulse. He'd been chasing them for over an hour, and he'd half-expected to be ambushed by now. *He* certainly would have tried it, he thought, and sniffed disdainfully.

He drew his holstered pistol and turned to the hatch. It slid open—quietly to unenhanced ears, but thunderous to his—and bright sunlight spilled out.

He slipped through the hatch and selected telescopic vision for his left eye. He kept his right adjusted to normal ranges (he did lots better with his eyes than with his ears) and peered into the dappled shadows of the whispering leaves.

Oaks and hickories drowsed under the "sun" as he slithered across the picnic area into the gloss-green rhododendrons that ran down to the lake. He moved quietly, holding the pistol against his chest two-handed, ready to whirl, point, and fire with all the snakelike quickness of his enhanced reflexes, but search as he might, he heard

1

and saw nothing except wind, birds, and the slop of small waves.

He worked his way clear to the lake without finding a target, then paused in thought. The park deck, one of many aboard the starship *Dahak*, was twenty-odd kilometers across. That was a big hiding place, but Harriet was impatient, and she hated running away. She'd be lurking somewhere within a few hundred meters, hoping to ambush him, and that meant—

Motion flickered, and he froze, vision zooming in on whatever had attracted it. He smiled as he saw a flash of long, black hair duck back behind an oak, but he didn't scoot out after her. Now that he'd found Harry, there was no way she could sneak away from her tree without his seeing her, and he swept his eyes back and forth, searching for her ally. She'd be part of the ambush, too, so she had to be pretty close. In fact, she should be . . .

A hand-sized patch of blue caught his eye, just visible between two laurels. Unlike Harry, it was patiently and absolutely still, but he had them both now, and he grinned and began a slow, stealthy move to his left. A few more meters and—

Zaaaaaaaaaaa-*ting!*

Sean jerked in disbelief, then punched the ground, and used a word his mother would not have approved. The chime gave way to a raucous buzzing that ripped at his augmented hearing, and he snatched his ears back to normal and stood resignedly.

The buzz from the laser-sensing units on his harness stopped at his admission of defeat, and he turned, wondering how Harry had slipped around behind him. But it wasn't Harry, and he ground his teeth as a diminutive figure splashed ashore. She'd shed her bright blue jacket (Sean knew exactly where), and she was soaking wet, but her brown eyes blazed with delight.

"I *got* you!" she shrieked. "Sean's dead! Sean's dead, Harry!"

He managed not to use any more of his forbidden vocabulary when the eight-year-old ninja began an impromptu war dance, but it was hard, especially when his twin threw herself into the dance with her half-pint ally. Bad enough to lose to *girls*, but to be ambushed by Sandy MacMahan was insupportable. She was two years younger than he, this was the first time she'd even been allowed to play, and she'd killed him with her first shot!

"Your elation at Sean's death is scarcely becoming, Sandra." The deep, mellow voice coming from empty air surprised none of them. They'd known Dahak all their lives, and the self-aware computer's starship body was one of their favorite playgrounds.

"Who cares?" Sandy demanded gleefully. "I got him! *Zap!*" She pointed her pistol at Sean and collapsed with a wail of laughter at his expression.

"Luck!" he shot back, holstering his own pistol with dignity he knew was threadbare. "You were just lucky, Sandy!"

"That is incorrect, Sean," Dahak observed with the dispassionate fairness Sean hated when it was on someone else's side. " 'Luck' implies the fortuitous working of chance, and Sandra's decision to conceal herself in the lake—which, I observed, you did not check once—was an ingenious maneuver. And as she has cogently if unkindly observed, she 'got' you."

"So there!" Sandy stuck out her tongue, and Sean turned away with an injured air. It didn't get any better when Harriet grinned at him.

"I told you Sandy was old enough, didn't I?" she demanded.

He longed to disagree—violently—but he was an honest boy, and so he nodded begrudgingly, and tried to hide his shudder as a vision of the future unrolled before him. Sandy was Harry's best friend, despite her youth, and now the little creep was going to be underfoot *everywhere*. He'd managed to fend that off for over a year by claiming she was too little. Until today. She was already two course units ahead of him in calculus, and now this!

The universe, Sean Horus MacIntyre concluded grumpily, wasn't exactly running over with justice.

✧   ✧   ✧

Amanda Tsien and her husband stepped out of the transit shaft outside *Dahak*'s command deck. Her son, Tamman, followed them down the passage, but he was almost squirming in impatience, and Amanda glanced up at her towering husband with a twinkle. Most described Tsien Tao-ling's face as grim, but a smile flickered as he watched Tamman. The boy might not be "his" in any biological sense, yet that didn't mean he wasn't Tamman's father, and he nodded when Amanda quirked an eyebrow.

"All right, Tamman," she said. "You can go."

"Thanks, Mom!" He turned in his tracks with the curiously catlike awkwardness of his age and dashed back towards the transit shaft. "Where's Sean, Dahak?" he demanded as he ran.

"He is on Park Deck Nine, Tamman," a mellow voice responded.

"Thanks! See you later, Mom, Dad!" Tamman ran sideways for a moment to wave, then dove into the shaft with a whoop.

"You'd think they hadn't seen each other in months," Amanda sighed.

"I do not believe children live on the same time scale as adults," Tsien observed in his deep, soft voice as she tucked a hand through his elbow.

"You can say that again!"

They turned the final bend to confront the command deck hatch. *Dahak*'s crest coiled across the bronze-gold battle steel: a three-headed dragon, poised for flight, clawed forefeet raised to cradle the emblem of the Fifth Imperium. The crowned starburst of the Fourth Empire had been retained, but now a Phoenix of rebirth erupted from the starburst, and the diadem of empire rested on its crested head. The twenty-centimeter-thick hatch—the first of many, each fit to withstand a kiloton-range warhead—slid soundlessly open.

"Hello, Dahak," Amanda said as they walked forward and other hatches parted before them.

"Good evening, Amanda. Welcome aboard, Star Marshal."

"Thank you," Tsien replied. "Have the others arrived?"

"Admiral Hatcher is en route, but the MacMahans and Duke Horus have already joined Their Majesties."

"One day Gerald must learn there are only twenty-eight hours even in Birhat's day," Tsien sighed.

"Oh, really?" Amanda glanced up at him again. "I suppose *you*'ve already learned that?"

"Perhaps not," he agreed with another small smile, and she snorted as a final hatch admitted them to the dim vastness of *Dahak*'s Command One.

A sphere of stars engulfed them. The diamond-hard pinheads burned in the ebon depths of space, dominated by the cloud-banded green-and-blue sphere of the planet Birhat, and Amanda shivered. Not from cold, but with the icy breeze that always seemed to whisper down her spine whenever she stepped into the perfection of the holographic display.

"Hi, Amanda. Tao-ling." His Imperial Majesty Colin I, Grand Duke of Birhat, Prince of Bia, Sol, Chamhar, and Narhan, Warlord and Prince Protector of the Realm, Defender of the Five Thousand Suns, Champion of Humanity, and, by the Maker's Grace, Emperor of Mankind, swiveled his couch to show them his homely, beak-nosed face and grinned. "I see Tamman peeled off early."

"When last seen, he was headed for the park deck," Tsien agreed.

"Well, he's in for a surprise." Colin chuckled. "Harry and Dahak finally bullied Sean into letting Sandy try her hand at laser tag."

"Oh, my!" Amanda laughed. "I'll bet that was an experience!"

"Aye." Empress Jiltanith, slender as a sword and as beautiful as Colin was homely, rose to embrace Amanda. "Belike he'll crow less loud anent her youth henceforth. His pride hath been humbled—for the nonce, at least."

"He'll get over it," Hector MacMahan remarked. The Imperial Marine Corps' commandant leaned on the gunnery officer's console while his wife occupied the couch before it. Like Amanda, he wore Marine black and silver, but Ninhursag MacMahan wore Battle Fleet's midnight-blue and gold, and she smiled.

"Not if Sandy has anything to say about it. One of these days that girl's going to make an excellent spook."

"You should know," Colin said, and Ninhursag managed a seated bow in his direction. "In the meantime, I—"

"Excuse me, Colin," Dahak murmured, "but Admiral Hatcher's cutter has docked."

"Good. Looks like we can get this show on the road pretty soon."

"I hope so," Horus said. The stocky, white-haired Planetary Duke of Terra shook his head. "Every time I poke my nose out of my office, something's waiting to crawl out of the 'in' basket and bite me when I get back!"

Colin nodded at his father-in-law in agreement, but he was watching the Tsiens. Tao-ling seated Amanda with an attentiveness so focused it was almost unconscious . . . and one that might seem odd to those who knew only Star Marshal Tsien's reputation or knew General Amanda Tsien only as the tough-as-nails commandant of Fort Hawter, the Imperial Marines' advanced training base on Birhat. Colin, on the other hand, understood it perfectly, and he was profoundly grateful to see it.

Amanda Tsien feared nothing that lived, but she was also an orphan. She'd been only nine years old when she learned a harsh universe's cruelest weapon could be love . . . and she'd relearned that lesson when Tamman, her first husband, died at Zeta Trianguli Australis. Colin and Jiltanith had watched helplessly as she hid herself in her duties, sealing herself into an armored shell and investing all the emotion she dared risk in Tamman's son. She'd become an automaton, and there'd been nothing even an emperor could do about it, but Tsien Tao-ling had changed that.

Many of the marshal's personnel feared him. That was wise of them, yet something in Amanda had called out to him, despite her defenses, and the man the newsies called "the Juggernaut" had approached her so gently she hadn't even realized he was doing it until it was too late. Until he'd been inside her armor, holding out his hand to offer her the heart few people believed he had . . . and she'd taken it.

She was thirty years younger than he, which mattered not at all among the bio-enhanced. After all, Colin was over forty years younger than Jiltanith, and she looked younger than he. Of course, chronologically she was well over fifty-one thousand years old, but that didn't count; she'd spent all but eighty-odd of those years in stasis.

"How're Hsu-li and Collete?" he asked Amanda, and she chuckled.

"Fine. Hsu-li was a bit ticked we didn't bring him along, but I convinced him he should stay to help take care of his sister."

Colin shook his head. "That wouldn't have worked with Sean and Harry."

"That's what you get for having twins," Amanda said smugly, then bent a sly glance on Jiltanith. "Or for not having a few more kids."

"Nay, acquit me, Amanda." Jiltanith smiled. "I know not how thou findest time for all thy duties and thy babes, but 'twill be some years more—mayhap decades— ere *I* again essay that challenge. And it ill beseemeth thee so to twit thine Empress when all the world doth know thee for a mother o' the best, while I—" She shrugged wryly, and her friends laughed.

Horus was about to say something more when the inner hatch slid open to admit a trim, athletic man in Battle Fleet blue.

"Hi, Gerald," Colin greeted the new arrival, and Admiral of the Fleet Gerald Hatcher, Chief of Naval Operations, bowed with a flourish.

"Good evening, Your Majesty," he said so unctuously his liege lord shook a fist at him. Admiral Hatcher had spent thirty years as a soldier of the United States, not a sailor, but BattleFleet's CNO was the Imperium's senior officer. That made it a logical duty for the man who'd served as humanity's chief of staff during Earth's defense against the Achuultani, yet not even that authority could quash Hatcher's cheerful irreverence.

He waved to Ninhursag, shook hands with Hector, Tsien, and Horus, then planted an enthusiastic kiss on Amanda's cafe-au-lait cheek. He bent gracefully over Jiltanith's hand, but the Empress tugged shrewdly on the neat beard he'd grown since the Siege of Earth and kissed his mouth before he could recover.

"Thou'rt a shameless fellow, Gerald Hatcher," she told him severely, "and mayhap that shall teach thee what fate awaiteth when thou leavest thy wife behind!"

"Oh?" He grinned. "Is that a threat or a promise, Your Majesty?"

"Off with his head!" Colin murmured, and the admiral laughed.

"Actually, she's visiting her sister on Earth. They're picking out baby clothes."

"My God, is *everybody* hatching new youngsters?"

"Nay, my Colin, 'tis only everyone *else*," Jiltanith said.

"True," Hatcher agreed. "And this time it's going to be a boy. I'm perfectly happy with the girls, myself, but Sharon's delighted."

"Congratulations," Colin told him, then waved at an empty couch. "But now that you're here, let's get down to business."

"Suits me. I've got a conference scheduled aboard Mother in a few hours, and I'd like to grab a nap first."

"Okay." Colin sat a bit straighter and his lazy amusement faded. "As I indicated when I invited you all, I want to talk to you informally before next week's Council meeting. We're coming up on the tenth anniversary of my 'coronation,' and the Assembly of Nobles wants to throw a big shindig to celebrate. That may be a good idea, but it means this year's State of the Realm speech is going to be pretty important, so I want a feel from the 'inner circle' before I get started writing it."

His guests hid smiles. The Fourth Empire had never

required regular formal reports from its emperors, but Colin had incorporated the State of the Realm message into the Fifth Imperium's law, and the self-inflicted annual duty was an ordeal he dreaded. It was also why he'd invited his friends to *Dahak*'s command deck. Unlike too many others, they could be relied upon to tell him what they thought rather than what they thought he wanted them to think.

"Let's begin with you, Gerald."

"Okay." Hatcher rubbed his beard gently. "You can start off with a piece of good news. Geb dropped off his last report just before he and Vlad headed out to Cheshir, and they should have the Cheshir Fleet base back on-line within three months. They've turned up nine more *Asgerds*, too. They'll need a few more months to reactivate them, and we're stretched for personnel—as usual—but we'll make do, and that'll bring us up to a hundred and twelve planetoids." He paused. "Unless we have another *Sherkan*."

Colin frowned at his suddenly bitter tone but let it pass. All the diagnostics had said the planetoid *Sherkan* was safe to operate without extensive overhaul—but it had been Hatcher's expedition that found her, and he'd been the one who'd had to tell Vladimir Chernikov.

So far, Survey Command had discovered exactly two once-populated planets of the Fourth Empire which retained any life at all—Birhat, the old imperial capital, and Chamhar—and no humans had survived on either. But much of the Empire's military hardware *had* survived, including many of its vast fleet of enormous starships, and they needed all of those they could get. Humanity had stopped the Achuultani's last incursion— barely—but defeating them on their own ground was going to be something else again.

Unfortunately, restoring a derelict four thousand kilometers in diameter to service after forty-five millennia was a daunting task, which was why Hatcher had been so pleased by *Sherkan*'s excellent condition. But the tests had missed a tiny flaw in her core tap, and its governors had blown the instant her engineer brought it on-line to suck in the energy for supralight movement. The resultant explosion could have destroyed a continent, and six thousand human beings had died in it, including Fleet Admiral Vassily Chernikov and his wife, Valentina.

"Anyway," Hatcher went on more briskly, "we're coming along nicely on the other projects, as well. Adrienne will graduate her first Academy class in a few months, and I'm entirely satisfied with the results, but she and Tao-ling are still fiddling with fine-tuning the curriculum.

"On the hardware side, things are looking good here in Bia, thanks to Tao-ling. He had to put virtually all the surviving yard facilities back on-line to get the shield operational—" Hatcher and the star marshal exchanged wry smiles at that; reactivating the enormous shield generators which surrounded Birhat's primary, Bia, in an inviolate sphere eighty light-minutes across had been a horrendous task "—so we've got plenty of overhaul capacity. In fact, we're ready to start design work on our new construction."

"Really?" Colin's tone was pleased.

"Indeed," Dahak answered for the admiral. "It will be approximately three-point-five standard years—" (the Fifth Imperium ran on Terran time, not Birhatan) "—before capacity for actual construction can be diverted from reactivation programs, but Admiral Baltan and I have begun preliminary studies on the new designs. We are combining several concepts 'borrowed' from the Achuultani with others from the Empire's Bureau of Ships, and I believe we will attain substantial increases in the capabilities of our new units."

"That's good news, but where does it leave us on Stepmother?"

"I fear that will require considerably longer, Colin," Dahak replied.

"'Considerably' is probably optimistic," Hatcher sighed. "We're still stubbing our toes on the finer points of Empire computer hardware, even with Dahak's help, and

Mother's the most complex computer the Empire ever built. Duplicating her's going to be a bitch—not to mention the time requirement to build a five-thousand-kilometer hull to put said duplicate inside!"

Colin didn't like that, but he understood. The Empire had built Mother (officially known as Fleet Central Computer Central) using force-field circuitry that made even molycircs look big and clumsy, yet the computer was still over three hundred kilometers in diameter. It was also housed in the most powerful fortress ever constructed by Man, for it did more than simply run Battle Fleet. Mother was the conservator of the Empire, as well—indeed, it was she who'd crowned Colin and provided the ships to smash the Achuultani. Unfortunately (or, perhaps, fortunately) she was carefully designed, as all late-Empire computers, to preclude self-awareness, which meant she would disgorge her unimaginable treasure trove of data only when tickled with the right specific question.

But Colin spent a lot of time worrying over what might happen to Battle Fleet if something happened to Mother, and he intended to provide Earth with defenses every bit as powerful as Birhat's . . . including a duplicate of Mother. If everything went well, Stepmother (as Hatcher had insisted on christening the proposed installation) would never come fully on-line, but if Mother was destroyed, Stepmother would take over automatically, providing unbroken command and control for Battle Fleet and the Imperium.

"What kind of time estimate do you have?"

"Speaking very, very roughly, and assuming we get a firm grip on the computer technology so we don't have to keep pestering Dahak with questions, we may be able to start on the hull in six years or so. Once we get that far, we can probably finish the job up in another five."

"Damn. Oh, well. We won't be hearing from the Achuultani for another four or five centuries, minimum, but I want that project completed ASAP, Ger."

"Understood," Hatcher said. "In the meantime, though,

we ought to be able to put the first new planetoids on-line considerably sooner. Their computers're a lot smaller and simpler-minded, without any of Mother's wonder-what-the-hell's-in-'em files, and the other hardware's no big problem, even allowing for the new systems' test programs."

"Okay." Colin turned to Tsien. "Want to add anything, Tao-ling?"

"I fear Gerald has stolen much of my thunder," Tsien began, and Hatcher grinned. Technically, everything that wasn't mobile belonged to Tsien—from fortifications and shipyards to R&D to Fleet training—but with so much priority assigned to rounding up and crewing Hatcher's planetoids there was a lot of overlap in their current spheres of authority.

"As he and Dahak have related, most of the Bia System has now been fully restored to function. With barely four hundred million people in the system, our personnel are spread even more thinly than Gerald's, but we are coping and the situation is improving. Baltan and Geran, with much assistance from Dahak, are doing excellent work with Research and Development, although 'research' will continue, for the foreseeable future, to be little more than following up on the Empire's final projects. They are, however, turning up several interesting new items among those projects. In particular, the Empire had begun development of a new generation of gravitonic warheads."

"Oh?" Colin quirked an eyebrow. "This is the first I've heard of it."

"Me, too," Hatcher put in. "What kind of warheads, Tao-ling?"

"We only discovered the data two days ago," Tsien half-apologized, "but what we have seen so far suggests a weapon several magnitudes more powerful than any previously built."

"Maker!" Horus straightened in his own couch, eyes half-fascinated and half-appalled. Fifty-one thousand years ago, he'd been a missile specialist of the Fourth

Imperium, and the fearsome efficiency of the weapons the Empire had produced had shaken him badly when he first confronted them.

"Indeed," Tsien said dryly. "I am not yet certain, but I suspect this warhead might be able to duplicate your feat at Zeta Trianguli, Colin."

Several people swallowed audibly at that, including Colin. He'd used the FTL Enchanach drive, which employed massive gravity fields—essentially converging black holes—to literally squeeze a ship out of "real" space in a series of instantaneous transitions, as a weapon at the Second Battle of Zeta Trianguli Australis. An Enchanach ship's dwell time in normal space was very, very brief, and even when it came "close" (in interstellar terms), a ship moving at roughly nine hundred times light-speed didn't spend long enough in the vicinity of any star to do it harm. But the drive's initial activation and final deactivation took a considerably longer time, and Colin had used that to induce a nova which destroyed over a million Achuultani starships.

Yet he'd needed a half-dozen *planetoids* to do the trick, and the thought of reproducing it with a single warhead was terrifying.

"Are you serious?" he demanded.

"I am. The warhead's total power is far lower than the aggregate you produced, but it is also much more focused. Our most conservative estimate indicates a weapon which would be capable of destroying any planet and everything within three or four hundred thousand kilometers of it."

"Jesu!" Jiltanith's voice was soft, and she squeezed the hilt of her fifteenth-century dagger. "Such power misliketh me, Colin. 'Twould be most terrible if such a weapon should by mischance smite one of our own worlds!"

"You got that right," Colin muttered with a shudder. He still had nightmares over Zeta Trianguli, and if the accidental detonation of a gravitonic warhead was virtually impossible, the Empire had thought the same thing about the accidental release of its bio-weapons.

"Hold off on building the thing, Tao-ling," he said. "Do whatever you want with the research—hell, we may *need* it against the Achuultani master computer!—but don't produce any hardware without checking with me."

"Of course, Your Majesty."

"Any other surprises for us?"

"Not of such magnitude. Dahak and I will prepare a full report for you by the end of the week, if you wish."

"I wish." Colin turned his eyes to Hector MacMahan. "Any problems with the Corps, Hector?"

"Very few. We're making out better than Gerald in terms of manpower, but then, our target force level's lower. Some of our senior officers are having trouble adjusting to the capabilities of Imperial equipment—most of them are still drawn from the pre-Siege militaries—and we've had a few training snafus as a result. Amanda's correcting most of that at Fort Hawter, and the new generation coming up doesn't have anything to unlearn in the first place. I don't see anything worth worrying about."

"Fine," Colin said. If Hector MacMahan didn't see anything worth worrying about, then there *was* nothing, and he turned his attention to Horus. "How're we doing on Earth, Horus?"

"I wish I could tell you the situation's altered, Colin, but it hasn't. You can't make these kinds of changes without a lot of disruption. Conversion to the new currency's gone more smoothly than we had any right to expect, but we've completely trashed the pre-Siege economy. The new one's still pretty amorphous, and a lot of people who're getting burned are highly pissed."

The old man leaned back and folded his arms across his chest.

"Actually, people at both ends of the spectrum are hurting right now. The subsistence-level economies are making out better than ever before—at least starvation's no longer a problem, and we've made decent medical care universally available—but virtually every skilled trade's become obsolete, and that's hitting the Third World hardest. The First World never imagined anything like Imperial technology before the Siege, and even there, retraining programs are mind-boggling, but at least it had a high-tech mind-set.

"Worse, it's going to take at least another decade to make modern technology fully available, given how much of our total effort the military programs are sucking up. We're still relying on a lot of pre-Imperial industry for bread-and-butter production, and the people running it feel discriminated against. They see themselves as stuck in dead-end jobs, and the fact that civilian bio-enhancement and modern medicine will give them two or three centuries to move up to something better hasn't really sunk in yet.

"Bio-enhancement bottlenecks don't help much, either. As usual, Isis is doing far better than I expected, but again, the folks in the Third World are getting squeezed worst. We've had to prioritize things somehow, and they simply have more people and less technical background. Some of them still think biotechnics are magic!"

"I'm glad I had someone else to dump *your* job on," Colin said with heartfelt sincerity. "Is there anything else we can give you?"

"Not really." Horus sighed. "We're running as hard and as fast as we can already, and there simply isn't any more capacity to devote to it. I imagine we'll make out, and at least I've got some high-powered help on the Planetary Council. We learned a lot getting ready for the Siege, and we've managed to avoid several nasty mistakes because we did."

"Would it help to relieve you of responsibility for Birhat?"

"Not much, I'm afraid. Most of the people here are tied directly into Gerald's and Tao-ling's operations, so I'm only providing support for their dependents. Of course—" Horus flashed a sudden grin "—I'm sure my lieutenant governor thinks I spend too much time off Earth anyway!"

"I imagine he does." Colin chuckled. "But then *my* lieutenant governor probably felt the same way."

"Indeed he did!" Horus laughed. "Actually, Lawrence has been a gift from the Maker," he added more seriously. "He's taken a tremendous amount of day-to-day duties off my back, and he and Isis make a mighty efficient team on the enhancement side."

"Then I'm glad you've got him." Colin knew Lawrence Jefferson less well than he would have liked, but what he knew impressed him. Under the Great Charter, imperial planetary governors were appointed by the Emperor, but *a lieutenant* governor was appointed by his immediate superior with the advice and consent of his Planetary Council. After so many centuries as an inhabitant (if not precisely a citizen) of the North American continent, Horus had chosen to turn that advice and consent function into an election, soliciting nominations from his Councilors, and Jefferson was the result. A U.S. senator when Colin raided Anu's enclave, he'd done yeoman work throughout the Siege, then resigned midway through his third senatorial term to assume his new post, where he'd soon made his mark as a man of charm, wit, and ability.

Now Colin turned to Ninhursag. "Anything new from ONI, 'Hursag?"

"Not really." Like Horus and Jiltanith, the stocky, pleasantly plain woman had come to Earth aboard *Dahak*. Like Horus (but unlike Jiltanith, who'd been a child at the time), she'd joined Fleet Captain Anu's mutiny, only to discover to her horror that it was but the first step in *Dahak*'s chief engineer's plan to topple the Imperium itself. But whereas Horus had deserted Anu and launched a millennia-long guerrilla war against him, Ninhursag had been stuck in stasis in Anu's Antarctic enclave. When she was finally awakened, she'd managed to contact the guerrillas and provide the information which had made the final, desperate attack on the enclave possible. Now, as a Battle Fleet admiral, she ran Naval Intelligence and enjoyed describing herself as Colin's "SIC," or "Spook In Chief." Colin was fond of telling her her self-created acronym was entirely apt.

"We've still got problems," she continued, "because Horus is right. When you stand an entire world on its head, you generate a lot of resentment. On the other hand, Earth took half a billion casualties from the Achuultani, and everybody knows who saved the rest of them. Almost all of them are willing to give you and 'Tanni the benefit of the doubt on anything you do or we do in your names. Gus and I are keeping an eye on the discontented elements, but most of them disliked one another enough before the Siege to make any kind of cooperation difficult. Even if they didn't, they can't do much to buck the kind of devotion the rest of the human race feels for you."

Colin no longer blushed when people said things like that, and he nodded thoughtfully. Gustav van Gelder was Horus' Minister of Security, and while Ninhursag understood the possibilities of Imperial technology far better than he, Gus had taught her a lot about how *people* worked.

"To be perfectly honest," Ninhursag continued, "I'd be a bit happier if I *could* find something serious to worry about."

"How's that?" Colin asked.

"I guess I'm like Horus, worrying about what's going to bite me next. We're moving so fast I can't even identify all the players, much less what they might be up to, and even the best security measures could be leaking like a sieve. For instance, I've spent hours with Dahak and a whole team of my brightest boys and girls, and we still can't figure a way to ID Anu's surviving Terra-born allies."

"Are you saying we didn't get them all?!" Colin jerked upright, and Jiltanith tensed at his side. Ninhursag looked surprised at their reactions.

"Didn't you tell him, Dahak?" she asked.

"I regret," the mellow voice sounded unwontedly uncomfortable, "that I did not. Or, rather, I did not do so explicitly."

"And what the hell does *that* mean?" Colin demanded.

"I mean, Colin, that I included the data in one of your

implant downloads but failed to draw your attention specifically to them."

Colin frowned and keyed the mental sequence that opened the index of his implant knowledge. The problem with implant education was that it simply stored data; until someone *used* that information, he might not even know he had it. Now the report Dahak referred to sprang into his forebrain, and he bit off a curse.

"Dahak," he began plaintively, "I've *told* you—"

"You have." The computer hesitated a moment, then went on. "As you know, my equivalent of the human qualities of 'intuition' and 'imagination' remain limited. I have grasped—intellectually, I suppose you would say— that human brains lack my own search and retrieval capabilities, but I occasionally overlook their limitations. I shall not forget again."

The computer actually sounded embarrassed, and Colin shrugged.

"Forget it. It's more my fault than yours. You certainly had a right to expect me to at least read your report."

"Perhaps. It is nonetheless incumbent upon me to provide you with the data you require. It thus follows that I should inquire to be certain that you do, in fact, realize that you have them."

"Don't get your diodes in an uproar." Colin turned back to Ninhursag as Dahak made the sound he used for a chuckle. "Okay, I've got it now, but I don't see anything about how we missed them . . . if we did."

"The how's fairly easy, actually. Anu and his crowd spent thousands of years manipulating Earth's population, and they had a tremendous number of contacts, including batches of people with no idea who they were working for. We got most of their bigwigs when you stormed his enclave, but Anu couldn't possibly have squeezed *all* of them into it. We managed to identify most of the important bit players from his captured records, but a lot of small fry have to've been missed.

"Those people don't worry me. They know what'll happen if they draw attention to themselves, and I expect most have decided to become *very* loyal subjects of the Imperium. But what does worry me a bit is that Kirinal seems to have been running at least two top secret cells no one else knew about. When you and 'Tanni killed her in the Cuernavaca strike, not even Anu and Ganhar knew who those people were, so they never got taken into the enclave before the final attack."

"My God, 'Hursag!" Hatcher sounded appalled. "You mean we've still got top echelon people who worked for Anu running around loose?"

"No more than a dozen at the outside," Ninhursag replied, "and, like the small fry, they're not going to draw attention to themselves. I'm not suggesting we forget about them, Gerald, but consider the mess *they're* in. They lost their patron when Colin killed Anu, and as Horus and I have been saying, we've turned Earth's whole society upside-down, so they've probably lost a lot of the influence they may've had in the old power structure. Even those who haven't been left out in the cold have only their own resources to work with, and there's no way they're going to do anything that might draw attention to their past associations with Anu."

"Admiral MacMahan is correct, Admiral Hatcher," Dahak said. "I do not mean to imply that they will never be a menace again—indeed, the fact that they knowingly served Anu indicates not only criminality on their part but ambition and ability, as well—yet they no longer possess a support structure. Deprived of Anu's monopoly on Imperial technology, they become simply one more criminal element. While it would be folly to assume they are incapable of building a new support structure or to abandon our search for them, they represent no greater inherent threat than any other group of unscrupulous individuals. Moreover, it should be noted that they were organized on a cell basis, which suggests members of any one cell would know only other members of that cell. Concerted action by any large number of them is therefore improbable."

"Huh!" Hatcher grunted skeptically, then made himself

relax. "All right, I grant you that, but it makes me nervous to know *any* of Anu's bunch are still around."

"You and me both," Colin agreed, and Jiltanith nodded beside him. "On the other hand, it sounds to me like you, Dahak, and Gus are on top of the situation 'Hursag. Stay there, and make sure I find out if anything—and I mean *anything*—changes in regard to it."

"Of course," Ninhursag said quietly. "In the meantime, it seems to me the greatest potential dangers lie in three areas. First, the Third World resentment Horus has mentioned. A lot of those people still see the Imperium as an extension of Western imperialism. Even some of those who truly believe we're doing our best to treat everyone fairly can't quite forget we imposed our ideas and control on them. I expect this particular problem to ease with time, but it'll be with us for a good many years to come.

"Second, we've got the First World people who've seen their positions in the old power structures crumble. Some of them have been a real pain, like the old unions that're still fighting our 'job-destroying new technology,' but, again, most of them—or their children—will come around with time.

"Third, and most disturbing, in a way, are the religious nuts." Ninhursag frowned unhappily. "I just don't understand the true-believer mentality well enough to feel confident about dealing with it, and there's a bunch of true believers out there. Not just in the extreme Islamic blocs, either. At the moment, there's no clear sign of organization—aside from this 'Church of the Armageddon'—but it's mighty hard to reason with someone who's convinced God is on his side. Still, they're not a serious threat unless they coalesce into something bigger and nastier . . . and since the Great Charter guarantees freedom of religion, there's not much we can do about them until and unless they try something overtly treasonous."

She paused, checking back over what she'd said, then shrugged.

"That's about the size of it, at the moment. A lot of rumbles but no present signs of anything really dangerous. We're keeping our eyes peeled, but for the most part it's simply going to take time to relieve the tensions."

"Okay." Colin leaned back and glanced around. "Anyone have anything else we need to look at?" A general headshake answered him, and he rose. "In that case, let's go see what the kids have gotten themselves into."

Eight hundred-plus light-years from Birhat, a man swiveled his chair towards a window and gazed down with unfocused yet intent eyes, staring through the view below to examine something far beyond it.

He rocked the old-fashioned swivel chair back with a gentle creak and steepled his fingers, tapping his chin with his index fingers as he considered the changes which had come upon his world . . . and the other changes he proposed to create in their wake. It had taken almost ten years to attain the position he needed, but attain it he had—not, he admitted, without the help of the Emperor himself—and the game was about to begin.

There was nothing inherently wrong, he conceded, in the notion of an empire, nor even of an emperor for all humanity. Certainly *someone* had to make the human race work together despite its traditional divisions, and the man in the chair had no illusions about his species. With the best of intentions (assuming they existed—a point he felt no obligation to concede), few of Earth's teeming billions would have the least idea of how to create some sort of democratic world state from the ground up. Even if they'd had one, democracies were notoriously short-sighted about preparing for problems which lay beyond the horizon, and the job of ultimately defeating the Achuultani was going to take centuries. No, democracy would never do. Of course, he'd never been particularly attached to that form of government, or Kirinal would never have recruited him, now would she?

Not that his own views on democratic government mattered, for one thing was clear: Colin I intended to exercise his prerogatives of direct rule to provide the central authority mankind required. And, the man in the chair reflected, His Imperial Majesty was doing an excellent job. He was probably the most popular head of state in Earth's history, and, of course, there was the tiny consideration that the Fifth Imperium's armed forces were deeply—one might almost say fanatically—loyal to their Emperor and Empress.

All of which, the man in the chair admitted, made things difficult. But if the game were easy, anyone could play, and think how inconvenient *that* would be!

He chuckled and rocked gently, listening to his chair's soft, musical creaking. Actually, he rather admired the Emperor. How many people could have resurrected an empire which had died with its entire population over forty-five thousand years before and crowned himself its ruler? That was a stellar accomplishment, whatever immediate military advantages Colin MacIntyre might have enjoyed, and the man in the chair saluted him.

Unfortunately, there could be only one Emperor. However skilled, however determined, however adroit, there could be but *one* of him . . . and he was not the man in the chair.

Or, the man in the chair corrected himself with a smile, not yet.

Chapter Two

"Finished, Horus?"

The Planetary Duke of Terra looked up and grimaced as Lawrence Jefferson stepped into his office.

"No," he said sourly, dropping a data chip into his security drawer, "but I'm as close as I'll be for the next decade, so we might as well go. It's not every day my grandchildren have a twelfth birthday, and that's more important than this."

Jefferson laughed as Horus stood and sent his desk computer a command to lock the drawer, and an answering smile flickered on the old man's lips. He glanced at Jefferson's briefcase.

"I see you're not leaving *your* work home."

"*I'm* not going to the party. Besides, this isn't 'my' work—it's Admiral MacMahan's copy of Gus' report on that anti-Narhani demonstration."

"Oh." Horus sounded as disgusted as he felt. "You know, I've learned to handle prejudice. We all suffer from that, to some extent, but this anti-Narhani thing is plain, old-fashioned bigotry."

"True, but then the difference between prejudice and bigotry is usually stupidity. The answer's education. The Narhani are on *our* side; we just have to prove that to these idiots."

"Somehow I doubt they'd appreciate your terminology, Lawrence."

"I call them as I see them." Jefferson grinned. "Besides, you're the only person here. If it leaks, I'll know who to come after."

"I'll bear that in mind." Horus finished shutting down

his computer through his neural feed as they strolled out of the office, and two armed Marine guards snapped to attention. Their presence was a formality, but Hector MacMahan's Marines took their responsibilities seriously. Besides, Horus was their Commandant's great-great-great-etc.-grandfather.

The two men took the old-fashioned elevator to the ground floor. White Tower at NASA's old Shepherd Center had been Horus' HQ throughout the Siege, and he'd resisted all pressure to relocate from Colorado on the basis that the fact that Shepherd Center had never been anyone's capital would help defuse nationalist jealousies. Besides, he liked the climate.

They crossed the plaza to the mat-trans terminal, and Jefferson was grateful for his bio-enhancement as his breath steamed. He wasn't in the military, so he lacked the full enhancement that gave Horus ten times the strength of an unenhanced human, but what he had sufficed to deal with little things like sub-freezing temperatures. Which was handy, since Earth hadn't yet fully emerged from the mini-ice age produced by the Siege's bombardment.

They chatted idly during the walk, enjoying the moment of privacy, but Jefferson was still a bit bemused by the absence of bodyguards. He'd grown to adulthood on a planet where terrorism was the chosen form of "protest" by have-not nations, and the report in his brief-case was proof his home world frothed with resentment as it strained to make a nine- or ten-millennium leap in technology. Yet for all that, violence directed at Earth's Governor was virtually unthinkable. Horus had not only led Earth's people through the carnage of the Siege, he was also the father of their beloved Empress, and only a particularly stupid maniac would attack *him* to make a statement.

Not, Jefferson reflected, that history didn't abound with stupid maniacs.

They entered the mat-trans facility, and Jefferson felt himself tense. It didn't look like much—merely a railed platform twenty meters on a side—but knowing what it could do turned that brightly lit dais into something that made the primitive tree-dweller within the Lieutenant Governor gibber.

His stride slowed, and Horus grinned at him.

"Don't take it so hard. And don't think you're the only one it scares!"

Jefferson managed a nod as they stepped onto the platform and the bio-scanners Colin MacIntyre had ordered incorporated into every mat-trans station considered them at length. The mat-trans had been the Fourth Empire's executioner, the vector by which the rogue bio-weapon infected worlds hundreds of light-years apart, and he had no intention of allowing that particular bit of history to repeat itself.

But the scanners cleared them, and Jefferson clutched his briefcase in a sweaty hand, trying very hard to appear nonchalant, as heavy capacitors whined. The mat-trans' power requirements were astronomical, even by Imperial standards, and it took almost twenty seconds to reach peak load. Then a light flashed . . . and Horus and Lawrence Jefferson stepped down from another platform on the planet Birhat, eight hundred light-years from Earth.

The thing that made it so damned scary, Jefferson thought as he left the mat-trans receiver gratefully behind, was that you didn't feel a thing. *Nothing.* It just wasn't natural . . . and wasn't that a fine thing for a man stuffed full of sensors and neural boosters to be thinking?

"Hi, Granddad." Jefferson looked up as General MacMahan held out his hand to Horus then turned to shake his own. "Colin asked me to meet you. He's tied up with something over at the Palace."

"Tied up with what?" Horus asked.

"I'm not sure, but he sounded a bit harassed. I think—" Hector grinned impishly "—it's got something to do with Cohanna."

"Oh, Maker! What's she been up to *now?*"

"Don't know. Come on, I've got transport waiting."

✧   ✧   ✧

"Damn it, 'Hanna!" Colin paced back and forth before the utilitarian desk from which he ran the Imperium, tugging on his nose in a gesture his subordinates knew only too well. "I've told you and *told* you you can't just go chasing off after any wild hare that takes your fancy!"

"But, Colin—" Cohanna began.

"Don't 'But, Colin' me! Did I or did I not tell you to check your next genetic experiment with me before you started on it?"

"Well, of course you did. And I *did* clear it with you," Baroness Cohanna, Imperial Minister of Bio-Sciences added virtuously.

"You *what?*" Colin wheeled on her in disbelief.

"I said I cleared it with you. I sat right here in this office with Brashieel and told you what I was going to do."

"You—!" Colin turned to the saurian-looking, long-snouted, quarter-horse-sized centauroid resting comfortably on his folded legs in the middle of the rug, who returned his gaze with mild, double-lidded eyes. "Brashieel, do *you* remember her saying anything about this?"

"Yes," Brashieel replied calmly through the small black box mounted on one strap of his body harness. His vocal apparatus was poorly suited to human speech, but he'd learned to use his neural feed-driven vocoder's deep bass to express emotion as well as words.

Colin drew a deep breath, then perched on his desk and folded his arms. Brashieel seldom made mistakes, and Cohanna's triumphant expression made Colin unhappily certain she had mentioned it. Or something about it.

"All right," he sighed, "what, exactly, did she say?"

Brashieel closed his inner eyelids in concentration, and Colin waited patiently. The alien's mere presence was enough to give some members of humanity screaming fits, which Colin understood even if he rejected their attitude. To be sure, Brashieel *was* an Achuultani. Worse, he was the sole survivor of the fleet which had come within hours of destroying the planet Earth. He was also, however, the being who'd emerged as the natural leader of the prisoners of war Colin had captured after defeating the incursion, and most of those prisoners—not all, but most—were even more committed to the ultimate defeat of the rest of the Achuultani than humanity was.

For seventy-eight million years, the people of the Nest of Aku'Ultan had quartered the galaxy, destroying every sentient species they encountered. Of all their potential victims, only humanity had survived—not just once, but three times, earning it the Achuultani appellation of "the Demon Nest-Killers"—but Brashieel and his fellows knew something the rest of their race did not. They knew their entire species was enslaved by a self-aware computer which used their unending murder of races who meant them no ill to sustain the "state of war" its programming required to maintain its tyranny.

Not all humans were ready to accept their sincerity, which was why Colin had turned the planet Narhan over to those who had applied for Imperial citizenship. Narhan had avoided the bio-weapon for a simple reason; no one had lived on it, since its 2.67 gravity field produced a sea-level atmosphere lethal to unenhanced humans. Its air was a bit dense even for Achuultani lungs, and it was inconveniently placed—it was far enough from Birhat that travelers by mat-trans had to stage through Earth to reach the capital planet—but its settlers had fallen under the spell of its rugged beauty as they set about carving out their new Nest of Narhan as loyal subjects of their human overlord on a world beyond the reach of hysterical xenophobes.

"Cohanna had reported on progress with the genetic engineering to recreate Narhani females," Brashieel said at last. The rogue computer had eliminated all sexual reproduction by eliminating all Achuultani females. Every Achuultani was male, either a clone or an embryo fertilized in vitro. "Thereafter, she turned to discussion of her suggestion to increase our life spans to something approaching those of humans."

Colin nodded. Achuultani—Narhani, he corrected himself—were bigger and far stronger than humans.

They also matured much more rapidly, but their normal span was little more than fifty years. Bio-enhancement, which all adult Narhani who'd taken the oath of loyalty had received as quickly as Cohanna got a grip on their alien physiology, stretched that to almost three hundred years, but that remained much shorter than for enhanced humans.

Extending Narhani lives was a challenge, but unlike humans, Narhani had no prejudice against bioengineering. They regarded it as a fact of life, given their own origins and the cloned children Jiltanith's Terra-born sister Isis had managed to produce over the last few years, and the possibility of recreating females of their species simply strengthened that attitude.

"We discussed the practical aspects," Brashieel continued, "and I mentioned Tinker Bell."

"I know you did, but surely I never okayed *this*."

"I regret that I must disagree," Brashieel said, and Colin frowned.

Hector MacMahan's big, happy half-lab half-rottweiler bitch Tinker Bell had fallen in love with the Narhani. It amused Colin, given the way the dogs in every bad science-fiction movie ever made hated the "alien menace" on sight, but it was more than amusing to the Narhani. The Nest of Aku'Ultan had nothing remotely like her—indeed, one of the most alien things about the nest was the absence of any form of pet—and they found her fascinating. Almost every Narhani had speedily acquired a dog of his own, but they, like any other Terrestrial animal, would have been unable to survive on Narhan, and the Narhani were fiercely devoted to their four-footed friends.

"Look, I know I authorized limited bio-enhancement so you could take the dogs with you, but I never contemplated anything like this."

"I cannot, of course, know what was in your mind, but the point was raised." Colin clenched his teeth. The Narhani were as intelligent as humans but less imaginative and far more literal-minded. "Cohanna pointed out that genetic engineering would permit her to produce dogs who required no enhancement, and you agreed. She then reminded you of Dahak's success in communicating with Tinker Bell and suggested the capability for meaningful exchanges might also be enhanced."

Colin opened his mouth, then shut it with a snap as his own memory replayed the conversation. She *had* mentioned it, and he'd agreed. But, damn it, she should have known what he meant!

He closed his eyes and counted to five hundred. Dahak had insisted for years that Tinker Bell's barks, growls, and yips were more value-laden than humans believed, and he'd persisted with an analysis of her sounds until he proved his point. Dogs were no mental giants. Their cognitive functions were severely limited, and their ability to manipulate symbols was virtually nonexistent, but they had lots more to say than mankind had guessed.

"All right," he said finally, opening his eyes and glowering at Cohanna, who returned his gaze innocently. "All right. I admit the point came up, but you never told me you had anything like this in mind."

"Only because I thought it was self-evident," she said, and Colin bit off an acid response. He sometimes toyed with the notion that the millennia Cohanna had spent in stasis had affected her mind, but he'd known Terraborn humans just like her. She was brilliant and intensely curious, and little things like political realities, wars, and nearby supernovas were totally unimportant compared to her current project—whatever it might be.

"Look," he tried again, "I've got several million Terraborn who find simple biotechnics scary, 'Hanna." Her nose wrinkled with contempt for such benighted ignorance, and he sighed. "All right, so they're wrong. But that doesn't change the way they feel, and if *that* upsets them, how are they going to react to your fooling with the natural order of evolution?"

"Evolution," she replied, "is an unreasoning statistical process which represents no more than the blind conservation of accidental life forms capable of surviving within their environments."

"*Please* don't say things like that!" Colin ran his hands through his hair and tried not to look harried. "Maybe you're right, but too many Terra-born regard it as the working out of God's plan for the universe. And even the ones who don't tend to remember the bio-weapon and wake up screaming!"

"Barbarians!" Cohanna snorted, and Colin sighed.

"I ought to order you to destroy them," he muttered, but he shied away from the rebellion in her eyes. "All right, I won't. Not immediately, anyway. But before I promise not to, I want to see them with my own eyes. And you are *not* to conduct any more genetic experiments outside a Petri dish without my specific—and written!—authorization. Is that understood?"

The doctor nodded frigidly, and Colin walked around his desk to flop into his chair. "Good. Now, I've got a meeting with Horus and Lieutenant Governor Jefferson in ten minutes, so we're going to have to wrap this up. But before we do, are there any problems—or surprises—with Project Genesis?"

"No." Cohanna's spine relaxed. One thing about her, Colin reflected; she was a tartar when her toes got stepped on, but she recovered. "Although," she added pointedly, "I'm a bit surprised you don't object to the name."

"I wish I'd thought about it when Isis suggested it, but I didn't. And we're only using it internally and all the reports are classified, so I don't expect it to upset anyone."

"Hmph!" Cohanna sniffed, then smiled wryly. "Well, it's really more her project than mine, anyway, so I suppose I shouldn't complain. Anyway, we should be ready to move within the next year or so."

"That soon?" Colin was impressed, and he cocked his head to gaze at Brashieel. "How do you folks feel about that, Brashieel?"

"Curious," the alien said, "and possibly a bit frightened. After all, the concept of females is still quite strange, and the notion of producing nestlings with a nestmate is . . . peculiar. Most of us, however, are eager to see what they're like. For myself, I look forward to it with interest, though I'm highly satisfied with the way Brashan has turned out."

"Yeah, you might say he's a chip off the old block." Brashieel, whose race was given neither to clichés nor puns, looked blank, but Cohanna winced, and Colin grinned. "Okay, that's going to have to be it." His guests rose, and he wagged a finger at Cohanna. "But I meant what I said about experiments, 'Hanna! And I want to see them myself."

"Understood," the doctor said. She and Brashieel walked from the office, pausing to exchange greetings with Horus, Hector, and Jefferson on their way out, and Colin leaned back in his chair with a sigh. Lord! Combining Narhani literal-mindedness with someone like Cohanna was just begging for trouble. He'd have to keep a closer eye on her.

He opened his eyes to see his father-in-law studying the carpet. A quirked eyebrow invited explanation, and Horus chuckled.

"Just checking to see how deep the blood was."

"You don't know how close to right you are," Colin growled. "Jesus! After all the times I've lectured her on the subject—!" He stood to embrace Horus, then extended a hand to Jefferson. "Good to see you again, Mister Jefferson."

"Thank you, Your Majesty. You might see more of me if I didn't have to come by mat-trans." His shudder was only half-feigned, and Colin laughed.

"I know. The first time I used a transit shaft I almost wet my pants, and the mat-trans is worse."

"But efficient," the stocky, brown-haired Lieutenant Governor replied with a small smile. "Most efficient— damn it!"

"True, too true."

"Tell, me, Colin, just what has 'Hanna been up to now?" Horus asked.

"She—" Colin paused, then shrugged. "It stays in this office, but I guess I can tell you. You know she's bioengineering dogs for Narhan?" His guests nodded. "Well, she's gone a bit further than I intended. She's been working with a couple of Tinker Bell's litters to give them near-human intelligence."

"What?" Horus blinked at him. "I thought you told her not to—"

"I did. Unfortunately, she told me she wanted to 'enhance their ability to communicate with the Narhani' and I told her to go ahead." He grimaced. "Silly me."

"Oh, Maker," Horus groaned. "Why can't she have half as much common sense as she does brainpower?"

"Because she wouldn't be Cohanna." Colin grinned, then sobered. "The worst of it is, the first litter's fully adult, and she's been educating them through their implants," he went on more somberly. "My emotions are having a little trouble catching up with my intellect, but if she's really given them human or near-human intelligence, the whole equation shifts. I mean, if she's gone and turned them into *people* on me, it's not like putting a starving stray to sleep. 'Lab animals' or not, I'm not sure I even have a legal right, much less a moral one, to have them destroyed, whatever the possible consequences."

"Excuse me, Your Majesty," Jefferson suggested diffidently, "but I think, perhaps, you'd better consider doing just that." Colin raised an eyebrow, and Jefferson shrugged. "We're having enough anti-Narhani problems without adding this to the fire. The last demonstration was pretty ugly, and it wasn't in one of our more reactionary areas, either. It was in London."

"London?" Colin looked sharply at Horus, instantly diverted from Cohanna's experiment. "How bad was it?"

"Not good," Horus admitted. "More of the 'The Only Good Achuultani Is a Dead Achuultani' kind of thing. There were some tussles, but they started when the marchers ran into a counter-demonstration, so they may actually have been a sign of sanity. I hope so, anyway."

"Oh, Lord!" Colin sighed. "You know, it was an awful lot easier fighting the Achuultani. Well, simpler, anyway."

"True. Still, I think time is on our side." Colin made a face and Horus chuckled. "I know. I'm getting as tired of saying that as you must be of hearing it, but it's true. And time is one thing we've got plenty of."

"Maybe. But while we're on the subject, who organized this thing?"

"We're not entirely certain," Jefferson replied. "Gus is looking into it, but the official organizers were a bunch called HHI—'Humans for a Human Imperium.' On the surface, they're a batch of professional rowdies backed up by a crop of discontented intellectuals. The 'highbrows' seem to be academics who resent finding everything they spent their lives learning has become outdated overnight. It would seem—" he smiled thinly "—that some of our fearless intellectual pioneers are a bit less pioneering than they thought."

"Hard to blame them, really," Horus pointed out. "It's not so much that they're rejecting the truth as that they feel betrayed. As you say, Lawrence, they spent their lives establishing themselves as intellectual leaders only to find themselves brushed aside."

"I know." Colin frowned down at his hands for a moment, then looked back up. "Still, that sounds like a pretty strange marriage. Professional rowdies and professors? Wonder how they made connections?"

"Stranger things have happened, Your Majesty, but Gus and I are asking the same question, and he thinks the answer is the Church of the Armageddon."

"Oh, shit," Colin said disgustedly.

"Inelegant, but apt," Horus said. "In fact, that's what bothers me most. The church started out as a simple fusion of fundamentalists who saw the Achuultani as the true villains of the Armageddon, but this is a new departure, even for them. They've hated the Achuultani all along, but this is a shift to open racism—if I may use the term—of a particularly ugly stripe."

"Yeah. Anything more on their leadership, Mister Jefferson?"

"Not really, Your Majesty. They've never tried to hide their membership—why should they when they enjoy legal religious toleration?—but they're such an untidy agglomeration of splinter groups the hierarchical lines are pretty vague. We're still working on who actually calls the shots. Their spokesperson seems to be this Bishop Hilgemann, though I'm afraid I don't agree with Gus about her real authority. I think she's more a mouthpiece than a policy-maker, but we're both just guessing."

"You're going to discuss this with Ninhursag?"

"Of course, Your Majesty. I've brought Gus' report and I'm going up to Mother after this meeting. Admiral MacMahan and I will put our heads together, and perhaps Dahak can help us pull something out of the data."

"Good luck. 'Hursag's been trying to get a handle on them for over a year now. Oh, well." Colin shook his head and rose, holding out his hand to the Lieutenant Governor once more. "In that case, I won't keep you, Mister Jefferson. Horus and I have a birthday party to attend, and two pre-adolescent hellions who'll make us both miserable if we're late."

"Of course. Please give the Empress and your children my regards."

"I will—in between the presents, cake, punch, and general hullabaloo. Good luck with your report."

"Thank you, Your Majesty." Jefferson withdrew gracefully, and Colin and Horus headed for the imperial family's side of the Palace.

Chapter Three

Colin MacIntyre tossed his jacket into a chair, and his green eyes laughed as a robot butler clucked audibly and scooped it up again. 'Tanni was as neat as the cat she so resembled, and she'd programmed the household robots to condemn his sloppiness for her when she was busy elsewhere.

He glanced into the library in passing and saw two heads of sable hair bent over a hologram. It looked like the primary converter of a gravitonic conveyor's main propulsion unit, and the twins were busily manipulating the display through their neural feeds to turn it into an exploded schematic while they argued some abstruse point.

Their father shook his head and continued on his way. It was hard to remember they were only twelve—when they were studying, anyway—but he knew that was only because he'd grown up without implant educations.

With neural interfacing, there was no inherent limit to the data any individual could be given, but raw data wasn't the same as *knowledge*, and that required a whole new set of educational parameters. For the first time in human history, the *only* thing that mattered was what the best educators had always insisted was the true goal of education: the exploration of knowledge. It was no longer necessary for students to spend endless hours acquiring data, but only a matter of making them aware of what they already "knew" and teaching them to use it—teaching them to *think*, really—and that was a good teacher's delight. Unfortunately, it also invalidated the traditional groundwork and performance criteria. Too many teachers were lost without the old rules—and even more of them, led by the West's unions, had waged a bitter scorched earth campaign against accepting the new. The human race in general seemed to think the Emperor possessed some sort of magic wand, and, in a way, they were right. Colin could do just about anything he decided needed doing . . . as long as he was prepared to use heavy enough artillery and convinced the battle was worth the cost.

It had taken him over three years to reach that conclusion where Earth's teaching establishment was concerned. For forty-three months, he'd listened to reason after reason why the changeover could not be made. Too few Earth schoolchildren had neural feeds. Too little hardware was available. Too many new concepts in too short a time would confuse children already in the system and damage them beyond repair. The list had gone on and on and on, until, finally, he'd had enough and announced the dissolution of all teachers' unions and the firing of every teacher employed by any publicly funded educational department or system anywhere on the planet.

The people he'd fired had tried to fight the decree in the courts only to discover that the Great Charter gave Colin the authority to do just what he'd done, and when they came up against the cold steel his homely, usually cheerful face normally hid so well, their grave concern for the well-being of their students had undergone a radical change. Suddenly the only thing they wanted to do was make the transition as quick and painless as possible, and if the Emperor would only let them have their jobs back, they would get down to it immediately.

They had. Still not without a certain amount of foot dragging when they thought no one was looking, but they had gotten down to it. Of course, every one of their earlier objections had had its own grain of truth, which made the introduction of an entirely new educational system difficult and often frustratingly slow, but once they accepted that Colin was serious, they'd really buckled down and pushed. And, along the way, the ones who had the makings of true teachers rather than petty bureaucrats had rediscovered the joy of teaching. The ones who didn't make that rediscovery tended to disappear from the profession in ever greater numbers, but their earlier opposition and lingering guerrilla warfare had delayed the full-scale implementation of modern education on Earth by at least ten years.

Which meant, of course, that children on Birhat had a measurable advantage over those educated on Earth. Dahak spent most of his time in Birhat orbit, and while Earth's teaching establishment grappled with Imperial education theories, Dahak had already mastered them. More, he, unlike they, had no institutional or personal objections to adopting them, and it required only a tithe of his vast capacity to institute what amounted to a planet-wide system of small-group studies. His students responded with an insatiable hunger to learn, and, to Colin's knowledge the twins had *never* played hooky, which was almost scary.

He walked into the study, and Jiltanith smiled at him from her desk. He took the time to kiss her properly, then flopped into his chair and sighed contentedly as it adjusted to his body's contours.

"Thou soundest well content to leave thine office behind thee, my love," Jiltanith observed, putting her own computer on hold, and he nodded.

"*You* oughta try it sometime," he said pointedly, and she laughed.

"Nay, my Colin. 'Twould drive me to bedlam's brink did I have naught to which to set my hands, and this—" she gestured at the hardcopy and data chips strewn over her desk "—is a study most interesting."

"Yeah?"

"Aye. Amanda hath begun to think how best we may use Tao-ling's Mark Twenty hyper gun in small unit tactics."

Colin shook his head wryly. Jiltanith didn't love combat—she knew too much of what it cost—yet there were dark and dangerous places in her soul. He suspected that no one, not even he, would ever be admitted into some of them, but a lifetime of bitter guerrilla warfare had left its mark, and, unlike him, she saw war not as a last response but as a practical option that worked. She wasn't merciless, but she *was* far more capable of slaughter—and less inclined to give quarter—than he. That was why he'd made her Minister of War. As Warlord, Colin was the Imperium's commander-in-chief, but it was 'Tanni who ran their growing military establishment on a day-to-day basis.

"Well, if you can tear yourself away, we're about to have visitors."

"Ah?" She cocked her head at him.

"Isis, Cohanna, and Cohanna's . . . project," he said less cheerfully. "I'm afraid Jefferson may be right about the logic of ordering them destroyed, but I can't say I'm looking forward to making that decision."

"Nor shouldst thou." His wife stood and walked around her desk. "Logic, as thou hast said time without number, my love, may be naught but a way to err wi' confidence."

"You got that right, babe," he sighed, snaking an arm around her as she passed. She paused to ruffle his sandy hair, then sank into her own chair. "The thing is, I think I'm trying to psych myself up to decide against them 'cause I think I ought to, and that makes me feel sort of ashamed."

"The day thy self-doubt ceaseth will be the day thou becomest less than thy best self, Colin," she said gently.

He smiled, changed the subject to something more comfortable, and let 'Tanni's voice flow over him. He treasured the moments when they could forget the Imperium, forget their duties, forget the need to finish the Achuultani threat once and for all, and 'Tanni's soft, archaic speech wove a spell that helped him hold those things at bay, be it ever so briefly. She'd learned her English during the Wars of the Roses and flatly refused to abandon it. Besides, as she'd pointed out upon occasion, she spoke *true* English, not the debased dialect *he'd* learned.

"Excuse me, Colin," a mellow voice injected into a break in their conversation, "but Cohanna and Isis have arrived."

"Thanks." Colin sighed and set the moment aside, feeling the universe intruding upon them once more but revitalized by the temporary escape. "Tell them we're in the study."

"I have already done so. They will arrive momentarily."

"Fine. And hang around yourself. We may need your input."

"Of course," Dahak agreed. Colin knew a tiny bit of the computer's attention always followed him about, ready to respond to questions or advise him of new developments, but Dahak had designed a special subroutine to monitor his Emperor's whereabouts and needs without bringing them to the front of his attention unless certain critical parameters were crossed. It was his way of assuring Colin's privacy, a concept he didn't entirely understand but whose importance to his human friends he recognized.

The study door opened, and Cohanna marched in like a grenadier with a delicate, white-haired woman whose aged eyes were remarkably like Jiltanith's. Isis Tudor was over ninety, and there'd been no bio-enhancement for the Terra-born in her girlhood. By the time it became available, her body was too old and fragile for full enhancement, and age pared away more of her strength with every year. Yet there was nothing wrong with her mind, and the enhancement she could tolerate gave her an energy at odds with her growing frailty.

Jiltanith stood to embrace her while Cohanna met Colin's gaze with an edge of challenge and four black-and-tan dogs followed her through the door. They moved in formation, with a most undoglike precision, and arranged themselves in a neat line as they sat on the rug.

They looked, Colin thought, like fireplugs on legs. Tinker Bell's pups had been sired by a pedigreed rottweiler, and the lab side of their heritage was scarcely noticeable. They had a solid, squared-off appearance, with powerful muzzles, and the biggest must have massed almost sixty kilos.

He studied them for signs of the changes Cohanna had wrought. There weren't many. The massive rottweiler head was perhaps a little broader, with a more pronounced cranial bulge, though he doubted he would have noticed without looking for it, yet there was something. And then he realized. The eyes fixed upon him with unwavering attention betrayed the intelligence behind them.

"All right, Colin." Cohanna's voice wrenched his attention from the dogs. "You wanted to see them. Here they are."

He looked up quickly, but her expression gave him pause. He was accustomed to her testiness, but her dark eyes were fierce. This, he realized with a sinking sensation, was no bloodless project for her.

"Sit down, 'Hanna," he said quietly, and knelt before the dogs as she sank into an empty chair. Heads cocked to look at him, and he ran a hand down the biggest's broad back. His sensory boosters were on high, and he felt the usual bunchy muscle of the breed . . . and something more. He looked at Cohanna, and she shrugged.

" 'Hanna," he sighed, "I have to tell you I'm less worried, in a way, about the genetic stuff than the rest of it. Do you have any idea how the anti-techies will react to fully enhanced *dogs?* The idea of a dog with that kind of strength and toughness is going to terrify them."

"Then they're idiots!" Cohanna glared at him, then sighed herself, and something very like guilt diluted her fierceness. A knot of tension inside him relaxed slightly as he saw it and realized how much of her anger at him came from an awareness that perhaps she *had* gone too far.

"All right," she said finally, her voice low. "Maybe *I* was an idiot. I still maintain—" her eyes flashed "—that they're superstitious savages, but, damn it, Colin, I can't understand how their minds work! These dogs represent no more danger to them than another enhanced human would!"

"I know you think they don't, 'Hanna, but—"

"I don't 'think' anything, Colin—I *know!* And so will you if you take the time to get to know them."

"That," he admitted, "is what I'm more than half afraid of." He turned back to the dogs, and the big male he'd touched returned his gaze levelly. "This is Galahad?" he asked Cohanna . . . but someone else answered.

"Yes," a mechanically produced voice said, and Colin's eyes widened as he saw the small vocoder on the dog's collar. A shiver ran down his spine as a "dumb animal" spoke, but it vanished in an instant. Wonder replaced it, and a strange delight he tried hard to suppress, and he drew a deep breath.

"Well, Galahad," he said quietly, "has Cohanna explained why I wanted to meet you?"

"Yes," the dog replied. His ears moved, and Colin realized it was a deliberate gesture—an expression intended to convey meaning. "But we do not understand why others fear us." The words came slowly but without hesitation.

"Excuse me a moment, Galahad," Colin said, feeling only a slight sense of unreality at extending human-style courtesies to a dog. He looked back up at Cohanna. "How much of that was computer enhanced?"

"There's some enhancement," the doctor admitted. "They tend to forget definite articles, and their sentence structure's very simple. They never use the past tense, either, but the software is limited to 'filling in the holes.' It doesn't provide any expansion of their meaning."

"Galahad," Colin turned back to the dog, "you don't frighten *me*—or anyone else in this room—but some people will find you . . . unnatural, and humans are afraid of things they don't understand."

"Why?" Galahad asked.

"I wish I could explain why," Colin sighed.

"Danger is cause for fear," the dog said, "but we are no danger. We wish only to be. We are not evil."

Colin blinked. A word like "evil" implied an ability to manipulate concepts light-years in advance of anything Tinker Bell had ever managed.

"Galahad," he asked carefully, "what do you think 'evil' is?"

"Evil," the mechanically-generated voice replied, "is danger. Evil is hurting when not hurt or when hurting is not needed."

Colin winced, for Galahad had cut to the heart of his own definition of evil. And whether he'd meant to or not, he'd thrown Colin's decision about his own fate into stark focus.

Colin MacIntyre stared into his own soul and disliked what he saw. How could he explain that much of humanity was incapable of understanding what Galahad saw so clearly, or why he felt so ashamed that it was so?

"Colin-human," Colin looked up as Galahad spoke again, "I try to understand, for understanding is good, but I cannot. We know—" a toss of a massive canine head indicated his litter-mates "—you may end us. We do not want to end. You do not want to end us. If we must end we cannot stop you. But it is not right, Colin-human." Canine eyes held his with heart-tearing dignity. "It is not right," Galahad repeated, "and this is something you know."

Colin bit his lip. He turned to Jiltanith, and when her eyes—the black, subtly alien eyes of a full Imperial—met his, they, too, shone with tears.

"He hath the right of it, my Colin," she said quietly. "Should we decree their deaths, 'twill be fear that moveth us—fear that maketh us do what we know full well is wrong. Nay, more than wrong." She knelt beside him, touching a slender hand to Galahad's heavy head. "E'en as Galahad hath said, 'twould evil be to hurt where hurting need not be."

"I know." His voice was equally quiet, and then he shook himself. "Isis?"

" 'Tanni's right. If I'd known what 'Hanna was planning I'd've pitched a fit right alongside you, but look at them. They're magnificent. *People*, Colin—good people who happen to have four feet and no hands."

"Yes." Colin looked down at his hands—the hands Galahad didn't have—and felt the decision make itself. He rose and tugged on his nose, thinking hard. "How many are we talking about here, 'Hanna?"

"Ten. These four and two smaller litters."

"Okay." He turned back to Galahad and his siblings. "Listen to me, all of you. I know you don't understand why humans should be afraid of you, but do all of you accept that they might be?" Four canine heads nodded in unmistakable assent, and he chuckled despite his solemnity. "Good, because the only way we could keep you really safe would be for us to keep the humans you might scare from finding out you exist, and we can't do that forever.

"So here's what I'm going to do. From now on, you four will live with us—with 'Tanni and me—and except for when you're alone with us, you have to pretend to be just like other dogs. Can you do that?"

"Yes, Colin-human." It wasn't Galahad, but a smaller female who spoke, and her dignified mien vanished abruptly. She leapt up on him, wagging her tail and slurping his face enthusiastically, then tore around the room barking madly. She skidded to a halt, tongue lolling, dumped herself untidily on the carpet, rolled on her back, and waved all four feet in the air. Then she rolled back over and sat upright once more, eyes laughing at him.

"All right!" He wiped his face and grinned, then sobered again. "I don't know if you'll understand this, but we're going to take you lots of places and show you to lots of people, and I want you to behave like ordinary dogs. The news people'll get a lot of footage of you, and that's good. When the truth about you gets out, I want the rest of humanity to be used to seeing you. I want them used to the idea that you're not a threat. That you've been around a long time and never hurt anyone. Do you understand?"

"If we prove we are not evil, people will not fear us?" Galahad asked.

"Exactly. It's not fair—you shouldn't have to *prove* it any more than they should—but that's how it has to be. Can you do that?"

"We can, Colin-human," Galahad said softly.

Chapter Four

Fleet Admiral the Lady Adrienne Robbins, Baroness Nergal and Companion of the Golden Nova, dodged with a haste which ill accorded with her exalted rank. She flattened herself against the wall of the Palace corridor and shrank into the smallest possible space as four human children, a half-grown Narhani, and a pack of four leaping rottweilers thundered down upon her.

Fortunately for the admiral, the long-haired girl leading the charge saw her, and they hit the brakes as only children can, skittering to a halt in a tangled confusion of arms, legs, feet, hooves, and paws.

"Hi, Aunt Adrienne!" Princess Isis Harriet MacIntyre shouted, and Admiral Robbins stepped away from the wall. Sean and Harriet seemed unaffected by her glare, but Sandy MacMahan looked a bit abashed and Tamman studied his toes. Brashan, Brashieel's clone-child, looked dreadfully embarrassed, for if he was younger than any of the others, he was already a near-adult, given the speed with which his species matured. For their part, the various dogs flopped down and panted at her, but their canine insouciance didn't fool Adrienne, for she was one of the handful of people who knew the truth about them.

"I wonder," the admiral said darkly, "how Their Imperial Majesties would react to the way you young hellions came tearing down on me?"

"Oh, Dad wouldn't mind." Sean grinned.

"I was thinking more of *Her* Imperial Majesty," Adrienne said, and Sean suddenly looked more thoughtful. "That's what I thought, too. Can you give me one good reason I shouldn't tell her?"

"Because you wouldn't want us on your conscience?" he suggested, and she swallowed a laugh and frowned.

"My conscience is pretty resilient, Your Highness."

"Uh, *do* you have to mention this to Mom and Dad?" Harriet asked, and Adrienne considered her for a long, dreadful moment. Tamman wiggled, clearly picturing *his* parents' reaction, and Adrienne relented.

"Not this time, I suppose. *But*—" she held up an admonishing finger as relieved smiles blossomed "—I won't be so gooey-centered next time!"

An earnest chorus of thanks answered her, and she made shooing motions with her hands.

"Then *get*, you horrible brats!" she commanded, and the cavalcade leapt back into motion (albeit less impetuously than before) down the hall.

Adrienne smiled after them, then resumed her interrupted journey. Sean, she reflected, was a dark-haired version of his father, with the same beaky nose and jug ears no one would ever call handsome, but he was already bidding fair to be quite a bit taller than either of his parents.

Harriet, on the other hand, was a junior edition of her mother—a pretty child who was going to be an astoundingly beautiful woman. Both twins had Jiltanith's eyes, but Harriet's were softer. No less lively, but gentler. Actually, Adrienne reflected, *she* took more after Colin personality-wise, while Sean mingled his mother's absolute fearlessness and his father's humor into an amalgam all his own. One of these days, that boy was going to be a real heart-breaker.

She emerged from her reverie as she reached her destination, and the door slid open to admit her to Colin's office. The Emperor looked up from his paperwork and waved at a chair.

"Have a seat, Adrienne. I'll be with you a minute."

Admiral Robbins sat, smoothing her uniform sleeve fastidiously, and waited patiently for Colin to finish the current installment of his unending paper chase. He dumped the data—and his decision—back into the computer, then leaned back and crossed his legs.

"I see you evaded the thundering herd," he observed, and she glanced at him in surprise. "I've got surveillance systems in the public corridors, remember? 'Young hellions' is exactly right!"

"Oh, they're not that bad. Lively, mind you, but I don't mind."

"Nobody does. Well, nobody but 'Tanni, maybe. The little devils are cute as a crop of buttons, and they know it." He shook his head and sighed. "Oh, well. On to business. Thanks for coming so promptly, by the way."

"That's the way empires are run, Your Majesty. 'I say unto one go, and he goeth' and all that. But I have to admit you piqued my curiosity. What's so sensitive we couldn't discuss it over the com?"

"I'm probably just being paranoid," Colin said more seriously, "but those anti-Narhani demonstrations are getting worse, not better, so I didn't want to take any chance on this leaking. What I've got in mind is either going to make them a lot better . . . or a hell of a lot worse."

"I hate it when you get enigmatic, Colin," Adrienne sighed.

"Sorry. It's just that I beat my head against this for months before I made up my mind, and I'm pissed at myself for taking so long to do what I should've done in the first place. I'm opening the Academy to Narhani."

"Oh, Lord!" Adrienne clutched at her gun-metal hair and moaned. "Why is it always me? Do you have any idea how the newsies are going to react? They'll be all over my campus, stomping the shrubbery flat!"

"Oh, come on!" Colin chuckled. "The first-generation clones won't be ready until Sean and Harry are—you've got time for the spade work."

" 'Spade work,' he says! Bulldozer work, you mean! Fortunately," she smiled rather smugly, "I figured out this was coming over a year ago. We've been working on syllabus modification ever since."

"You have?"

"Of course we have. Lordy, Colin, don't you think I've been around long enough to realize how you think? It takes you a while, sometimes, but you usually get to the right decision sooner or later."

"You," Colin observed dryly, "don't have the most respectful demeanor of any naval officer in the galaxy."

"I do on duty. Want to see my 'official commandant's' face?" Her smile vanished instantly into a stern expression and cold, measuring eyes that impaled him for a ten-count before she relaxed with a grin. "I keep it in a box on my dresser till I need it."

"God, no wonder the middies are all scared spitless of you!"

"Better me than the bad guys."

"True. Actually, though, I want a bit more from you than adjustments to your curriculum. I want you to endorse the suggestion."

"Well, of course," she said with some surprise. "Why shouldn't I?"

"I mean I want you to go public and talk to the media," he explained, and she grimaced. One of the things she liked best about the Imperial Charter was that while it guaranteed freedom of speech it didn't regard reporters as tin gods. Imperial privacy laws and—even better—libel laws had come as a shock to Terran journalists, and if there was one life form Adrienne Robbins truly despised, it was newsies. They'd made her life hell after the Siege of Earth and the Zeta Trianguli campaign.

"Oh, shit, Colin. Do I *have* to?"

" 'Fraid so," he said with a twinge of guilt, for a large chunk of the Palace staff was devoted to keeping the press as far away from *him* as possible, helped by the fact that Jiltanith was not only far more photogenic but surprisingly comfortable with the public. Colin knew his subjects respected him, but they *loved* 'Tanni.

Which, he mused, indicated the public had a higher IQ than he'd once believed possible.

"Look," he went on persuasively, "you know my policy on Narhani civil rights. They're citizens, just like anyone else. Giving them their own planet may have defused the potential for direct unpleasantness, but we've got to integrate them into the government and military or that very isolation's only going to make things worse. I've got quite a few in civil service positions here on Birhat already, but I need to get them into the Fleet, too.

"I don't expect trouble from the military, but the civilians may be something else. I need all the help I can get selling the idea, and after 'Tanni, you're the best salesman I've got."

Adrienne made a face, but she knew it was true. She was the only living officer to have commanded a capital ship throughout both the Siege and the Zeta Trianguli campaign. More than that, she'd led the task force that died in Earth's last, hopeless counterattack, and hers had been the only ship to survive it. She was Battle Fleet's most decorated officer, belonged to more Terran orders of chivalry than she could count, and was the only person in history to have received the highest award for valor of *every* Terran nation, as well as the Golden Nova. It embarrassed her horribly, but it was true.

All of which meant Colin was right. If he was trotting out the big guns, she was going to have to come to battery.

"All right," she sighed finally, "I'll do it."

Francine Hilgemann took her time locking the car doors while she scanned her surroundings. She'd seen no sign of surveillance on the drive here, but paranoia was a survival tool which had served her well over the years.

She ambled across the parking lot to the pedestrian belt serving the enormous, brightly-lit Memorial complex. She was uneasy at the thought of meeting in the very heart of Shepherd Center, but she supposed it made sense. Who in his right mind would expect a pair of traitors to make contact here?

She stepped off the belt into the people flowing past the fifty-meter obsidian needle of the Cenotaph and the endless rows of names etched into its unadorned battle steel plinth. Those names listed every individual known to have fallen in the millennia-long battle against Anu, and even Hilgemann wasn't quite immune to the hush about her. But time was short, and she worked her way briskly through the fringes of the throng.

Another, even quieter crowd surrounded the broken eighty-thousand-ton hull that shared the Memorial with the Cenotaph. The sublight battleship *Nergal* remained where Fleet Captain Robbins had landed her, resting on her belly and ruined landing legs, preserved exactly as her final battle had left her. She'd been decontaminated; that was all, and crippled missile launchers and energy weapons hung like broken teeth from her twisted flanks. How she'd survived was more than Hilgemann could guess, and she couldn't even begin to imagine what it had taken to bring that wreck home and land her under her own power.

She turned away after a moment, walking to the service exit she'd been told to use. It was unlocked as promised, and she slipped through it into the equipment storage room and closed the door behind her.

"Well," she said a bit tartly, looking around at the deserted machinery, "I must say this has all the proper conspiratorial ambience!"

"Perhaps." The man who'd summoned her stepped out of the shadows with a thin smile. "On the other hand, we can't risk meeting very often . . . and we certainly can't do it in public, now can we?"

"I feel like an idiot." She touched the brunette wig which hid her golden hair, then looked down at her plain, cheap clothing and shuddered.

"Better a live idiot than a dead traitor," he replied, and she snorted.

"All right. I'm here. What's so important?"

"Several things. First, I've confirmed that they know they didn't get all of Anu's people." Francine looked up sharply and received another thin smile. "Obviously they don't know *who* they didn't get, or we wouldn't be having this melodramatic conversation."

"No, I suppose we wouldn't. What else?"

"This." A data chip was handed over. "That little item is too important to trust to our usual pipeline."

"Oh?" She looked down at it curiously.

"Indeed. It's a copy of the plans for Marshal Tsien's newest toy: a gravitonic warhead powerful enough to take out an entire planet."

Francine's hand clenched on the chip, and her eyes widened.

"His Majesty," the man said with a soft chuckle, "has decided against building it, but I'm more progressive."

"Why? To threaten to blow *ourselves* up if they ID us?"

"I doubt that bluff would fly, but there are other ways it might be useful. For now, I just want the hardware handy if we need it."

"All right." She shrugged. "I assume you can get us any military components we need?"

"Perhaps. If so, we'll handle that through the regular channels. In the meantime, how are your action groups coming along?"

"Quite nicely, actually." Hilgemann's smile was unpleasant. "In fact, their training's developing their paranoia even further, and keeping them on a leash isn't the easiest thing in the world. It may be necessary to give them the odd mission to work off some of their . . . enthusiasm. Is that a problem?"

"No, I can pick a few targets. You're certain they don't know about you?"

"They're too well compartmented for that," she said confidently.

"Good. I'll select a few operations that'll cost them some casualties, then. Nothing like providing a few martyrs for the cause."

"Don't get too fancy," she cautioned. "If they lose too many they're likely to get a bit hard to control."

"Understood. Then I suppose that's about it . . . except that you'll want to get your next pastoral letter ready."

"Oh?"

"Yes. His Majesty's decided to bite the bullet and begin

enlisting Narhani in the military." Hilgemann nodded, eyes suddenly thoughtful, and he smiled. "Exactly. We'll want something restrained for open distribution—an injunction to pray that His Majesty hasn't made a mistake, perhaps—but a little furnace-fanning among the more hardcore is in order, I believe."

"No problem," the bishop said with an equally thin smile.

"I'll be going, then. Wait fifteen minutes before you leave."

"Of course." She was a bit nettled, though she didn't let it show. Did he think she'd lasted this long without learning her trade?

The door closed behind him, and she sat on a floor cleaner, lips pursed, considering how best to fill her pen with properly diffident vitriol, while the hand in her pocket squeezed the data chip that could kill a world.

Chapter Five

Sean MacIntyre landed neatly in the clearing and killed the power.

"Nice one, Sean," Tamman said from the copilot's seat. "Almost as nice as I could've done."

"Yeah? Which one of us took the top off that sequoia last month?"

"Wasn't the pilot's fault," Tamman replied loftily. "*You* were navigating, if I recall."

"He couldn't have been; you got home," a female voice said.

Tamman smirked, and Sean raised his eyes to the heavens in a plea for strength. Then he punched Tamman's shoulder, and the female voice groaned behind them as they grappled. "They're at it *again*, Sandy!"

"Too much testosterone, Harry." The younger voice dripped sympathy. "Their poor, primitive male brains are awash in the stuff."

Tamman and Sean paused in silent agreement, then turned towards the passenger compartment with vengeful intent, but their purposeful progress came to an abrupt end as Sean ran full tilt into a large, solid object and *oofed*.

"Damn it, Brashan!" he complained, rubbing the prominent nose he'd inherited from his father to check for damage.

"I'm simply opening the hatch, Sean," a mechanically produced voice replied. "It's not *my* fault you don't watch where you're going."

"Some navigator!" Harriet sniffed.

"Fortunately for a certain loudmouthed snot," Tamman

observed, "she's a princess, so I can't paddle her fanny the way she deserves."

"Don't you just *wish* you could get your hands on my fanny, you lech!"

"Don't worry, Tam," Sean said darkly. "I'll be happy to deputize. As soon—" he added "—as a certain oversized polo pony gets out of my way!"

"Oooh, protect me, Brashan!" Harriet cried, and the Narhani laughed and stood aside, blocking off the cockpit as the hatch opened. The girls scampered out, and Galahad's litter-mate Gawain followed, raised muzzle already scenting the rich jungle air.

"Traitor!" Sean kicked his friend—which hurt his toe far more than his target. Brashan was only ten Terran years old, six years younger than Sean, but he was already sufficiently mature for full enhancement. The augmentation biotechnics provided was proportional to a being's natural strength and toughness, and the heavy-grav Narhani were very, very tough by human standards.

"Nonsense. Simply a more mature individual striving to protect you from your own impetuosity," Brashan returned, and trotted down the ramp.

"Yeah, sure," Sean snorted as he and Tamman followed.

It was noon, local time, and Bia blazed directly overhead. Birhat lay almost a light-minute further from its G0 primary than Earth lay from Sol, but they were almost exactly on the equator, and the air was hot and still. The high, shrill piping of Birhat's equivalent of birds drifted down, and a bat-winged pseudodactyl drifted high overhead.

Sean and Tamman paused to check their grav rifles. Without full enhancement, neither could handle a full-sized energy gun, but their present weapons were little heavier than Terran sporting rifles. The twenty-round magazines held three-millimeter darts of superdense chemical explosive, and the rifles fired them with a velocity of over five thousand meters per second. Which meant they had enough punch to take out a pre-Imperial tank . . . or the larger denizens of Birhat's ecosystem.

"Looks good here." Sean's crispness was far removed from his earlier playfulness, and Tamman nodded to confirm his own weapon's readiness. Then they turned towards the others, and Sean made a face. Sandy was already perched in her favorite spot astride Brashan's powerful back.

He supposed it made sense, even if she did look insufferably smug, for something had gone astray in Sandra MacMahan's genes. Neither of her parents were midgets, yet she barely topped a hundred and forty centimeters. If she hadn't had Hector MacMahan's eyes and Ninhursag's cheekbones, Sean would have suspected she was a changeling from his mother's bedtime stories. Of course, she wasn't quite fifteen, but Harriet had shot up to almost one-eighty by the time she was that age.

Not, he thought darkly, that Sandy let her small size slow her down. She was so far out ahead scholastically it wasn't funny, but the thing he really hated was that whenever they got into an argument she was invariably right. Like that molycirc problem. He'd been positive the failure was in the basic matrix, but, *nooooo*. She'd insisted a power surge had bridged the alpha block, and damned if she hadn't been right . . . again. It was maddening.

At least he had a good sixty centimeters on her, he thought moodily.

He and Tamman caught up with the others, and he tapped the grav pistol at Harriet's side pointedly. She made a face but drew it and checked its readiness. Sandy—of course—had already checked hers.

"Which way, Sean?" Brashan asked, and Sean paused to orient his built-in inertial guidance system to the observations he'd made on the way in.

"About five klicks at oh-two-twenty," he announced.

"Couldn't you set down any closer?" Harriet demanded, and he shrugged.

"Sure. But we're talking about tyranotops. You really want one of them stepping on the flyer? It might get sort of broken around the edges."

"True," she admitted, and drew her bush knife as they

approached the towering creepers and ferns fringing the clearing.

As always, she and Sean took point, followed by Tamman, while a wide-ranging Gawain burrowed through the undergrowth and Brashan covered the rear. Sean was well aware Brashan was the real reason his mother and father raised no demur to the twins' excursions. Even a tyranotops—that fearsome creature which resembled nothing so much as a mating of a Terran triceratops and tyrannosaurus—would find a fully enhanced Narhani a handful, and Brashan carried a heavy energy gun, as well. As baby-sitters went, Narhani took some beating, which suited Sean and his friends just fine. Birhat was ever so much more interesting than Earth, and Brashan meant they could roam it at will.

Odd birds and beasts fluttered and rumbled in the underbrush, starting up in occasional panic as Gawain flushed them, and many of them were species no one else had yet seen. That was one of the things they loved about Birhat. The old Imperial capital had reverted to its second childhood after the bio-weapon hit, for the toxin hadn't been able to reach the sealed, protected eco-systems of the Imperial family's extraplanetary zoos. By the time failing environmental equipment finally released the inhabitants of over a dozen different oxy-nitrogen planets, the weapon itself had died, and forty-odd thousand years of subsequent natural selection had produced a biosystem that was a naturalist's opium dream.

For all intents and purposes, Birhat was a virgin planet, and it was all theirs. Well, theirs and three-quarters of a billion other people's, but that left lots of empty space, since most of the Bia System's steadily growing population was concentrated in and around the new capital or out in the system's enormous spaceborne industrial complexes, working like demons to resurrect the Empire. And, of course, at the moment they were in the middle of the Sean Andrew MacIntyre Continental Nature Preserve the Crown had established to honor Sean's uncle, who'd died fighting Anu's mutineers.

Not that they'd have such freedom much longer. Sean had been vested with the first official sign of his status as Heir last year when he was presented to Mother, for under the Great Charter Mother passed on the acceptability of the Heir's intellect and psych-profile. He'd been accepted, and the subliminal challenge-response patterns and implant codes which identified him as Heir had been implanted, but it had been the scariest moment of his life—and a clear sign that adulthood was coming closer.

There were signs for his friends, as well. All of them were headed for Battle Fleet—they'd known that for years—but they were getting close to meeting the Academy's entry requirements. Another year, possibly two, Sean estimated, until their free time evaporated.

But for now the day was young, the pride of tyranotops they'd come to see awaited them, and he intended to enjoy himself to the full.

A cool breeze flowed over the balcony, for it was summer in Birhat's northern hemisphere, and Colin had switched off the force fields which walled the balcony against the elements at need.

The city of Phoenix lay before him in the night, the serpentine curve of the River Nikkan sparkling far below, and Tsien Tao-ling's engineering crews had done well by Birhat's settlers. Phoenix was the product of a gravitonic civilization, and its towers soared even above the mighty near-sequoias about them, but the Palace was the tallest spire of all. Perhaps some thought that was to reflect its inhabitants' rank, but the real reason was practicality. True, the imperial family had luxurious personal quarters, but that was almost a side effect of the Imperium's administrative needs. Even a structure as vast as the Palace was badly overcrowded by functionaries and bureaucrats, though the new Annex going up next door would help . . . for a while.

He sighed and slid an arm about Jiltanith, and silken hair brushed his cheek as she leaned against him. He kissed the top of her head, then swept his telescopic eyes over the city, enjoying the jeweled interplay of lights and the magical wash of shifting moonlight. The complex pattern never ceased to delight him, for he'd grown up with but a single moon.

He raised his gaze to the heavens, and the stars were hard to see. The gleaming disk of Mother's fortress hull hung almost directly overhead, and over fifty huge planetoids dotted the night sky beyond her. They were much farther out (the comings and goings of that many "moons" would play merry hell with Birhat's tides), but the sunlight reflected from their hulls gilded the Fifth Imperium's capital in bronze and ebony. And on the farside of the planet from Mother—indeed, just about directly over the spot where his children were even now observing their tyranotops—hung another vast sphere named *Dahak*.

"God, 'Tanni," he murmured, "*look* at that."

"Aye." She squeezed him gently. " 'Tis like unto God's own gem box."

"It really is," he agreed softly. "Sort of makes it all seem worthwhile, doesn't it?" She nodded against his shoulder, and he sighed, looking back up at the distant planetoids once more. "Of course, looking at all this also tends to make me think about how much we still have to do."

"Mayhap, my love. Yet have we done all Fate hath called us to thus far. I misdoubt not we'll do all else when time demands."

"Yeah." He inhaled deeply, savoring the night, and pressed his cheek against her hair in deep, happy contentment.

"How're the kids coming along, Dahak?"

"I regret to report that Sean has just tripped Harriet into a particularly muddy stream. Otherwise, things are proceeding to plan. Analysis of Harriet's personality suggests she will attain revenge shortly."

"Damn right," Colin agreed, and Jiltanith's laugh gurgled in his ear.

"Thou'rt worse by far than thy offspring, Colin Mac-Intyre!"

"Nah, just older and deeper in sin." He chuckled. "God, I'm glad they're growing up like normal kids!"

" 'Normal,' thou sayest? My love, the Furies themselves scarce could wreak the havoc those twain do leave strewn in their wake!"

"I know. Ain't it great?" Bio-enhanced fingers pinched his ribs like a steel vise and he yelped. "Just think what royal pains in the ass they *could* have turned into," he said, rubbing his side.

"Aye, there's that," Jiltanith said more seriously, "and 'twas thou didst save them from it."

"You had a hand in it, too."

"Oh, aye, there's truth in that, but thou'rt the one who taught them warmth, my Colin. I love them well, and that they know wi'out doubt, but life hath not fitted me o'er well to nourish younglings."

"You did good, anyway," Colin said. "Actually, it looks like we make a pretty good team."

"Indeed, 'Tanni," Dahak added. "Left to his own devices, Colin would undoubtedly have—I believe the proper term is 'spoiled them rotten.' "

"Oh, I would, would I? Well, mister energy-state smarty pants, who was smart enough to suggest finding them something to do besides sitting around sucking on silver spoons?"

"It was you," Dahak replied with a soft, electronic chuckle. "A fact which, I must confess, continues to surprise me." Colin muttered something rude, and Jiltanith giggled. "Actually," the computer went on, "it was an excellent idea, Colin. One which should have occurred to me."

"Oh, it probably would've come to you eventually. But unless something goes wrong in a big way, 'Tanni and I are gonna be around for centuries, and a professional crown prince could get mighty bored in that much time. Besides, we're young enough it's unlikely Sean will outlive us by more than a century or so. It'd be a dead waste of his life to wait that long for such a brief reign."

"Indeed. The classic example from your own recent history would, of course, be that of Queen Victoria and Edward VII. The tragic waste of Edward's potential did great disservice to his country, and—"

"Maybe," Colin interrupted, "but I wasn't thinking about the Imperium. I want our kids to *do* something, and not for the Imperium. I want them to be able to look back and know they were winners, not place-holders. And I want them to know all the nice perks—the rank and deference, the flattery they're gonna hear—don't mean a thing unless they *earn* them."

He fell silent for a moment, feeling Jiltanith's silent agreement as she hugged him tight, and stared up to where Mother hung overhead like the very embodiment of an emperor's power and treacherous grandeur.

"Dahak," he said finally, "Herdan's dynasty ruled for five thousand years. Five *thousand* years. That's not a long time for someone like you, but it's literally beyond the comprehension of a human. Yet long as it was, impossible as it is for me to imagine, our kids—and their kids, and their kids' kids—may rule even longer. I can't begin to guess what they'll face, the sorts of decisions they'll have to make, but there's one thing 'Tanni and I can give them, starting right here and now with Sean and Harry. Not for the Imperium, though the Imperium'll profit from it, but for them."

"What, Colin?" Dahak asked quietly.

"The knowledge that power is a responsibility. The belief that who they are and what they do is as important as what they're born to. A tradition of—well, of *service*. Becoming Emperor should be the capstone of a life, not a career in itself, and 'Tanni and I want our kids—our family—to remember that. That's why we're sending them to the Academy, and why we won't have anyone kowtowing to them, much as some of the jerks who work for us would love to."

Dahak was silent for a moment—a very long moment, for him—before he spoke again. "I believe I understand you, Colin, and you are correct. Sean and Harriet do not yet realize what you and 'Tanni have done for them, but someday they will understand. And you are wise to make service a tradition rather than a matter of law, for my observation of human polities suggests that laws are more easily subverted than tradition."

"Yeah, that's what we thought, too," Colin said.

"Nay, my love," Jiltanith said softly. " 'Twas what *thou* didst think, and glad am I thou didst, for thou hadst the right of it."

" 'Tanni is correct, Colin," Dahak said gently, "and I am glad you have explained it to me. I do not yet have your insight into individuals, but I will have many years to gain it, and I will not forget what you have said. You and 'Tanni are my friends, and you have made me a member of your family. Sean and Harriet are your children, and I would love them for that reason even if they were not themselves my friends. But they *are* my friends—and my family—and I see I have a function I had not previously recognized."

"What function?"

"Mother may be the guardian of the Imperium, Colin, but *I* am the guardian of our family. I shall not forget that."

"Thank you, Dahak," Colin said very, very softly, and Jiltanith nodded against his shoulder once more.

Chapter Six

It wasn't a large room, but it seemed huge to Sean MacIntyre as he stood waiting at the foot of the narrow bed, and his anxious eyes swept it again and again, scanning every surface for the tiniest trace of dust.

Sean had spent all his seventeen and a half years knowing he was Academy-bound, yet despite the vantage point his lofty birth should have given him, he hadn't really understood what that meant. Now he knew . . . and his worst nightmares had fallen far short of the reality.

He was a "plebe," the lowest form of military life and the legitimate prey of any higher member of the food chain. He remembered dinner conversations in which Adrienne Robbins had assured his father she'd eliminated most of the hazing the Emperor had recalled from his own days at the U.S. Navy's academy. Sean would never dream of disputing her word, of course, but it seemed unlikely to him that she could have eliminated very much of it after all.

Intellectually, he understood a plebe's unenviable lot was a necessary part of teaching future officers to function under pressure and knew it wasn't personal—or not, at least, for most people. All of which made no difference to his sweaty palms as he awaited quarters inspection, for this was a subject upon which his intellect and the rest of him were hardly on speaking terms. He'd embarrassed Mid/4 Malinovsky, his divisional officer, before her peers. The fact that he'd embarrassed himself even worse cut no ice with her, and understanding why she'd set her flinty little heart on making his life a living hell was no help at all.

He'd felt, to use one of his father's favorite deflating phrases, as proud as a peacock as he stood in the front rank of the newest Academy class, awaiting the Commandant's first inspection. Every detail of his appearance had been perfect—God knew he'd worked hard enough to make it so!—and he'd been excited and happy despite the butterflies in his midsection. And because he'd felt and been all those things, he'd done an incredibly stupid thing.

He'd *smiled* at Admiral Robbins. Worse, he'd forgotten to stare straight before him as she inspected the ranks. He'd actually *turned his head* to meet her eyes and *grinned* at her!

Lady Nergal hadn't said a word, but her brown eyes had held no trace of "Aunt Adrienne's" twinkle. Their temperature had hovered somewhere a bit below that of liquid helium as they considered him like some particularly repulsive amoeba, and the parade ground's silence had been . . . profound.

It only lasted a century or so, and then his eyes whipped back to their appointed position, his ramrod-straight spine turned straighter still, and his smile vanished. But the damage had been done, and Christina Malinovsky intended to make him pay.

The click of a heel warned him, and he snapped to rigid attention, thumbs against his trouser seams, as Mid/4 Malinovsky entered his quarters.

There were no domestic robots at the Academy. Some of the Fleet and Marine officers had pointed out that their own pre-Imperial military academies had provided their midshipmen and cadets with servants in order to free them from domestic concerns and let them concentrate on their studies. Admiral Robbins, however, was a product of the U.S. military tradition. She was a great believer in the virtues of sweat, and no one had quite had the nerve to argue with her when she began designing the Academy's syllabus and traditions. The fact that His Imperial Majesty Colin I sprang from the same tradition as Admiral Robbins may also have had a little something to do with that, but the mechanics behind the decision meant little to the plebes faced with its consequences, and Sean had labored manfully against this dreadful moment. Now he stood silent, buttons gleaming like tiny suns, boots so brightly polished it was difficult to tell they were black, and used the full enhancement he'd finally received to keep from sweating bullets.

Mid/4 Malinovsky prowled around the room, running white-gloved fingers over shelves and dresser top, regarding her stony face in the lavatory mirror as she checked his tooth glass for water spots. She opened his locker to examine its contents and his tiny closet to check the hangered garments and study the polish of his second pair of boots. Her perfectly turned out exec stood in the door, traditional clipboard tucked under his arm, watching her, and Sean could almost feel the sadistic glee with which he waited to inscribe Mid/1 MacIntyre's name on his gig list. But Malinovsky said nothing, and Sean fought down a sense of relief and reminded himself she wasn't done yet.

She straightened and closed the closet, looked about the room one more time, and crossed to his bed. She stopped where he could see her—not, he was certain, by accident—and reached into her pocket. She took her time, making an elaborate ritual of it, as she withdrew a shiny disk Sean recognized after a moment as an antique U.S. silver dollar. She balanced it consideringly on her crooked index finger and thumb, then flipped it.

The coin flashed through the air, then arced down to land precisely in the center of the bunk . . . and lie there.

Malinovsky's gray eyes glittered as it failed to bounce, and Sean's heart fell. He kept his face impassive—with an effort—as she reclaimed the coin and weighed it in her palm a moment before pocketing it once more. Then she reached down, gripped the blanket and sheets, and stripped the mattress bare with a single jerk.

She turned on her heel, and her exec's stylus was poised.

"Five demerits," she said flatly, and stalked away.

❖   ❖   ❖

Colin MacIntyre looked around the gleaming conference table at the members of his Imperial Council. Two of them were absent, for Lawrence Jefferson had been called in as a last-minute substitute for Horus, and Life Councilor Geb, the Minister of Reconstruction was seldom on Birhat. For the most part, that was because he spent his time following close on the heels of Survey Command, but Geb was also the last surviving citizen of the original Birhat, and the monumental changes his home world had suffered hurt.

That was one reason Colin had recalled Vlad Chernikov from his post as Geb's assistant. Tsien and Horus had needed an engineer on Birhat, so Colin had created the Ministry of Engineering and Vlad had agreed to accept it. Now the blond, blue-eyed ex-cosmonaut finished his summary of the Bia System's ongoing civilian projects, and Colin nodded approval.

"Sounds like you're on top of things, Vlad . . . as usual." Vlad smiled, and Colin smiled back. "Having said that, how's Earth's shield coming?"

"Quite well," Vlad said. "The only real problem is the task's simple magnitude. We have emplaced forty percent of the primary generators and work is beginning on the subordinate stations. I fear the asteroid belt has all but vanished, but the Centauris freighters are keeping pace."

Colin nodded. Spaceborne Imperial "smelters" could render almost any material down to its basic elements to synthesize the composites and alloys Imperial industry needed, like the battle steel which formed Battle Fleet's planetoids, but even Imperial synthetics required some starting point. The raw materials to build things the size of Mother or *Dahak* had to come from somewhere, and the huge freighters of the Imperium's "mining expeditions" could—and did—transport the rubble of entire planets to the fabrication centers. The Centauris System, unfortunately for it, was conveniently close to Sol, and its original eleven planets had already been reduced to nine. Soon there would be only eight as gravitonic warheads blew yet another to splinters to feed the insatiable appetite of Earth's orbital shipyards.

"In the meantime, Baltan and Dahak have completed plans for Stepmother." Several councilors' eyes narrowed with interest. "We have yet to fully explore Mother's memory, but we are confident we have extracted all the essential programs for her Battle Fleet and constitutional functions. Stepmother's final core programming parameters remain flexible, however, as it seems probable additions will be required as our studies here in Bia continue. Of course, the entire project will require many years, but Horus, Tao-ling and I intend to initiate construction within three months."

"And thank God we're finally ready," Colin said. "Dahak, you and Baltan have my sincere thanks for your efforts."

"You are, of course, welcome, Sire," Dahak replied, on his best formal behavior for the meeting. "I feel certain I speak for Admiral Baltan as well as for myself."

"Well, remind me to thank him in person the next time I see him." Colin turned back to Vlad. "And the new planetoids?"

"Those are much further advanced, despite the usual unforeseen delays. *Imperial Terra* should commission within four years."

"Any problems with the computers, Vlad?" Gerald Hatcher asked.

"I'll take that, if I may, Colin," Sir Frederick Amesbury said. The wiry Englishman, one of Hatcher's fellow chiefs of staff during the Siege, had become Minister of Cybernetics, and Colin nodded for him to go on.

"The pilot computers have been up and running for over two years, Ger," Amesbury said, "and Dahak's original figures have been spot on. Incorporating that Achuultani logic circuit into our energy-state designs has raised the speed of operations another five percent, and we've included more responsiveness to nonspecific prompts in the software. They aren't self-aware, of course, but they have about thirty percent more autonomous decision-making capability. I believe you'll be quite pleased with the results."

"Excuse me, Sir Frederick," it was Lawrence Jefferson, "but that's something I'm still not quite clear on. I can see why we wouldn't want Mother or Stepmother to be self-aware, but why don't we want our warships that way? If we had more ships like *Dahak*, wouldn't we have a far more effective fleet?"

"Yes and no," Amesbury said. "The ships would certainly be more efficient, but they'd also be far more dangerous."

"Why?"

"If I may, Sir Frederick?" Dahak said, and Amesbury nodded. "The problem, Lieutenant Governor, is that such ships would be too powerful for our own safety. As you know, the Fourth Imperium was incapable of building fully self-aware computers at the time of my construction. My own awareness evolved accidentally during fifty-one thousand years of unsupervised operation, and even now, we have not fully determined the reasons for this.

"The Fourth Empire, however, was so capable yet chose not to utilize that capacity for reasons which, upon consideration, particularly in light of facts we have discovered but which the Empire could not have known, seem entirely valid. Consider: there is no proof cybernetic intelligences are immune to 'insanity,' and the Achuultani computer is ample proof not all are immune to ambition. Should an *Asgerd*-class planetoid go 'insane,' it could do incalculable damage. Indeed, true prudence might suggest that I myself should be transferred from my present hull to some less dangerous location."

"Dahak," Colin sighed, "we are *not* going to argue about that again! I'll accept your argument against creating any more self-aware computers, but *you've* certainly proven yourself to us!"

"Besides," Vlad said dryly, "why should the possibility that *you* might go crazy disturb us when we have an Emperor who has done so already?"

A chuckle ran around the table, but Colin didn't share it. His mind was already moving on to the next point, and he glanced at his Minister of Biosciences with a pang of sorrow. In many ways, Isis would have made a better councilor than Cohanna . . . if not for her age. She had far better "people sense," but Colin was unhappily certain Project Genesis was going to be not simply the crowning achievement of Isis Tudor's life but its last.

"All right, I believe that covers just about everything," he said quietly, "but before we close, Cohanna has something to report. 'Hanna?"

Cohanna looked down at her hands with uncharacteristic sadness for a moment, then cleared her throat.

"I wish Isis were here to tell you this herself, but she wasn't up to the trip. However—" she raised her eyes "—I'm pleased to announce that the first free Narhani female in seventy-eight million years was born at oh-two-thirty-four Greenwich time this morning." A soft sound of surprise ran around the table, and Cohanna smiled mistily. "Isis was there, and she's named the child 'Eve.' So far as we can tell, she's absolutely healthy."

Gerald Hatcher's quiet voice broke the long, still silence.

"I never really believed you could do it, 'Hanna."

"I didn't." Cohanna's voice was very soft. "Isis did."

There was another moment of silence before Vlad Chernikov spoke again, and his earlier levity had vanished.

"How *is* Isis, 'Tanni?" he asked gently.

"Not well, Vlad," Jiltanith said sadly. "She faileth quickly, and so Father doth stay at her side. She feeleth no pain, and she hath seen her life's work yield its fruit, yet do I fear her time is short."

"I am sorry to hear that." Vlad looked around the silent table for a moment, then back at Jiltanith. "Please tell her how proud we are of her . . . and give her our love."

"I shall," Jiltanith said softly.

Francine Hilgemann activated her antisnooping devices

before taking the new Bible from its package. Her security systems were every bit as good as those of the Imperial government (since they'd *come* from government sources), which meant she was as safe from observation as anyone could be, and she inhaled the rich smell of printer's ink appreciatively as she opened the book. She'd always loved beauty, and she was both amused and genuinely pleased by the effect neural computer feeds had produced on the printing industry. Man had rediscovered that books were treasures, not simply a means of conveying information, and the volume she held was a masterpiece of the printer's art.

She leafed through it admiringly, then paused at the Lamentations of Jeremiah. The tissue-thin paper slid out with pleasing ease—unlike the last time, when some idiot had used glue and wrecked two pages of Leviticus.

She unfolded the sheets, careful of their fragility, and spread them on her blotter. Datachips were far smaller and easier to hide. She and her allies knew that, but they also knew few modern security people thought in terms of anything as clumsy as written messages, which meant few looked for them. And, of course, data that was never *in* electronic storage couldn't be extracted *from* electronic storage by a computer named Dahak.

She got out her code book, translated the message, and read through it slowly twice, committing it to memory. Then she burned the sheets, ground the ash to powder, and leaned back to consider the news.

MacIntyre and his crowd were finally ready to begin on Stepmother, and she agreed with her ally's assessment. By rights, Stepmother ought to represent an enormous threat to their long-term plans, but that could be changed. With a little luck and a great deal of hard work, the "threat" was going to become the advantage that let them bring off the most ambitious coup d'etat in human history, instead.

She gnawed her thumbnail thoughtfully. In many ways, she'd prefer to strike now, but Stepmother had to be closer to completion. Not complete, but within sight of it. That gave them their time frame, and she was beginning to understand the purpose that godawful gravitonic warhead would serve. Her eyes gleamed appreciatively as she considered the implications. It would be their very own Reichstag fire, and the Narhani gave them such a splendid "internal threat" to justify the "special powers" their candidate for the crown would invoke to insure Stepmother got finished the right way.

But that was for the future. For now, there was this latest news about the Narhani to consider, and she pondered it carefully. Officially, she was simply the general secretary of the Church's coequal bishops—but then, Josef Stalin had been "simply" the General Secretary of the Central Committee, hadn't he?—and it would be her job to soothe her flock's anxiety when the information was officially released. Still, the Achuultani *were* the Spawn of the Anti-Christ, and with a little care, her soothing assurance that Narhani weren't *really* Achuultani—except, perhaps, in a purely technical sense, which, of course, loyal subjects of the Imperium could never hold against their fellow subjects when no one could *prove* they had Satanic origins—would convey exactly the opposite message. Add a particularly earnest pastoral letter reminding the faithful of their duty to pray for the Emperor's guidance in these troubled times, and the anti-Narhani ferment would bubble along very nicely, thank you.

And, in the meantime, there were those *other* members of her flock whom she would see got the news in somewhat less soothing form.

The Reverend Robert Stevens sat in the dingy room beneath his church and watched the shocked eyes of the men and women seated around him. He felt their horror rising with his own, and more than one face was ashen.

"Are you *sure*, Father Bob?" Alice Hughes asked hoarsely.

"Yes, Alice." Stevens' grating, high-pitched voice was ill-suited to prayers or sermons, but God had given him a mission which put such paltry burdens into their proper perspective. "You know I can't reveal my source's identity—" in fact, he had no idea who the ultimate source was, though its information had always proven reliable "—but I'm sure."

"God forgive them," Tom Mason whispered. "How could they actually help the Anti-Christ's spawn *breed?*"

"Oh, come on, Tom!" Yance Jackson's lip curled and his green eyes blazed. "We've known the answer to that ever since they started cloning their precious *'Narhani.'* " He made the name a curse. "They've been corrupted."

"But how?" Alice asked hesitantly. "They fought the Achuultani as God's own champions! How could they do that . . . and then do *this?*"

"It's this new technology," Jackson growled. "Don't you see, where fear couldn't tempt them, power has. They've set *themselves* up as gods!"

"I'm afraid Yance is right," Stevens said sadly. "They were God's champions, Alice, but Satan knows that as well as we do. He couldn't defeat them when they fought in His armor, so Satan's turned to temptation, seducing where he couldn't conquer. And this—" he tapped the piece of paper on the table before them "—is the proof he's succeeded."

"And so is the name they've given this demon of theirs," Jackson said harshly. " *'Eve!'* It should've been 'Lilith'!"

Stevens nodded even more sadly, but a new fire kindled in his eyes.

"The Emperor and his Council have fallen into evil," cold certitude cleansed his voice of sorrow, "and God-fearing people are under no obligation to obey evil rulers." He reached out to the people sitting on either side of him, and more hands rose, joining in a circle of faith under the humming fluorescent light. Stevens felt their belief feeding his own, making it strong, and a fierce sense of purpose filled him.

"The time is coming, brothers and sisters," he told them. "The time of fire, when the Lord shall call us to

smite the ungodly in His name, and we must be strong
to do His will. For the Armageddon is truly upon us, and
we—" his eyes swept around the circle, glittering with
an inner flame "—are the true Sword of God!"

Chapter Seven

The planet Marha, seventeen light-minutes from Bia and smaller than Mars, had never been much of a planet, and it had become less of one when the Fourth Imperium made it a weapons testing site. For two thousand years, until antimatter and gravitonic warheads made planetary tests superfluous, fission, fusion, and kinetic weapons had gouged and ripped its near-airless surface into a tortured waste whose features defied all logical prediction.

Which was precisely why the Imperial Marines loved Marha. It was a wonderful place to teach infantry the finer points of killing other people, and Generals Tsien and MacMahan were delighted to share it with Admiral Robbins' midshipmen. Naval officers might not face infantry combat often, but they couldn't always avoid it, either, and not knowing what they were doing was a good way to get people (especially their Marine-type people) killed.

At the moment, Admiral Robbins rode the command deck of the transport *Tanngjost*, sipping coffee, and her brown eyes gleamed as her scanners watched her third-year class deploy against the graduating class. That Sean was a sneaky devil, she thought proudly. He'd made an absolute ass of himself at his first parade, but he'd survived it, and he stood first in the Tactics curriculum by a clear five points. He was a bit audacious for her taste, but that wasn't too surprising, and his parents would have just loved this one.

Mid/3 MacIntyre hand-signaled a stop, and his

company of raiders slumped in the knife-sharp shadow of the tortured ring wall. He slumped with them, panting hard, and tried to remember he was being brilliant. If he managed to pull this off, he might even find two or three people to agree with him; if he screwed up, everybody would be waiting to tell him what a jackass he'd been.

He glanced at Sandy, more worried than he cared to admit as he noted how wearily she sat. This was her company, and she'd loved the idea when he sketched it out, but her small size was working against her.

An enhanced person could move in powered-down combat armor, if its servos were unlocked. It wasn't easy (especially for someone Sandy's size), but the sheer grunt work could be worth it under the right circumstances. Unpowered armor had no energy signature, and it even hid any emissions from its wearer's implants, which meant his raiders were virtually invisible.

The only real threat was optical detection, and he'd noticed that while his peers gave lip service to the importance of optical systems, they *relied* on more sophisticated sensors. He'd started to mention that during the critique of the last field exercise, but then he'd remembered *he* would be leading this one . . . and that the Academy didn't give out prizes for losing.

He slithered up the ring wall, unhooked the passive scanner from his harness, poked it over the crest, and grinned at its display. Onishi and his staff were exactly where The Book said they ought to be, safely tucked away at the heart of the sensor net guarding their HQ site. But The Book hadn't envisioned having a company of raiders barely half a klick away, well inside the sensor perimeter which should have protected Onishi's tactical HQ and ready to decapitate his entire command structure before Tamman (who'd always wanted to be a Marine anyway, for some strange reason) led in the main force.

He slid back down beside Sandy and pressed his helmet to hers. The face behind her visor was sweat-streaked and weary, but her brown eyes were bright, and he grinned and slapped her armored shoulder.

"We got 'em, Sandy!" Their helmets conducted his voice to her without the betraying pulse of a fold-space com. "Get the troops saddled up."

She nodded and began waving hand signals, and her support squad set up with gratifying speed, even without their armor's "muscles." He left them to it and reclimbed the slope to double-check the target coordinates. A standard saturation pattern would work just fine, he thought gleefully.

He glanced up. Sandy's heavy weapons types were set, and her other people were creeping up beside him, "energy guns" ready. It was just like laser tag, he thought, prepping his implants to activate his armor. And then he energized his com for the first time in almost six hours.

"*Now!*" he snapped.

Mid/4 Onishi Shidehara frowned as he stepped out of his HQ van to stretch. Crown Prince or no, MacIntyre was a hot dog, and the cautious sparring being reported by the outposts wasn't like him. It was only skirmishing, and along the most logical line of advance, at that. Mid/4 Onishi expected to kick His Imperial Highness's ass most satisfyingly, but so far he'd seen barely ten percent of the opposition, which suggested MacIntyre meant to try something fancy. For Onishi's money all that razzle-dazzle might look good to the instructors, but only MacIntyre's luck had let him get away with it so long. *This* time he was going to have to do things the hard way, and—

Something kicked dust in front of him. In fact, *dozens* of somethings were falling all over his position! He just had time to feel alarm before they erupted in the brilliant flashes of "nukes" and "warp grenades," and he went down in an astonished cloud of dust as the flash-bangs' override pulses locked his armor and blanked out his com implant to simulate a casualty.

He whipped his head around, trapped in his inert armor, and saw his entire HQ staff falling about him. A second wave of flash-bangs deluged his position, catching most of the handful who'd escaped the first, and then a horde of armored figures came down off the ring wall shooting.

It was over in less than thirty seconds, and Mid/4 Onishi gritted his teeth as one armored figure loped over to squat beside him with a toothy grin.

"*Zap!*" Sean MacIntyre said insufferably.

It had taken Horus months to learn to smile again after Isis' death, but today his grin was enormous as he entered Lawrence Jefferson's office.

"What's so funny?" the Lieutenant Governor asked.

"I just got back from Birhat," Horus said, still grinning, "and you should've heard Colin and 'Tanni describing Dahak's latest brainstorm!"

"Oh?" Unlike most people, Jefferson preferred an old-fashioned swivel chair, and it creaked as he leaned back. "What 'brainstorm'?"

"Oh, it was a beaut! You know how protective he is of the kids?" Jefferson nodded; Dahak's devotion to the imperial family was legendary. "Well, their middy cruise's coming up in a few months, and he had the brilliant idea that they should make it aboard him." The old man laughed, and Jefferson frowned.

"Why not? They couldn't possibly be in safer hands, after all!"

"That was his point," Horus agreed, "but Colin and 'Tanni won't hear of it, and I don't blame them." Jefferson still looked puzzled, and Horus shook his head and hitched a hip onto the Lieutenant Governor's desk.

"Look, *Dahak*'s the flagship of the Imperial Guard, right? Not even a unit of Battle Fleet at all."

Jefferson nodded again. Colin MacIntyre had lost ninety-four percent of the Fourth Empire's resurrected Imperial Guard Flotilla in the Zeta Trianguli Campaign. Only five ships remained, and repairing them had taken years, but they were back in service now. They were also fundamentally different from the rest of the Fifth

Imperium's planetoids, for their computers lacked the Alpha imperatives which compelled the rest of Battle Fleet to obey *Mother*, not the Emperor directly. Herdan the Great, the Fourth Empire's founder, had set Battle Fleet up that way as an intentional safeguard, since Mother wouldn't obey an emperor who'd been constitutionally removed by the Assembly of Nobles or whose actions violated the Great Charter stored in her memory. That neatly cut the legs out from under a monarch with tyranny on his mind, but the Guard was the Emperor's personal command, and its units *weren't* hardwired to obey Mother.

"All right," Horus continued, "every midshipman makes his senior-year cruise aboard a unit of Battle Fleet, so how would it look if Colin sends *his* kids out in *Dahak*? Bad enough that their fellows might resent it, but what kind of message does it send the twins? Besides, Dahak dotes on them; he'd find it mighty hard to treat them like any other snotties!"

"I suppose that's true." Jefferson swung his chair gently from side to side and grinned. "One doesn't tend to think of emperors and empresses as harassed parents. But if they're not using *Dahak*, what are they doing?"

"Well, Colin was all for letting the assignments be made randomly, but Dahak can be a bit mulish." Horus' eyes twinkled, and Jefferson laughed. He'd been present on one occasion when the computer had been moved to intransigence, and the Emperor's expression had been priceless.

"Anyway, they argued about it for a while and finally reached a compromise. *Imperial Terra*'s almost ready to commission—they're working up her final programming now—and Dahak 'suggested' using her. She'll be the newest and most powerful ship in Battle Fleet, and Dahak's personally vetted every detail of her design. Nothing's going to happen to them aboard *her*."

"It *is* a bit hard to conceive of anything threatening her," Jefferson mused. "In fact, I think that's a very good idea. With all due respect to Their Majesties, we shouldn't run risks with the succession."

"That's how Dahak brought them around in the end, and just between you and me, I'm glad he did," Horus agreed, and Jefferson nodded slowly.

"Here." Father Al-Hana took the data chips from his bishop and crooked his heavy eyebrows. "We've only got about two weeks to set this one up," Francine Hilgemann continued, "but don't take any chances."

"I see." Al-Hana slipped the chips into his pocket and wondered what they said. "Which group should I route them to?"

"Um." Hilgemann frowned down at her desk, playing with her pectoral cross as she considered. "Which is closest to Seattle?"

"That would be Stevens' group, I believe."

"Oh?" Hilgemann's smile wasn't pleasant. "That's nice. They've been spoiling for a mission. Are they ready for one?"

"I'd say so. The training cadre reports very favorably on them. And, as you say, they're eager. Shall I activate them?"

"Yes, they'll do nicely. But if *this* one goes sour the consequences are going to be fairly dire, so make sure of your cutouts. Use someone else if there's *any* way they could be traced back to us."

"Of course," Al-Hana said, and tried almost successfully to hide his surprise. Whatever was on the chips, it was important.

Vincente Cruz parked his rented flyer outside the cabin and inhaled deeply as he popped the hatch. Imperial technology had long since healed the worst scars from the Achuultani bombardment of Earth. Even the temperature was coming back to normal, and the terrible rains following the Siege had produced one beneficial side effect by washing centuries of accumulated pollution out of the atmosphere. The mountain air was crystal clear, and while he knew many of his fellow Bureau of

Ships programmers thought he was crazy to spend his vacations on Earth instead of the virgin surface of Birhat, he and Elena had always loved the Cascade Mountains.

He climbed out to unload the groceries, then paused with a frown, wondering why the kids weren't already here to help carry them in.

"Luis! Consuela!"

There was no response, and he shrugged. Luis had been in raptures over the fishing. No doubt he'd finally talked Consuela into trying it, and Elena had taken the baby and gone along to keep an eye on them.

He gathered up a double armload of groceries—no particular problem to a fully-enhanced set of arms—and climbed the steps to the porch. It was a bit awkward to work the door open, but he managed, and stepped through it, pushing it shut behind him with a toe. He started for the kitchen, then froze.

A man and a woman sat in front of the fireplace, and their faces were concealed by ski masks. He was still staring at them when he grunted in anguish and crashed to the floor. Cascading milk cartons burst like bombs, drenching him, but he hardly noticed. Only one thing could have produced his sudden paralysis: someone had just shot him from behind with a capture field!

He tried desperately to fight, but the police device had locked every implant in his body—even his com had been knocked out. He could neither move nor call for help, and panic filled him. His family! *Where was his family?*

The man from the fireplace rose and turned him onto his back with a toe, and Vincente stared up into the masked face, too consumed by terror for his family to feel any fear for himself even as the man knelt and pressed the muzzle of an old-fashioned Terran automatic into the base of his throat.

"Good afternoon, Mister Cruz." The high-pitched voice was unpleasant, but menace made its timbre utterly unimportant. "We have a job for you."

"W-who are you?" Just getting out those few words against the capture field took all Vincente's strength.

"Where are my—"

"Be quiet!" The voice was a whiplash. The pistol muzzle pressed harder, and Vincente swallowed, more frightened for his family than ever.

"That's better," the intruder said. "Your wife and children will be our guests, Mister Cruz, until you do exactly as we tell you."

Vincente licked his lips. "What do you want?" he asked hoarsely.

"You're a senior programmer for *Imperial Terra*," his captor said, and even through his fear Vincente was stunned. His job was so classified even Elena didn't know precisely what he did! How could these people—?

"Don't bother to deny it, Mister Cruz," the masked man continued. "We know all about you, and what you're going to do is add this—" he waved a data chip before Vincente's eyes "—to the ship's core programs."

"I-I *can't!* It's impossible! There's too much security!"

"You have access, and you're bright enough to find a way. If you don't—" The man's shrug was a dagger in Vincente's heart. He stared into the eyes in the mask slits, and their coldness washed away all hope. This man would kill him as easily as he might a cockroach . . . and he had Vincente's family.

"That's better." The masked man dropped the chip on his chest and straightened. "We have no desire to hurt women and children, but we're doing the Lord's work, and you've just become His instrument. Make no mistake; if you fail to do exactly as you're told, we *will* kill them. Do you believe me?"

"Yes," Vincente whispered.

"Good. And remember this: we knew where to find you, we know what you do, and we even know what ship you're working on. Think about that, because it also means we'll know if you're stupid enough to tell anyone about this."

The masked man stepped back, joined by his female companion and a tall, broad-shouldered man with the capture gun. They backed to the door, and he lay helpless, watching them go.

"Just do as you're told, Mister Cruz, and your family will be returned safe and sound. Disobey, and you'll never even know where they're buried."

The leader nodded to his henchman, and Vincente screamed as the capture field suddenly soared to maximum and hammered him into the darkness.

Chapter Eight

Senior Fleet Captain Algys McNeal sat on his command deck and watched his bridge officers with one eye and the hologram beside him with the other. Physically, Admiral Hatcher was several hundred thousand kilometers away, but fold-space coms let them maintain their conversation without interruptions. Not that Captain McNeal felt overly grateful. Commanding Battle Fleet's most powerful warship on her maiden cruise was quite enough to worry about; having both heirs to the Crown aboard made it worse, and he did *not* need the CNO sitting here flapping his jaws while *Imperial Terra* prepared to get underway!

". . . then take a good look around Thegran," Hatcher was saying.

"Yes, Sir," McNeal replied while he watched Midshipman His Imperial Highness Sean MacIntyre running final checks at Astrogation. The Prince had obviously hoped for assignment to Battle Comp, but he was already a competent tactician. He'd learn far more as an assistant astrogator, and so far, McNeal was cautiously pleased with Midshipman MacIntyre's cheerfulness in the face of his disappointment.

"And bring back some green cheese from Triam IV," Hatcher continued.

"Yes, Sir," McNeal said automatically, then twitched and jerked both eyes to his superior's face. Hatcher grinned, and McNeal returned it wryly.

"Sorry, Sir. I guess I *was* a bit distracted."

"Don't apologize, Algys. I should know better than to crowd you at a time like this." The admiral shrugged.

"Guess I'm a bit excited about your new ship, too. And frustrated at being stuck here in Bia."

"I understand, Sir. And you're not really crowding me."

"The hell I'm not!" Hatcher snorted. "Good luck, Captain."

"Thank you, Sir." McNeal tried to hide his relief, but Hatcher's eyes twinkled as he flipped a casual salute. Then he vanished, and McNeal's astrogator roused from her neural feeds to look up at him.

"Ship ready to proceed, Sir," she said crisply.

"Very good, Commander. Take us out of here."

"Aye, aye, Sir," Commander Yu replied.

Birhat's emerald and sapphire gem began to shrink in the display as they headed out at a conservative thirty percent of light-speed, and *Imperial Terra*'s officers were too busy to note a brief fold-space transmission. It came from the planetoid *Dahak*, and it wasn't addressed to any of them, anyway. Instead it whispered to *Terra*'s central computer for just an instant, then terminated as unobtrusively as it had begun.

"Well, they're off," Hatcher's hologram told Colin. "They'll drop off a dozen passage crews at Urahan, then move out to probe the Thegran System."

Colin nodded but said nothing, for he was concentrating on the neural feed he'd plugged into Mother's scanners. *Imperial Terra* had to be at least twelve light-minutes from Bia to enter hyper, and he sat silent for the full ten minutes she took to reach the hyper threshold. Then she blinked out, with no more fuss than a soap bubble, and he sighed.

"Damn, Gerald. I wish I was going with them."

"They'll be fine. And they've got to try their wings sometime."

"Oh, that's not my problem," Colin said with a crooked grin. "I'm not worried—I'm envious. To be that young, just starting out, *knowing* the entire galaxy is your own private oyster. . . ."

"Yeah. I remember how I felt when Jennifer made her middy cruise. She was cute as a puppy—and she'd have killed me on the spot if I'd said so!"

Colin laughed. Hatcher's older daughter was attached to Geb's Reconstruction Ministry, with three system surveys already under her belt, and she was about due for promotion to lieutenant senior grade.

"I guess all the good ones start out confident they can beat anything the universe throws at them," he said. "But you know what scares me most?"

"What?" Hatcher asked curiously.

"The fact that they may just be right."

The Traffic Police flyer screamed through the Washington State night at Mach twelve. That was pushing the envelope in atmosphere, even for a gravitonic drive, but this one looked bad, and the tense-faced pilot concentrated on his flying while his partner drove his scan systems at max.

An update came in from Flight Control Central, and the electronics officer cursed as he scanned it. Jesus! An entire family—*five* people, three of them kids! Accidents were rare with Imperial technology, but when they happened they tended to happen with finality, and he prayed this one was an exception.

He turned back to his sensors as the crash site came into range and leaned forward, as if he could force them to tell him what he wanted to see.

He couldn't, and he slumped back in his couch.

"Might as well slow down, Jacques," he said sadly.

The pilot looked sideways at him, and he shook his head.

"All we've got is a crater. A big one. Looks like they must've gone in at better than Mach five . . . and I don't see any personnel transponders."

"*Merde*," Sergeant Jacques DuMont said softly, and the screaming flyer slowed its headlong pace.

Underway holo displays had always fascinated Sean,

especially because he knew how little they resembled what a human eye would actually have seen.

Under the latest generation Enchanach drive, for example, a ship covered distance at eight hundred and fifty times light-speed, yet it didn't really "move" at all. It simply flashed out of existence *here* and reappeared over *there*. The drive built its actual gravity masses in less than a femtosecond, but the entire cycle took almost a full trillionth of a second in normal space between transpositions. That interval was imperceptible, and there was no Doppler effect to distort vision, since during those tiny periods of time the ship was effectively motionless, but any human eye would have found it impossible to sort out the visual stimuli as its point of observation shifted by two hundred and fifty-four million kilometers every second.

So the computers generated an artificial image, a sort of tachyon's-eye view of the universe. The glorious display enfolded the bridge in a three-hundred-sixty-degree panorama whose nearer stars moved visibly and gave humanity the comforting illusion of moving through a comprehensible universe.

The imaging computers confronted different parameters at sublight speeds. The Fifth Imperium's gravitonic drive had a maximum sublight velocity of a smidgen over seventy percent of light-speed (missiles could top .8 *c* before their drives lost phase lock and Bad Things happened) and countered mass and inertia. That conferred essentially unlimited maneuverability and allowed maximum velocity to be attained very quickly—not instantly; a vessel's mass determined the efficiency curves of its drive—without turning a crew into anchovy paste. But unlike a ship under Enchanach drive, sublight ships *did* move relative to the universe, and so had to worry about things like relativity. Time dilation became an important factor aboard them, and so did the Doppler effect. To the unaided eye, stars ahead tended to vanish off the upper end of the visible spectrum, while those astern red-shifted off its bottom.

Sean found the phenomenon eerily beautiful, and he'd loved the moments when his instructors had allowed him to switch the computer imaging out of the display to enjoy the "starbow" on training flights. Unfortunately, it wasn't very useful, so the computers and FTL fold-space scanners normally were called upon once more to produce an artificially "real" view.

Then there was hyper-space. *Imperial Terra*, like all Battle Fleet planetoids, had three distinct drive systems: sublight, Enchanach, and hyper, and her top speed in hyper was over thirty-two hundred times that of light. Yet "hyper-space" was more a convenient label for something no human could envision than an accurate description, for it consisted of many "bands"—actually a whole series of entirely different spaces—whose seething tides of energy were lethal to any object outside a drive field. Even with Imperial technology, human eyes found h-space's gray, crawling *nothingness* . . . disturbing. Vertigo was almost instantaneous; longer exposure led to more serious consequences, up to and including madness. Ships in normal space could detect the hyper traces of ships in hyper; ships in hyper were blind. They could "see" neither into normal space nor through hyper-space, and so their displays were blank.

Or, more precisely, they showed other things. Aboard *Imperial Terra*, Captain McNeal preferred holo projections of his native Galway coast, but the actual choice depended on who had the watch. Commander Yu, for example, liked soothing, abstract light sculptures, while Captain Susulov, the exec, had a weakness for Jerusalem street scenes. The only constant was the holographic numerals suspended above the astrogator's station: a scarlet countdown showing the time remaining to emergence at the ship's programmed coordinates.

Now Sean sat at Commander Yu's side, watching the sun set over Galway Bay while Captain McNeal waited for his ship to emerge from hyper in the Urahan System, twelve days—and over a hundred light-years—from Bia.

❖　　　　❖　　　　❖

Imperial Terra dropped back into humanity's universe sixty-three light-minutes from the F3 star Urahan. The Urahan System had never been a Fleet base, but a survey ship had found a surprising number of planetoids orbiting in its outer reaches . . . for reasons which became grimly clear once the survey crew managed to reactivate the first derelict's computers.

No one had ever lived on any of Urahan's planets, so starships contaminated by the bio-weapon could do no harm there. As ship after ship became infected and their people began to sicken, their officers had taken them to Urahan or some other unpopulated system and placed them in parking orbit.

And then they'd died.

Galway Bay vanished. Scores of planetoids appeared, drifting against the stars, gleaming dimly in the reflected light of Urahan, and Sean shivered as he watched six of *Terra*'s parasites move across the display, carrying forty thousand people towards the transports and repair ships of the Ministry of Reconstruction keeping station on those dead hulls.

All his life, Sean MacIntyre had known what had overwhelmed the Fourth Empire. He'd seen the ships brought back to Bia and read about the disaster, studied it, written papers on it for the Academy. He knew about the bio-weapon . . . but now he *understood* something he'd never quite grasped.

Those dead ships were real, and each had once been crewed by two hundred thousand people who'd worn the uniform he now wore. Real people who'd died because they'd tried to assist planets teeming with billions of other real people. And when they knew they, too, were infected, they'd come here to die rather than seek help for themselves and endanger still others.

The bio-weapon itself had died at last, but through all the dusty millennia, those ships had remained, waiting. And now, at last, humanity had returned to reclaim them and weigh itself against the criminal folly which had killed their crews . . . and the courage with which they'd died.

He watched the display, measuring himself against those long-dead crews, and a part of him that was very young hoped Captain McNeal would hyper out for Thegran soon.

Fleet Commander Yu Lin had been to Urahan before, and she'd watched her snotty as they dropped out of hyper. It would never do to admit it, but she rather liked Mid/4 MacIntyre. Crown Prince or no, he was hardworking, conscientious, and unfailingly polite, yet she'd wondered how such a cheerful extrovert would react to Urahan's death fleet.

Now she filed the ghosts in his eyes away beside the other mental notes she was making for his evaluation. It was interesting, she thought.

He seemed to feel exactly the way she did.

Imperial Terra considered her options as the coordinates for her next hyper jump were entered.

Although her Comp Cent wasn't self-aware, it came closer than those of older Battle Fleet units. *Terra* was actually a good bit brighter than Dahak had been when he first arrived in Earth orbit, yet trying to reconcile the two sets of Alpha Priority commands no one knew she had was a problem.

Normally, she would have asked for guidance, but Alpha commands took absolute precedence, and her directive to seek human assistance didn't carry Alpha Priority. There'd never seemed any reason why it should, but one of Vincente Cruz's commands prohibited any discussion of his other orders with her bridge officers, which meant Comp Cent was faced with devising a course of action which would satisfy both sets of commands all on its own.

It did.

Sean sat beside the park deck lake, skimming stones across the water. A bio-enhanced arm could send them for incredible distances, and he watched the skittering splashes vanish into the mist while his implants' low-powered force field shielded him from the falling rain.

Feet crunched on wet gravel behind him, and he read the implant codes without looking.

"Hi, guys," he said. "How d'you like Commander Godard's weather?"

He stood and turned to grin at his friends. This was the first time they'd all been off watch at once since leaving Urahan, and *Terra*'s logistics officer had decided the park decks needed a good rain. Fleet Commander Godard was a nice guy, and Sean didn't *think* he'd done it on purpose.

"I like it." Brashan trotted down to the lake and waded out belly-deep into the water. Unlike his human friends, he was in uniform, but Narhani uniform consisted solely of a harness to support his belt pouches and display his insignia, and Sean felt a familiar spurt of envy. Brashan had to spend more time polishing his leather and brightwork, but he'd never had to worry about getting a spot out of his dress trousers in his life.

"It reminds me of spring on Narhan," Brashan added, folding down into the water until only his shoulders showed and extending the fan of his cranial frill in bliss. "Of course, the air's still too thin, but the weather's nice."

"You *would* think so." Tamman kicked off his deck shoes and perched on the outer hull of a trimaran, dangling his feet in the water. "For myself, I'd prefer a bit less drizzle."

"You and me both," Sean agreed, though he wasn't sure that was entirely true. The humidity emphasized the smell of life and greenery, and he had his sensory boosters on high to enjoy the earthy perfume.

"Still want to go sailing?" Sandy asked.

"Maybe." Sean skimmed another stone into the mist. "I checked the weather schedule. This is supposed to clear up in about an hour."

"Well I'd rather wait until it does," Harriet said.

"Yeah." Sean selected another stone. "I suppose we could go up to Gym Deck Seven while we wait."

"No way." Tamman shook his head. "I poked my head in on the way down, and Lieutenant Williams is running another 'voluntary participation' unarmed combat session up there."

"Yuck." Sean threw his rock with a grimace. His human friends and he had played and worked out with Dahak's training remotes since they could walk. They were about the only members of the crew who were both junior to Williams and able to give him a run for his money, but he kept producing sneaky (and bruising) moves they hadn't seen yet whenever they got him in trouble.

"Double yuck," Sandy agreed. She was nimble and blindingly fast, even for an enhanced human, but her small size was a distinct disadvantage on the training mat.

"Oh, well," Harriet sighed, heading for the trimaran and beginning to unlace the sail covers, and Sean laughed as he climbed aboard to help her.

Deep in *Imperial Terra*'s heart Comp Cent silently oversaw her every function, monitoring, adjusting, reporting back to its human masters.

Terra was somewhat larger than an *Asgerd*-class planetoid, but she carried far fewer people, mostly because her sublight parasites, while larger and more powerful than their predecessors, had been designed around smaller crews. Horus' old *Nergal* had required three hundred crewmen, and even the Fourth Empire's sublight battleships had needed crews of over a hundred. With their Dahak-designed computers, *Imperial Terra*'s were designed for core crews of only thirty, and even that was more of a social than a combat requirement.

Yet *Terra*'s personnel still numbered over eighty thousand. Each of them was superbly trained, ready for any emergency, but all of those eighty thousand people depended upon what their computers told them and relied upon Comp Cent to do what it was told. From the engineers tending the roaring energy whirlpool of her core tap to the logistics staff managing her park decks and life support, they worked in an intimate fusion with their cybernetic henchmen, united through their neural feeds.

Continuous self-diagnostic programs scrutinized every aspect of those computers' operations, alert for any malfunction while *Imperial Terra*'s crewmen stood their watches and monitored their displays, and those displays told them all was well as their ship tore through hyper. But all was not well, for none of *Imperial Terra*'s crew knew about the Alpha Priority commands a programmer now dead with his entire family had inserted into their ship's computer, and so none of them knew Comp Cent had become a traitor.

Sandy MacMahan crossed the cool, cavernous bay to the gleaming flank of the sublight battleship *Israel*. Number six personnel hatch stood open, and she trotted up the ramp, wondering where Fleet Commander Jury was.

She poked her head in through the hatch and blinked in surprise.

"Sean? What're you doing here?"

"Me? What're *you* doing here? I got a memo from Commander Jury to report for an unscheduled training exercise."

"So did I." Sandy frowned. "Dragged me out of the sack, too."

"Too bad, considering how much you need your beauty sleep."

"At least beauty sleep does *me* some good, Beak Schnoz," she shot back, and Sean grinned and rubbed his nose, acknowledging her hit. "But speaking of Commander Jury, where is she?"

"Dunno. Let's check the command deck."

Sandy nodded, and they stepped into the transit shaft. The gravitonic system whisked them away . . . and the hatch closed silently behind them.

The midshipmen stepped out of the shaft onto the command deck and into a fresh surprise. Harriet,

Tamman, and Brashan were already there, and they looked just as puzzled as Sandy and Sean felt. There was a moment of confused questions and counter-questions, and then Sean held up his hands.

"Whoa! Hold on. Look, Sandy and I both got nabbed by Commander Jury for some extra hands-on parasite training time. What're you guys doing here?"

"The same thing," Harriet said. "And I don't understand it. I just finished a two-hour session in the simulator last watch."

"Yeah," Tamman said, "and if we're here, where's Commander Jury?"

"Maybe we'd better ask her." Sean flipped his neural feed into *Imperial Terra's* internal com net . . . and his eyes widened as the system kicked him right back out. *That* had never happened before.

He thought for a moment, then shrugged. Procedure frowned on using fold-space coms aboard ship, but something decidedly strange was going on, so he activated his implant com. Or, rather, he *tried* to activate it.

"Shit!" He glanced up and saw the others looking at him. "I can't get into the com net—and something's blanketing my fold-space com!"

Sandy stared at him in astonishment, and then her face went blank as *she* tried to contact Jury. Nothing happened, and a tiny flame of uncertainty kindled in her eyes. It wasn't fear—not yet—but it was closer to that than Sean liked to see from Sandy.

"I can't get in, either."

"I don't like this," Tamman muttered. Harriet nodded agreement, and Brashan stood and headed for the transit shaft.

"I think we'd better find out what's going on, and—"

"Three-minute warning," a calm, female voice interrupted the Narhani. "Parasite launch in three minutes. Assume launch stations."

Sean whirled to the command console. *Launch stations?* You couldn't launch a parasite in hyper-space without destroying parasite and mother ship alike—any moron knew that!—but the boards were blinking to life, and his jaw clenched as the launch clock began to count down.

"Oh, my God!" Harriet whispered, but Sean was already hammering at the console through his neural feed, and his dark face went white as the computer refused to let him in.

"Computer! Emergency voice override! Abort launch sequence!"

Nothing happened, and Brashan's voice was taut behind him.

"The transit shaft has been closed down, Sean."

"Jesus Christ!" With the shaft down, it would take over five minutes to reach the nearest hatch.

"Two-minute warning," the computer remarked. "Parasite launch in two minutes. Assume launch stations."

"What do we do, Sean?" Tamman asked harshly, and Sean scrubbed his hands over his face. Then he shook himself.

"Man your stations! Try to get into the system and shut the damned thing down, or this crazy computer'll kill us all!"

Commander Yu had been on watch for two hours. As most watches in hyper-space, they'd been deadly dull hours, and her attention was on the slowly shifting light sculptures, so it took her a few seconds to note the peculiar readings from Launch Bay Forty-One.

But then they began to register, and she straightened in her couch, eyes widening. The bay was entering launch cycle!

Commander Yu was an experienced officer. She paled as she realized what breaching the drive field in hyper would do to her ship, yet she didn't panic. Instead, she threw an instant abort command into Comp Cent's net and the computer acknowledged, but the bay went right on cycling!

She snapped her feed into a standby system and tried to override manually. The launch count went steadily on, and her face was bloodless as she began punching alarm circuits . . . *and nothing at all happened!*

Time was running out fast, and she did the only thing left. She ordered a complete, emergency computer shut down.

Comp Cent ignored her, and then it was too late.

Imperial Terra dropped out of hyper. There was no warning. She shouldn't have been able to do it. A ship in hyper *stayed* in hyper until it reached its programmed coordinates, and *Terra* hadn't reached the coordinates Commander Yu had given her. But she *had* reached the ones she'd selected under the overriding authority of her Alpha Priority commands.

She reappeared in normal space, over a light-year from the nearest star, and the battleship *Israel* screamed out of her bay under full emergency power. Her drive field shredded centimeter-thick battle steel bulkheads and splintered hatches the size of an aircraft carrier's flight deck. She massed over a hundred and twenty thousand tons, and *Imperial Terra*'s alarms screamed as she reamed the access shaft into tangled ruin.

Sean MacIntyre gasped in fear, pressed back into his couch by a cold-start, full-power launch. The battleship was moving at twenty percent of light-speed when she erupted from the air-spewing wound of her bay, and her speed was still climbing!

He stared at the holo display as it sprang to life, too confused and terrified to grasp what was happening. He should be dead, and he wasn't. The display should show only the gray swirls of hyper-space; it was spangled with diamond-chip suns in the velvet immensity of n-space, and *Imperial Terra* was a rapidly dwindling dot astern.

Comp Cent watched *Israel* accelerate clear and noted the faithful discharge of one set of Alpha Priority commands. With that detail out of the way, it could turn to its other imperatives.

✧   ✧   ✧

Harriet cried out in horror, and Sean cringed as *Imperial Terra*'s core tap blew, and eighty thousand people vanished in an eye-searing glare.

Chapter Nine

Baroness Nergal curled up on her couch with Fleet Vice Admiral Oliver Weinstein's head in her lap and popped another grape into his mouth.

"You do realize you're going to have to *earn* these grapes, don't you?" she purred as he swallowed.

"I don't think of it that way," he said with a chuckle.

"No? Then how *do* you think of it, pray tell?"

"The way I see it, *I* don't have to do anything. First my superior officer wines and dines me, spoiling me rotten and softening me up so she can have her wicked way with me. And second—"

"And second?" she prompted, poking his ribs as he paused with a grin.

"Why, second, she *does* have her way with me."

"You," she examined her remaining grapes with care, "are a despicable person of weak moral fiber." He nodded, and she shook her head in sorrow. "I, on the other hand, as a virtuous and upright person, am so shocked by the depths of your decadence that I think—" she paused as she finally found the perfect grape "—I'm going to shove this grape up your left nostril!"

Admiral Weinstein tried to whip upright and dodge, but Admiral Robbins was a clever tactician and tumbled him to the floor in a squirming, tickling heap. Her intended instrument of retribution pulped harmlessly against the tip of his nose, but things were progressing satisfactorily indeed when an urgent tone sounded.

Adrienne stopped dead, head rising in shock as the priority tone repeated, then vaulted to her feet. Weinstein sat up and started to speak, then froze as the tone sounded yet again. His confused expression vanished as the priority of the signal registered, and he rose to his knees.

Adrienne paused only to jerk a robe over her negligee, then answered the call with an impatient implant flick. Gerald Hatcher's hologram materialized before her, sitting in Mother's Command Alpha command chair, and his face was grim.

"Sorry to disturb you, Adrienne," his voice was flat, and her dread grew, "but we may have a serious problem." He drew a breath and met her eyes squarely. "Algys McNeal's Thegran sitrep is three hours overdue."

Robbins went white, and Hatcher continued in that same flat voice.

"We've double-checked with Urahan. They hypered out on schedule, and they should've reached Thegran five hours ago."

Adrienne nodded slowly, eyes huge. Many of the Fourth Empire's system governors had erected defenses in desperate efforts to quarantine their planets against the bio-weapon, but communications had been so chaotic as the Empire died that no one knew what any given governor might have cobbled up. The only way to find out was to go see, and if no one had yet encountered anything capable of standing up to a planetoid, there was always the possibility someone would. That was why all survey ships were required to report by hypercom within two hours of arrival in any unexplored system.

"It might be a hypercom failure," she suggested, but her own tone told her how little she believed it.

"Anything's possible," Hatcher said expressionlessly. The hypercom was massive and complex, but its basic technology had been refined for over six millennia. One might fail once in four or five centuries: certainly no more often. They both knew that, and they stared at one another in sick silence.

"Oh, Jesus, Ger," she whispered at last.

"I know."

"Was their hyper field unbalanced when they left Urahan?"

"I don't *know*." Frustration harshened Hatcher's voice. "They dropped off their passengers and hypered straight out, and none of the reconstruction people had any reason to run a trace on them. All we know is they hit the threshold and kicked over right on the tick."

"Oh, shit." The expletive was a prayer, and Adrienne raked fingers through her hair. "I simply can't believe they could've hit anything that could take *Terra*—not with Algys in command. It *has* to be a com failure!"

"You mean you *hope* it is," Hatcher said, then closed his eyes. "And so do I. But hoping won't change things if it's not." Adrienne nodded unhappily, and he drew a deep breath. "I'm mobilizing BatRon One for search and rescue with *Herdan* as Flag. Do you want it?"

"Of course I do!" Adrienne began unbelting her robe. Weinstein was already there, holding out her uniform, and she spared him a strained smile. "I'll be ready by the time my cutter gets here."

"Thank you," Hatcher said softly, and Adrienne swallowed.

"Will you—?" she began, and he nodded, face grimmer than ever.

"I'm leaving for the Palace now."

Fifteen *Asgerd*-class planetoids erupted from hyperspace ten light-minutes from the G4 star Thegran. They came out in battle formation, with shields up and enough weapons on-line to destroy an entire solar system. Every sensor was at max, seeking any threat and searching for any lifeboat's beacon.

But there was nothing to engage . . . and no beacons.

Adrienne Robbins sat on *Emperor Herdan*'s command deck, staring into the display, and her eyes burned. Thegran II, once known as Triam, was a sphere of bare rock and lifeless dirt, surrounded by a fraying necklace of near-space satellites and derelicts as dead as Triam herself.

She fought her tears. She'd hoped so *hard*! But there was no sign of *Imperial Terra* . . . or of anything that could have destroyed her. And if a hyper ship failed to reach its destination it never emerged from hyper at all. She drew a deep breath and rubbed her stinging eyes once, angrily, before she looked at her white-faced communications officer.

"Calibrate the hypercom, Commander," she said in a voice leached of all emotion.

"I'm sorry, Colin," Gerald Hatcher said quietly. "God, I'm sorry."

Colin sat in his study, trying not to weep while Jiltanith pressed her face into his shoulder and her tears soaked his tunic, and Hatcher started to reach out to them, then stopped. His hand hung in midair for a moment while he stared down at it as if at an enemy, then dropped it back into his lap.

"I'd hoped Adrienne would find something. Or that they'd have returned themselves if it *was* a com failure, but—" He broke off, and his jaw tightened. "It's my fault. I should never have let them all go in one ship."

"No." Colin's frayed voice quivered despite his effort to hold it steady. He shook his head almost convulsively. "It . . . it was *our* idea, Ger. Ours." He closed his eyes and felt a tear trickle down his cheek.

"I should've argued. God, how could I *be* so stupid! *Both* of them, and Sandy and Tam—" Hatcher stopped, cursing himself as Colin's face clenched. Venting his self-hate could only hurt his friends, but he would never forgive himself. Never. *Terra* had seemed so powerful, so *safe* . . . and so he'd let not merely both heirs to the throne but the children of *all* of his closest friends sail aboard a single ship, never reflecting for a moment that even the mightiest starship might malfunction and die. Of course it was unlikely, but it was his *job* to expect the unlikely.

"Have you told the others?" Colin asked, and Hatcher shook his head.

"No. I— Well, you and 'Tanni needed to know first, and—"

"I understand." Colin cut him off softly, hugging

Jiltanith as she wept. "It's not your fault, Ger. I don't want to hear that from you ever again." He held the admiral's eyes until Hatcher gave a tiny nod, then drew a deep, ragged breath.

" 'Tanni?" His voice was gentle, and Jiltanith raised her face. She stared at him in mute agony, and he remembered the final engagement at Zeta Trianguli as their ship shuddered and bucked under the pounding of Achuultani warheads and Tamman's *Royal Birhat* vaporized before their eyes. She'd wept then, too, wept for the friends dying about them, but her commands had come firm and steady through her tears, with all the invincible courage he loved so much. The courage that had broken at last.

He cupped her face between his palms, and her diamond tears wrenched at him, for he understood her too well. She'd been wounded too often in the endless battle against Anu. Her softness had withdrawn behind a fiery temper and a warrior's armor forged by a lifetime of warfare and lost friends. But it was still there, however hard she found showing it, and when she loved, she loved as she did everything else—with all she was.

"We have to go, 'Tanni." Fury sparked suddenly within her hurt, but he made himself meet it. "We have to," he repeated. "They're our friends."

She drew a quick, angry breath . . . then held it and closed her eyes. One hand rose to his cheek, and she nodded and pressed a kiss upon his wrist. Anguish still filled her eyes when she opened them once more, but there was understanding as well. The understanding that she had to go on, not simply because her friends needed her, but because if she didn't there was nothing left but a dark, bottomless gulf, waiting to suck her under forever.

"Aye," she whispered, and looked at Hatcher. "Forgive me, dear Gerald." She held out a trembling hand, and the admiral took it. "Well I know thy grief, sweet friend. 'Tis ill done to heap mine own upon it."

" 'Tanni, I—" Tears fogged Hatcher's voice, and she squeezed gently.

"Nay, Gerald. 'Tis no more fault o' thine than mine. And Colin hath the right. Our dearest friends do need our aid . . . e'en as we need theirs." She managed a soft, sad smile and stood. "Let us go to them."

A chair squeaked as the man in it finished the report and turned to look out his office window. The Imperium was in mourning, and even the most fiery malcontents were muted by the shock and sorrow of a race. Every flag of humankind flew at half-mast, but there was no sorrow in *his* heart. The heirs were gone, and the children of the imperial family's closest friends had gone with them. Grief and loss would weaken them, make them less vigilant, blunt their perceptions and reactions, and that was good.

He rose and walked to the window, hands folded behind him, looking down on the crowds below, then rested his eyes upon the spire of the Cenotaph. The names on the memorial were endless, and once he'd hated every one of them, for they named the people who'd toppled his patron. But he hated them no longer, for in toppling Anu they'd cleared *his* path to power, and his palms tingled as he waited to reach out and grasp it.

He pursed his lips, pondering his preparations. The gravitonic warhead was almost ready, and so was his plan for delivering it when the time was right. He'd been more worried about that than he'd cared to admit to Francine, but not anymore. It wouldn't be easy, but with his foreknowledge and the holos of the artist's sketches he could fabricate his duplicate in plenty of time. And, of course, it would never do to deliver it too soon, anyway. He needed Stepmother closer to operational, for it was essential to reduce delay to an absolute minimum if his coup was to succeed.

And it *would* succeed. He was like a spider, he thought, weaving his webs at the very heart of empire, unnoticed yet perfectly placed to observe and thwart every countermove even before it was launched. Just as he'd been placed to act on the opportunity *Imperial Terra* presented.

He smiled again—a thin, triumphant smile. With a little luck, the heirs' deaths might even drive a wedge between the imperial family and Dahak, for it was Dahak who'd designed *Imperial Terra*, supervised her construction, and suggested sending them out aboard her. With Cruz and his family dead, no one would ever know what had really happened, and the grieving parents would be more than human if some secret part of them didn't blame Dahak for their loss.

The time would come. Not this year, perhaps, but soon, and then Colin and Jiltanith MacIntyre would die, as well, in one deadly stroke which would decapitate the Imperium . . . and there would be nothing anyone could do about it. Nothing at all.

He smothered a soft laugh, savoring the victory to come and the exquisite irony which would make him Colin's legal successor. He, the Terra-born "degenerate" Kirinal and Anu had despised even while they groomed him as their tool, would achieve what Anu had only dreamed of: utter and complete dominion. And it would all be *legal*!

A soft sound warned him, and he turned, banishing his smile and replacing it with soft, sad sympathy as Horus walked into his office. The old man's shoulders slumped, and his eyes were haunted, but like his daughter and son-in-law, he was making himself go on. Making himself discharge his duties, never guessing how futile it all truly was.

"Sorry to bother you," Horus said, "but I wondered if you'd finished that report on the Calcutta bio-enhancement center?"

"Yes, I have." He crossed to his desk and handed over the datachip folio from the blotter.

"Thanks." Horus took it and started back to his office, then stopped and turned as a throat cleared itself behind him.

"I just . . . Well, I just wanted to say I'm sorry, Horus.

If there's anything I can do—anything at all—please let me know."

"I will." Horus managed a sad smile of his own. "It helps just to know friends care," he said softly.

"I'm glad. Because we *do* care, Horus," Lawrence Jefferson said gently. "More, perhaps, than you'll ever know."

Chapter Ten

"I don't think we're going to nail it down any closer, Harry," Sean sighed from the captain's couch. He rubbed his forehead in a futile effort to relieve the subliminal ache of hours of concentration on his neural feeds, then rose and stretched hugely.

"I'm afraid you're right." His sister sat up in the astrogator's couch and twisted a lock of sable hair around a fingertip.

Sandy lay like a dead woman in the tactical officer's couch, but Sean was used to her utter concentration on the task in hand. Besides, he could see her breathing. He flipped his feed into her net, nudging her gently, and felt her acknowledgment. She began to disengage from her painstaking computer diagnostics, and he fired another message off to Tamman and Brashan, summoning them from their examination of Engineering for a conference.

He clasped his hands behind him and watched the display while Harriet rose and worked through a few tension-relieving stretches. *Israel* drifted in interstellar space, drive down while her tiny crew examined her every system. Before they did anything else, they were going to be *certain*—or as close as was humanly (or Narhanily) possible—no more booby traps awaited them. But once they were certain they still had to decide what to do, and the display's glittering stars offered few options.

He looked up as Tamman and Brashan entered the command deck. Tamman still looked drawn and pinched, but Brashan seemed almost calm. Which, Sean reflected, might owe something to the famed Narhani lack of imagination. Personally, he'd always thought of it more as pragmatism. Narhani were more concerned with the nuts and bolts of a problem than with its implications, and he was glad of it. Brashan's levelheadedness was exactly what they all needed just now, for, to use the current Academy phrase, they were up to their eyebrows in shit.

Tamman perched on the assistant tactical officer's couch beside Sandy while Brashan keyed a reconfiguration command into the exec's couch. It twitched for a moment, then reformed itself into a Narhani-style pad, and he folded onto it just as Sandy shook her head and roused. She sat up with a wan smile that still held a ghost of her familiar humor, and Sean grinned back wryly. Then he cleared his throat.

"All right. I know our system checks are still a long way from finished, but I think it's time to compare notes."

Their nodded agreement was a relief. He was senior to all of them, yet his authority, while real and legal, rested solely on their class standings. He stood first in their Academy class, but less than five points separated him from Tamman, their most "junior" officer, and there was a bare quarter-point between him and Sandy. Which was due solely to his higher scores in Tactics and Phys-Ed, for she'd waxed him in Math and Physics.

"Okay. Harry and I have done our best to figure out where we are, but we can't be as precise about it as we'd like. Or, rather, we know where *we* are; we just don't have any idea what the neighborhood looks like. Harry?" He passed the discussion to her, and she propped a hip against the astrogator's console.

"First of all, we're nowhere near where we're supposed to be. *Israel*'s astro data is limited—normally, sublight units don't much need interstellar data—but we've got the old basic Fourth Empire cartography downloads. Working from them and allowing for forty-odd thousand years of stellar motion, we're just about smack in the middle of the Tarik Sector."

"The *Tarik* Sector?" Tamman sounded dubious, and Sean didn't blame him.

"Exactly." Harriet's voice was calmer than Sean knew she was. "Whatever happened took *Terra* off her programmed course by something like plus seventy-two degrees declination and fifty degrees left ascension from Urahan, then brought her out of hyper three days early on top of it. At the moment, we're five-point-four-six-seven light-centuries from Birhat, as near as Colin and I can figure it, on a bearing no one could possibly have predicted."

Sean watched the implications sink home. It didn't make much real difference—they'd known from the start that their battleship was a hopelessly tiny needle in a galactic haystack—but now they also knew no one had even the faintest idea where to start looking for them. Harriet gave them a few moments to consider it, then went on even more dispassionately.

"Unfortunately, *Israel*'s database was loaded for the Idan Sector, where we were supposed to be going. We've figured out where we are relative to Bia, but we don't have *any* data on the Tarik Sector, so we don't have the least idea what it contained forty thousand years ago, much less today. No Survey people have penetrated this far, and they probably won't for at least fifty years or so. All of which means we're not in real good shape for making informed guesses about where we ought to go next."

She paused again, then returned the floor to Sean with a small nod.

"Thanks, Harry." He looked at the others and shrugged. "As Harry says, we don't have much guidance about possible destinations, but then, we don't have much choice, either." He flipped his neural feed into the display computers, and a red sighting ring circled a bright star.

"That," he said, "is an F5 star at about one-point-three light-years. We don't know which one it is, so we don't know if it had any habitable planets even before the bioweapon hit, but the next nearest candidate for a life-bearing world is this G6—" a second sighting ring blossomed "—over eleven light-years away. It's going to take us a while to reach either of them at our best sustained sublight speed, but it'd take something like nine hundred years to get back to Bia—assuming *Israel's* systems would hold up for a voyage that long. On the other hand, we can get to the F5 in just under two-point-two years. At point-six cee, we'll have a tau of about point-eight, so the subjective time will be about twenty-one months. That's a long time, and we've only got two stasis pods, so we'll have to put up with each other awake the whole way, but I don't see that we have any other option. Comments?"

"I have one, Sean," Brashan said after a moment, and Sean nodded for him to go on. "It's more of an observation, really. It occurs to me that, given such a long voyage time, it may be a fortunate thing we Narhani still think of ourselves as having only one sex."

The other three stared at Brashan, but Sean astonished himself with a chuckle. After a moment the others began to grin, too, though Harriet was a little pink. Sean coughed into his fist, smothering the last of his chuckles, and regarded the Narhani sternly.

"Contrary to what you poor, benighted aliens may believe, Brashan, not all humans are helpless slaves to their hormones."

"Indeed?" Brashan cocked his head and looked down his long snout at him, raising his crest in an expression of polite disbelief. "I would never dispute your veracity, Sean, but I must say my personal observation of human mating behavior invalidates your basic premise. And while we Narhani are quite different from humans, it seems to me that a disinterested perspective is less prone to self-deception. As you know, my people have given this matter of sex a great deal of thought in the last few years, and—"

"All right, Brashan Brashieel-nahr!" Sandy hurled a boot at the centauroid. Sean hadn't seen her take it off, but a six-fingered hand darted up and caught it in midflight, and Brashan made the bubbling noise that always reminded Sean of a clogged drain trying—vainly—to clear itself.

The laughing Narhani returned Sandy's boot without rising, inclining his saurian-looking head in a gallant bow, and Sean shook his head. Like most Narhani clone-children, Brashan had spent so much time with humans his elders found his sense of humor quite incomprehensible, but he was also a far shrewder student of human psychology than he cared to pretend. He understood humans needed to laugh in order not to weep. And, Sean thought with heightened respect, perhaps he also understood how his teasing could help set his human friends at ease with a topic which was certainly going to rear its head.

"If we can turn to a less prurient subject?" he said loudly. The others turned back towards him, and their faces, he was pleased to see, were much more relaxed.

"Thank you. Now, Harry and I have already plotted our course, but before we head out I want to know we can rely on our systems." Heads nodded more soberly, and he turned to Tamman. "How does Engineering look, Tam?"

"Brash and I haven't quite finished our inspection, but as far as we've been everything looks a hundred percent. The power plant's nominal, anyway, and the catcher field shows a green board. Once we get up above about point-three cee we'll be sucking in more hydrogen than we're burning. And the drive looks fine, despite that crash launch."

"Environmental?"

"First thing we checked. No problems with the plant, but we may have one with rations." Sean raised an eyebrow, and Tamman shrugged. "There were only five Narhani in *Terra's* entire complement, Sean. I haven't had a chance to run a Logistics inventory yet, but we could be low on supplementals."

"Uh." Sean tugged at an earlobe and frowned. Narhani body chemistry incorporated a level of heavy metals lethal to humans; Brashan could eat anything his friends could, but he couldn't metabolize all of it, nor would it provide everything he needed.

"Don't worry," Sandy said. Sean looked at her and saw the absent expression of someone plugged into her computers. "Logistics shows a heap of Narhani supplementals. In fact, we've got six or seven times our normal food supplies in all categories, and the hydroponic section's way overstocked. Which—" her eyes refocused and she grimaced "—isn't too surprising, really."

"No?" Sean was relieved to hear food wouldn't become a problem, but Sandy's last comment required explanation.

"Nope. While I was checking out the tactical net I found out why we couldn't get into *Terra*'s internal com net, and I'll be very surprised if we find anything at all wrong with *Israel*'s systems."

"Why?"

"Because this—" she waved at the command deck "—is basically a lifeboat, specifically selected for the five of us." Sean frowned, and she shrugged. "I'm not sure what zapped *Terra*, but I'm pretty sure I know why it didn't zap *us*. Unless I miss my guess, we've got a guardian angel named—"

"Dahak," Harriet interrupted, and Sandy nodded.

"You got it. While I was running through the test cycles I hit an override in the core command programs. It went down the instant I challenged it, but that's because it was supposed to. Before *Terra* decided to blow her core tap, she shanghaied the five of us and ordered *Israel*'s computers to ignore us until *after* we'd launched."

"But why?" Tamman sounded confused.

" 'Why' which?" Harriet asked. "Why did *Terra* blow? Or why did she shove us out the tube first?"

" 'Why' both," he replied, and she shrugged.

"I'd have to guess to answer either of them, but from what Sandy's saying I think I can come pretty close to guessing right." She glanced at Sean, and he nodded for her to continue.

"Okay. First, it's obvious someone sabotaged *Terra*. Planetoids don't just casually change their own headings, drop out of hyper early, and then blow their core taps. Theoretically, I suppose, any one of those actions could have been a malfunction, but all of them?" She shook her head. "Somebody got to her core programming, and it seems pretty likely *we* were the targets."

"Us? You mean someone waxed *Terra* just to get at *us?*" Tamman clearly disliked that thought as much as Sean did.

"Harry's right," Sandy said. "I wouldn't want us to get swelled heads, but it's the only answer that makes sense. Although," she added more thoughtfully, "I doubt they were after *all* of us. More likely they were out to get Sean and Harry."

"Oh, *shit*," Tamman breathed. He scratched an eyebrow, frowning at the deck, then sighed. "Yeah, it makes sense. But, Jesus, Sean, if they could do that, who knows what else they can do? And nobody back home knows what happened. If these creeps—whoever they are—try something else, nobody'll be expecting a thing!"

"I fear Tam has a point," Brashan murmured, and Sean shrugged.

"So do I, but I don't see what we can do about it. We don't have a hypercom, and there's no way we can build one." A hypercom massed five times as much as *Israel*'s entire hull and required synthetic elements they couldn't possibly fabricate from shipboard resources. "All we can hope for is that the star system we head for was, in fact, inhabited. If it was, we may find an orbital yard we can kick back into operation, and then we *can* build one."

All five of them shuddered at the thought. With only five sets of hands, the gargantuan task of reactivating even one of the Fourth Empire's heavily automated fabrication centers, while not exactly impossible, would take years. On the other hand, Sean reflected mordantly, it wasn't like they'd have anything else to waste their time on.

"But getting back to what happened," Harriet went on, "*Terra* was set up to destroy herself and make sure no evidence ever turned up. That has to be why she took herself way out here first. But I'll bet you that was *her* idea. Whoever programmed her expected her to scuttle herself while she was still in hyper, in which case there wouldn't have been any n-space debris at all. That's how I would've handled it."

"Me, too," Sean agreed. "And the reason she didn't do it?"

"Dahak," Harriet said with utter certainty. "You know how he looks out for us. Whoever sabotaged *Terra* had to be working inside her Alpha programming, and that means whatever caused her not to kill *us* was also buried in her Alpha priorities. And who do we know who worries about us *and* has the capability to get in and out of any computer ever built?"

"Dahak." It was Sean's turn to nod.

"Exactly. We'll probably never know, but I'll bet anything you like whoever set up the sabotage program ordered *Terra* to make sure there was no evidence but never specifically told her to actually kill her crew. Lord," Harriet turned to Sandy and rolled her eyes, "can you *imagine* what would've happened if they'd tried? They'd have hit so many Alpha overrides against harming humans Comp Cent would've burned to a crisp!"

She crossed her arms and pursed her lips.

"Whoever did this was slick, Sean," Harriet said soberly. "*Real* slick. Even a simple self-destruct command would've hit—I don't know. Nine overrides, Sandy? Ten?"

"Something like that." Sandy frowned as she ran over a mental checklist. "At least that. So they had to cut and paste around them. And those're *hardwired*." She frowned harder. "*I* couldn't have done it even if you gave me a couple of years to work on it. It would've taken somebody pretty darn senior over at BuShips to get away with it."

"Well, of course," Tamman said. Sandy looked at him, and he shrugged. "Doesn't matter how sneaky he had to be, Sandy. He had to have *access*."

"Oh, sure. Well," Sandy's sudden, unpleasant smile reminded Sean very forcefully of her mother, "that's nice to know. Whenever we do get back in touch with Bia, Mom'll be able to narrow it down mighty quick. Can't be more than twenty or thirty people. Probably more like ten or fifteen."

"So we've got an order to blow herself up and hide the evidence," Sean mused, "but not an actual order to kill her crew."

"Yep," Harriet said, "and that's why we're still alive, 'cause Dahak parked his own Alpha command somewhere in Comp Cent and instructed *Terra* to keep an eye on us. On us, specifically—the five of us. Mom and Dad'd probably have killed him if they'd known, but thank God he did it! *Terra* couldn't blow herself without getting us out first without violating *his* commands, and whoever set her up never guessed what he might do, so there was no way they could counter it. *That*, people, is the only reason she came out of hyper at all. And, now that I think about it, it's probably why we wound up way out here. She couldn't hide the evidence in hyper without killing us, but she could sure put us somewhere no one would think to look!"

"Makes sense," Sean agreed after a moment, then shivered. It hadn't felt nice to realize how close they'd come to dying, but it felt even less nice to know eighty thousand people had died as a casual by-product of an effort to murder him and his sister. The hatred—or, even worse, the cold calculation—of such an act was appalling. He shook himself free of the thought and hoped it wouldn't return to haunt his nightmares.

"All right. If that's what happened—and I think you and Sandy are probably right, Harry—then we shouldn't run into any more 'programs from hell' in *Israel*'s software. On the other hand, the trip's going to take long enough I don't mind spending a few days making certain. Do any of you?"

Three human heads shook emphatically and Brashan curled his crest in an equally definite expression of disagreement. Sean grinned crookedly.

"I'm glad you agree. But in the meantime, it's been

over six hours since everything went to hell. I don't know about you, but I'm starved."

The others looked momentarily taken aback by his prosaic remark, but all of them had young, healthy appetites. Surprise turned quickly into agreement, and he smiled more naturally.

"Who wants to cook?"

"Anyone but you." Sandy's shudder elicited a chorus of agreement. Sean MacIntyre was one of the very few people in the universe who could burn boiling water.

"All right, Ms. Smartass, I hereby put *you* in charge of the galley."

"Suits me. Lasagna, I think, and a special side dish delicately spiced with arsenic for Brashan." She eyed *Israel's* youthful commander. "And maybe we can convince him to share it with *you*, Captain Bligh," she added sweetly.

Chapter Eleven

The Emperor of Mankind opened his eyes at the desolate sounds, and for just a moment, as he hovered on the edge of awareness, he felt only anger. Anger at being awakened from his own tormented dreams, anger that he must find the strength to face another's sorrow. And, perhaps most of all, anger that the sobs were so soft, so smothered, so . . . ashamed.

He turned his head. Jiltanith was curled in a wretched knot, far over on her side of their bed, arms locked about a pillow. Her shoulders jerked as she sobbed into the tear-soaked pillowcase, and waking anger vanished as he listened to her sounds and knew what truly spawned his rage. Helplessness. He couldn't heal her hurt. Her grief was nothing he could fight. He couldn't even tell her everything would "be all right," for they both knew it wouldn't, and that tormented him with a sense of inadequacy. It wasn't his fault, and he knew it, but the knowledge was useless to a heart as badly wounded by the anguish of the woman he loved as by his own.

He rolled over and wrapped her in his arms, and she drew into an even tighter knot, burying her face in the pillow she clutched. She *was* ashamed, he thought. She condemned herself for her "weakness," and another flash of irrational anger gripped him—anger at *her* for hurting herself so. But he strangled it and murmured her name and kissed her hair. She clenched the pillow tautly an instant longer, and then every muscle unknotted at once and she wept in desolation as he gathered her close.

He stroked her heaving shoulders, caressing and kissing her while his own tears flowed, but he offered no clichés, no ultimately meaningless words. He was simply there, holding her and loving her. Proving she was not alone as she'd once proved he was not, until gradually— so heartbreakingly gradually—her weeping eased and she drifted into exhausted slumber on his chest while he stared into the dark from the ache of his own loss and hated a universe that could hurt her so.

Dahak closed the file on *Imperial Terra*'s hyper drive once more. Had he possessed a body of flesh and blood he would have sighed wearily, but he was a being of molycircs and force fields. Fatigue was alien to him, a concept he could grasp from observation of biological entities but never feel . . . unlike grief. Grief he'd learned to understand too well in the months since the twins had died, and he'd learned to understand futility, as well.

It was odd, a tiny part of his stupendous intellect thought, that he'd never recognized the difference between helplessness and futility. He'd orbited Earth for fifty thousand years, trapped between a command to destroy Anu and another which forbade him to use the weapons that would have required on a populated world. Powerful enough to blot the planet from the cosmos yet impotent, he'd learned the full, bitter measure of helplessness in a way no human ever could. But in all that time, he'd never felt *futile*—not as he felt now—for he'd understood the reason for his impotence . . . then.

Not now. He'd reconsidered every aspect of *Imperial Terra*'s design with Baltan and Vlad and Geran, searching for the flaw which had doomed her, and they'd found nothing. He'd run simulation after simulation, reproducing every possible permutation on *Imperial Terra*'s performance envelope in an effort to isolate the freak combination of factors which might have destroyed her, and no convincing hypothesis presented itself.

The universe was vast, but it was governed by laws and processes. There was always more to learn, even (or especially) for one like himself, yet within the parameters of what one could observe and test there should be understanding and the ability to achieve one's ends. That was the very essence of knowledge, but he'd used every scrap of knowledge he owned to protect the people he loved . . . and failed.

He'd already decided never to tell Colin about the Alpha Priority command he'd given *Imperial Terra*. It had failed, and revealing it would only hurt his friends as one more safeguard—one more effort on his part—which had saved nothing. They had not said a word to condemn him for insisting upon that particular ship, nor would they. He knew that, and knowing only made the hurt worse. He'd done harm enough; he would not wound them again.

He was different from his friends, for he was potentially immortal and, even with enhancement, they were such ephemeral beings. Yet the brevity of their span only made them more precious. He would have the joy of their company for such a short time, and then they would live only in his memory, lost and forgotten by the universe and their own species. That was why he fought so hard against the darkness, the reason for his fierce protectiveness.

And it was also why, for the first time in his inconceivable lifetime, a wounded part of him cried out in anguish and futility against a universe which had destroyed the ones he loved for no reason he could find.

". . . and so," Vlad Chernikov said quietly, "we must conclude *Imperial Terra* was lost to 'causes unknown.'" He looked around the conference table sadly. "I deeply regret—all of us do—that we can give no better answer, but our most exhaustive investigation can find no reason for her destruction."

Colin nodded and gripped Jiltanith's hand.

"Thank you for trying, Vlad. Thank you *all* for trying." He inhaled sharply and straightened. "I'm sure I speak for all of us in that."

A soft murmur of agreement answered, and he saw Tsien Tao-ling slip an arm around Amanda's shoulders.

Her eyes were dry but haunted, and Colin thanked God for her other children and for Tsien.

He glanced at Hector and bit his lip, for Hector's face was dark and shuttered, and Ninhursag watched him with anxious eyes. Hector had withdrawn, building barricades about his pain and buttressing them by burying himself in his duties. It was as if he couldn't—or wouldn't—admit how savagely Sandy's loss had scarred him, and until he did, he could never deal with his grief.

Colin shook himself with a silent, bitter curse. Of course Hector couldn't "deal with his grief"—and who was he to be surprised by that? They were all wise enough to seek assistance, but the Imperium's best mental health experts could tell him nothing he didn't already know. Jiltanith wept less often now, but even as he comforted her and drew comfort from her, there was a festering hatred in his own heart. A deep, bitter rage for which he could find no target. He knew what he felt was futile, even self-destructive, yet he needed to lash out . . . and there was nothing to lash out against. He pushed the rage down once more, praying his counselor was right and that time would someday mute its acid virulence.

"All right," he said. "In that case, I see no reason not to resume construction on the other class units. Gerald? Do you or Tao-ling disagree?"

"No," Hatcher said after a brief glance at the star marshal.

"Then let's do it. Is there anything else we need to discuss?" Heads shook, and he sighed. "Then we'll see you all Thursday." He stood, still holding Jiltanith's hand, and the others rose silently as they left the room.

Senior Fleet Admiral Ninhursag MacMahan was angry with herself. Few would have guessed it from looking at her, but after a century of hiding her feelings from Anu's security thugs, her face said exactly what she told it to.

She sat behind her desk and drew a deep breath. It

was time to return to the needs of the living. Gus van Gelder and her ONI assistants had been carrying her load, and that they'd done it superlatively was scant comfort. It was *her* job; if she couldn't do it, it was time to curl up and die. For a time she'd considered doing just that, but even at her worst, a stubborn part of her had mocked the bad melodrama of the thought.

Now, deliberately, she buried the temptation forever and felt herself coming back to life as she set her grief aside. It wasn't easy, and it hurt, but it also felt good. Not as it once had, but so much better than the dull, dead disinterest which had gripped her for far too long, and she plugged her feed into her computer and called up the first intelligence summary.

Colin sat on the rug, watching the fire and rubbing Galahad's ears. The dog lay beside him before the library hearth, eyes half-closed, massive head resting on Colin's thigh while they both stared into the crackling flames. To the outward eye they must present the classic picture of a man and his dog, Colin thought, but Galahad certainly wasn't his pet. Galahad and his litter-mates shared a very dog-like exuberant openness, insatiable curiosity, and a need for companionship, but they belonged only to themselves.

Now Galahad emitted a contented snuffle and rolled onto his back, waggling his feet in the air to invite his friend to scratch his chest. Colin complied with a grin, and chuckled as the dog wiggled with soft, chuffling sounds of sensual delight. That grin felt good. The four-footed members of the imperial family had done more than anyone else would ever suspect to help with his and 'Tanni's grief. They shared it, for they, too, had loved the twins, but there was a clean, healthy simplicity to their caring, without the complex patterns of guilt and subliminal resentment even the best humans felt while they grappled with their own loss.

"Like that, do you?" he said, working his scratching fingertips into Galahad's "armpits," and the big dog sighed.

"Of course," his vocoder replied. "It is a pity we do not have hands. I would enjoy doing this for the others."

"But not as much as you'd enjoy having them do it for you, huh?" Colin challenged, and Galahad sneezed explosively and rolled upright.

"Perhaps not," he agreed, and Colin snorted. None of the dogs ever lied. That seemed to be a human talent they couldn't (or didn't want to) master, but they were getting pretty darn good at equivocating.

"I think humans are a bad influence on you. You're getting spoiled."

"No. It is only that we are honest about things we enjoy."

"Yeah, sure." Colin reached under Galahad's massive chest and stroked more gently. The standing dog's chin rested companionably on his shoulder, and he glanced over at the corner where Galahad's sister Gwynevere sat very upright, watching Jiltanith move her queen. Gwynevere cocked her head, ears pricking as she considered the move. She was the only one of the dogs to develop a taste for chess—it was a bit too cerebral for the others—and by human standards she wasn't all that good. Galahad and Gawain were killers at Scrabble, and he'd been horrified to discover Horus had taught all of them to play poker (though none of them—except, perhaps, Gaheris—could bluff worth a damn), but Gwynevere was determined to master chess. And, to be fair about it, she was improving steadily.

The really funny thing, he thought, was that while Jiltanith was an excellent strategist in real life, Gwynevere beat her quite often. 'Tanni was too direct—and impatient—for a game which emphasized the indirect approach.

"Excuse me, Colin," Dahak's voice said, "but Ninhursag has just arrived at the Palace."

"She's here *now?*" Colin looked up, and Jiltanith met his eyes with matching surprise. It was very late in Birhat's twenty-eight-hour day.

"Indeed. And she appears quite agitated."

" 'Hursag is agitated?" Colin shook his head and scrambled to his feet. "Tell her to come on down to the library."

"She is already on her way. In fact—"

The library door burst open. Admiral MacMahan came through it like a thunder squall, and Colin rocked back on his heels—literally. Ninhursag was only middling tall, and the mood he usually associated with her was one of deliberate consideration, but tonight she was a titan wrapped in vicious, killing rage.

" 'Hursag?" he said tentatively as she came to a halt just inside the door. Every movement was rigidly overcontrolled, as if each of them took every ounce of will she had, and she chopped a nod.

"Colin. Jiltanith." Her voice was harsh, each word bitten off with utter precision. "Sit down, both of you. I have something to tell you."

Colin looked at Jiltanith, wondering what could have transformed Ninhursag so, but 'Tanni met his eyes with a shrug of ignorance and a slight gesture at the chairs before the hearth. They settled into them, listening to the crackle of burning logs as Galahad and his siblings ranged themselves to either side, and every eye, human and canine alike, watched Ninhursag grip her hands behind her and make herself take a quick, wordless turn about the room. When she turned to face them, her face was calmer, but it was a surface calm, built solely from professionalism and self-discipline.

"I'm sorry to burst in on you, but I just turned up something . . . interesting. Or, rather, I just *confirmed* something interesting."

She inhaled again, sharply, and gave herself a tiny shake.

"I've been slacking off at ONI for months," she continued in a flat voice. "You know that, Colin, though you haven't said anything. I'm sorry. You know why I have. But I'm getting myself back together, and yesterday I started through a stack of reports that've been accumulating since, well—" She broke off with another shrug, and Colin nodded. Jiltanith held out a hand to him, and he took it as Ninhursag cleared her throat.

"Yes. Anyway, most of them were fairly routine. Gus and Commodore Sung have handled the hot stuff as it came in. But one of them—an accidental death report—caught my attention. It was the date, I think. It happened two days after *Imperial Terra* hypered out for Urahan, and it covered an entire family." Fresh pain tightened her lips, but she went harshly on.

"They were civilians, and it was a traffic accident, so I wondered why ONI had it, until I looked more closely," Ninhursag went on in that flat voice. "The husband was Vincente Cruz. He wasn't military, strictly speaking, but—" she paused, and her eyes were cold "—he worked for BuShips."

Colin felt Jiltanith's hand twitch in his and stiffened. It was no more than a vague stirring of suspicion, but the bitterness in Ninhursag's eyes turned something cold and wary deep inside him.

"I don't know why that stuck in my mind, but it did, and when I looked more closely I found a couple of things that seemed . . . out of kilter.

"The Cruzes lived on Birhat, since he worked for BuShips, but they were killed on Earth. I checked and found out they usually vacationed in North America, but Cruz had returned from there less than three months before, so I wondered why they'd gone back so soon. Then I found out his wife and family had stayed there—visiting friends—and he'd gone back to collect them.

"Again, I don't know why that bothered me, but it did. So I did some more checking. Cruz's two older children were enrolled for education here on Birhat, and I discovered that he hadn't warned the education people they'd be staying on Earth. He notified them only after he got back, but two years ago, when he left them to visit family in Mexico, he'd notified their teachers over a month before they left. He was concerned with making certain they didn't lose any ground shifting back and forth between the two school systems.

"That seemed odd, so I checked the hypercom and mat-trans logs. In the ten weeks they stayed on Earth, he neither sent to them nor received from them a single hypercom message. Nor did he use the mat-trans to visit them in person. There was *no communication* between them at all for ten weeks . . . and he and his wife had a ten month-old baby."

Colin's eyes began to burn with a green fire that matched the fury in Ninhursag's bitter brown stare, and the admiral nodded slowly.

"The accident report looks completely aboveboard, if a bit freakish. It was a high-speed event—a ridge-line collision at almost Mach six—and the flight recorder was totaled, but the altimeter was recovered, and analysis indicated it was under-reading by about two hundred meters. That was enough to put it into the ridge, but when I did a little discreet checking, no one seemed to know who Cruz's family had been visiting. I did a computer search of Earth's credit transactions—as a BuShips employee, he and his wife both held Fleet cards—and I couldn't find a single transaction for Elena Cruz on Earth.

"I can't prove it wasn't an 'accident,' but there are too many coincidences. Especially—" Ninhursag's hands went back behind her, clenched about one another, and her voice was very, very quiet "—when Vincente Cruz was assistant project chief for *Imperial Terra's* cybernetics."

"Son-of-a-*bitch!*" Colin whispered, and she nodded coldly.

"I haven't checked his work logs yet—that comes next—but I'm already certain what I'm going to find," she said, and this time Colin understood her murderous fury perfectly.

Chapter Twelve

The mood around the conference table was very different this time.

". . . so there's a fifteen-minute hole in his work log," Ninhursag said, "smack in the middle of his work on *Terra's* core software. Unfortunately, there are eight other holes, from just under a minute to almost an hour long, in the same log, and we've found an intermittent defect in his terminal that looks completely normal." Her curled lip showed what she thought of that.

"But why?" Horus asked softly. "I don't question your conclusions, 'Hursag, but in the Maker's name, *why?*"

"We can't prove 'why' until we know 'who,'" Ninhursag's voice was harsh, "but I see only two motives. Destroy *Imperial Terra*, one, because of *what* she was—our most powerful warship—or, two, because of who was aboard."

"Sean and Harry," Colin grated, and Ninhursag nodded.

"Whoever set this up went to tremendous lengths—and ran tremendous risks. What else could his objective have been?"

"Sweet Jesu," Jiltanith whispered. "Full eighty thousand people and the children of our dearest friends to kill my babes?" Her face was drawn, but more than despair burned in her black eyes, and her knuckles were white about the hilt of the dagger she always wore.

"*Bastards!*" Hector MacMahan's stylus snapped in his hand. He looked down at the broken pieces and slowly and carefully crushed each of them between enhanced fingertips.

"Agreed," Colin's voice was ice, "but the other kids may have been targets as well. Look how it's affected all of us. 'Hursag blames herself for 'slacking off,' but have any of us done better? And whoever the son-of-a-bitch is, he damned well *knew* what it would do to us!"

"I must agree," Tsien said. Amanda nodded beside him, eyes smoking, and he touched her hand where it lay upon the table. "Yet I am also certain 'Hursag's other deduction is equally correct. Whoever did this must have a powerful organization and penetration at the highest levels. Without such an organization he could not have acted; without such penetration he could have known neither which ship to attack nor whom to use for that attack."

"Agreed," Gerald Hatcher sounded even grimmer. "They had to pick someone with access who was also vulnerable. Anybody this ruthless might have popped one of his own people to cut the chain of evidence, but why kill an entire family? No, they knew exactly which poor bastard to pick, held his family hostage to make him play, then killed them all to cover their tracks."

"There's another pointer." Adrienne Robbins' voice was cold; Algys McNeal had been her friend, and twenty more of her midshipmen had been aboard *Imperial Terra*. "Cruz didn't pop a single security flag. He must have known how small a chance he had of getting them back alive, but he went for it without telling *anyone*. He never even *tried* to get help, so maybe he *knew* they had enough penetration to know if he'd talked to any of 'Hursag's people."

Cold, bitter silence enveloped the council room, then Colin nodded.

"All right. There's someone out there cold enough to murder an entire family and eighty thousand of our people, and I want the son-of-a-bitch. How do we get him?"

"Dust off the lie detectors and put everybody—and I mean *everybody*—on them," MacMahan grated.

"We can't," Horus said. Eyes turned to him, and he

shrugged. "If we're right about how far we've been penetrated, the bad guys—whoever they are—will know the instant we start that. If they're our own people, well and good; all they can do is run and identify themselves for us. But if they're tapped in from the *outside*, they'll be operating through a blizzard of cutouts, and whoever's really in charge will just pull in his horns. If he disengages, we may never get another shot at him."

"It's worse than that," Colin sighed. "We don't have 'probable cause' for that kind of sweep."

"Bullshit!" MacMahan snarled. "This is a security matter. We can pull in anybody in uniform we want to!"

"No, we can't." MacMahan started to speak again, but Colin raised a hand. "Hold it, Hector. Just wait a minute. Goddamn it, I want this bastard as badly as you do, but think about it. *We* know 'Hursag's right, but there's not a single piece of hard evidence. Everything except the disappearance of Cruz's family is covered by plausible 'technical failures.' And while it's true his family *did* disappear from our records, that by itself doesn't prove a thing. No law requires people to report their whereabouts to us—our subjects are also free citizens. The fact that we don't know where they were actually works against us; Cruz never indicated they were being held against their will, and if we don't even know where they were, we can hardly prove they were prisoners!

"Even if we could, we'd have to be very specific about who we questioned. The Charter provides no protection against self-incrimination, so we can ask anything we like under a lie detector . . . but only in a court. That particular civil right is absolutely guaranteed specifically *because* there's no protection against self-incrimination.

"Now, you're right that we can question anyone in uniform as long as we make it a security matter, but we still have to furnish them and their counsel with a list of areas we intend to cover—approved by a judge—before we start asking. There's no way we could process legal paperwork on the scale we need without its coming to the attention of anyone with the sources to target Cruz, and what happens when our Mister X finds out about it? We don't want his sources, Hector—we want *him*."

MacMahan looked rebellious, but he subsided with a muttered curse and a grudging nod. Colin was glad to see it, and even gladder to see the life flowing back into his eyes as he realized he had an enemy. Sandy's death was no longer a senseless act by an uncaring universe. Hector had someone besides God to hate, and perhaps that would bring those inner barricades down.

"Very well, then," Tsien said, "what steps *shall* we take?"

"First we start taking security *real* serious," Amanda said. "Whoever went after the kids may be religious nuts, anarchists, out of their fucking minds, or planning a coup, but they *don't* get you two—or Horus—by God!"

"Damn straight," Adrienne approved amid a snarl of agreement, and Colin swallowed. He heard their hunger to destroy whoever had done this to them, but these weren't just his senior officers or angry, bereaved parents. These were friends, determined to protect him and Jiltanith.

"For Colin and 'Tanni, yes," Horus said after a moment, "but not me." Colin raised his eyebrows, and the old man shrugged. "We can reinforce your security quietly, but we can't slap armed guards all over White Tower. Your 'Mister X' could hardly miss that."

"Nay, Father! Shalt not risk thyself thus!"

"Oh, hush, 'Tanni! Who'd want to kill me? Unless we're talking about a total maniac, and I don't think we are, given how smoothly this whole thing went down, what possible motive could he have? Maybe *after* they got the two of you I'd become a target—not before."

"I believe Horus has a point, 'Tanni," Dahak put in. "While it is possible this was a crime of hate and not of logic, whoever perpetrated it did so in a most rational fashion." The computer's voice was as mellow as ever, but they all heard its anger. "At present, this would appear to be the first step in an attempt to decapitate the Imperium, and if that is, indeed, the case, Horus becomes a logical target only in the endgame of the conspiracy."

"Umm." Ninhursag rubbed her forehead. "I don't know, Dahak. You may be right, but you're a bit prone to believe everyone operates on the basis of logic. And whoever it is *did* go for the kids first."

"True, yet analysis suggests this was a crime of opportunity. Security for the twins was very tight, however it might appear to the uninformed. In the Bia System, they were attended by my own scanners at all times and, save for their field trips, continuously guarded by other security arrangements, as well. I do not say it would have been impossible to assassinate them, but it would have been difficult—and it could not have been done without being recognized as an act of murder. In this instance, the killer was able to strike when they were beyond my own surveillance or that of any regular security agency. Moreover, had you not pursued your own intuition in the matter of the Cruz family's murders, the fact that Sean and Harriet's deaths had been deliberately contrived would never have been known."

"That makes sense," Adrienne said slowly, "but I can't shake the feeling that there was more behind it."

"Indeed there was," Dahak agreed. "The twins were not murdered for personal motives, My Lady, but for who—and what—they were. For whatever reason, our enemy elected to strike at the succession. It is for this reason I believe it to be the start of an effort to destroy the monarchy."

"Which *does* make Horus a target," Colin sighed. "Oh, crap!"

"That is an incorrect assumption. Horus is a member of the imperial family, true, but he is not your heir. He would become a potential heir only should you and 'Tanni die without issue, and with all due respect, I believe the Assembly of Nobles would be unlikely to select one of Horus' advanced years as Emperor. Mother might do so if she were required to execute Case Omega yet again, but she would do so only if there were no

Assembly of Nobles to discharge that function. Moreover, Horus would not be the first choice even under Case Omega. The proper successor choice under Case Omega would be Admiral Hatcher, as CNO, followed by Star Marshal Tsien. Horus, as the highest civil official of the Imperium, would become the legal heir only if both of the Imperium's senior military officers were also dead. In addition, any open attack upon Horus would clearly risk awakening the suspicion the twins' 'accidental' deaths were intended to avoid. Thus any attempt to kill him before killing you, 'Tanni, Admiral Hatcher, and Star Marshal Tsien would be pointless unless we are, indeed, dealing with an irrational individual."

"I hate it when you get this way, Dahak," Colin complained, and several of the angry people around the table surprised themselves by smiling.

"Maybe, but he's right," Ninhursag said. "I don't want to get complacent, but tightening security for you two—and Gerald and Tao-ling—should have the effect of covering Horus, as well. And he's right, too. If we boost *his* security, it's a gold-plated warning to whoever we're up against."

"All right, we'll handle it that way—for starters. Hector, can you manage the security details?"

"Yes," MacMahan said tersely, and Colin nodded. The protection of the imperial family was the responsibility of the Imperial Marines, and MacMahan's expression was all the reassurance he needed.

"Good. But that's only a defensive action—how do we nail this bastard?"

"Whatever we do, Colin, we do it very carefully," Ninhursag said. "We start by putting all of this on a strict need-to-know basis. I don't want to bring in anyone else—not even Gus. Without knowing how 'Mister X' gets his information, every individual added to the information net gives him another possible conduit, however careful our people are."

"All right, agreed. And then?"

"And then Dahak and I sit down with every bit of

security data we have. Everything, military and civilian, from Day One of the Fifth Imperium. We find *any* anomalies, and then we eliminate them one at a time.

"In addition," she leaned back in her chair and frowned up at the ceiling, "we step up efforts to infiltrate every known group of malcontents. Those're underway already, so we don't have to give any new reasons for them. And while we flesh-and-bloods're doing that, Dahak, *you* jump into the datanets here in Bia and start setting up your own taps. Cruz could futz his terminal, but no one can get to *you*, so I want you tied into everything."

"Understood. I must point out, however, that I cannot achieve the same penetration of Earth's datanets."

"No, but until we figure out what's going on, Colin and 'Tanni will never visit Earth simultaneously. We know someone's after them now, and as long as 'Mister X' has to get through you, ONI, Hector's Marines, and Battle Fleet to reach them, I think they're pretty safe, don't you?"

Darin Gretsky leaned his broom in a corner and surveyed the well-lit workshop with a thin smile. He'd worked thirty years to prepare himself as a theoretical physicist, and during all those years he'd felt disdain for most of his fellows. He'd shared their thirst for knowledge, but for them, acclaim, respect, even power, were by-products of knowledge. For him, they were what knowledge was all about. His calculating pursuit of the lifestyle promised by corporate and governmental research empires had earned the contempt of his fellow students, but he hadn't cared, and the wealth and—especially—power he craved had been just within his reach . . . until Dahak and the explosion of Imperial science snatched them away.

Gretsky felt his jaw ache and made himself relax it. Overnight, he'd been transformed from a man on the cutting edge to an aborigine trying to understand that the strange marks on the missionary's white paper actually had meaning. He'd had the stature to be included in the first implant education programs, and, for a time during the Siege, he'd thought he might catch the crest of this new wave as he had the old. But once the emergency was past, Darin Gretsky had realized a horrible thing: he'd become no more than a *technician*. A flunky using knowledge others had amassed. Knowledge, he'd been forced to admit with bowel-churning hatred, he didn't truly understand.

It had almost destroyed him . . . and it *had* destroyed the life he'd planned. He'd become but one more of the thousands of Terra-born scientists exploring millennia of someone else's research and watching it invalidate much of what they'd believed was holy writ. There were no fellow students whose work he might steal, and it couldn't matter less who "published first." And worst of all, the ones for whom he'd felt contempt—the naive ones to whom it was knowledge itself which mattered—were better at it than he. The Terra-born scientists exploring the rarefied stratosphere of the Fourth Empire's tech base came from their number, and there was no room for Darin Gretsky save as one more hewer of wood and drawer of water in the dust about their feet.

But things would change once more, and his smile grew ugly at the thought. His work here had filled his secret bank account with enough Imperial credits to buy the life he'd always craved, and that was good, yet far more satisfying to his wounded soul was what his work could bring about. He didn't know how it would be used, but contemplating the cataclysmic power of the device he'd built gave him an almost sexual thrill. It had taken longer than he'd expected, and he'd had to reinvent the wheel a time or two to work around components that didn't exist, but money had been no object, and he'd succeeded. He'd *succeeded*, and someday soon, unless he was sadly mistaken, his handiwork would topple the smug cretins who'd pushed him aside.

He gave the workshop one more glance, then walked down the hall to the office in which he became not Shiva, Destroyer of Worlds, but one more freelance consultant helping Terran industry cope with the flood of concepts pouring like water from the new Imperial Patent Office. Even that was merely picking the bones of the dead past, he thought acidly. *Emperor Colin*—the title was an epithet in his soul—had declared all civilian Imperial technology public knowledge, held by the Imperial government and leased at nominal fees to any and all users. The free flow of information was unprecedented, and old, well-established firms were being challenged by thousands of newcomers as the manna tumbled down and imagination became more important than mere capital.

He hated the people he worked for. Hated all the bright-eyed, smiling people reaching out for the new world which had robbed him. He had to hide that, but not for much longer. Soon what he'd wrought would—

He looked up in surprise as the office door opened, for it was after midnight. The well-groomed young woman in the doorway looked at him with an odd little smile and raised her eyebrows.

"Dr. Gretsky?" He nodded. "Dr. *Darin* Gretsky?" she pressed.

"Yes. What can I do for you, Ms.——?" He paused, waiting for her name, and she reached into her outsized purse.

"I have a message for you, Doctor." Something in her voice set off a distant alarm, and his muscles tightened as the door opened once more and four or five men stepped through it. "A message from the Sword of God."

He leapt to his feet as her hand came out of the purse, but the last thing Darin Gretsky ever saw was the white, bright glare of a muzzle flash.

Lawrence Jefferson closed the report and leaned back in his swivel chair with a thoughtful expression. Over the past decade he'd assumed ever more of Horus' day-to-day responsibilities, freeing the Governor to concentrate on policy issues, and Gus van Gelder reported directly to him on routine matters now, which was a very useful thing, indeed.

He swung his chair gently from side to side, considering his strategy yet again in light of the latest report. The Sword of God was becoming quite a headache, he thought cheerfully. They were growing bolder, applying all the lessons of the terrorist organizations Colin MacIntyre and his fellows had smashed, and they were far harder to destroy. These terrorists knew the strengths—and weaknesses—of the Imperial technology opposed to them, and none of the security people trying to defeat them suspected their most priceless advantage. Knowledge was power, and through Gus van Gelder, Lawrence Jefferson knew exactly what moves were being made against his tools.

For example, he knew Gus was getting uncomfortably close to Francine. *Gus* didn't know it yet, but Jefferson did, and so Bishop Hilgemann was driving the Sword from the Church of the Armageddon. The excesses of zealotry must be forever anathema to the godly, and she was horrified by the thought that such misguided souls might be numbered among her flock. They must recognize the error of their ways or be cut off from the body of the faithful, for they had embraced a fundamental error. Hatred for the Achuultani and all other works of the Anti-Christ was every godly person's duty, but that hate must not be extended to the leadership which stood against the foe. Rather the errors of that leadership must be addressed nonviolently, by prayer and remonstrance, lest all the undeniable good it had achieved be lost, as well.

It was all very touching, and it had Gus a bit confused, since he didn't know about the conduits through which she directed those same zealots. What Gus hadn't quite grasped yet was that the Sword no longer required the infrastructure of the Church. No doubt Gus *would* figure it out, but by then it should be too late to find any institutional links to Bishop Hilgemann.

Security Councilor van Gelder nodded to the Marine sentry as the elevator deposited him on an upper floor of White Tower. He walked down the hall and knocked on the frame of an open door.

"Busy?" he asked when the man behind the desk looked up.

"Not terribly." Lieutenant Governor Jefferson rose courteously, waving to a chair, then sat again as van Gelder seated himself. "What's up?"

"Horus still on Birhat?"

"Well, yes." Jefferson leaned back, steepling his fingers under his chin, and raised his eyebrows. "He's not scheduled to return until tomorrow night. Why? Has something urgent come up?"

"You might say that," van Gelder said. "I've finally got a break on the Sword of God."

"You have?" Jefferson's chair snapped upright, and van Gelder smiled. He'd thought Jefferson would be glad to hear it.

"Yes. You know how hard it's been to break their security. Even when we manage to take one or two of them alive, they're so tightly compartmented we can't ID anyone outside the cell *they* come from. But I've finally managed to get one of my people inside. I haven't reported it yet—we're playing her cover on a strict need-to-know basis—but she's just been tapped to serve as a link in the courier chain to her cell's main intelligence pipeline."

"Why, that's wonderful, Gus!" Jefferson cocked his head, considering the implications, then rubbed his blotter gently. "How soon do you expect this to pay off?"

"Within the next few weeks," van Gelder replied, smothering a small, familiar spurt of exasperation. Jefferson couldn't help it any more than any other bureaucratic type, but even the best of them had a sort of institutional impatience that irritated intelligence officers immensely. They couldn't appreciate the life-and-death risks his field people ran, and a "why can't we move quicker on this?" mind-set seemed to go with their jobs.

"Good. Good! And you want to report this directly to Horus?"

"Yes. As I say, I've been running this agent very carefully. I'm the only one in the shop who knows everything about the job, and I just got her report this afternoon. Horus and I set the concept up several months ago, and I need to let him know what's happening before I brief anyone on my staff."

"I see. Do you have a formal report for him, then?"

"Not a formal one, but—" van Gelder reached into his jacket pocket and extracted a small security file "—these are my briefing notes."

"I see." Jefferson regarded the security file thoughtfully. Such files were keyed to randomly generated implant access codes when they were sealed. Any attempt to open them without those codes would reduce the chips within them to useless slag.

"Well, as I say, he won't be back until tomorrow night. Is this really urgent? I mean—" he waved his hand apologetically at van Gelder's slightly affronted expression "—are we facing a time pressure problem so we *have* to get the word to him immediately?"

"It's not exactly a crisis, but I'd like to brief him as soon as possible. I don't want to be too far from the office in case something breaks, but maybe I should mat-trans out to Birhat and catch him there. If he agrees, I could brief Colin and Jiltanith, too."

"That might be a good idea," Jefferson mused, then paused with an arrested air. "In fact, the more I think about it, the more I think we ought to get it to him ASAP. It's the middle of the night in Phoenix right now, but I'm already scheduled to mat-trans out tomorrow morning their time. Could I drop your notes off with him, or is he going to need a personal briefing?"

"We do need to discuss it," van Gelder said thoughtfully, "but the basic information's in the notes. . . . In fact, it might help if he had them before we sat down to talk."

"Then I'll take them out with me, if you like."

"Fine." Van Gelder handed over the file with a grin. "Never thought I'd be using a courier quite *this* secure!"

"You flatter me." Jefferson slid the file into his own pocket. "Does Horus have the file access code?"

"No. Here—" Van Gelder flipped his feed into

Jefferson's computer and used it to relay the code to the Lieutenant Governor, then wiped it from the computer's memory. "I hope you don't talk in your sleep," he cautioned.

"I don't," Jefferson assured him, rising to escort him to the door. He paused to shake his hand. "Again, let me congratulate you. This is a tremendous achievement. I'm sure there are going to be some very relieved people when they get this information."

Chapter Thirteen

"We've got another one, Admiral."

Ninhursag MacMahan grimaced and took the chip from Captain Jabr. She dropped it into the reader on her desk, and the two of them watched through their neural feeds as the report played itself to them. When it ended, she sighed and shook her head, trying to understand how the slaughter of nineteen power service employees possibly served the "holy" ends of the Sword of God.

"I wish we'd gotten at least one of them," she said.

"Yes, Ma'am." Jabr rubbed his bearded jaw, dark eyes hard. "I would have liked to entertain those gentlemen myself."

"Now, now, Sayed. We can't have you backsliding to your bloodthirsty Bedouin ancestors. Not that you might not be onto something." She drummed on her desk for a moment, then shrugged. "Pass it on to Commander Wadisclaw. It sounds like part of his bailiwick."

"Yes, Ma'am."

Captain Jabr carried the chip away, and Ninhursag rubbed weary eyes, propped her chin in cupped palms, and stared sightlessly at the wall.

The "Sword of God's" escalating attacks worried her. One or two, like the one on Gus, had hurt them badly, and even the ones that weren't doing that much damage—except, she amended with a wince, to the people who died—achieved the classic terrorist goal of proving they could strike targets despite the authorities. Open societies couldn't protect every power station, transit terminal, and pedestrian belt landing, but anyone with

136

the IQ of a rock knew that, and at least this time humanity seemed to have learned its lesson. Not even the intellectuals were suggesting the Sword might, for all its deplorable choice of tactics, have "a legitimate demand" to give it some sort of sick quasirespectability. Yet as long as these animals were willing to select targets virtually at random, no analyst could predict where they'd strike next, and they were killing people she was supposed to protect. Which was why they had to get someone *inside* the Sword if they ever expected to stop them.

She winced again as her roving thoughts reminded her of the single agent they *had* gotten inside. Janice Coatsworth had been an FBI field agent before the Siege, and Gus had been delighted to get her. She'd been one of his star performers—one of his "aces" as he called them—and she'd died the same day he had. Somehow she'd been made by the Sword, and they'd dumped what was left of her body on Gus's lawn the same day they killed him, his wife, and two of their four children. Four of his personal security staff had died, as well, two of them shielding his surviving children with their own bodies.

Ninhursag's eyes were colder and harder by far than Captain Jabr's had been. If anything could be called a "legitimate" terrorist target, it was certainly the head of the opposing security force, but she'd been as astounded as any by the attack. Indeed, the van Gelder murders had shaken everyone into a reevaluation of the Sword's capabilities, for Gus' security had been tight. Penetrating it had taken meticulous planning.

She chewed her lip and frowned over a familiar, nagging question. Why was the Sword so . . . spotty? One day they carried out a meaningless massacre of defenseless power workers and left clues all over the countryside; on another they executed a precision attack on a high-security target and left the forensic people damnall. She knew the Sword was intricately compartmented, but did it have a split personality, too? And where had a bunch of yahoos who could be as clumsy as that power station attack gotten a tight, cellular organization in the first place? Anyone who could put that together could choose more effective targets, and hit them more cleanly, too.

She sighed and put the thought aside once more. So far, they had no idea how the Sword was organized. For all she knew, the meaningless attacks were the work of some splinter group or faction. For that matter, they might actually be the work of some totally different organization which was simply hiding behind the Sword while it pursued an agenda all its own! They needed a better look inside to answer those kinds of questions, and that was up to the folks on Earth, where the Sword operated. Gus had managed it once, and since his death, Lawrence Jefferson had managed to break no less than three of its cells. It was unfortunate that none of them had led to any others—indeed, it seemed likely they were among the more inept members of their murderous brotherhood or they wouldn't have been so easy to crack—but they were a start.

And, she reminded herself, at least the slaughter of Gus' family had given them a reason to beef up Horus' security at White Tower without arousing their real enemy's suspicions.

"Sweet mother of God!" Gerald Hatcher blurted. "Are you *serious*?"

"Of course I'm not!" Ninhursag snarled back. "I just thought *pretending* I was would be really hilarious!"

She quivered with frightened anger Colin understood only too well, and he touched her shoulder, watching her relax with a hissing sigh before he turned his attention back to Hatcher's hologram. Vlad Chernikov also attended by holo image from his office aboard Orbital Yard Seventeen, but Tsien was present with Colin and Ninhursag in the flesh.

"Sorry, 'Hursag," Hatcher muttered. "It's just that— Well, Jesus, how did you *expect* us to react?"

"About the same way I did," Ninhursag admitted with a crooked grin. Then real humor flickered in her eyes. "Which, I might add, you did. You should've heard what *I* said when Dahak told me!"

"But there is no question?" Tsien's deep voice was harder than usual, for it was his files which had been penetrated this time.

"None, Star Marshal," Dahak replied. "I have checked my findings no less than five times with identical results."

"Shit." Colin rubbed the fatigue lines which had formed in the long, dreary months since his children died. After almost a year and a half they were still playing catch-up. Ninhursag and Lawrence Jefferson had managed to pick off a few Sword of God cells, a few score terrorists had been killed in shoot-outs with security forces when they'd struck at guarded sites, and they'd identified exactly seven spies in their military.

And each of those spies had been dead by the time they found him.

"The bastards have us penetrated six ways to Sunday," he said through his fingers, tugging on his nose while his other hand pushed the chip of Ninhursag's report in an aimless circle.

"Yes and no, Colin," Dahak said. "True, we are uncovering evidence of past penetration, yet we are also clearing a progressively higher number of senior personnel of suspicion. I cannot, of course, be certain that we have sealed all breaches in the Bia System, yet recall that I am now monitoring all hypercom traffic between Bia and Sol as well as all datanets in this system. And while I cannot assure you that no information is being transmitted via courier, ONI now maintains permanent surveillance of *all* visitors from Earth."

"Yeah, but it looks like we just found out we didn't get the door locked till after the barn burned down!"

"Perhaps and perhaps not." For a moment Tsien sounded so much like Dahak Colin suspected him of deliberate humor, but that wasn't Tao-ling's style.

"Meaning what?"

"Meaning, Colin, that this particular piece of hardware, while undoubtedly dangerous, is of limited utility to whoever has it."

"What do—" Hatcher began, then stopped. "Yeah, you've got something, Tao-ling. What the hell can they do with it even if they've got it?"

"I would not invest too much confidence in that belief, Admiral Hatcher," Dahak said, "but my own analysis does tentatively support it."

"But how did they get their hands on it in the first place?" Vlad asked, for he'd arrived a few moments late for the initial briefing.

"We're not positive," Ninhursag answered. "All Dahak's discovered for certain is that there's at least one more copy of the plans for the new gravitonic warhead than there should be. We don't know where it is, who has it, or even how long whoever stole it has had it in his possession."

"I believe we may venture a conjecture on the last point," Tsien disagreed. "Dahak has examined the counter in the original datachip from Weapons Development's master file, Vlad." Vlad's holo image nodded understanding. Each Fleet security chip was equipped with a built-in counter to record the numbers of copies which had been made of it, and while the counter could be wiped, it could not be altered. "According to our records, there should be ten copies of the plans—including the original chip—and all ten of those have now been accounted for. However, a total of ten copies were made of the *original* chip, and we do not know where that eleventh copy is.

"On the other hand, that original has been locked in the security vault at BuShips since the day all authorized copies were made, and none of the external or internal security systems show any sign of tampering. I therefore believe the additional copy was made at the same time as the authorized ones."

"Oh, *shit*," Hatcher moaned. "That was—what, six years ago?"

"Six and a half," Ninhursag confirmed. "And while I wouldn't care to bet my life on it, I'd say Tao-ling is probably right. Particularly since a certain Senior Fleet Captain Janushka made the authorized copies. Two years ago, *Commodore* Janushka, who was then assigned to the Sol System as part of the Stepmother team, died of a 'cerebral hemorrhage.'"

She grimaced, and the others snorted. A properly pulsed power surge in a neural feed implant produced something only the closest examination could distinguish from a normal cerebral hemorrhage. But pulsed surges like that couldn't happen by accident, and an ME with no reason to suspect foul play might very well opt for the natural explanation.

"I see." Vlad pursed his lips for a moment, then gave a Slavic shrug. "On that basis, I am inclined to share your conclusion as to the timing, Tao-ling. Yet this weapon is an extremely sophisticated piece of hardware. Building it would require either military components or a civilian workshop run by someone thoroughly familiar with Imperial technology."

"I'm sure it would," Colin said, "but whoever we're up against had the reach and sophistication to sabotage *Imperial Terra*—unless anyone cares to postulate two separate enemies with this level of penetration?" Clearly no one wished to so postulate, and he smiled grimly. "I think we have to assume Mister X wouldn't have stolen it if he didn't believe he could produce it."

"True." Hatcher was coming back on balance, and his voice was calmer and more thoughtful. "But Tao-ling's still right about its utility. They can blow up a planet with it, but if that's all they had in mind, six years plus is plenty of time to build the thing—assuming they could build it at all—and it's also plenty long enough to have used it."

"Precisely," Tsien agreed. "They undoubtedly had some plan for its use, either actual or threatened, else they had not stolen the plans, but what that use may be eludes me. The conspirators must be human—there were far too few Narhani contacts with humans for any of them to have penetrated our security so deeply so long ago—so the destruction of Earth would be an act of total madness. If, on the other hand, their target is here on Birhat, any of our much smaller gravitonic warheads or even a simple thermonuclear device would satisfy their needs. Nor is a weapon of this power required to destroy any conceivable deep space installation."

"What about Narhan?" Ninhursag asked quietly, and Tsien frowned.

"That, Ninhursag, is a very ugly thought," he conceded after a moment. "Again, I can see no sane reason to destroy the planet—that sounds much more like something the Sword of God would wish to attempt—yet Narhan would seem a more likely target than either Earth or Birhat."

"God, all we need is for Mister X to be tied in with a bunch of crazies like the Sword of God!" Colin groaned.

"On the surface, that appears unlikely," Dahak said. "The pattern of 'Mister X's' operations indicates a long-term plan which, while criminal, is rational. The Sword of God, on the other hand, is fundamentally *ir*rational. Moreover, as Admiral Hatcher has pointed out, they have had ample time to destroy Narhan if they possessed the weapon. It is possible 'Mister X' might attempt to capitalize upon the activities of the Sword of God or even to influence those activities, but his ultimate goals are quite different from their xenophobic nihilism."

"Then what do *you* think he's going to do with it?"

"I have no theory at this time, unless, perhaps, he intends to use it as a threat to extort concessions. If that is the case, however, we are once more faced by the fact that he has had ample time to build the device and thus, one would anticipate, to make whatever demands he might present."

"Maybe Vlad has a point, then," Colin mused. "Maybe they *have* hit a snag that's kept them from building it at all."

"I would not depend upon that assumption," Dahak cautioned. "I believe humans refer to the logic upon which it rests as 'whistling in the dark.'"

"Yeah," Colin said morosely. "I know."

Chapter Fourteen

The fist in his eye woke Sean MacIntyre.

He twitched aside, one hand jerking up to the abused portion of his anatomy, even before he came fully awake. Damn, that hurt! If he hadn't been bio-enhanced himself, the punch would have cost him the eye.

He wiggled further over on his side of the bed and rose on one elbow, still nursing his wound, as Sandy lashed through another contortion. That one, he judged, could have done serious damage if he hadn't gotten out of the way. She muttered something even enhanced hearing couldn't quite decipher, and he sat further up, wondering if he should wake her.

They'd all had problems dealing with the reality of *Imperial Terra*'s loss. Just being alive when all those others were dead was bad enough, but their conviction that *Terra* had been destroyed in an attempt to kill *them* made it worse, as if it were somehow their fault. Logic said otherwise, but logic was a frail shield against psyches determined to punish them for surviving.

Sandy twisted in her nightmare, fighting the sheet as if it had become an enveloping monster, and it ripped with a sound of tearing canvas. Her breasts winked at him, and he chastised himself as he felt a stir of arousal.

This was hardly the time for that! He wished—again—that even one of them had been interested in a psych career. Unfortunately, they hadn't, and now that they needed a professional, they were on their own. The first weeks had been especially rough, until Harriet insisted they all had to face it. She didn't know any more about running a therapy session than Sean did, but her instincts seemed good, and they'd drawn tremendous strength from one another once they'd admitted their shared survival filled them with shame.

Sandy twisted yet again, her sounds louder and more distressed. She was the most cheerful of them all when she was awake; in sleep, the rationality which fended off guilt deserted her and, perversely, made her the most vulnerable member of their tiny crew. Her nightmares had become blessedly less frequent, yet their severity remained, and he made up his mind.

He leaned over her, stroking her face and whispering her name. For a moment she tried to jerk away, but then his quiet voice penetrated her dreams, and her brown eyes fluttered open, drugged with sleep and shadowed with horror.

"Hi," he murmured, and she caught his hand, holding it and nestling her cheek into his palm. Fear flowed out of her face, and she smiled.

"Was I at it again?"

"Oh, maybe a little," he lied, and her smile turned puckish.

"Only 'a little,' huh? Then why's your eye swollen?" The tattered sheet fell about her waist as she sat up and reached out gently, and he winced. "Oh, my! You're going to have a black eye, Sean."

"Don't worry about it. Besides—" he treated her to his best leer "—the others'll just think you were maddened with passion."

His heart warmed at the gurgle of laughter which answered his sally, and she shook her head at him, still exploring his injury with tender fingers.

"You're an idiot, Sean MacIntyre, but I love you anyway."

"Uf course you do, Fräulein! You cannot help yourzelf!"

"Oh, you *creep!*" Her caressing hand darted to his nose and twisted, and he yelped in anguish and grabbed her wrists, pinning her down—not without difficulty. He was sixty centimeters taller, but she wiggled like a lithe, naked

eel until a final shrewd twist toppled him from the bed.
He sat up on the synthetic decksole, then stood, rubbing
his posterior with an aggrieved air while she laughed at
him, the last of her nightmare banished.

"Jeez, you play rough! I'm gonna take my marbles and
go home."

"Now there's an empty threat! You can't even *find* your
marbles."

"Hmph!" He took a step towards the bed, and her fingers curved into talons. Her eyes glinted, and he stopped
dead. "Uh, truce?" he suggested.

"No way. I demand complete and unconditional surrender."

"But it's my bed, too," he said plaintively.

"Possession is nine points of the law. Give?"

"What'll you do with me if I do?"

"Something horrible and disgustingly debauched."

"Well, in *that* case—!" He hopped onto the bed and
raised his hands.

Brashan looked up from the executive officer's station
and waved without disconnecting his feed from the console as the others stepped through the command deck
hatch. With Engineering slaved to the bridge, one person
could stand watch under normal conditions, though it
would have taken at least four of them to fight the ship
effectively.

Sean dropped into the captain's couch. Harriet and
Tamman took the astrogator's and engineer's stations, and
Sandy flopped down at Tactical. She looked into the display at the star burning ever larger before them, and the
others' eyes followed hers.

Their weary voyage was drawing to an end. Or, at least,
to a possible end. They didn't talk a great deal about what
they'd do if it turned out that blazing star had no reclaim-
able hardware, but so far they'd detected no habitable
world which might have provided it.

Sean glanced at the others from the corner of an eye.
In many ways, they'd made out far better than he'd

hoped. It helped that they were all friends, but being trapped so long in so small a universe with anyone made for problems. There'd been the occasional disagreement—even the odd furious argument—but Harriet's basic good sense, with a powerful assist from Brashan, had held them together. Solitude didn't really bother Narhani much, and Brashan had spent enough time with humans—especially these humans—to understand their more mercurial moods. He'd poured several barrels of oil on various troubled waters in the past twenty months, and, Sean thought, it helped that he still regarded sex primarily as a subject for intellectual curiosity.

His attention moved to Tamman and Harriet. Despite *Israel*'s size, she was intended for deployment from her mother ship or a planet, not interstellar voyaging, but at least she was designed for a nominal crew of thirty. That gave them enough room to find privacy, and the humans had fallen into couples without much fuss or bother. For him and Sandy, he knew, the pairing would be permanent even if—when!—they got home, but he didn't think it was for Harry and Tamman. Neither of them seemed particularly inclined to settle down, though they obviously enjoyed one another's company . . . greatly.

He grinned and inserted his own feed into the captain's console for a systems update. As usual, *Israel* was functioning perfectly. She really was an incredible piece of engineering, and he'd had an unusual amount of time to learn to appreciate her design and capabilities. They'd spent endless hours running tactical exercises, as much for a way to keep occupied as anything else, and he'd discovered a few things he'd never imagined she could do.

Still, it was Sandy who'd unearthed the real treasure in *Israel*'s computers. Her original captain had been a movie freak—not for HD or even pre-Imperial tri-vid, but for old-fashioned, flat-image movies, the kind they'd put on film. There were hundreds of them in the ship's memory, and Sandy had tinkered up an imaging program to convert them to holo via the command bridge display.

They'd worked their way through the entire library, and some of them had been surprisingly good. Sean's personal favorite was *The Quest for the Holy Grail* by someone called Monty Python, but the ones they'd gotten the most laughs out of were the old science fiction flicks. Brashan was especially fascinated by something called *Forbidden Planet*, but they'd all become addicted. By now, their normal conversation was heavily laced with bits of dialogue none of their Academy friends would even begin to have understood.

He withdrew from the console, maintaining only a tenuous link as he tucked his hands behind his head and crossed his ankles.

"Behold the noble captain, bending his full attention upon his duties!" Sandy remarked. He stuck out his tongue, then looked at Harriet.

"Looks like our original position estimates were on the money, Harry. I make it about another two and a half days."

"Just about," she agreed, an edge of anticipation sharpening her voice. "Anything more on system bodies, Brash?"

"Indeed," the Narhani said calmly. "The range is still well beyond active scanner range, but passive instrumentation continues to pick up additional details. In particular—" he gave his friends a curled-lip Narhani grin "—I have detected a third planet on this side of the star."

Something in his tone brought Sean up on an elbow. The others were staring at him just as hard, and Brashan nodded.

"It would appear," he said, "to have a mean orbital radius of approximately seventeen light-minutes—well within the liquid water zone."

"Hey, that's great!" Sean exclaimed. "That ups the odds a bunch. If there used to be people here, we may find something we can use after all!"

"So we may." Brashan's voice was elaborately calm, even for him; so calm Sean looked at him in quick suspicion. "In fact," the Narhani went on, "spectroscopic analysis confirms an oxygen-nitrogen atmosphere, as well."

Sean's jaw dropped. The bio-weapon had killed *everything* on any planet it touched, and when all life died, a planet soon ceased to be habitable, for it was the presence of life which created the conditions that allowed life to exist. Birhat was life-bearing only because the zoo habitats had cracked before her atmosphere had time to degrade completely, and Chamhar had survived only because no one had lived there, anyway. Earth, never having been claimed by the Fourth Empire, was a special case.

But if this planet had breathable air, then perhaps it hadn't been hit by the bio-weapon at all! And if they could get word of their find home again, humanity had yet a third world onto which it might expand anew.

Then his spirits plunged. If the planet hadn't been contaminated, it probably hadn't had any people, either. Which, in turn, meant no chance at all of finding Imperial hardware they could use to cobble up a hypercom.

"Well," he said more slowly, "that *is* interesting. Anything else?"

"No, but we are still almost sixty-two light-hours from the star," Brashan pointed out. "With *Israel's* instrumentation, we can detect nothing smaller than a planetoid at much above ten light-hours unless it has an active emissions signature."

"In which case," Sean murmured, "we might begin seeing something in the next eighty hours. Assuming, of course, that there's anything to see."

The talmahk were returning early this spring.

High Priest Vroxhan stood by the window, listening to the Inner Circle with half an ear while he watched jeweled wings flash high above the Sanctum. One gleaming flock broke away to dart towards the time-worn stumps of the Old One's dwellings, and he wondered yet again why such lovely creatures should haunt places so wrapped in damnation. Yet they also nested in the

Temple's spires and were not struck dead, so it must not taint them. Of course, unlike men they had no souls. Perhaps that protected them from the demons.

Corada's high-pitched voice changed behind him, and he roused to pay more heed as the Lord of the Exchequer came to the conclusion of his report.

". . . and so Mother Church's coffers have once more been filled by God's grace and to His glory, although Malagor remains behind time in its tithing."

Vroxhan smiled at the last, caustic phrase. Malagor was Corada's pet hate, the recalcitrant princedom whose people had always been least amenable to Church decrees. No doubt Corada put it down to the influence of the Valley of the Damned, but Vroxhan suspected the truth was far simpler than demonic intervention. Malagor had never forgotten that she and Aris had dueled for supremacy for centuries, and Malagor's mines and water-powered foundries made her iron-master to the world, a princedom of stubborn artisans and craftsmen who all too often chafed under the Church's Tenets. That chafing had been the decisive factor in starting the Schismatic Wars, but The Temple used those wars to put an end to such foolishness forever. Today Prince Uroba of Malagor was The Temple's vassal, as (if truth be known) were all the secular lords, for Mother Church made and broke the princes of all Pardal at will.

"Frenaur?" Vroxhan raised his eyes to the Bishop of Malagor. "Does your unruly flock truly mean to distress Corada this year?"

"Not, I think, any more than usual." Frenaur's eyes twinkled as Corada's jowls turned mottled red. "The tithe is late, true, but the winter has been bad, and the Guard reports the wagons have passed the border."

"Then I think we can wait a bit before resorting to the Interdict," Vroxhan murmured. It was unkind, and not truly befitting to his office, but Corada was such an old gas-bag he couldn't help himself. The fussy bishop's bald pate flushed dark against its fringe of white hair as he sniffed and gathered his parchments more energetically than necessary, and Vroxhan felt a pang of remorse. Not a very painful one, but a pang.

He turned back to the window, hands folded in the sleeves of his blue robe with the golden starburst upon its breast. A company of Guard musketeers marched across his view, headed for the drill field with voices raised in a marching hymn behind their branahlk-mounted captain, and he admired the glitter of their silvered breastplates. Polished musket barrels shone in the sunlight, and scarlet cloaks swirled in the spring breeze. As a second son, Vroxhan had almost entered the Guard instead of the priesthood. Sometimes he wondered rather wistfully if he might not have enjoyed the martial life more—certainly it was less fringed with responsibilities! But the Guard's power was less than that of the Primate of all Pardal, too, he reminded himself, and sat in his carven chair, returning his attention to the council room.

"Very well, Brothers, let us turn to other matters. Fire Test is almost upon us, Father Rechau—is the Sanctum prepared?"

Faces which had been amused by Corada's fussiness sobered as they turned towards Rechau. A mere underpriest might be thought the lowest of the low in this chamber of prelates, but appearances could be deceiving, for Rechau was Sexton of the Sanctum, a post which by long tradition was always held by an under-priest with the archaic title of "Chaplain."

"It is, Holiness," Rechau replied. "The Servitors spent rather longer in their ministrations this winter—they appeared soon after Plot Test and labored for two full five-days. Such a ministration inspired my acolytes to even greater efforts, and the sanctification was completed three days ago."

"Excellent, Father!" Vroxhan said sincerely. They had three five-days yet before Fire Test, and it was a good start to the liturgical year to be so beforehand with their preparations. Rechau bent his head in acknowledgment of the praise, and Vroxhan turned his eyes to Bishop Surmal.

"In that case, Surmal, perhaps you might report on the new catechism."

"Of course." Surmal frowned slightly and looked around the polished table. "Brothers, the Office of Inquisition recognizes the pressure brought upon the Office of Instruction by the merchant guilds and 'progressives,' yet I fear we have grave reservations about certain portions of this new catechism. In particular, we note the lessened emphasis upon the demonic—"

The council chamber doors flew open so violently both leaves crashed back against the walls. Vroxhan surged to his feet at the intrusion, eyes flashing, but his thunderous reprimand died unspoken as a white-faced under-priest threw himself to his knees before him and trembling hands raised the hem of his robe to ashen lips in obeisance.

"H-holiness!" the under-priest blurted even before he released Vroxhan's robe. "Holiness, you must come! Come quickly!"

"Why?" Vroxhan's voice was sharp. "What is so important you disturb the Inner Circle?!"

"Holiness, I—" The under-priest swallowed, then bent to the floor and spoke hoarsely. "The Voice has spoken, Holiness!"

Vroxhan fell back, and his hand rose to sign the starburst. Never in mortal memory had the Voice spoken save on the most sacred holy days! A harsh, collective gasp went up from the seated Circle, and when he darted a quick glance at them he actually saw the blood draining from their faces.

"What did the Voice say?" His question came quick and angry with his own fear.

"The Voice spoke Warning, Holiness," the under-priest whispered.

"God protect us!" someone cried, and a babble of terror rose from the Church's princes. An icy hand clutched at Vroxhan's heart, and he drew a deep breath and clutched his pectoral starburst. For one, dreadful instant he closed his eyes in fear, but he was Prelate of

Pardal, and he shook himself violently and whirled upon the panicky prelates.

"Brothers—Brothers! This is not seemly! Calm yourselves!" His deep, powerful voice, trained by a lifetime of liturgical chants, lashed out across the confusion, stinging them into brief silence, and he hurried on.

"The Warning has come upon us, possibly even the Trial, but God will surely protect us as He promised to our fathers' fathers these many ages past! Did He not give us the Voice against this very peril? There will be panic enough among our flock—let us not begin that panic in the Inner Circle!"

The bishops stared at him, and he saw reason returning to many faces. To his surprise, old Corada's was one of them. Bishop Parta's was not.

"Why?" Parta moaned. "Why has this come to *us*? What sin have we committed that God sends the very Demons upon us?"

"Oh, be quiet, Parta!" Corada snapped, and Vroxhan swallowed an hysterical giggle at the way the old man's vigor widened every eye. "You know your Writ better than that! The demons come when they come. Sin won't bring them any sooner; it will only turn God's favor from us when they come."

"But what if He *has* turned His favor from us?" Parta blathered, and Corada snorted.

"If He has, would His Voice give us Warning?" he demanded, and Parta blinked. "You see? I know it's never happened before, but the Writ says no man can know when the Trial may come. Put your trust in God where it belongs, man!"

"I—" Parta cut himself off and gasped in a breath like a drowning man's, then nodded sharply. "Yes, Corada. Yes. You're right. It's just—"

"Just that it's scared the tripes out of you," Corada grunted, then gave a lopsided grin. "Well, don't think it hasn't done the same for me!"

"Thank you, Corada," Vroxhan said gratefully, making a mental promise never to tease the old man again. "Your

faith and courage are an inspiration to us." He swept his
bishops' eyes once more, and nodded. "Come, Brothers.
Join me in a brief prayer of rededication before we
answer the Voice's call."

Vroxhan had never vested in such unseemly haste,
but neither had he ever faced a moment like this. For
thousands upon thousands of years God had warded
His faithful from the demons whose very touch was
death to body and soul. Not in recorded history had
He allowed the enemies of all life whose vile trickery
had cast Man from the starry splendor of God's Heaven
to earth to approach so near as to rouse the Voice to
Warning, but Vroxhan reminded himself of Corada's
words. God had not abandoned His people; the Voice's
Warning was proof of that.

He jerked the golden buttons closed, suppressing a
habitual stab of annoyance as the tight-fitting collar
squeezed his neck. He checked the drape of the dark
blue fabric in the wavery reflection of a mirror of polished silver, for it would never do to come before God
improperly vested at this of all times. He passed inspection, and he stepped quickly through the door of imper-
ishable metal onto the glassy floor of the Sanctum.

His bishops waited, clad as he in their tight-fitting
vestments, as he walked to his place at the center of
the huge chamber and felt a wash of familiar awe as
the night sky rose above him. The dark sphere of midnight enveloped him, blotting out the polished, trophy-
hung walls with the glory of God's own stars, but awe
was replaced by dread as he looked up and saw the
scarlet sigil of the demons rising slowly in the eastern
sky.

The sight chilled his blood, for it burned still and
bright, the color of fresh blood and not the pulsing yellow
flicker of Fire Test, Plot Test, or System Check. But he
squared his shoulders, reminding himself he was God's
servant. He marched to the altar, and the inhuman
beauty of the Voice's unhurried, inflectionless speech

rolled over him, calm and reassuring in its eternal, unchanging majesty.

"Warning," it said in the Holy Tongue, every word sweet and pure as silver, "passive system detection warning. Hostiles approach." The Voice continued, speaking words not even the high priest knew as it invoked God's protection, and he felt a shiver of religious ecstasy. Then it returned to words he recognized, even though he did not fully understand them. "Contact in five-eight-point-three-seven minutes," it said, and fell silent. After a moment it began again, repeating the Warning, and Vroxhan knelt to press his bearded lips reverently to the glowing God Lights of the high altar with a silent prayer that God might overlook his manifest unworthiness for the task which had come to him. Then he rose, and sang the sacred words of benediction.

"Arm systems," he sang, and a brazen clangor rolled through the Sanctum, but this time no one showed fear. This they had heard before, every year of their religious lives, at the Feast of Fire Test. Yet this time was different, for this time its familiar, martial fury summoned them to battle in God's holy cause.

The challenge of God's Horn faded, and the Voice spoke once more.

"Armed," it said sweetly. "Hostiles within engagement parameters."

Amber circles sprang into the starry heavens, entrapping the crimson glare of the demons, ringing it in the adamantine rejection of God's wrath, and Vroxhan felt himself tremble as the ultimate moment of his life rushed to meet him. He was no longer afraid—no longer even abashed, for God had raised him up. He was God's vessel, filled with God's power to meet this time of Trial, and his eyes gleamed with a hundred reflected stars as he turned to his fellows. He raised his arms and watched them draw strength from his own exaltation. Other arms rose, returning his blessing, committing themselves to the power and the glory of God while the demons' red glare washed down over their faces and vestments.

"Be not afraid, my brothers!" Vroxhan cried in a great voice. "The time of Trial is upon us, but trust in God, that your souls may be exalted by His glory and the demons may be confounded, for the power is His forever!"

"Forever!" The answering roar battered him, and there was no fear in it, either. He turned back to the high altar, lifting his eyes defiantly to the demon light, rejecting it and the evil for which it stood, and his powerful, rolling voice rose in the sonorous music of the ancient Canticle of Deliverance.

"Initiate engagement procedure!"

Chapter Fifteen

"Coming into range of another one," Harriet announced from Plotting as a display sighting ring circled yet another dot. "A big one."

Sean felt—and shared—her stress. They were finally close enough for *Israel*'s scanners to detect subplanetary targets, and the tension had been palpable ever since the first deep-space installation was spotted. There'd been more in the last two hours—lots more—and his hopes had soared with the others'. The first one hadn't been much to look at, only a remote scanner array crippled by what appeared to have been a micrometeorite strike, but the ones deeper in-system were much bigger. In fact, they looked downright promising, and he kept reminding himself not to let premature optimism carry him away.

"I'm on it, Harry," Sandy reported from Tactical. Her active scanners had less reach than Harriet's passive sensors but offered far better resolution once a target had been pointed out to them. "Coming in now. Comp Cent calls it a *Radona*-class yard module, Tam."

"*Radona*, *Radona*," Tamman muttered, running through his Engineering files. "Aha! I *thought* I remembered! It's a civilian yard, but with the right support base, a *Radona* class could turn out another *Israel* in about eight months, Sean. If we get it on-line, we can build us a hypercom no sweat."

"That," Sean said quietly, "is the best news I've had in the last twenty-one months. People, it looks like we're going to make it after all."

"Yes, I—" Sandy began, then broke off with a gasp. "Sean, that thing's live!"

"*What?*" Sean stared across at her, and she nodded vigorously.

"I'm getting standby level power readings from at least two Khilark Gamma fusion plants—maybe three."

"That's ridiculous," Sean muttered. He twisted back around to glare at the bland light floating in Harriet's sighting ring. "She'd need hydrogen tankers, maintenance services, a resource base . . . She *can't* be live!"

"Try telling that to my scanners! I've definitely got live fusion plants, and if her power's up, we won't even have to activate her!"

"But I still don't see how—"

"Sean," Harriet cut him off, "I'm getting more installations. Look."

Scores of sighting rings blossomed as her instruments came in range of the new targets, and Sean blinked.

"Sandy?"

"I'm working them, Sean." Sandy's voice was absent as she communed with her systems. "Okay, these—" three of Harriet's amber rings turned green "—look like your 'resource base.' They're processing modules, but they're not Battle Fleet designs, either. They might be modified civil facilities." She paused, then continued flatly. "And *they're* live, too."

"This," Sean said to no one in particular, "is getting ridiculous. Not that I'm ungrateful, but—" He shook himself. "What about the others?"

"Can't tell yet. I'm getting some very faint power leakage from them, but not enough for resolution at this range." She closed her eyes and frowned in concentration. "If they're live, it doesn't look like they've got much on-board generation capacity. Either that, or . . ." Her voice trailed off.

"Or what?"

"Those *might* be stasis emissions." She sounded unhappy at suggesting that, and Sean grunted. No stasis field could maintain itself from internal power, and there wasn't enough available from the powered-down plants of the other facilities to sustain that many fields with broadcast power.

"Humph. Goose us back up to point-five cee and take us in, Brashan."

"Coming up to point-five cee, aye," Brashan replied from Maneuvering, and Sean frowned even more thoughtfully. Something about those installations bothered him. They floated in distant orbit around the third planet, not in a ring but in a wide-spaced sphere. There were too many of them—and they were much too small—to be more yard modules, but each was almost a third of *Israel's* size, so what the devil *were* they?

"Sean!" Harriet's exclamation was sharp. "I've got a new power source—a monster—*and it's on the planet!*"

His head whipped back up as still another sighting ring appeared in the display and the new emission source crept into sight over the planetary horizon. Harry was right; it was huge. But it was also . . . strange, and he frowned as its light code flickered uncertainly.

"Can you localize it?"

"I'm trying. It's— Sean, my scanners say that thing's *moving*. It's almost like . . . like some weird ECM, but I've never seen anything like it."

Sean frowned. That single massive power source was all alone down there, and that made it the most maddening puzzle yet. Obviously the population and tech base which had produced the system installations hadn't survived, or they would have been challenged by now. Besides, if the planet had fusion power, there should be dozens of planetary facilities down there, not just one. But without people, how had even one power plant survived the millennia? And what did Harry mean by "moving"? He plugged into her systems and watched it with her, and damned if she wasn't right. It *was* like some sort of ECM, as if something were trying to prevent them from locking in its coordinates.

"Can you crack whatever it is, Harry?"

"I think so. It's a weird effect, but it looks like . . . Oh, that's sneaky!" Her tone took on a mix of admiration and excitement. "That source isn't as big as we thought, Sean. It *is* big, but there's at least a dozen—probably more like two or three dozen—false emitters down there, and they're jumping back and forth between them. Their generators aren't moving, they're just reshaping the main emission source. I don't know why, but now that I know *what* they're doing it's only a matter of ti—"

"Status change." Sandy's voice was flat with tension. "The satellite power readings are going up like missiles. They're coming on-line, Sean!"

His eyes darted back to the satellites. Those *had* been stasis fields; now they were gone, and whole clusters of new sources were coming up while they watched. Sean chewed his lip, wondering what the hell was going on. But until he knew—

"Bring us about, Brashan. Let's not get in too deep."

"Coming onto reciprocal course, aye," Brashan confirmed, and Sean watched the changing tactical symbols in the display as *Israel* came about.

"I've got a bad feeling about this," he muttered.

"First phase activation complete. All platforms nominal."

Vroxhan listened to the Voice's ancient, musical words as a net of emeralds blazed against the night sky. God's Shields glowed with the color of life, yet he'd never seen so many of them at once, not even at the once-a-decade celebration of High Fire Test. Truly this was the time of Trial, and he licked his lips as he proceeded to the second verse of the Canticle.

"Activate tracking systems," he intoned sonorously.

"Status change!" This time Sandy almost screamed the words. "Target system activation! *Those things are weapons platforms!*"

"Settle down, Sandy!" Sean snapped. "Brashan, take us to point-seven! Evasion pattern Alpha Romeo!"

"Alpha Romeo, aye," Brashan replied with reassuring Narhani calm.

$\diamond$ $\diamond$ $\diamond$

"Target acquisition," the Voice announced. Its singing power filled the Sanctum, and the golden ring about the demons' sigil turned blood-red. Tiny symbols appeared within it—some steady and unwinking, others changing with eye-bewildering flickers. Vroxhan had never seen anything like that; none of the symbols which appeared during Plot Test and Fire Test ever changed, and mingled terror and exaltation filled him as he chanted the third verse.

"Initiate weapon release cycle."

Israel leapt to full speed, and the power of her drive quivered in bone and sinew as Brashan threw her into the evasion pattern. A corner of Sean's thoughts stole a moment to be thankful for all the drills they'd run and another to curse how undermanned they were, but it was only a tiny corner. The rest of his mind had suddenly gone cold, humming with a strange, deep note unlike anything he'd ever experienced in a training exercise, and his thoughts came like a dance of lightning, automatic, almost instinctive.

"Tactical, get the shields up and initiate ECM! Download decoys for launch on my signal but do not engage."

"Shields—up!" Sandy snapped back, her earlier edge of panic displaced by trained reactions. "ECM—active. Decoys prepped and downloaded."

"Acknowledged. Have you localized that power source, Harry?"

"Negative!"

Sean felt himself tightening inwardly as his queerly icy brain raced. Every instinct screamed to open fire to preempt whatever those weapons might do, but even if his assumption that the planetary power source was the command center was right, he couldn't hit it if Harry couldn't localize it. That only left the platforms themselves, and they were such small targets—and there were so many of them—that going after them would be a losing proposition. Perhaps more importantly, they hadn't fired yet. If he initiated hostilities, they most certainly would, and although *Israel* was beyond energy weapon range, maximum range for the Fourth Empire's hyper missiles against a target her size was thirty-eight light-minutes. They were ten light-minutes inside that. At maximum speed, they needed fourteen minutes to clear the planet's missile envelope, and every second the platforms spent thinking about shooting was one priceless second in which they *weren't* shooting.

"Target evading."

Vroxhan's heart faltered as the Voice departed from the Canticle of Deliverance. It had never said those words before, and the symbols inside the bloody circle danced madly. The demon light pulsed and capered, and his faith wavered. But he felt ripples of panic flaring through the bishops and upper-priests. He had to do *something*, and he forced his merely mortal voice to remain firm as he intoned the fourth verse of the Canticle.

"Initiate firing sequence!" he sang, and his soul filled with relief as the Voice returned the proper response.

"Initiating."

"Launch activation! Multiple launch activations!"

Sean paled at Sandy's cry. The platforms had brought their support systems on-line; now their hyper launchers were cycling. They'd need several seconds to wind up to full launch status, but there were *hundreds* of them!

He tasted blood. This was a survey ship's worst nightmare: an intact, active quarantine system. An *Asgerd*-class planetoid would have hesitated to engage this kind of firepower, and he had exactly one parasite battleship.

"Launch decoys!"

"Launching, aye." A brief heartbeat. "First decoy salvo away. Second salvo prepping."

Blue dots speckled the display with false images, each

a duplicate of *Israel's* own emissions signature as it streaked away from her.

"Activate missile battery. Designate launch platforms as primary targets but do not engage."

"Missile battery active," Sandy said flatly.

"Hostile decoys deployed," the Voice announced sweetly.

Vroxhan clutched at the altar, and a terrified human voice cried out behind him, for the high priest's portion of the Canticle was done! There *was* no more Canticle! But the Voice was continuing.

"Request Tracking refinement and update," it said, and the High Priest sank to his knees while the demon light spawned again and again. Dozens of demons blazed in the stars, and he didn't know what the Voice wanted of him!

"Initiate firing sequence!" he repeated desperately, and his trained voice was broken-edged and brittle.

"Probability of kill will be degraded without Tracking refinement and update," the Voice replied emotionlessly.

"*Initiate firing sequence!*" Vroxhan screamed. The Voice said nothing for a tiny, terrible eternity, and then—

"Initiating."

"Hostile launch! I say again, hostile launch!"

A deathly silence followed Sandy's flat announcement. The Fourth Empire's hyper missiles traveled at four thousand times the speed of light. It would take them almost seven seconds to cross the light-minutes to the battleship, but there was no such thing as an active defense against a hyper missile, for no one had yet figured out a way to shoot at something in hyper. They could only take it . . . and be glad the range was so long. At seventy percent of light-speed, *Israel* would have moved almost one-and-a-half million kilometers between the time those missiles launched and the time they arrived. But that was why defensive bases had prediction and tracking computers.

Israel had never been intended to face such firepower

single-handed, but her defenses had been redesigned and refined by Dahak and BuShips to incorporate features gleaned from the Achuultani and new ideas all their own. Her shields covered more hyper bands, her inner shield was far closer to her hull than the Fourth Empire's technology had allowed, and she had an outer shield, which no earlier generation of Imperial ship had ever boasted.

It was as well she did.

Only a fraction of those missiles were on target, but *Israel* bucked like a mad thing, and Sean almost ripped the arms from his couch as warheads smashed at her and she heaved about him. Damn it! *Damn* it! He'd forgotten to activate his tractor net! The gravity wells of a dozen stars sought to splinter his ship's insignificant mass, and shield generators screamed in her belly.

The familiar musical note of Fire Test rang in his ears, and Vroxhan stared up from his knees, eyes desperate, waiting for the demon lights to vanish, praying that they would. He didn't know how long he would have to wait; he never did, even during Fire Test, for no one had ever taught him to read the range notations within the targeting circles.

Then, suddenly, all but one of the demon lights *did* vanish. A great sigh went up from the massed bishops, and Vroxhan joined it. The demons might have spawned, but God had smitten all but one of them! Yet that one remained, and that, too, had never happened during Fire Test.

His terrible fear ebbed just a bit, but only a bit, for yet again the Voice spoke words no high priest had ever heard.

"Decoys destroyed. Engagement proceeding."

A ship of the Fourth Empire would have died. Five of those mighty missiles had popped the hyper bands covered by *Israel's* outer shield, but they erupted outside her inner shield . . . and it held. Somehow, it held.

"Jesus!" Sean shook his head and activated his couch

tractor net as soon as the universe stopped heaving. They couldn't take many more like that!

"Shift to evasion pattern Alpha Mike. Launch fresh decoy salvo."

This time there were no verbal acknowledgments, but they flowed back to him through his feed. He felt his friends' fear, but they were doing their jobs. And they were still alive. He didn't understand that. With this much fire coming at them, they should be dead. But there wasn't time to wonder why they weren't—and no longer any reason not to fight back.

"Engage the enemy!" he snapped.

The first salvo spat from *Israel*'s launchers, and it was odd, but his own fear had disappeared.

"Incoming fire," the Voice said. "Request defense mode."

Vroxhan covered his face, trying to understand while faith, terror, and confusion warred within him. He knew what "request" meant, but he had no idea what a "defense mode" was.

"Urgent," the Voice said. "Defense mode input required."

Israel twisted in agony as the second salvo erupted into normal space about her, and a damage warning snarled. One of those missiles had gotten too close, and armor that would have sneered at a nuclear warhead tore like tissue under the fraction of power that leaked through the inner shield.

But Sean had more time to watch this attack's pattern, and it told him something. Whatever was on the other end of those missiles was fighting dumb, spreading its fire evenly between *Israel* and her decoys, and that was crazy. Any defensive system ought to be able to refine its data enough to eliminate at least a few false images.

He felt Tamman activate his damage control systems, yet a quick check told him nothing vital had gone, and he looked back at the display just as Sandy's first salvo went home.

Sweat stung Vroxhan's eyes as a dozen of God's emerald Shields vanished from the stars. The demons! The demons had done that!

"Urgent," the Voice repeated. "Defense mode input required."

The high priest racked his brain. Thought had never been required during any of the high ceremonies, only the liturgy. His mind ran desperately over every ritual, seeking the words "defense mode," but he couldn't think of any canticle that used them. Wait! He couldn't think of any that used *both* words, but the Canticle of Maintenance Test used "mode"!

He trembled, wondering if he dared use another canticle's words. What if they were the *wrong* words? What if they turned God's wrath against *him*?

Sean bit down on a yell of triumph. The ground source might be hiding, but the weapon platforms were stark naked! Not even a shield!

"Hit them, Sandy!" he snapped, and *Israel*'s next salvo went out even as the third hostile salvo came in.

Vroxhan groaned as another dozen emeralds vanished. That was almost a tenth of them all, and the Demons still lived! If they destroyed all of God's Shields, nothing would stand between them and the world's death!

"Warning." The Voice was as beautiful as ever, yet it seemed to shriek in his brain. "Offensive capability reduced nine-point-six percent. Defense mode input required."

Blood ran into Vroxhan's beard as his teeth broke his lip, but even as he watched the demons were spawning yet again. He had no choice, and he spoke the words from the Canticle of Maintenance Test.

"Cycle autonomous mode selection!" he cried.

He felt the others stare at him in horror, but he made

himself stand upright, awaiting the stroke of God's wrath. Silence stretched to the breaking point, and then—

"Autonomous defense mode selection engaged," the Voice said.

"Shit!"

Sean smashed a clenched fist against the arm of his couch. They'd gotten in a third salvo, but the quarantine system had finally noticed they were killing its weapons. Shields popped into existence around the scores of surviving orbital bases, and decoys of their own blinked into life. They were only Fourth Empire technology, nowhere near as good as the improved systems Dahak and BuShips had provided *Israel*, but they were good enough. It would take every missile they could throw to take out even one of them now, yet they had no other target. They still hadn't localized the ground base controlling them and the range was now too great to try.

He started to order Sandy to reprioritize her fire, massing it on single targets, but she was already doing it.

The battleship writhed again, yet the ferocity was less and he felt a surge of hope. Sandy had nailed almost forty bases; maybe she'd thinned them enough they could survive yet!

They'd been engaged for four minutes, and they'd started running a full minute before the enemy opened fire. The range was up to over thirty-one light-minutes, and that would help, too. If they got to at least thirty-five and managed to break lock, they might be able to go into stealth and—

Israel heaved yet again, and another damage signal snarled. Crap! That one had taken out two of Sandy's launchers.

Vroxhan stared at the stars, and hope rose within him. Only one of the Shields had vanished that time. Perhaps none of them might have perished if he'd known what God and the Voice truly demanded, but at least he was still alive and the rate of destruction had slowed. Did that mean God smiled upon him after all? The Writ said man could but do his best—had God granted him the mercy of recognizing his best when he gave it?

Israel sped outward, bobbing and weaving as Sean, Brashan, and the maneuvering computers squirmed through every evasion they could produce, and Harriet abandoned Plotting and plugged into the damage control sub-net to help Tamman fight the battleship's damage. Two more near-misses had savaged her, and her speed was down to $.6\ c$ from the loss of a drive node, but the incoming fire was less and less accurate. Sandy had picked off thirteen more launch stations, ripping huge holes in the original defensive net, but Sean could see the surviving weapon platforms redeploying, with more coming around from the far side of the planet. Still, Sandy's fire might just have whittled them down enough to make the difference in the face of *Israel*'s ECM.

Even as he thought that, he knew he didn't really believe it.

He rechecked the range. Thirty-four light-minutes. Another seven minutes to the edge of the missile envelope at their reduced speed. Could they last that long?

Another salvo shook the ship. And another. Another. A fresh damage signal burned in his feed. They weren't going to make it out of range before something got through, but they were coming up on thirty-five light-minutes, and each salvo was still spreading its fire to engage their decoys. They hadn't managed to break lock, but if the bad guys' targeting was so bad it couldn't differentiate them from the decoys, they might be able to get into—

Vroxhan watched the demons spawn yet again. They must have an inexhaustible store of eggs, but God smote every one they hatched. A fresh cloud of crimson dots profaned the stars—and then they vanished.

They *all* vanished, and the ring of God's wrath was empty. Empty!

Silence hovered about him and his pulse thundered as the assembled priests held their breath.

"Target destroyed," the Voice said. "Engagement terminated. Repair and replacement procedures initiated. Combat systems standing down."

"They've lost lock," Sandy reported in a soft, shaky voice as *Israel* vanished into stealth mode, and Sean MacIntyre exhaled a huge breath.

He was soaked in sweat, but they were alive. They shouldn't have been. No ship their size could survive that much firepower, however clumsily applied. Yet *Israel* had. Somehow.

His hands began to tremble. Their stealth mode ECM was better than anything the Fourth Empire had ever had, but to make it work they'd had to cut off all detectable emissions. Which meant Sandy had been forced to cut her own active sensors and shut down both her false-imaging ECM and the outer shield, for it extended well beyond the stealth field. He'd hoped synchronizing with the decoys' destruction would convince the bad guys they'd gotten *Israel*, as well, but if their tracking systems *hadn't* lost lock, they would have been a sitting duck. They wouldn't even have been covered by decoys against the next salvo.

His hands' shakiness spread up his arms as he truly realized what a terrible chance he'd just taken, and not with his own life alone. It had worked, but he hadn't even thought about it. Not really. He'd reacted on gut instinct, and the others had obeyed him, trusting him to get it right.

He made himself breathe slowly and deeply, using his implants to dampen his runaway adrenaline levels, and thought about what he'd done. He made himself stand back and look at the logic of it, and now that he had time to think, maybe it hadn't been such a bad idea. It had worked, hadn't it? But, Jesus, the risk he'd taken!

Maybe, he told himself silently, Aunt Adrienne's homilies on overly audacious tactics contained a kernel of truth after all.

Chapter Sixteen

Stardrift glittered overhead, and a smaller, fiercer star crawled along the battle steel beneath his feet as the robotic welder lit a hellish balefire in Sean MacIntyre's eyes while *Israel* drifted in sepulchral gloom almost a light-hour from the system primary.

His wounded ship lay hidden in an asteroid's ink-black lee while he coaxed the welder through his neural feed. Other robotic henchmen had already cut away the jagged edges of the breach, rebuilt sheared frame members, and tacked down replacement plates of battle steel. Now the massive welding unit crept along, fusing the plates in place. Under other circumstances, damage control could have been left to such a routine task unsupervised, but one of *Israel*'s hits had taken out a third of her Engineering peripherals. Until Tamman and Brashan finished putting them back on-line—*if* they finished—the damage control sub-net remained far from reliable.

"How's it coming?"

He turned his head in the force field globe of his "helmet" as Sandy walked down the curve of the hull towards him.

"Not too bad."

Fatigue harshened his voice, and she studied him as she came closer. A massive, broken pylon towered behind him, shattered by the hit that had demolished the heavily armored drive node it had supported. He stood between stygian blackness and the welder's fire, half his suited body lost in shadow, the other glowing demon-bright, and his face was drawn. It was his turn to wake from nightmares these nights, but he met her eyes squarely.

"You're doing better than I expected," she said after a moment.

"Yeah. We'll have this breach finished by the end of the watch."

"The end of which watch, dummy?" she teased gently. "You're supposed to be in the sack right now."

"Really?" He sounded genuinely surprised, and she didn't know whether to laugh or cry at his tired, bemused expression as he checked the time.

"I'll be damned. Is that why you came out here? To get me?"

"Yep. A MacMahan always gets her man—and in this instance, my man better get his ass inside before he goes to sleep on his big, flat feet."

"I do believe," he stretched, "you have a point, Midshipwoman MacMahan. But what about junior?" He waved at the welder.

"It's only got fifty meters to go, Sean. You can trust it that far on its internal programming. And if you come along and let her tuck you in, Aunt Sandy promises she'll come back out and check on it in about an hour. Deal?"

"Deal," he sighed. The two of them turned away, disappearing over the rise of the battleship's flank, and the lonely star of the welder crawled on behind them, blazing like a lost soul in the depths of endless night.

Even Brashan looked drawn, and the humans were downright haggard, but three weeks of exhausting labor had repaired everything they could repair.

"Okay, people," Sean called the meeting to order. "It doesn't seem to me that going on to our next stop is a real good idea. Anybody disagree?"

Wry, weary grins and headshakes answered him. The G6 star of their second-choice destination was twelve and a half light-years away from their present position. At barely half the speed of light—the best *Israel* could sustain with a primary drive node shot away—the voyage would take seventy-five months, even if it would be "only" five and a half years long for them.

"Good. I'd hate to make a trip that long and then not find anything at the other end. Especially since we *know* there's an active shipyard here."

"Cogently put," Brashan agreed with one of his curled-lip grins. "Of course, there remains the small problem of gaining control of that shipyard."

"True," Sean lay back in his couch and stared up into the display, "but maybe that's not as tough as it looks. For instance, we know the power for the platform stasis fields is beamed up from that ground source, so that's probably the HQ site. If so, taking it over should give us control of the platforms, too. Failing that, taking it out should shut them down, right?"

"I agree that seems a logical conclusion, but how do you intend to penetrate its orbital defenses to get at it?"

"Sleight of hand, Brashan. We'll fool the suckers."

"Oh, dear. This sounds like something I'm not going to like."

Sean smiled and the others chuckled as Brashan fanned his crest in a Narhani expression of abject misery.

"It won't be that bad—I hope." Sean turned to Sandy and his sister. "Did your analysis reach the same conclusion I did?"

"Pretty much," Sandy said after a glance at Harriet. "We agree they detected us on passive, at least. We didn't pick up any active systems till their launcher fire control came up."

"And their tactics?"

"That's a lot more speculative, Sean, and one point still worries us," Harriet replied. "Your theory sounds logical, but it's *only* a theory."

"I know, but look at it. Much as it pains me to admit it, that much firepower should have swatted us like a fly, however brilliant my tactics were. Whatever runs those defenses was slow, Harry. Slow and clumsy."

"Okay, but how do you explain its *defensive* tactics? Slow's one thing, but it let us take out thirty-six platforms before the others even began to defend themselves."

"So it's slow, clumsy, and *dumb*," Tamman said with a shrug.

"You're missing the point, Tam." Sandy came to Harriet's aid. "Properly designed automated defenses shouldn't have let us take any of them out unopposed, but anything dumb enough to let us zap any of them that way should have let us take them *all* out. Besides, how many other intact quarantine systems have we seen? None. That means this thing's original programming wasn't just good enough to control its weapons—it's run enough deep-space industry to keep the whole system functional for forty-five thousand years, as well."

She paused to let that sink in, and Tamman nodded. Harriet's stealthed sensor remotes, operating from a circumspect forty light-minutes, had given them proof of that. The *Radona*-class yard was no longer on standby; it was rebuilding the weapon platforms Sandy had destroyed.

"Another thing," she continued. "Those platforms' passive defenses are mighty efficient by Empire standards, and that razzle-dazzle trick by the ground source is pretty cute, too. It's not standard military hardware, but it works. Maybe its designer was a civilian, but if so he was a sneaky one—not exactly the sort to give anything away to an enemy. And if a sharp cookie like whoever set this all up built in defensive systems at all, why arrange things so they didn't come on-line until after our *third* salvo?"

"So what do you think happened?" Tamman countered.

"We don't know; that's what worries us. It's almost like there was something else in the command loop—something that really was slow, clumsy, and stupid. If there is, it probably saved our lives this time, but it may also surprise us, especially if we make any wrong assumptions."

"Fair enough," Sean said. "But given how long it waited to bring its weapons on-line, whatever it is must be pretty myopic, right?"

"There we have to agree with you," Harriet replied wryly. "But it's what you're planning on *after* we arrive that scares us, not the approach."

"Whoa! Hold on." Tamman straightened in the engineer's couch. "What approach? You been holding out on me and Brashan, Captain, Sir?"

"Not really. It's only that you both've been so buried in Engineering you missed the discussion."

"Well we're not buried *now*, so why don't you just fill us in?"

"It's not complicated. We came in fat and happy last time, radiating as much energy as a small star; this time we'll be a meteorite."

"I *knew* I wouldn't like it," Brashan sighed, and Sean grinned.

"You're just sore you didn't think of it first. Look, it let us get within twenty-eight light-minutes before it even began bringing its systems on-line, right?" Tamman and Brashan nodded. "Okay, why'd it do that? Why didn't it start bringing them up as soon as we entered missile range? After all, it couldn't know *we* wouldn't shoot as soon as we had the range."

"You're saying it didn't pick us up until then," Brashan said.

"Exactly. And that gives us a rough idea how far out its passive sensors were able to detect us. Sandy and Harry ran a computer model assuming it had picked us up at forty light-minutes—a half hour of flight time before it powered up. Even at that, the model says our stealth field should hide the drive to within a light-minute if we hold its power well down. That means we can sneak in close before we shut down everything and turn into a meteor."

"Seems to me you've still got a little problem there." Tamman sounded doubtful. "First of all, if *I'd* designed the system, it wouldn't let a rock *Israel's* size hit the planet in the first place. I'd've set it to blow the sucker apart way short of atmosphere. Second, we can't land, or even maneuver into orbit, without the drive, and we'll be way inside a light-minute by that point. It's going to spot us as a ship at that range, stealth field or no."

"Oh, no it won't." Sean smiled his best Cheshire Cat

smile. "In answer to your first point, you should have made time to read that paper I wrote for Commander Keltwyn last semester. Our survey teams have looked at the wreckage of over forty planetary defense systems by now, and every single one of them required human authorization to engage anything without an active emissions signature. Remember, over half these things were set up by civilians, not the Fleet, and the central computers were a hell of a lot stupider than Dahak. The designers wanted to be damned sure their systems didn't accidentally kill anything *they* didn't want killed, and none of the system's we've so far examined would have engaged a meteor, however big, without specific authorization."

"So? The whole point is that we *will* have an active signature when we bring the drive up."

"Sure, but not where it can see us long enough to matter. We come in under power to *two* light-minutes, then reduce to about twenty thousand KPS, cut the drive, and coast clear to the planet."

"Jesus Christ!" Tamman yelped. "You're going to hit atmosphere in a *battleship* at twenty thousand kilometers per second?"

"Why not? I've modeled it, and the hull should stand it now that we've got the holes patched. We come in at a slant, take advantage of atmospheric braking down to about twenty thousand meters, then pop the drive."

"You're out of your teeny-tiny mind!"

"What's the matter, think the drive can't hack it?"

"Sean, even with one node shot out, my drive can take us from zip to point-six cee in eleven seconds. Sure, if we program the maneuver right and leave it all on auto we've got the oomph to land in one piece. But we're gonna be one hell of a high-speed event when we hit air, and the drive'll create an awful visible energy pulse when you kill that kind of velocity that quick. There's no way— no way!—a stealth field will hide either of those!"

"Ah, but by the time the drive kicks in, we'll be inside atmosphere. I doubt whoever set this up programmed it to kill air-breathing targets!"

"Um." Tamman looked suddenly thoughtful, but Brashan regarded his captain dubiously.

"Isn't that a rather risky assumption—particularly if, as Harry and Sandy argue, there's an unpredictable element to the control system?"

"Not really." Harriet sounded a bit as if she were agreeing with Sean despite herself. "This is a quarantine system. It's probably programmed to wax people trying to escape after the bio-weapon hit as well as anyone coming from outside, but Sean's right. Every one we've seen before has required human authorization to engage anything that wasn't obviously a spacecraft. It shouldn't care a thing about meteors, and it's almost certainly not set to shoot before a target leaves atmosphere. Even if it is, you're forgetting reaction time. It'll take at least two minutes just to spin down the stasis fields on its platforms. There won't be enough time for it to see us and activate its weapons between the time the drive cuts in and we cut power, go back into stealth, and land."

"I suppose that's true enough. But what do we do once we're down?"

"That's where Sandy and I part company with our fearless leader. He wants to put down on top of the power source and take it over. Which sounds good, unless it's got on-site defenses. We won't be able to tell ahead of time—we can't use active sensors without warning it we're coming—but if it *does* have site-defense weapons, they may be permanently live. If they are, they'll get us before we can even go active and sort out the situation."

"We could just waste the whole site from space," Tamman suggested. "Coming in that slow, Harry should have plenty of time to localize it on passive. We could pop off a homing sublight missile from a few light-seconds out. And, as you say, even if it spotted the launch, it wouldn't have time to react before the bad news got there."

"We could, and it's something to bear in mind," Sean agreed, "but I'd rather take the place over intact. We can't use active scanners from stealth, but we *can* carry out visual observations once we come out of stealth. That's a huge power plant, and there must be some reason the automatics kept it running after everybody died. Let's take a peek and see if it's something we can generate any additional support from before we zap it. I'd rather not kill any golden egg-laying geese if I can help it."

"A point," Tamman conceded. "Definitely a point."

"Which brings us back to Sandy's and my objection," Harriet pointed out. "If we don't want to take the place out from space, then we shouldn't be landing on top of it, either. Not when we don't know whether the site's armed or what that 'something else' in the command loop is."

"I believe the girls are correct, Sean," Brashan said. "I confess your plan seems less reckless than I assumed, but they're still right, and there's no need to charge in precipitously."

"Tam? You agree with them?"

"Yes," Tamman said positively, and Sean shrugged.

"All right, I can be big about these things. What say we plan our insertion to set us down over the curve of the planet from the site?"

High Priest Vroxhan sat in his gilded throne and surveyed the worshipers with studied calm, trying to assess their mood.

Mother Church had been shaken to her foundations, but by God's blessing the Trial had been upon them and then past so quickly few outside the Inner Circle had known a thing about it till it was over. The word had spread on talmahk wings after that, and the people were abuzz with the story—which, he was certain, had grown more terrible with each telling—but they'd managed to suppress all mention of the Voice's unknown words and his own desperate improvisation. Vroxhan wasn't certain that was necessary, but he *was* certain it would be far wiser for the Inner Circle to sort it out themselves before they risked the faith of others by revealing all the facts.

Yet however unorthodox events might have been, the outcome was clear: the Trial had come, and the demons had been smitten as the Writ promised. Thousands of years of faith had been vindicated, and that was what this solemn festival of thanksgiving and the priestly conclave to follow were all about.

The last human soul entered the packed courtyard of the Sanctum, and he raised one hand in blessing from his throne as the choir sang the majestic opening notes of the Gloria.

The last four hours had been frustrating.

Israel had crept in at the paltry velocity of .2 c, wrapped in the stealth field that turned her into a black nothingness. Her passive systems had peered ahead, poised on a hair-trigger to warn of any active detection systems, but she'd been blind to anything but fairly powerful energy sources, and curiosity was killing her crew.

Harriet had, indeed, localized the power source to within fifty kilometers, which was ample for warheads of the power they carried, but Sean longed to examine the planet directly. Unfortunately, *Israel's* optical systems, pitiful compared to active fold-space scanners at the best of times, were degraded by the stealth field which protected her. They could have used the drive to impart a higher initial velocity and coasted the whole way without a stealth field, but they could neither have maneuvered nor slowed for atmospheric insertion without going into stealth. Sean had no idea how the defenses would react to an "asteroid" that popped in and out of detectability, and he didn't want to find out; he was taking a big enough chance by coming this close before he dropped stealth in the first place. More importantly, he wanted to be able to turn and creep away if he saw any sign of changing power levels on the orbital bases. It was always possible the defenses might pick up something without being able to localize *Israel* and shoot, and if he'd come in any faster the drive settings needed to kill the ship's velocity might have burned through the stealth field and given them a target.

But they were coming up on the two-light-minute mark, and he lay tense in his command couch as their speed fell still further. Tamman and Brashan coordinated their departments carefully, reducing drive power and velocity in tandem, and Sean grunted his satisfaction as the drive died at last. Right on the mark, he noted: exactly 20,000 KPS. The internal gravity was still up, but *Israel* no longer had any emission signature at all.

"Good, guys," he murmured, then glanced at Sandy. "Take the stealth field down."

"Coming down now," she replied tautly, and Sean watched through a cross feed as she powered down their cloak of invisibility with the same exquisite care Tamman had taken.

The entire crew held its collective breath as Harriet consulted her passive systems very, very carefully. Then she relaxed.

"Looks good, Sean." Her voice was hushed, as if she feared the defenses might hear. "The platform stasis fields're steady as a rock."

Her crewmates' breath hissed out, and Sandy looked up with a grin.

"We're *heeeere*," she crooned, and the others laughed out loud.

"Of course we are." Sean grinned back at her, elated by his ploy's success. "But we're just a great big rock." He glanced smugly at Tamman. "Looks like the defenses *are* programmed to kill only ships, and without emissions, we ain't a ship."

"I hate it when he's right," Sandy told the others. "Fortunately, it doesn't happen often."

That was good for another chuckle, and the last of the hovering tension faded as Sean waved a fist in her direction. Then he sat up briskly.

"All right. Bring up the optics and see what we can see, Harry."

"Bringing them up now," his sister said, and the blue

and white sphere of the planet swelled, displacing the starfield from the display as she engaged the forward optical head. They were almost thirty-six million kilometers away, but surface features leapt into startling clarity.

Sean stared eagerly at seas and rivers, the rumpled lines of mountain ranges, green swathes of forest. Theirs were the first human (or Narhani) eyes to behold that planet in forty-five thousand years, and it was lovely beyond belief. None of them had dared hope to see this living, breathing beauty at the end of their weary voyage, but incredible as it seemed, the planet lived. Here in the midst of the Fourth Empire's self-wrought devastation, it *lived*.

His eyes devoured it, and then he stiffened.

"Hey! What the—?"

"Look! *Look!*"

"My God, there's—!"

"Jesus, is that—?!"

An incredulous babble filled the command deck as all of them saw it at once. Harriet didn't need any instructions; she was already zooming in on the impossible sight. The holo of the planet vanished, replaced by a full-power closeup of one tiny part of its surface, and the confusion of voices died as they stared at the seaport city in silence.

"There's no question, is there?" Sean murmured.

"Damn." Tamman shook his head. "I wouldn't have believed it if I hadn't seen it. Hell, I'm still not sure I *am* seeing it!"

"You're seeing it," Sandy told him quietly. "And maybe it's a good thing we didn't just zap the control center after all."

"No question," Tamman agreed, and *Israel*'s crew shared a shudder at the thought of what they might have unleashed against a populated world.

"But I don't understand it," Brashan mused. "Life, yes—there's life on Birhat, so it has to be theoretically possible. But people? *Humans?*" His crest waved in perplexity and a double-thumbed hand rubbed his long snout.

"There's only one answer," Sean said. "This time quarantine worked."

"It seems impossible," Harriet sighed. "Wonderful, but impossible."

"You got that right." Sean frowned at the large, fortified town they were currently watching. "But this only raises more questions, doesn't it? Like what happened to their tech base? Their defenses are still operable, and the HQ is down there, so how come they're all running around like that?"

He waved at the image, where animal-drawn plows turned soil in a patchwork of fields. The small, low buildings looked well-enough made, but they were built of wood and stone, and many were roofed in thatch. Yet the eroded stumps of an ancient city of the Fourth Empire lay barely thirty kilometers from the town's crenulated walls.

"It *doesn't* make much sense, does it?" Sandy replied.

"You can say that again. How in hell can someone decivilize in the midst of that much technology? Just from the ruins we've already plotted, this planet had millions of people. You'd think poking around in the wreckage, let alone having at least one still operating high-tech enclave in their midst, would get the current population started on science. But even if it hasn't, where did the *original* techies go?"

"Some kind of home-grown plague?" Tamman suggested.

"Unlikely." Brashan shook his head in the human expression of negation. "Their medical science should have been able to handle anything short of the bioweapon itself."

"How about a war?" Sandy offered. "It's been a *long* time, guys. They could have bombed themselves out."

"I suppose so, but then why aren't more of those towers flattened?" Sean objected. "Imperial warheads shouldn't have left *anything*."

"Not necessarily." Harriet watched the display, toying with a lock of her hair. "Oh, you're right about gravitonics, but suppose they used small nukes or dusted each other? Or whipped up their *own* bio-weapons?"

"I suppose that's possible, but it still doesn't explain why they never rebuilt. Maybe they lost their original tech base—I can't see how, with that ground station still up, but let's concede the possibility. But we're still looking at a city-building culture spread over at least two continents. It looks to me like they've got about as many people as a pre-tech agrarian economy can support— more than I would have expected, in fact; their agriculture must be more efficient than it looks. But given that kind of population base, why haven't they developed their own indigenous technology?"

"Good point," Tamman agreed, "and I wish I could answer it, but I can't. It's like they've got some kind of technological blind spot."

"Yeah, but then they go and put their biggest city right on top of where we figure the defensive HQ has to be." Sean shook his head in disgust. "It's right in the middle of their largest land mass, and there's not a river within fifty kilometers. With the transportation systems we've seen, that's a hell of an unlikely place for a city to grow up naturally. Look at the canal system they've built. There's over two hundred klicks of it, all to move stuff into the city. There has to be *some* reason for its location, and I can only think of one magnet. Except, of course, that that particular magnet doesn't make any sense on a planet that doesn't know about technology!"

"Well," Sandy sighed, "I guess there's only one way to find out."

"Guess so." Sean's calm tone fooled none of his friends. Then he grinned. "And whatever the reason, Mom and Dad are going to be mighty glad to hear we've found another planet that's not only habitable but stuffed full of people as well!"

◆   ◆   ◆

The sublight battleship *Israel* split atmosphere in a long, shallow descent that wrapped her in a shroud of fire. Her crew rode their couches, feeling their ship quiver with the fury of her descent as her bow plating began to glow. Heat sensors soared as the thick battle steel armor burned cherry-red, then yellow, then white. The terrible glow crept back along her hull, the air blazed before her as she battered a column of superheated atmosphere out of her path, and Sean MacIntyre monitored his instruments and tried to stay calm.

The maneuvering computers waited patiently to engage their carefully written program and stop them dead in the bellow of the drive's fury. It was going to be a rough ride, but so far everything was nominal, and they'd already picked out an alpine valley hiding place fifteen hundred kilometers from the planet's largest city. It was going to be fine, he told himself for the thousandth time, and grinned mirthlessly at his own insistence.

High Priest Vroxhan stood on his balcony and watched the night sky burn. His servants had summoned him almost hysterically, and he'd charged out in only his under-robe to see the terrible strand of fire with his own eyes. Now he did see it, and it touched him with ice.

Shooting stars he had seen before, and wondered why the work of God's Hands should abandon the glorious firmament for the surface of the world to which the demons' treachery had banished man, but never had he seen one so huge. No one had, and he watched it blaze above The Temple like the very Finger of God and trembled.

Could it be—?

No! God's Wrath had slain the demons, and he suppressed the blasphemous thought quickly. But not quickly enough. He'd thought it, and if *he* had, how much more might the ignorant of his flock think the same thing?

He inhaled sharply as the beautiful, terrifying light vanished beyond the western peaks. Would it land? If so, where? Far beyond the borders of Aris—probably even beyond those of Malagor. In Cherist, then? Or Showmah?

He shook himself and turned away, hurrying back into the warmth of his apartments from the chill spring night. It couldn't be the demons, he told himself firmly, and if not they, then it must, indeed, be God's handiwork, as all the world was. He nodded with fresh assurance. No doubt God had sent it as a sign and reminder of His deliverance, and he must see the truth was spread before the less faith-filled panicked.

He closed the balcony door and beckoned to a servant. His messages must be ready for the semaphore tower by first light.

Chapter Seventeen

Colin MacIntyre paused outside the larger state dining room to watch three harassed humans and a dozen robots sorting the countless bags of old-fashioned mail into paper breastworks. No one noticed him in the doorway, and as he resumed his journey towards the balcony, he made a note to divert still more human staff to reading the letters while he tried to sort out his own feelings.

Those bags, and the hundreds which had preceded them in the past few days, proved that whatever outrages the Sword of God might wreak and however well-hidden their true enemy might be, his subjects cared. Those letters weren't just formal, official nothings from heads of state. They came from people all over the Fifth Imperium, expressing their joy—and relief—that their Empress was pregnant.

Yet his own joy, as 'Tanni's, was bittersweet. Over two years had passed, but the aching void remained. Perhaps the new children (for the doctors had already confirmed it would be twins once more) would fill that emptiness. He hoped so. But he also hoped he and 'Tanni could resist the need to *make* them fill it. Sean and Harriet had been special. No one could replace them, and their new children deserved the right to be special in their own ways, not compared, however lovingly, to ghosts.

The decision to have them hadn't been easy. It was fraught with grief, a guilty sense of betraying Sean and Harriet in some indefinable way, and fear of fresh loss. His and 'Tanni's enhancement would give them centuries of fertility, and the temptation to wait was great. Yet they faced the dilemma of all dynasts: the succession must be secured.

That wasn't something Lieutenant Commander MacIntyre, USN, had ever worried about, and it hadn't entered his or 'Tanni's head when Sean and Harriet were conceived, for it had seemed preposterous that the monarchical government of a long-dead empire might be maintained. But as Tsien Tao-ling had pointed out twenty years past, it was loyalty to the Crown—to Colin MacIntyre's person—which held humanity together despite its legacy of rivalries, and many years must pass before that primal source of loyalty could be buttressed by others. Colin had been amazed that someone who had been the commander-in-chief of the last Communist power on Earth could make that statement, but Tao-ling had been right. And because he had, Colin and Jiltanith had no option but to think in dynastic terms.

And perhaps, he mused, as he stepped out onto the balcony and saw his wife dozing in the summer sunlight, that was good. If their hands had been forced, the decision had still proved there was a future . . . and that they had the courage to love again after love had hurt them so cruelly.

He smiled and crossed to Jiltanith, bending over her under Bia's drowsy warmth, and kissed her gently.

"I'm afraid you're right, Dahak." Ninhursag scratched her nose and nodded. "We've put every senior officer under a microscope—hell, we're down to *lieutenants*— and the only bad apples we've found are deceased, so it looks like we've closed off Mister X's penetration there."

"I must confess I had anticipated neither that his penetration might be so limited," Dahak replied, "nor that he would dispose of his minions so summarily."

"Ummmm." Ninhursag leaned back and crossed her legs as she contemplated their findings. Dahak was an enormous asset for any security officer. The computer might not yet have developed the ability to "play a hunch," but he'd achieved total penetration of Bia's datanets, and he was a devastatingly thorough and acute analyst. He and Ninhursag had started with a top-down threat analysis of every officer outside Colin's inner circle, then used Dahak's access to every database in Bia to test their analyses. Where necessary, ONI agents had added on-the-ground investigation to Dahak's efforts, usually without even realizing what they were doing or why. By now, the computer could tell Admiral MacMahan where every Fleet and Marine officer in the Bia System had been at any given minute in the last fifteen years. Of course, he didn't have anything like that degree of penetration in the Sol System. Not even the hypercom was capable of real-timing data at that range, and Earth's datanets were still far more decentralized than Birhat's. But even with those limitations, his access to the military's every order and report had allowed him to clear most of Sol's senior officers, as well.

"Apparently Mister X takes the adage about dead men telling no tales to heart," Ninhursag observed now.

"True. Yet eliminating his agents, however much it may contribute to his security, also deprives him of their future services. That would seem somewhat premature of him—unless he has acquired all the access his plans, whatever they may be, require."

"Yeah." Ninhursag frowned at that unpalatable thought. "Of course, he may have been a bit too smart for his own good. We know about him now, and knowing he doesn't have a military conduit frees us up a lot."

"Yet by the same token, it deprives us of potential access into his own network. We have exhausted all leads available to us, Ninhursag."

"Yeah," she sighed again. "Damn. How I *wish* I knew what he was after! Just sitting here waiting for him to take another shot doesn't appeal to me at all. He's got too good a track record."

"Agreed." Dahak paused, then spoke rather carefully, even for him. "It has occurred to me, however, that our concentration on the military, while logical, may have had the unfortunate consequence of narrowing our vision."

"How so?"

"We have proceeded on the assumption that he himself was of or closely connected to the military, or that the military was in some wise essential to his objectives. If such is not, indeed, the case, may we not have devoted insufficient attention to other areas of vulnerability?"

"That's an endemic security concern, Dahak. We have to start someplace where we can establish a 'clear zone,' and we've got one now—physically, as well as in an investigative sense. We can be fairly confident the entire Bia System is clear, now, so we can assume Colin and 'Tanni are safe from direct physical attack, and knowing the military is clear—now—gives us the resources to mount a counteroffensive of our own. But if Mister X *is* a civilian—even one in government service somewhere—our chance of finding him's a lot lower."

Dahak made a soft electronic sound of agreement. Entry level positions for civilian politicians and bureaucrats were subject to less intensive background scrutinies, and civilian careers seldom included the periodic security checks military men and women took for granted. When it came to civilians, he and Ninhursag lacked anything remotely approaching Battle Fleet's central databases, and their ability to vet suspects was enormously reduced.

"Even worse," the admiral said after a moment, "Mister X knows what he's after, and that gives him the initiative. Until we figure out what he wants, we can't even predict what he's likely to do. Every security chief in history's worried about what he may have overlooked."

"Granted. I only raise the point because I feel it is important that we maintain our guard against all contingencies to the best of our ability."

"Point taken. And that's precisely why I see more reason than ever to keep this on a need-to-know basis. Especially since we *don't* know who in the civil service might have been suborned. Or who's vulnerable in the same way Vincente Cruz was."

"A wise precaution. But may this not create problems when your ONI agents begin operations on Earth? They will inevitably be seen as interlopers, and the decision not to inform even the highest levels of the civilian security forces as to why their presence is necessary will exacerbate that perception. Indeed, it may even lead to a certain degree of institutional obstructionism in what humans call 'turf wars.' "

"If there *are* any turf wars, I guarantee they'll be short. Ultimate responsibility for the Imperium's security rests right here, in my office. ONI's the senior service, and if anybody thinks different, I'll just have to show him the error of his ways, won't I?"

Admiral MacMahan's smile was cold. Which suited Dahak very well indeed.

Lawrence Jefferson's pleasant expression masked a most unpleasant mood as he and Horus walked together to the Shepherd Center mat-trans. Alert bodyguards watched over the Governor, and knowing his own actions had made them inevitable was irritating. Yet he'd had no choice. He'd known having Gus van Gelder killed would almost have to shake the Imperium's leadership into a fundamental reassessment of its security needs, but it had been essential to unmask Gus' mole. And, having done so, the only man who knew he'd had access to those briefing notes had to be removed, as well.

He rather regretted the deaths of Erika, Hans, and Jochaim van Gelder. Gus, of course, would have had to go eventually, but it had offended Jefferson's innate tidiness to eliminate him so messily. On the other hand, his early removal had worked out far better than Jefferson had dared plan for. A successful conspirator didn't base long-term strategy on a gift from the gods which made him the person charged with catching himself, but that didn't make him ungrateful when it was given. And if Horus' security was better now, it still wasn't impenetrable . . . particularly against his own security chief.

No, Jefferson's true unhappiness had less to do with defenses which couldn't, in the end, really matter than with the news from Birhat. The last thing he needed was for the imperial family to produce another heir! He'd already been forced to dispose of one pair, and now he might have to do the whole job over again—especially since Jiltanith had already announced her intention to visit her father on Earth for the birth. Which, he thought disgustedly, was precisely the sort of thing she *would* do just when he needed her and Colin in the same, neat crosshairs on Birhat.

Of course, he reminded himself as he and Horus stepped up onto the mat-trans platform, pregnancy wasn't something whose timing even Imperial bioscience could predict with absolute accuracy. But if the doctors were right, Jiltanith would not give birth, after all, for she—and her unborn children—would die two weeks before she did.

The Planetary Duke of Terra grinned as he and his lieutenant governor entered the conference room. Hector MacMahan—still grim, but no longer an ice-encased stranger—had brought Tinker Bell, and Brashieel had brought his own Narkhana, one of her genetically altered pups.

Horus watched Narkhana collapse as Tinker Bell leapt upon him and wrestled him to the floor. He rolled on the rug, thrusting back at her with all four feet while their happy growls mingled. For a dog well into her third decade, Tinker Bell was remarkably spry, thanks to her own limited biotechnics, yet she had no conception of the tremendous strength Narkhana was reining in to let her win, nor of just how far her son's intellect surpassed her own. Even if she'd been able to conceptualize such things, she would never have known, for her children would never tell her, and there was something both hilarious and poignant in watching them revert to utter doggishness in her presence.

Hector looked up and saw the late arrivals, and a whistle brought Tinker Bell instantly to his side. She flopped down at his feet, panting cheerfully as she prepared to put up with another of the incomprehensible human things her person did. Horus raised a sardonic eyebrow at his grandson, and Hector looked back with a bland innocence he'd forgotten how to assume for far too many months. For all her boisterousness, Tinker Bell was well behaved when Hector chose to remind her to be.

"Horus, Lawrence. Glad you could make it," Colin said, standing to shake hands. Horus squeezed back, then opened his arms to his daughter's embrace and slid into the chair beside Jefferson's.

"Now that you're here," Colin went on, "let me introduce someone very special. Horus, you've already met, but it's been a while since you've seen her. Gentlemen, this is Eve."

Horus inclined his head to the slender being on the pad beside Brashieel's. She was much more delicate than Brashieel, and several centimeters shorter, but her crest was magnificent. Brashieel's, like that of all male Narhani, was the same gray-green as the rest of his hide; Eve's was half again as large, proportionally, and shot with glorious color. Now that crest fanned in a graceful expression that conveyed greeting and thanks for his courtesy with an edge of embarrassment at the fuss being made over her, and it was hard for him to remember she wasn't quite seven years old.

Jefferson bowed in turn, and Brashieel preened with pride beside her. The Narhani were a hierarchical race, and there'd never been much doubt the first Narhani female would become the bride of the first Narhani nest lord, but it was clear that more than duty and mutual expectation flourished between these two. Horus was glad for them—and not just because Eve represented the culmination of his dead daughter's greatest project.

"We've got several things on today's agenda," Colin announced, "but first things first. Horus, 'Tanni and I want you to make sure the Earth-side news channels are ready for our broadcast."

"In truth." Jiltanith's smile was almost as lovely as of old. Not quite, but it was getting there, and the knowledge that she was to be a mother again showed. " 'Twas kindness greater than e'er any mother, be she sovereign lady or no, might expect of so many to wish her unborn babes so well, Father. 'Twill heal our souls to tell them all how greatly their letters have helped to heal our hearts."

"That," Horus said, "will be my very great pleasure."

"Thank you," Colin said warmly, then grinned. "I know the Council's got to talk about all those little niggling things like taxes, budgets, and engineering projects, but first there's something really important. Eve?"

"Of course, Your Majesty." Eve's vocoder had been set to produce a female human voice, and Horus felt a familiar stinging sensation in his eyes when he heard it. At Eve's own request, the voice was Isis Tudor's. It was her way of honoring her human "mother's" memory, and he'd once been afraid it would hurt to hear it. But there was no pain. Only pride.

The adolescent Narhani woman reached into her belt pouch and withdrew a half-dozen holo plates. She laid one before her with a slender, six-fingered hand, adjusting it with nervous precision, then looked up at the humans seated around the table.

"As you know," she said with a formality at odds with her youth, "the Nest of Narhan plans to commemorate the Siege of Earth with a gift to our human friends. We do this for many reasons, including our nest's desire to express sorrow for the deaths we caused and thanks for all humanity has given us when we might have expected only destruction. Memorials, such as your own Memorial at Shepherd Center, are important to us, as well, and it is our hope that this will be the beginning of an Imperial Memorial. One in which our nest shares and which will be completed when the Nest of Aku'Ultan has also been freed."

She paused, obviously relieved to have completed her formal statement without errors, and Brashieel's crest rose even higher in pride.

"Our gift," she said more naturally, "is now finished."

She pressed a button, and a soft gasp went up as a light sculpture appeared above the plate. It wasn't in the abstract style human artists were currently enamored of; it was representational, a reproduction of another sculpture worked in finest marble . . . and it was magnificent.

A rearing Narhani rose high on his rear hooves to fight the bonds which held him captive. The cruel, galling collar about his neck drew blood as he pitted his frenzied strength against its massive chain, and the humans who looked upon him knew Narhani expressions well enough to read the despair in his eyes and flattened crest, but his teeth were bared in snarling defiance. He was without hope yet unconquered, and the anguish of his captivity wrenched at them.

Yet he was not alone. Broken chains flailed from his wrists, the exquisitely detailed links shorn by some sharp edge, and a human knelt beside him, torso naked but clothed from the waist down in the uniform of the Imperial Marines. His face was drawn with fatigue, but his eyes were as fierce as the prisoner's, and he held a chisel in one hand, its honed sharpness hard against the iron ring which held the Narhani pent, while the other raised a hammer high to bring it smashing down.

The detail was superb, the anatomy perfect, the two species' very different expressions captured with haunting fidelity. Sweat beaded the human's bare skin, and each drop of Narhani blood was so real the viewer held his breath, watching for it to fall. They were trapped forever in the stone—human and Narhani, fleshed in marble by a master's hand—and for all their alienness, they were one.

"My God," Colin whispered into the silence. "It's . . . it's— I don't have the words, Brashieel. I just . . ." His voice trailed off, and Brashieel lowered his own crest.

"What you see in it is only truth, Colin," he said softly.

"My people are not so gifted with words as yours; we put our truths in other things. But while this lasts—" he gestured at the light-born statue before them "—we of the Nest of Narhan will never forget what humans have given us. We came against you thinking you nest-killers, but you taught us who the true nest-killer is and, when you might have slain us, gave us life. You gave us more than life." His hand stoked Eve's crest gently. "But most of all, you gave us truth, and so we return that truth to you. To all your people, but especially to you, for you are our nest lord now."

"I—" Colin blushed as he had not in years, then looked up and met Brashieel's eyes squarely. "Thank you. I will never receive anything more beautiful . . . or that I will treasure more."

"Then we are content, High Nest Lord."

Lawrence Jefferson gazed raptly at the statue through the buzz of admiration which followed, and not even his reverence was completely feigned. He cleared his throat when the first rush of conversation slowed.

"Brashieel, may I—" He paused, then shrugged slightly. "I hesitate to ask it, but may I have a holo of this for a place of honor in my office?"

"Of course. We have brought several copies for our friends, although we hope they will not be made public before the formal gifting."

"May I display it if I promise to hide it from any newsies?"

"We would be honored."

The Lieutenant Governor of Earth was almost as carefully protected as her Governor. Whenever he was in residence, security troops, unobtrusive but alert, prowled the grounds of the Kentucky estate the Jeffersons had owned for generations. But none of those protectors knew of the secret measures which let him elude their guardianship at need.

Lawrence Jefferson stepped from the concealed tunnel exit eight kilometers from his home. Once it had served

the Underground Railroad, but it had been refurbished
and extended in more recent years when Senator Jefferson had been recruited by Anu's chief operations officer. Not even Kirinal's most trusted subordinates had
known of its existence, but Jefferson had labored upon
it under her direction, incorporating certain unobtrusive
elements of Imperial technology to make it undetectable.
At the time, those measures had been aimed at Horus
and the scanners of the hidden battleship *Nergal*, yet
they'd proved equally efficacious against those of a planetoid named *Dahak*.

A flyer waited in a carefully dilapidated old barn, and
Jefferson climbed aboard and set the holo plate almost
lovingly on the empty seat beside him. He'd managed
to obtain copies of the preliminary study, but he'd never
expected to receive the exact image of the finished sculpture, and his smile was unpleasant as he activated the
drive and, even for him, highly illegal stealth field and
lifted quietly into the night.

It wasn't a long trip, though reason told him he
shouldn't be making it, but he wanted to make this deliv-
ery in person, and the risk was slight. Yet even had it
been greater, he would have made this flight himself.
There were times when the elaborate deception of his
life palled upon him, when he wanted—needed—to be
about his work himself. He built his strategies like a chess
master, but there was a gambler within him, as well, one
who sometimes felt the need to throw the dice from his
own hand.

He landed outside a shed-like structure and keyed a
complicated admittance code through his neural feed.
There was a moment of hesitation, and then its door slid
open. Imperial machinery stood silent in the bright overhead lights as he walked to stand beside the heroically
scaled sculpture that machinery had wrought in exact
duplicate of the sketches he'd provided.

A stoop-shouldered man turned to greet him. His
artist's eye told him he had never seen his employer's
undisguised face, and he was glad, for he believed that

made him safe. He didn't know he, too, would be eliminated anyway when his task was done. Lawrence Jefferson took no chances.

"Good evening," the stoop-shouldered man said. "No one told me you were coming in person, sir."

"I know. But I've brought you a gift." Jefferson set the holo plate on a work table and pressed the button.

"Magnificent," the man breathed. He looked back and forth between the sculpture and his own handiwork. "I see a few details will need changing. I must say, sir, that this is even more spectacular than the sketches indicated."

"I quite agree," Jefferson said sincerely. "Will there be any schedule problems?"

"No, no. It's only a matter of arranging the input and then letting the sculpting unit do its job."

"Excellent. In that case, I'd like you to go ahead and input it now; I need to take this with me when I leave."

"Of course. If you'll excuse me?"

The stoop-shouldered man bent over his equipment, and Jefferson stood back, hands folded behind him while he admired the work his doomed henchman had already produced. It looked just like real marble, and so it should, given how much it was costing.

Perfect, he thought. It was perfect. And no one who looked at it would ever guess the secret it concealed, for the gravitonic warhead and its arming circuits were quite, quite invisible.

Chapter Eighteen

Israel's captain was in a grumpy mood.

It wasn't anyone's fault, but *Israel*'s crew were bright, competent, confident . . . and young. And, as bright, confident people are wont to do, they'd underestimated their task—which made their lack of progress enormously irritating. Still, Sean told himself with determined cheer, for people who'd found out they were approaching a populated world only in the last half hour of their flight they weren't doing all that badly. And Sandy *had* said she and Harry had some good news for a change.

He lay back in the captain's couch, studying the image from one of the stealthed remotes. They'd decided to rely on old-fashioned, line-of-sight radio, something an Imperial scan system probably wouldn't even think to look for, rather than more readily detected fold coms to operate their remotes. That limited their operating radius, but it gave them enough reach for a fair sampling, and Sean watched a kneeling row of villagers weed their way across a field of some sort of tuber and wondered how whatever they were tending tasted.

He glanced up as Tamman arrived, completing their gathering, then turned his gaze to Sandy. She and Harriet relied heavily on Brashan's hard-headed pragmatism to shoot down their wilder hypotheses and upon Tamman to build and maintain their surveillance systems, but the major burden of analysis was theirs, and Sean was delighted to leave them to it.

"Okay, Sandy," he said now. "You've got the floor."

She rubbed the tip of her nose for a moment, then cleared her throat.

"Let's start with the good news: we finally have a language program of sorts." Sean sat up straighter, and she smiled. "As I say, that's the good news. The bad news is that without a proper philologist, we've had to fall back on a 'trial and error' approach, with predictably crude results.

"It helps that they're literate and use movable type, but it would've helped more if the old alphabet had survived. Out of forty-one characters, we've found three that *might* be derived from Universal; the rest look like somebody tried to transcribe Old Norse into cuneiform. Working at night, we've managed to scan several printed books through our remotes, but they didn't do us much good until about six weeks ago when Harry found *this*."

The display changed to a recorded view looking down from some high vantage point on a circle of children. A bearded man in a robe of blue and gold stood at its center, holding up a picture of one of the native's odd, bipedal saddle beasts to point at a line of jagged-edged characters beneath it.

"This," Sandy resumed after a moment, "is a class in one of those temples of theirs. Apparently the Church believes in universal literacy, and Tam built a teeny-tiny remote for Harry to land on top of a beam so we could eavesdrop. It was maddening for the first month or so, but we set up a value substitution program in the linguistics section of *Israel*'s comp cent, and things started coming together early last week."

Sean nodded, glad something had finally worked as he'd hoped it might. English was the common tongue of the Imperium and seemed likely to remain so. Its flexibility, concision, and adaptability were certainly vastly preferable to Universal! Age had ossified the language of the Fourth Imperium and Empire, and, given the availability of younger, more versatile Terran languages, the Fifth Imperium had no particular desire to speak it.

Yet all Fourth Empire computers spoke only Universal, at least until they could be reprogrammed. Worse, in some cases—like Mother's hardwired constitutional functions—they *couldn't* be reprogrammed, so all Battle Fleet personnel had to speak Universal whether they wanted to or not.

Cohanna's Bio-Sciences Ministry had met that need with a dedicated implant, and with the enormous "piggyback" storage molycircs made possible, Battle Fleet had decided to give its personnel all major Terran languages. That made sense in view of their diversity—and also meant each of *Israel's* crewmen had a built-in "translating" software package. True, none of the languages in their implants' memories were quite *this* foreign, but if *Israel's* computers could cobble up a local dictionary . . .

"As I say, it's still patchy, but we ought to be able to make a stab at understanding what someone says. It's going to be another matter if we try to talk back, though. So far Harry and I have identified seven distinct dialects and what may be one minor language, and there's no way we could mingle with the locals without a lot more work."

"How much more?" Tamman asked.

"I can't say, Tam—not for certain—but I'd estimate another month of input. At the moment, we can read about forty percent of the printed material we collect, and the percentage is expanding, but that's a far cry from understanding the spoken language, much less conversing coherently. And we need more than simple coherency, unless we want to scare the natives to death."

"Umph." Sean frowned at the frozen image of the teacher. He'd hoped for better, but even while he'd hoped, he'd known it was unreasonable.

"In the meantime, one of our 'borrowed' books—an atlas—has given us a running start on figuring out the geopolitics of the planet, which, by the way, the natives call 'Pardal.' We can't find the name in any of *Israel's* admittedly limited records, so I suspect it's locally evolved.

"As near as we can tell, this is what Pardal currently looks like." The display changed to a map of Pardal's five continents and numerous island chains. The biggest inhabited continent reminded Sean of an old-fashioned, air-foil aircraft, flying northeast towards the polar ice cap with a second, smaller land mass providing its tail assembly. "We made enough photomaps on the way in to know the atlas maps aren't perfectly scaled, and we still can't read all of its commentary, but it appears Pardal is split into hundreds of feudal territories." Scarlet boundary lines flashed as she spoke. "At the moment, we're located just inside the eastern border of this one, which is called, as nearly as I can translate it, the Kingdom of Cherist.

"Now, North Hylar—" she indicated the fuselage and wings of the "aircraft" "—seems to be the wealthiest and most heavily populated land mass. The 'countries' are larger and seem to contain more internal subdivisions, which suggests they may be older. It looks to us like there's been a longer period of absorption and consolidation here, and that conclusion may be supported by the fact that our ground site is, indeed, underneath North Hylar's largest city." A red cursor flashed approximately dead center in North Hylar.

"South Hylar, connected to North Hylar by this isthmus down here, is less densely populated, probably because it doesn't have much in the way of rivers—aside from this one big one out of the southern mountains— but that's a guess. As you can see, the other two populated continents, Herdaana and Ishar, are located across a fairly wide body of water—the Seldan Sea—to the west of the Hylars. These other two continents to the east are uninhabited. As far as we can tell, the Pardalians don't even realize they exist, and from the aerial maps, they seem to have less human-compatible vegetation. Looks like they were never terraformed—which, in turn, suggests they never *were* inhabited, even before the bio-weapon.

"Of the settled continents, both Hylars are extremely mountainous, and Ishar's on the desert side. Herdaana's much flatter and seems to be the bread basket of Pardal, and a lot of the territories in Herdaana and Ishar alike have Hylaran names prefixed by '*gyhar*,' or 'new,' which

probably means they were colonized—or conquered—
by North Hylar. It may or may not imply a continuing
relationship between those territories and their 'mother
countries' back home. Some evidence suggests that; other
evidence, particularly the small size and apparent com-
petition between the Herdaana states, suggests otherwise,
but we simply can't read the atlas well enough to know,
and the entire continent's out of range of our remotes."

She paused, brow wrinkled in frustration, then
shrugged.

"All right, that's the political structure, but there's a
catch, because despite all these nominally independent
feudal states, the entire planet seems to be one huge the-
ocracy. That surprised us, given Pardal's primitive technology. I'd have thought simple communication delays
would do in any planet-wide institution, but that was
before we figured out what *this* is."

The display changed to a tall, gantry-like structure with
two massive, pivoted arms, and she shook her head
almost admiringly.

"That, gentlemen, is a semaphore tower. They've got
chains of them across most of the planet. Not all; they'd
need ships to reach Herdaana and Ishar, and given the
mountains on the isthmus, they probably send over-water
couriers to South Hylar, too. It's a daylight-only system,
but it still means they can send messages a *whole* lot
faster than we'd suspected."

"Ingenious," Sean murmured.

"Exactly. Obviously we're still guessing, but it looks like
the Church deliberately keeps political power decentralized, and control of the communications net would give
them a heck of a tactical edge. I'd say they push it to
the max; when the Church says jump, it's a good bet the
local prince only asks how high. In addition to the semaphore towers, every town—and most of the villages—
in range of our remotes contains at least one Church
complex. Some larger towns have dozens, and they do
a *lot* of business. Our reading class is only a tiny part of
it.

"More to the point, our power-source city is where the semaphore chains converge—the Pardalian equivalent of the Vatican. In fact, the entire city is simply called 'The Temple,' and as far as we can tell, it's ruled by the high priest as both secular and temporal lord. Interestingly enough, the title of said high priest appears to be *eurokat a'demostano*." Sean looked up sharply, and she nodded. "Even allowing for several millennia of erosion, that sounds too much like *eurokath adthad diamostanu* to be a coincidence."

" 'Port Admiral,' " Sean translated softly, frowning at the city's light dot. "You think the Church is tied directly to the quarantine system?"

"Probably," Harriet answered for Sandy. "The Temple's site certainly suggests it, especially given this 'port admiral' priestly title. And if they have, in fact, preserved any access to the computer running the system, it'd have to be purely vocal; there can't be anyone out there with neural feeds. If they're running it on some sort of rote basis, that might explain why the system seemed so slow and clumsy when it attacked us; they literally didn't know what they were doing. On the other hand, if they *do* have voice access, think what it might mean for a religion. It'd be like the very voice of God."

"Which might help explain the Church's authority," Sean mused aloud.

"Exactly," Sandy said, "though we've turned up a few suggestions that the Church's current *political* power is a relatively recent innovation. And it might also explain how they could have contact with high-tech without realizing it *was* technology. It isn't a machine; it's 'God.' "

"Which," Tamman observed sourly, "doesn't help us out at all, Sean. Not in terms of getting hold of the computer, I mean. If it's their holy of holies, access is going to be limited, I'd think—unless we want to shoot our way into neural feed range, anyway."

"We're a long way from crossing that bridge yet, Tam. Anyway, I'd prefer to do a personal recon on the ground before we make any plans."

"Perhaps," Brashan said, "but I fear you'll have a problem there." He changed the display image to a closeup from one of their approach opticals. "Observe a typical citizen of the Temple."

"Oy vey!" Sean sighed, and Sandy laughed at his disgusted tone. The image was far from clear, but the individual in it was perhaps a hundred and fifty centimeters tall, red-haired and blue-eyed—the complete antithesis of any of *Israel's* human crew.

"Indeed," Brashan replied. "Obviously, I could never pass as anything other than an alien, but I fear the same is true of all of you in the Temple."

"Not necessarily," Sandy said, and Sean brightened as the image changed again. This time the man standing before him had dark hair. His eyes were brown, not the black of the old Imperial Race—or of Sean or Harriet, for that matter—but the newcomer stood just over a hundred seventy centimeters, far short of Sean's own towering height but getting closer.

"This," Sandy continued, "is a citizen of something called the Princedom of Malagor. It's one of the bigger national units—a bit larger, in fact, than the Kingdom of Aris, which contains the Temple—and it's just over the Cherist border from us. We've been watching it through our remotes, and I'd say the Malagorans are an independent sort. Malagor's very mountainous, even for North Hylar, and these seem to be typical, stiff-necked mountaineers, without a lot of nobles. Their hereditary ruler's limited to the title of 'prince,' and I'd guess there's a lot of local government, but that doesn't make them stay-at-homes. There's an historical maps section in our atlas, and there've been *lots* of battles in the Duchy of Keldark, which lies between Malagor and Aris. It looks like Malagor and Aris were probably political rivals and Aris came out on top because of the Temple."

"Not so good," Sean muttered. "If there's a tradition of hostility, trying to pass as Malagorans wouldn't exactly get us a red carpet in Aris."

"Perhaps not," Brashan said, "but consider: the Temple is the center of a *world* religion."

"Oho! Pilgrims!"

"Maybe, but let's not get carried away, Sean," Sandy cautioned. "Remember all of this is still guesswork."

"Understood. Can you bring your map back up?"

Sandy obliged, and Sean frowned as he stared at it. *Israel* lay hidden in the spine of the westernmost of North Hylar's major mountain ranges, while Aris lay to the east of an even higher range. Malagor occupied a rough, tumbled plateau between the two before they merged to form the craggy spine of the isthmus into South Hylar.

"I wish we had a line of sight to run remotes into the Temple," he muttered.

"Perhaps," Brashan replied. "On the other hand, our position puts the mountains between us and any surveillance systems the Temple might boast."

"True, true." Sean shook himself. "All right, Sandy. It looks to me like you guys are doing good. I'm impressed. But—"

"But what've we done for you lately?" She smiled, and he grinned back.

"More or less. We need to refine your data a lot before we poke our noses out. Would it help if we took a stealthed cutter over closer to the Temple and ran some additional remotes in on it?"

"Maybe." Sandy considered, then shook her head. "Nope, not yet. We're already pulling in more data than we can integrate, and I'd rather not risk running afoul of any on-site detection systems until we know more."

"Makes sense to me," Sean agreed. "That about it for now, then?"

"I'm afraid so. We've spotted a Church library in one of the towns just west of here, and Tam and I are going to run in a couple of remotes tonight. Harry and I may be able to develop something out of that."

Father Stomald kilted his blue robe above his knees

and waded out into the icy holding pond to examine the new waterwheel. Folmak Folmakson, the millwright, fidgeted while he waited, and Stomald frowned. A priest must be eternally vigilant this close to the Valley of the Damned, especially with the Trial so recently past and the strange shooting star to remind him of his duties. At moments like this he was unhappily aware of his own youth, but, he reminded himself, a man need not be aged to hear God in his heart.

He sloshed up onto the bank of the millrace and peered down at the wheel. To be sure, it *did* look odd. Stomald had never heard of a wheel driven by water which fell from above rather than turning submerged paddles, but he could see several advantages. For one thing, it required much less water, and that meant it could run for far more of the year in drier regions. Lack of rain was seldom a problem in Malagor, but the new design's efficiency meant more wheels could be run with the same water supply even here.

He frowned again, listening to the creak of the wheel while he applied the Test. It was a particularly important task here, for Malagor's artisans had always been notoriously restive under Mother Church's injunctions, even since the Schismatic Wars. Indeed, he sometimes suspected they'd grown still more so since then . . . and he knew many of them still harbored dreams of Malagoran independence. Within the last six five-days alone, he'd heard no less than four people whistling the forbidden tune to "Malagor the Free," and he was deeply concerned over how he ought to respond to it. Yet he was relieved to note that this wheel, at least, didn't seem to violate any of the Tenets. It was powered by water and required the creation of no new tools or processes. It might be suspiciously innovative, but Stomald could see no demonic influence. It was still a water wheel, and those had been in use forever.

He banished his frown and replaced it with a properly meditative expression as he splashed back towards his anxious audience. He could, he decided, pronounce on this without bothering Bishop Frenaur, and that was a distinct relief. Like most senior prelates, the bishop was unhappy at being called away from the Temple for anything other than his twice-a-year pastoral visitation. Stomald didn't like to think how he might react if some village under-priest, especially a native-born Malagoran, suggested a special conclave was required, and the fact that Folmak hadn't introduced a single new technique gave him an out.

Which, Stomald thought a bit guiltily, might be fortunate in more ways than one. The new catechism suggested Mother Church was entering one of her more dogmatic periods, and some of the Inquisition's recent actions boded ill for Stomald's stubborn countrymen. Bishop Frenaur just might have felt compelled to make an example of Folmak.

He stepped out of the water, trying to hide an unpriestly shiver, and Folmak shifted from foot to foot, almost wringing his hands. The millwright was twice Stomald's age and more, and it struck the priest—not for the first time—how absurd it was for someone older than his own father to look at him so appealingly. He scolded himself—again, not for the first time—for the thought. Folmak wasn't looking to Stomald Gerakson for guidance; he was looking to Father Stomald of Cragsend, and Father Stomald spoke not from the authority of his own years but with that of Mother Church Herself.

"Very well, Folmak, I've looked at it," the young priest said. He paused, unable to resist the ignoble desire to cloak his pronouncement in mystery a moment longer, then smiled. "As far as I can tell, your contraption satisfies all the Tenets. If you'll walk to the vicarage with me, I'll fill out the Attestation right now."

A huge grin transfigured the millwright's bearded face. Stomald permitted himself to grin back, then clapped Folmak on one brawny shoulder, and the unsullied joy of serving his flock made him look even younger.

"In fact," he chuckled, "I believe I've a small cask of Sister Yurid's winter ale left, and it strikes me that this might be an appropriate moment to broach it. Don't you think so?"

This time Sandy's eyes actually sparkled. Harriet seemed almost as excited, and Sandy started talking even before the others were all seated.

"People," she said, "we still haven't figured out how Pardal lost its tech base in the first place, but at least we know now why it hasn't built another one! We spent several hours in the Church library night before last, reading the books into memory through the remotes. We didn't have time to do any content scans then, but it turns out one of our finds is a book on Church doctrine and a couple of others are Church histories. For whatever reason, the Church has anathematized technology."

"Wait a minute," Sean said. "I considered that, but it doesn't hold up. Not for forty-five thousand years, anyway."

"Why not?"

"Just think about it for a minute. Let's say that at some point in the past—some pretty long ago point, judging from what's left of the Imperial ruins—the Church *did* proscribe technology. I can think of a few scenarios which might lead to that, like Harry's original suggestion that they dusted themselves out or whipped up a bio-weapon all their own. Either of those could have killed off most of the techies, and I suppose the destruction could have created an anti-technical revulsion that resulted in a 'religious' anti-tech stance. Certainly *something* caused them to lose their original alphabet, their original language, science—all of it—and that sounds more like systematic suppression than simple damage to the tech base.

"But having done that, the Church wouldn't even know what technology *was* by the time it got a few thousand years down the road. How could they prevent it from reemerging in a homegrown variety? Without some term of reference to know what constituted 'high tech,' how could they recognize it to snuff it when it turned up again?"

"Fair enough," Sandy agreed, "but you don't have the full picture. First, they *didn't* completely lose Universal. We thought they had, but that was before we hit the Church documents. They're written in something called the 'Holy Tongue,' using an alphabet restricted to the priesthood, and for all intents and purposes the Holy Tongue is a corrupted version of Universal.

"Second, the Church is definitely connected to the quarantine system. There are several references in here to 'the Voice of God'; in fact, their whole liturgical year is set up around what has to be the quarantine system's central computer—there are festivals called 'Fire Test,' 'Plot Test,' 'High Fire Test,' and the like. There are also references to something called 'Holy Servitors' that I'd guess are maintenance mechs from the shipyard, since they appear mysteriously to tend the inner shrine. There's no sign these people understand what's really going on, but they seem to recognize that the system's purpose is to protect their world from contamination, though they've turned it into a religious matter. The Voice is part of God's plan to protect them from demons, and it not only 'proves' God's existence but their own rectitude. If they weren't doing what God wants, His Voice would tell them so, right?

"Third, way back whenever, the Church set up a definition of what constitutes acceptable technology. In essence, Pardalians are forbidden anything but muscle, wind, or water power, so they don't have to know what high tech is; they've set up preconditions which preclude its existence.

"There's more to it than that—there's a whole, complicated evaluating procedure called the Test of Mother Church. Bear in mind that we're talking about something written in this debased version of Universal rather than the vulgar tongue, so we can make lots more sense of it. Apparently the Test consists of applying a number of Tenets which consider whether or not any new development violates the power restrictions or requires new tools, new procedures, or new knowledge. If it does, it's right out."

"Hold it." It was Tamman's turn to object. "These people have gunpowder, and that doesn't rely on muscles, wind, or water!"

"No," Harriet agreed, "but *Earth* certainly had gunpowder before it got beyond waterwheels and windmills, and the Church occasionally—*very* occasionally—grants dispensations through a system of special Conclaves. It takes a long time to work through, but it means advances aren't entirely impossible. We've found several dispensations scattered over the last six hundred local years—almost a thousand Terran years—and most of them seem to be fairly pragmatic things like kitchen-sink chemistry and pretty darn empirical medicine and agriculture. We're still groping in the dark, but it *looks* like there've been some 'progressive' periods—which, unfortunately, seem to provoke backlash periods of extreme conservatism. The key thing, though, is that the Church is continually on the lookout to suppress anything that even looks like the scientific method, and without that there's no systematic basis for technological innovation."

"And people put up with it?" Tamman shook his head. "I find that hard to accept."

"That's because of your own cultural baggage," Sandy said. "You come from a technical society and you accept technology as good, or at least inevitable; these people have the opposite orientation. And remember that the Church *knows* God is on its side; they have proof of it several times a year when the Voice speaks. Not only that," her excited voice turned grimmer, "but their version of the Inquisition has some pretty grisly punishments for anybody who dares to fool around with forbidden knowledge."

"Inquisition?" Sean looked up. "I don't like the sound of that."

"Me neither," Harriet said. "I had to stop after the first little bit, but Sandy and Brashan waded through the whole ghastly thing." She shuddered. "Even the little I read is going to give me nightmares for a week."

"Me, too," Sandy murmured. Her bright eyes were

briefly haunted, and she brooded down at the deck for a long, silent moment. Then she shook herself. "Like a lot of intolerant religions, their Inquisition stacks the deck. First, they're only doing it to 'save souls,' including that of the 'heretic' in question, and they've picked up on the theory of the mortification of the flesh to 'expiate' sins. That means they're actually *helping* the people·they murder. Worse, they're never wrong. Their religious law enshrines the use of torture during questioning, which means the accused always confess, even knowing how they'll be put to death, and—" she looked up and met Sean's gaze "—the actual executions are even worse. *Pour de'courager les autres*, I suppose."

"Brrrr." Sean's lips twisted in revulsion. "I suppose any 'church' that packs that kind of whammy probably *could* keep the peasants in line."

"Especially with the advantage of a whole secret language. They can promote universal literacy in the vulgar tongue and still have most of the advantages of a priestly monopoly on education. And they've got a pretty big carrot to go with their stick. The Church collects a tithe—looks like somewhere around twelve percent—from every soul on the planet. A lot of that loot gets used to build temples, commission religious art, and so forth, but a big chunk is loaned out to secular rulers at something like thirty percent, and another goes into charitable works. You see? They've got their creditor nobles on a string, and the poor look to them for relief when times get bad. Sean, they've got this planet sewed up three ways to Sunday!"

"Damn. And they're the ones sitting on top of the quarantine ground station!" Sean shook his head in disgust.

"They sure are," Harriet sighed.

"Yes, they are," Sandy agreed, "but remember that we're still putting the whole picture together. We've just filled in a big piece, and discovering this 'Holy Tongue' gives us a Rosetta Stone of sorts for the vulgar languages, as well, but there's a lot we haven't even begun on. For instance, there's something called 'The Valley of the Damned' that sounds interesting to me."

" 'Valley of the Damned'?" Sean repeated. "What sort of valley?"

"We don't know yet, but it's utterly proscribed. There may be other, similar sites, but this is the only one we've found so far. It's up in the mountains of northern Malagor, outside the reach of our remotes. Anyone who goes in is eternally damned for consorting with demons. If they come back out again, they have to be ritualistically—and hideously—killed. It looks to me like the preliminaries probably take at least a couple of days, and then they burn the poor bastards alive," she finished grimly.

"It sounds," Sean mused, "like whatever's in there must represent a mighty serious threat to the Church's neat little social structure. Or *they* think it does, anyway." He frowned, and then his eyes began to gleam. "Just where, exactly, did you say this valley is?"

Chapter Nineteen

Sean snaked around the feet of the towering summits at a cautious four hundred KPH. His sluggish speed had made the journey long and dragging, but it was the best he could manage, for the cutter's terrain-following systems were down. That forced him to fly hands-on, which was a pain. But few things were harder to spot than a stealthed cutter with no active emissions and flying low, slow, and nape-of-the-earth through mountains, and until they *knew* the quarantine system wouldn't swat atmospheric targets, anything that might draw its attention was right out.

Inconsequential thoughts flickered as he concentrated on his flying. All the unoccupied seats in the twenty-man cutter made *Israel*'s human crewmen uncomfortably aware of just how alone—and how far from home—they were, yet it was even worse for Brashan. They had to leave someone aboard the battleship at all times, and his nonhuman appearance made him the obvious choice. He'd taken it better than Sean could have, especially since they'd agreed to forego any com signals that might be detected. Not only was Brashan barred from sharing their exploration trip, he couldn't even know what they'd found until they got back to tell him!

The cramped valley narrowed further, and he dumped another fifty KPH. It was nerve-wracking to fly solely by Mark One Eyeball (well, Mark Two or Three, given his enhancement) through the inevitable distortion of its stealth field, and he swore softly as they came up on an acute bend.

"The Force, Sean," Sandy whispered in his ear. "Use the Force!"

"Jerk!" he snorted, but there was an edge of laughter in his retort and tense muscles loosened back up a bit. He spared her a brief smile, then returned his attention to his console as their valley joined another. He checked his nav systems and headed up the new gorge with a small surge of excitement. It was even narrower and twistier, but they were getting close enough that this one might take them all the way in.

He made another forty kilometers, then cursed again—less softly—as the valley ended in a steep cliff. He halted the cutter and lifted it vertically, hugging the rock wall. The dim light of Pardal's small moon washed scrubby trees and bare rock as tumbled mountains fell away on every side, and Harriet sucked in a sharp breath beside him as they topped out.

"I'm getting something on passive!" Sean went into an instant hover, and his sister closed her eyes, communing with her sensors, then scowled. "I can't resolve it, Sean, but it's coming from just beyond that next mountain."

Sean banked the cutter, angling down and around the side of the next peak, and she opened her eyes.

"Now I've lost it entirely!" she groused.

"Good," he said. "If it's line-of-sight, it can't see us, either. And for your information, sister mine, our objective is 'just beyond that next mountain,' if you and Sandy have it plotted right, so it sounds like we're going to find *something* when we get there!"

Tamman grinned at him, but Sandy plugged her own feed into Harriet's console to study her recorded scanner readings.

"Not much, is it, Harry?"

"No." Harriet turned her own attention back to the data. "I make it at least six distinct point sources, though."

"Yeah. But did you notice the one at about oh-two-one?"

"Hm?" Harriet frowned, then nodded. "Lots stronger than the others, isn't it? And there's something about it . . . Damn. I *wish* I had a link to *Israel*'s computers! It reminds me of something, but I can't think what."

"Me neither. Tam?"

Tamman glanced at the emissions through his own feed and shrugged. "Beats me. Most of those look like power leakages, not detection systems, but the biggie *is* something else." He tapped his teeth. "Hmm. . . . You know, that just might be an orbital power feed. Look there—see the smaller source tucked in to the east? That looks like a leak from a big-assed bank of capacitors, and the big one's definitely some sort of transmission. How about a ground beacon for an orbital broadcast power system?"

"Could be," Sandy mused. "Hard to believe it could still be up after all this time, but you're right about it's being a transmission, and it'd sure explain why it's so much more powerful than the others—not to mention how there could still be power for *any* active installations. But if it really is a receptor, that means the Valley of the Damned has an active link to at least one power satellite. Even if it's only a passive solar job, you'd think the quarantine system would spot the transmission."

"So?" Tamman countered. "If you and Harry are right, the Temple's running the system by rote, so what could they do about it? For that matter, why should they even understand what their 'Voice' was talking about?"

"Yeah." Harriet twisted hair around a finger and glanced at her twin. "I think Tam's right, Sean. Either way, the transmission's just a steady tone, not a detection system. I don't see anything that looks like one, either, but I'd rather not take the cutter much closer or give away any more scan image than we have to until we're certain of that."

"You and me both. What d'you think about that for a landing site?" He pointed to a wide ledge. It was at least thirty meters across, covered in the local equivalent of grass and brush, but a visible depression had been worn through the vegetation. "That looks like some sort of game trail, and it's headed just about the right way."

"How far out are we?" Tamman asked.

" 'Bout thirty klicks, straight-line. Don't know how far by foot."

"Suits me," Tamman agreed, and Harriet and Sandy nodded.

Sean slid closer, studying the ledge. A swell of rock broke the grass close beside the game trail, promising no hidden surprises for his landing legs, and he set the cutter down. He held the drive until the gear stabilized, then cut power but left the stealth field up.

"End of the line." He tried unsuccessfully to keep the excitement out of his voice. "Let's get our gear."

He rose from his couch and opened the weapons locker while Sandy and Harriet slipped into the shoulder harnesses of a pair of scanpacks. He strapped on a gun belt and grav gun and handed matching weapons to the others. The Malagoran mountains were home to at least two nasty predators—a sort of bear-sized cross between a wolf and a wolverine called a "seldahk," and a vaguely feline carnivore called a "kinokha"—both of whom had bellicose and territorial personalities. None of them felt like walking around unarmed, and Sean wished privately that *Israel*'s equipment list had offered something a bit tougher than their uniforms. The synthetic fabric the Fleet used for its uniforms was incredibly rugged by pre-Imperial Terran standards. He had no doubt it would resist even a kinokha's claws, but it wasn't going to stop a seldahk's jaws, nor would it stop bullets. Of course, it was unlikely, to put it lightly, that they'd meet any armed natives this close to the Valley of the Damned in the middle of the night, yet kevlar underwear would have been very reassuring. Unfortunately, neither Battle Fleet nor the Imperial Marines issued such items, which he supposed made sense, given that nothing short of battle armor could hope to resist Imperial weaponry.

He grinned at his own thoughts as he and Tamman clipped extra magazines to their belts and shrugged into knapsacks heavy with spikes, pitons, ropes, and assorted mountaineering gear Sean hoped they weren't going to need. Then he eased his pack straps more comfortably, opened the hatch, and led the way out into the night.

✧   ✧   ✧

The game trail helped, but it was far from straight, and many of its slopes were almost vertical. Tamman took the lead while Sean brought up the rear. The formation freed Harriet and Sandy to focus on their scanpacks (which had far more reach than implant sensors), without worrying about anything they might meet, and the four of them moved at a pace which would have reduced any unenhanced human to gasping exhaustion in minutes.

The moon was still high when Harriet threw up a hand and beckoned them all to a halt. Sean closed up from behind as the other three clustered to wait for him, and his eyes brightened as he looked down at last into the valley they'd come so far to find.

It was bigger than he'd expected—at least twenty kilometers across at its widest point and winding deep into the mountains. A sharp bend fifteen kilometers to the north blocked their vision, and the shallow, rushing river down its length gleamed dull pewter under the moon. He adjusted his eyes to telescopic vision and felt a shiver of excitement. The shapes clumped on either bank of the river at mid-valley were half-buried in drifted ages of soil, but they were too regular and vertical to be natural.

"I'm getting those same readings." Harriet swung the hand-held array of her passive backpack unit slowly from side to side and frowned. "There's a batch of new ones, too. They're lots weaker and more spread out; that's probably why we didn't spot them before."

Sandy turned, directing her own attention down-valley, and nodded.

"You're right, Harry. Most of what we saw before seems to be clustered in those ruins, but I'm getting a line of weak point sources about ten klicks to the south. Looks like they run clear across the valley."

"Yeah." Harriet shaded her eyes with her free hand as if it could help her see farther. "And there's another line just like it up there where the valley curls back to the west. I'm not too sure I like that. I can't lock in well enough to prove it, but they *could* be passive sensors, and those're logical places to put some sort of defensive system."

"Good point," Sandy agreed.

"Um." Sean moved a few meters south, peering in the direction of Sandy's find, but not even enhanced eyes could pick out any details. The valley floor was too heavily covered in scrub trees and tall alpine grasses, and moonlight and shadow did funny things to depth perception even in low-light mode. He pinched his nose in thought, then turned back to the others.

"Anything right in front of us?" he asked, pointing down the steep-sloped valley wall, and his sister shook her head.

"Not on this side, but that big one's just about opposite us. And I'm getting something else from it now. Do you have it, Sandy?"

"No, I—oh. That's funny." She made painstaking adjustments. "The darn thing isn't steady, almost like it's got some sort of intermittent short." It was her turn to frown. "See how the beacon power level fluctuates just a bit in time with it? Think it's some kind of control system?"

"If it is, it looks kind of senile. Then again, from the state of the ruins this whole place must've been abandoned thousands of years ago." Harriet tinkered with her own scanpack, then shrugged. "Let's spread out a little and see if we can triangulate on it, Sandy. I'd feel better if I at least knew exactly where whatever-it-is is."

"Suits me." The two of them separated and took very careful bearings, and Sandy nodded and pointed across the valley.

"Okay, I see it . . . sort of," she said, and Sean stood behind her and followed the line of her finger until he saw the more solid patch of shadows. He couldn't make out much in light-gathering mode, but when he switched to infrared things popped into better resolution. Not a lot better, but better. The ruins were built out from a bare stone precipice and whatever they were made of had different thermal properties from the cliff. Small

trees sprouted from a thick roof of collected dirt, but the
vertical walls were clear.

"Any better ideas about that intermittent source now
that you know where it is?" he asked, but Sandy shook
her head. He glanced at Harriet and sighed as he got
a shrug of equal mystification. "That's what I was afraid
of. Well, whatever else this is, it's clearly the leftovers
of some Imperial site, and I'm not too surprised it's in
such lousy shape. In fact, if I'm surprised at all it's that
anything's live down there. But it looks like we have to
go on down if we want any more to go on. Any objections?"

There were none, though Harriet looked a bit dubious, and he nodded.

"Okay, but we'll play this as smart as we can. Let's rope
up, Tam, and since you're the closest we've got to a
Marine, you take point. Sandy, you stay up here and play
lookout till the rest of us get down. Keep an eye on the
whole place, but especially on that thing on the far side.
Harry, you follow Tam with your scanpack, and I'll bring
up the rear."

Tamman nodded and slid out of his pack to extract a
two hundred-meter coil of synthetic rope. While he and
Sean rigged safety harnesses, Harriet and Sandy went on
trying to analyze their readings without much success.
Sean wasn't too happy about that, yet there wasn't a lot
he could do about it, and he waved Tamman over the
side.

Tamman picked his way as carefully as he could, but
the hundred-meter slope, while less sheer than the bare
rock face to the west, was both steep and treacherous.
The soil was soft and shifting despite a covering of grass,
and he slipped several times. Harriet had it easier. She
was taller than he but as slender as her mother; even with
her scanpack she was much lighter, and she had the
advantage of watching where he'd put his feet ahead of
her.

Sean should have found the descent easiest of all,
despite his height and weight, since he was behind both

of them and placed to learn by their mistakes, but much as he knew he ought to, he couldn't seem to keep his mind on where he was going. He kept looking up at the ruins on the far side of the valley, and when he wasn't doing that his attention kept trying to stray to the ones out in the middle. He knew he should ignore them—after all, Sandy was keeping watch on them and he was anchor man for the safety rope—but he just couldn't. Which was another reason he'd put Tamman in front, where they needed someone who wouldn't let curiosity distract him from the task in hand.

Yet perhaps it was as well he was distracted. It meant he was looking up, not at his feet, when Sandy suddenly screamed.

"Something's coming up over th—!"

A boulder two meters to Harriet's right exploded, and she cried out in pain as a five-kilo lump of stone slammed into her shoulder. It didn't break her bio-enhanced skin, but the impact threw her from her feet, and that, Sean realized later, was what saved her life. The heavy energy gun needed a handful of seconds to reduce the boulder to powder; by the time the first energy bolt hit where she'd been standing, she wasn't there anymore.

He dug in his heels instinctively, hurling himself backward to anchor her, but the next bolt of gravitonic disruption sliced the rope like a thread. Her fall accelerated, and she tumbled downslope, slithering and bouncing. She tried frantically to avoid Tamman, clawing for traction as she gathered speed, but the loose soil betrayed her and he couldn't get out of the way in time. Her careening body cut his feet from under him, sending them both crashing downward in a confusion of arms and legs, and more bolts of energy came screaming out of the night. Gouts of flying dirt erupted all about them as ancient, erratic tracking systems tried to lock on them, and only their unpredictable movement and the senility of the defenses kept them alive.

Sean almost fell after them as soil crumbled under his heels, but he managed to hold his position, and his grav gun leapt into his hands in pure reflex. The scarcely visible energy gun fire was a terrible network of fury to his enhanced vision, and a fist squeezed his heart as it reached out for his sister and his friend. But he'd been looking in exactly the right direction when it started. Whatever was firing on them wasn't shooting at *him*— apparently he was still outside its programmed kill zone— but his implants told him where its targeting systems were, and his weapon snapped up into firing position without conscious thought.

It hissed, spitting explosive darts across the valley at fifty-two hundred meters per second, and savage flashes lit the dark as they ripped into the ruins. Each armor-piercing dart had the power of a half-kilo of TNT, and the crackle of their explosions was a single, ripping bellow as ancient walls blew outward in a tornado of splinters.

He held the trigger back, firing desperately and cursing himself for not having brought any heavy weapons. Even his implants couldn't "see" well enough to target the energy guns; he could only pour in fire and pray he hit something vital before their control systems killed Harriet and Tamman.

A fist of pulverized soil slammed the side of his head, and a corner of his mind noted that the defenses had finally noticed him, but it was a distant thought as his three-hundred round magazine emptied. He ripped a fresh one from his belt, then grunted in anguish as the energy bloom of a bolt of disruption clawed at him. He rolled desperately to his left and managed—somehow—not to plunge downward after the others. Sandy had gotten her grav gun into action as well, and the thunder of her fire filled the valley as he finished reloading and opened up again. He cursed viciously as Harriet and Tamman slithered to a halt, but Tamman had figured out what was happening. He wrapped a powerful arm around Harriet and hurled both of them back into motion a split second before the automated guns could lock on.

Flames licked at the brush atop the ruined structures as Sean and Sandy pounded them, and Sean cried out as an energy bolt blew his backpack apart. His nervous system whiplashed in agony, the stunning shock threw the grav gun from his hands, and he heard Sandy screaming his name through the roar of her fire. He clawed after his weapon with numb, desperate fingers, and then an explosion far more violent than any grav gun dart lit the valley like a sun at midnight. The ruins vomited skyward as the capacitors feeding the energy guns tore themselves apart, and the concussion blew Sean MacIntyre into unconsciousness at last.

"Sean?" The soft, anxious voice penetrated his darkness, and his eyes slid open. He was still on the slope, but his head was in Sandy's lap. He blinked groggily, and she smiled and brushed dirt from his face.

"Are you all right? Are you hurt?"

"I—" He coughed and broke off, wincing as a fresh wave of pain spun through him. His implant sensors had been wide open as he tried to find a target, and the corona of the energy bolt had bled through them. His nerves were on fire, and he moaned around a surge of nausea, but he was alive, and he wouldn't have been without his enhancement. Not after taking a shot that close to his heart and lungs.

"I'm okay," he rasped as his implants recovered and began damping the pain. He swallowed bile, then stiffened. "Harry! Harry and Tam! Are they—?"

"They're all right," Sandy soothed, pressing him back as he tried to sit up. "The guns never managed to line up on them, and—" a ghost of humor lit her face "—at least they got to the bottom faster than they'd expected. See?"

He turned his head, and Harriet waved up at him from the valley floor. Tamman wasn't looking in their direction; he was down on one knee, grav gun ready as he scanned the valley for any fresh threat. Not, Sean thought muzzily, that there was likely to be another. All the ruckus they'd raised dealing with the first one should have drawn the attention of anything else that was still active, and he relaxed.

"Thanks. If you hadn't gotten to it in time—"

"Hush." Sandy's hand covered his mouth, and his eyes smiled up at her as she kissed his forehead. "*We* got to it, and we're all lucky you left me behind. Now kindly shut your mouth and let your implants finish unscrambling themselves before we hike down after Tam and Harry. Hopefully—" her free hand caressed his hair and her lips quirked primly "—a bit more sedately than *they* did."

Chapter Twenty

Harriet watched Sandy and Sean work their way down the valley wall, and her anxious eyes noted the way her twin favored his left side and leaned on Sandy. She'd almost started back up when she realized he couldn't get up at once, but Sandy's wave had reassured her . . . some.

She ran to meet them as they slithered down the last few meters, and Sean gasped as she enveloped him in a fierce hug.

"Hey, now!" He raised a hand to her dust-smutted black hair. "I'm in one piece, and everything's still working, more or less."

"Sure it is," she said tartly, accessing his implants with her own, but then he felt her relax as they confirmed what he'd told her. What that near miss had done to his enhanced musculature was going to leave him stiff for a week, yet the damage was incredibly minor.

"Sure it is," she repeated at last, softly, and raised her head to peer up into his eyes, then kissed his cheek. He smiled and touched her face, then tucked one arm around each young woman and limped over to Tamman.

"See the conquering hero comes," he said smugly. Tamman chuckled, yet he, too, reached out and cupped the back of Sean's head, and the four of them clung together.

"Well!" Sean said at last. "The last step was a lulu, but at least we're here. Let's see what we've found. You still reading anything, Sandy?"

Sandy gave him a last little hug and returned her attention to her scanpack—the only one they had after

Harriet's tumbling descent. She turned in a complete circle, then sighed.

"I think you were right about the power receptor, Tam. Most of the power sources're gone, and the ones that're left are fading fast. Looks like we finally killed the Valley of the Damned."

"Pardon me if I don't cry," Tamman replied dryly.

"True, true." She pivoted back to the ruins at mid-valley and nodded. "Looks like at least one of them had some reserve, but the others are gone."

"Let's go see the one that's still up," Sean decided, "but cautiously. *Very* cautiously."

"You got it," Tamman agreed, and swung out to take the lead towards the ancient, half-buried buildings.

Sean studied their surroundings as they moved up the valley. Waist-high waves of grass rippled between clumps of dense thicket and tangled trees, slashed with moonlight and hard-edged shadow under the cold night wind. It was a wild and desolate place, still more haunted somehow after the thunder and lightning of their battle. Yet that very desolation, coupled with the effectiveness the automated weapons had displayed even in their senescence, brightened his eyes, for it was clear no one had gotten through to disturb whatever of pre-bio-weapon Pardal might have survived.

They reached the ruined buildings at last. Centuries of windblown dirt had buried their lower stories, but the worn walls were intact, and tough, transparent Imperial plastic, cloudy with age, still filled most of the window frames. Others gaped like open wounds in the dark, and he felt himself shiver as they stopped outside the ancient tower which contained the single remaining power source, for those age-sick walls had brooded over this lonely valley for nine times the life of Egypt's Sphinx.

The tower stood in the center of the long-dead settlement. Faint swirls of decoration still clung to its ceramacrete facade, and the roots of a tree in its lee—a stubby, thick-trunked thing with peeling, hairy bark—had invaded a window frame. Their inexorable intrusion had pried and twisted at the plastic, and the entire pane fell inward with a clatter when Tamman tapped it.

Sean swallowed. That tree grew on almost level earth heaped twenty meters high against the tower, and he expected to *feel* the centuries when he touched the hard solidity of the frame.

Tamman dug into his knapsack (which, unlike Sean's, had survived the trip down the valley wall) for a hand lamp far more powerful than the smaller, individual lights clipped to their gun belts, and all of them gazed into the building as he trained its diamond-bright spear through the opening. A drift of dirt fanned down from the sprung window, but the bare, stained floor beyond it looked sound, and Tamman picked his way cautiously down the dirt ramp, then turned in a circle, flashing his lamp over the walls.

"Seems pretty stout, Sean. We've got water damage to the floor, but it looks like it all came through the window; no sign of seepage on the walls. Want me to try the door?"

"Sounds like the next logical step." Sean tried to hide how much his left side hurt as he limped down after his friend, but Sandy and Harriet were there instantly, offering him support with such obvious tact he chuckled. Sandy grinned up at him, and he shook his head and abandoned his attempted machismo to lean gratefully on her small, sturdy shoulder.

Harriet crossed to help Tamman with the door, but it refused to move, and he finally dipped back into his pack for a cutter. Brilliant glare chiseled his intent face from the darkness, and Harriet coughed on the stench of burning plastic as a line of fire knifed through the ancient barrier.

Tamman sliced clear around the door frame, then kicked sharply. The cut-out panel toppled away from him, and it was his turn to sneeze as pyramid-dry dust billowed. He flashed his lamp through the opening and grinned.

"No sign of water damage in here, people! And there's

something else to be grateful for." His light settled on a spiral-shaped well. "Good old-fashioned stairs. I was afraid we'd have to rappel down dead transit shafts!"

"That's because you have a poor, limited Marine's brain," Sean said. "If that receptor was their only power source, they couldn't have had the juice to spare for things like transit shafts." He smiled pityingly. "Obviously."

"Go ahead—pretend you figured that out ahead of time. In the meantime, smartass, do we go up or down?"

"Sandy?"

She consulted her scanpack, then pointed at the floor.

"We go down, Tam," Sean said, stooping to clear the edge of door still filling the top of the frame.

They inched downward, unwilling to trust the stairs' stability until they'd tested it, yet the building's interior was remarkably intact. One or two of the dust-encrusted rooms they passed still contained furniture, but not even Imperial materials had been intended to last this long, and Sandy touched one chair only to snatch her hand back with a soft sound of distress as the upholstery crumbled. She shivered, and Sean tucked his arm about her and pretended to lean on her only for support.

It took half an hour to reach the tower's basement, for it was buried deep in bedrock and they had to deal with several more frozen doors along the way. Yet the stair finally ended, and Tamman's lamp showed half a dozen sealed doors circling the central access core. He raised an eyebrow at Sandy.

"That one." She pointed, and he gave it a shove. To their collective surprise, it moved a centimeter sideways, and he set down his lamp as Harriet joined him. They locked their fingers through the opening and heaved, grunting with effort, until the stubborn panel groaned open, and Tamman bit off a surprised expletive as a tiny glow leaked back out at them through it.

"Well, *something's* still live," he announced unnecessarily, and the four explorers edged into the room beyond.

The wan light came from a computer console, and Harriet and Tamman scurried over to it, all caution forgotten. It was a civilian model, with more visual telltales than military equipment, but very few were green. Most burned amber or red—those that weren't entirely dark—but they bent over it like a pair of mother hens and probed delicately for a live neural interface.

Sean and Sandy stayed out of their way, and Sean sighed as he found a counter sturdy enough to support him. He sank down on it gratefully and watched Sandy explore with her beltlight while the others fussed over the computer.

Clearly this had been a control center, for the one live console was flanked by a dozen more that were completely dead. But it had been more, as well, for it was cluttered with an incongruous mix of utilitarian equipment and personal furnishings. Someone had lived here, and he wondered if whoever it was had moved in to baby the computers as the settlement began to die.

"Sean?" He looked up at Sandy's hushed voice. She stood in a doorway across the room, and her shadowed expression was strange. He rose at her gesture and hobbled across the room to peer through it beside her, and his own face tightened. It was a bedroom, as time-conquered as the rest of the building, and the bed was occupied.

He limped further into the room, staring down at the dust-covered body. The bone-dry air had mummified him, and his parchment face showed the unmistakable features of a full Imperial framed in tangled white hair. He must, Sean thought, have been the oldest human being any of them had ever seen, and the fact that he lay here still was chilling.

Sean turned away from the sunken eye sockets with a shudder. What must it have been like, he wondered, to be the last? To lie here in the emptiness of the ruins, knowing he would die as he had lived—alone?

He slipped an arm around Sandy, urging her away, and they crossed silently to stand behind Harriet as she and Tamman concentrated obliviously on the computer.

Forty minutes passed before the two of them straightened, and their expressions were a curious blend of delight and disappointment.

"Well?" Sean asked, and Harriet glanced at Tamman and shrugged.

"We don't know. We can get into the operating system, sort of, but it's in terrible shape. I've never seen one this bad off—as far as I know, *no one*'s ever seen one this bad—and we can't access any of its files."

"Crap," Sean muttered, but Tamman shook his head.

"It may not be quite that bad. The main memory core's shot, but there's an auxiliary wired into the system. I'd guess somebody hooked in his personal unit as a peripheral—it's all that's keeping anything up, and there's a chance we can recover some of its memory."

"How much?" Sean asked eagerly, and Tamman and Harriet laughed.

"Spoken like a true optimist." Tamman grinned. "We can't tell you that till we can get at it properly, and we can't do that here. It's going to take *Israel*'s 'tronics shop to access this, Sean. We'll have to pull the unit and haul it back with us."

"Oh, lord!" Sandy knelt and ran her fingers over the dusty console, peering into it through her implants. "That's gonna be a real bitch, Tam."

"I know." He propped his hands on his hips and frowned at the glowing telltales. "I'm not real crazy about carting it out of here by hand, either. Molycircs or no, this thing's fragile as hell. Dropping it down a cliff or two wouldn't be real good for it."

"Then let's take it out the easy way," Harriet suggested. "Sandy and Sean blew what was left of the defenses into dust bunnies, so why don't I go back and collect the cutter while you and she take it apart?"

"Now that," Tamman murmured, "sounds like an excellent idea."

"I don't know, Harry," Sean said. "You're all better techs than me. Maybe I should go back while all three of you work on it."

She snorted. "Seen yourself moving lately, brother dear? It'd take you till dawn to hobble back to the cutter!"

"Hey, I'm not that bad off!"

"Maybe not, but you wouldn't enjoy the hike, and Tam and Sandy are better mechanics than me. That makes me the logical choice, now doesn't it? Besides, I haven't had a good jog since *Terra* kicked us overboard."

Sean didn't like the thought of splitting up and letting any of them out on his (or her) own, yet they hadn't met anything worrisome on the way in. None of the native predators, if any, had put in an appearance, and this was the Valley of the Damned. No Pardalian was likely to be wandering about in its vicinity in the middle of the night. And she was right about how he felt. The trek back to the cutter was more than he cared to face, and he discovered he'd been dreading the thought of it.

"All right," he agreed finally. "I'll stay here and hold lights and pass tools or something, but keep your belt light lit. That ought to discourage any of the local beasties from wondering what you taste like. And you take a *real* close look through your passive sensors before you try to land out there! You're probably right about the defenses being down, but don't take any chances."

"Aye, aye, Captain!" She tossed him an impudent salute, then whipped about and fled with a trill of laughter as he started for her. She paused at the outer door just long enough to stick out her tongue, and then her light, quick step receded rapidly up the stairs. Sean shook his head, then smiled and eased down to sit on the floor beside Sandy and Tamman as they produced tools and began removing the front of the console.

Harriet jogged happily through the darkness at a steady forty kilometers per hour. Sean might be fourteen centimeters taller, but he had their father's long body and broad shoulders; her legs were almost as long, despite his height advantage, and she was *much* lighter. Without even the weight of her scanpack she was free to attack the steep slopes, burdened only by her holstered grav gun, and she savored the opportunity. The moon had set, but her belt light was more than enough for someone with enhanced eyes, and running on *Israel*'s treadmill paled beside the sheer joy of filling her lungs with the crisp, cold mountain air as her feet spurned the ground.

It took her just under eighty minutes to reach the ledge they'd landed the cutter on. She paused, jogging in place, to wipe sweat from her forehead, then trotted onward a bit more cautiously in light of the hundred-meter drop to her right.

She was less than a kilometer from the cutter when her head came up in sudden surprise. Her eyes widened, and she slithered to a halt as the sound of human voices cut the darkness.

Her head whipped around and she went active with every implant, probing the night. People! At least a *dozen* people, coming around the bend ahead of her! Her implants should have picked them up sooner, and she cursed herself for not paying more attention to her surroundings and less to the pleasure of running. But even as she raged at her foolishness a part of her mind whirred with questions. She hadn't looked for them, but, damn it, what were they *doing* out here in the middle of the night without even a torch?

Questions could wait. She killed her belt lamp and turned back the way she'd come, and a voice shouted, loud and harsh with command. Crap! She'd been seen!

She abandoned her attempt to sneak away for a blinding pace no unenhanced human could have matched, and her thoughts flashed. They'd agreed not to use their coms in case they were picked up, but if there were people *here*, there might be more of them, closer to the Valley, as well. The others had to be warned, and—

Light glared and thunder barked behind her. Something whizzed past her ear, and something else slammed into her left shoulder blade. She staggered and snatched for her grav gun, spun to the side by the brutal impact, and the beginning of pain exploded up her nerves. A second fiery hammer hit her in the side, throwing the grav gun from her hand, but before it really registered there was another flash, and a sixty-gram lead ball smashed her right temple.

Chapter Twenty-One

"Come *out* of there, you—*aha!*"

Tamman broke off in mid-exasperation and eased the glittering block of molecular circuitry gently to the floor with a wide, triumphant smile.

Removing it had proved even harder than Sandy had feared. Not even implants could trace circuits in three dimensions without a schematic, and they'd found too late that it would have been far simpler to disconnect the console from the wall and go in from the back. Dust had infiltrated the ancient seals, as well, drifting up to irritate eyes and inspire bursts of sneezing, and Tamman had had an interesting moment when he bridged what he'd thought was a dead circuit. But two and a half painstaking hours had finally yielded their prize, and Sean met Tamman's grin with one of his own.

"*Foosh!*" Sandy fanned herself with a dirty hand. "When I think how much quicker we could have done this in a proper shop—!" Sean switched his grin to her. Then he frowned.

"Hey—shouldn't Harry be back by now?"

Sandy and Tamman stared at him, and he felt their matching surprise. All three of them had been oblivious to time as they concentrated on eviscerating the console; now their eyes met his, and he saw them darken as surprise gave way to the beginnings of concern.

"Damn right she should!" Tamman rose and snatched up the hand lamp. "The way she likes to run, it shouldn't've taken her more than two hours—tops—to get to the cutter!"

Sean started for the stairs and drew up with a gasp,

for his injured side had stiffened as he watched his friends work. Pain beaded his forehead with sweat, and he muttered a curse and hit his implant overrides. He knew he shouldn't—pain was a warning a body did well to heed, lest it turn minor injuries into serious ones—but that was the least of his worries.

Sandy frowned as his suddenly brisker movement told her what he'd done, yet she said nothing, and the two of them half-ran up the treads on Tamman's heels.

They scrambled out past the tree, panting from their hurried ascent, and stared into the darkness. There was no sign of the cutter, and Sean bit his lip as cold wind ruffled his hair.

Tamman was right—Harriet should have been back thirty minutes ago. He should have noticed her absence sooner . . . and he should *never* have let her out on her own! He'd known better at the time, damn it, but he'd let himself worry more over the possibility of losing an hour or two than her safety. He pounded his fists together and stared up at the sky with bitter eyes, but the alien stars mocked him, and his jaw clenched as he powered his com implant and sent out a full-powered omnidirectional pulse, heedless of the quarantine system's sensors.

There was no response, and the others looked at him with matching horror. Harriet should have heard that signal from forty light-minutes away!

"Oh, Jesus!" His whisper was a plea, and then he was running for the valley wall with no thought for such inconsequentials as his injuries, and his friends were on his heels.

They ran with implants fully active. It took them less than fifty minutes to reach the cutter, despite their feverish concentration on their search, and if Harriet had been within five hundred meters of the trail in any direction, they would have found her.

Sean leaned on a landing leg, sucking in air, enhanced lungs on fire, and tried to think. Even if she were dead—his mind shied from the thought like a terrified animal—

they should have spotted her implants. It was as if she'd never come this way at all, but she must have! She *had* to have!

"All right," he grated, and his panting companions turned to him anxiously. "We should have spotted her. If we didn't, she's not here, and I can't think of any reason she shouldn't be. We can use the cutter for an aerial search, but if she's unconscious or . . . or something—" his voice quavered, and he wrenched it back under iron control "—we might miss something as small as implant emissions. We need better scanners."

"Brashan." Tamman's voice was flat, and Sean nodded choppily.

"Exactly. If he puts up a full-powered array he can cover five times the ground twice as fast. And *Israel*'s med computers can access her readouts for a full diagnostic if she's hurt." He forced his hands down to his sides. "It'll also be a flare-lit tip-off to the quarantine system when he goes active." He bit the words off in pain, but they must be said, for if they threw away caution now, it might kill them all. "If it *is* watching the planet, there's no way it'll miss something like that."

"So what?" Tamman snarled. "We have to find her, goddamn it!"

"Tam's right," Sandy agreed without a flicker of hesitation, and Sean's hand caressed her face for just a moment. Then he opened the cutter hatch and went up the ramp at a run.

"I've found her."

The people in the cutter jerked upright, staring at Brashan's tiny hologram, and the centauroid's crest was flat. Another endless hour had passed, and even the fact that the quarantine system hadn't reacted in the slightest had meant nothing beside their growing fear as seconds dragged away.

Brashan straightened on his pad, his holographic eyes meeting Sean's squarely, and his voice was very quiet. "She's dying."

"No," Sean whispered. "*No*, goddamn it!"

"She is approximately seven kilometers from your current position on a heading of one-three-seven," Brashan continued in that same flat, quiet voice. "She has a broken shoulder, a punctured lung, and severe head injuries. The medical computer reports a skull fracture, a major eye trauma, and two subdural hematomas. One of them is massive."

"*Skull fracture?*" All three humans stared at him in shock, for Harriet's bones—like their own—were reinforced with battle steel appliqués. But under their shock was icy fear. Unlike muscle tissue and skin, the physical enhancement of the brain was limited; Harriet's implants might control other blood loss, but not bleeding inside her skull.

"I cannot say positively, but I believe her wounds to be deliberately inflicted," Brashan said, and Sean's dark eyes burned with sudden, terrible fire. "I say this because she is presently in the center of a small village. I hypothesize that she must have been carried thence by whoever injured her."

"Those fucking sons-of-bi—!"

"Wait, Sean!" Sandy cut him off in midcurse, and he turned his fury on her. He knew it was stupid, yet his rage needed a target—any target—and she was there. But if her brown eyes were just as deadly as his own, they were also far closer to rational.

"*Think*, damn it!" she snapped. "Somehow someone must have spotted her—and that means they probably know she came out of the Valley!"

Sean sank back, his madness stabbed through with panic as he recalled the fate the Church prescribed for any who dabbled with the Valley of the Damned. Sandy held his eyes a second longer, then turned to the Narhani.

"You said she's dying, Brashan. Exactly how bad is it?"

"If we do not get her into *Israel*'s sickbay within the next ninety minutes—two hours at the outside—she will be dead." Brashan's crest went still flatter. "Even now, her chances are less than even."

"We have to go get her," Tamman grated, and Sean nodded convulsively.

"Agreed," Sandy said, but her eyes were back on Sean. "Tam's right," she said quietly, "but we can't just go in there and start killing people."

"The hell we can't! Those motherfuckers are *dead*, Sandy! Goddamn it, they're trying to kill her!"

"I know. But you know why they are, and so do I."

"I don't fucking well *care* why!" he snarled.

"Well you fucking well ought to!" she snarled back, and the utterly uncharacteristic outburst rocked him even through his rage. "Damn it, Sean, they think they're doing what God wants! They're ignorant, superstitious, and scared to death of what she's done—are you going to kill them all for *that*?"

He stared at her, eyes hating, and tension crackled between them. Then his gaze fell. He felt ashamed, which only made his need for violence perversely stronger, but he shook his head.

"I know." Her voice was far more gentle. "I *know*. But using Imperial weapons against them would be pure, wanton slaughter."

He nodded, knowing she was right. Perhaps even more importantly, he knew even through his madness why she'd stopped him. He looked back up, and his eyes were sane once more . . . but colder than interstellar space.

"All right. We'll try to scare them out of our way without killing anyone, Sandy. But if they won't scare—" He broke off, and she squeezed his arm thankfully. She knew what killing the villagers would do to him after the madness passed, and she tried not to think about his final words.

Father Stomald knelt before his altar, ashen-faced and sick, and raised revolted eyes to the outsized beaker of oil. To pour that on a human being—*any* human being, even a heretic! To *light* it and watch her burn . . .

Bile rose as he pictured that blood-streaked, hauntingly

beautiful face and saw that slim, lovely body wreathed in flame, crisping, burning, blackening. . . .

He forced his nausea down. God called His priests to their duty, and if the punishment of the ungodly was harsh, it must be so to save their souls. Stomald told himself that almost tearfully, and it did no good at all. He loved God and longed to serve Him, but he was a shepherd, not an executioner!

Sweat matted his forehead as he dragged himself up. The beaker was cold between his palms, and he prayed for strength. If only Cragsend were big enough to have its own Inquisitor! If only—

He cut the thought off, despising himself for wanting to pass *his* duty to another, and argued with his stubborn horror. There was no question of the woman's guilt. The lightning and thunder from the Valley had waked the hunting party, and despite their terror, they'd gone to investigate. And when they called upon her to halt, she'd fled, proclaiming her guilt. Even if she hadn't, her very garments would convict her. Blasphemy for a woman to wear the high vestments of the Sanctum itself, and Tibold Rarikson, the leader of the huntsmen, had described her demon light. Stomald himself had seen the other strange things on her belt and wrist, but it was Tibold's haunted eyes which brought the horror fully home. The man was a veteran warrior, commander of Cragsend's tiny force of the Temple Guard, yet his face had been pale as whey as he spoke of the light and her impossible speed.

Indeed, Stomald thought with a queasy shiver as he turned from the altar, perhaps she was no woman at all, for what woman would still live? Three times they'd hit her—*three!*—at scarcely fifty paces, and if her long black hair was a crimson-clotted mass and her right eye wept bloody tears, her other wounds didn't even bleed. Perhaps she was in truth the demon Tibold had named her . . . but even as he told himself that, the under-priest knew why he wanted to believe it.

He descended the church steps into the village square,

and swallowed again as he beheld the heretic in the bloody light of the flambeaux.

She looked so young—younger even than he—as she hung from the stake by her manacled wrists, wrapped in heavy iron chains and stripped of her profaned vestments, and he felt a shameful inner stir as he once more saw her flimsy undergarments. Mother Church expected her priests to wed, for how could they understand the spiritual needs of husband or wife without experience? Yet to feel such things *now* . . .

He drew a deep breath and walked forward. Her bloody head drooped, and she hung so still he thought—prayed—she had already died. But then he saw the faint movement of her thinly covered breasts, and his heart sank with the knowledge that her death would not free him from the guilt he must bear.

He stopped and turned to face his flock as Tibold approached. The Guardsman bore a torch, and its flame wavered with the shaking of his hand. He stopped two paces from the priest, and the pity in his blunt, hard features made Stomald wonder if perhaps he, too, had tried to insist this woman was a demon out of revulsion for what they now must do to her.

He met Tibold's haunted eyes, and a flicker passed between them. One of understanding . . . and gratitude. Of thanks that they had no Inquisitor to break that slender body upon the wheel before her death as the letter of the Church's Law demanded, and that, demon or no, she had never waked. That she would die unknowing, spared the agony of her horrible end . . . unlike the men who would always remember wreaking it upon her.

He turned away from the Guardsman who must share his duty, facing his people, and wondered how they would look upon him in days to come. He couldn't see their faces beyond the fuming flambeaux, and he was glad.

He opened his mouth to pronounce the words of anathematization.

Harriet's weakening implant signals left no time to

return to *Israel*, and Sean landed the stealthed cutter
within a half-klick of the village. He selected a six-mil-
limeter grav rifle from the weapons locker to back up
his side arm, and Tamman chose an energy gun, but
Sandy bore only her grav gun and a satchel of grenades.
Sean wished she'd taken something heavier, yet time was
too short to argue, and he led them through the darkness at a run.

The torch-lit village square came in sight, and his
mouth twisted into a snarl. Harriet—*his Harriet!*—hung
by her wrists from a stake, heaped faggots piled about
her chained, half-naked body, and her hair was soaked
with blood. His hands tightened on his rifle's grips, but
he felt Sandy's anxious eyes, and he'd promised her.

"Go!" he snapped, and she hurled the first plasma
grenade.

Stomald cried out in horror as terrible white light
exploded against Cragsend's night. Its fiery breath
touched hay ricks to flame and singed the assembled
villagers' hair, and screams of terror lashed the priest.

He staggered back, blinded by the terrible flash. There
was another—*and another!*—and he heard Tibold's
hoarse bellow beside him and cringed, trying to understand, as three figures appeared. They seemed to step
forth from within the fury consuming the smithy, the gra-
nary, and tanning sheds. Their featureless black shapes
loomed before the glare, and the one in the center, a
towering giant out of some tale of horror, aimed a strange
musket shape at the slate roof of the church.

Sparkling flashes ripped stout stonework to shrieking
splinters in an endless roll of thunder that scattered
screaming villagers in panic, but Stomald's heart spasmed
with a terror even worse than theirs. It was his fault! The
thought leapt into his brain. He'd hesitated. He'd
rebelled in his heart, contesting God's will, and this—
this—was the result!

Tibold seized him, trying to drag him away, but he
stared transfixed as the shape beside the giant aimed its

own weapon at a trio of freight wagons. There was no flash this time, and that was even worse. A hurricane of chips and snapped timbers erupted, and the only sound was rending wood and the whine as fragments flew like bullets.

It was too much for Tibold. He abandoned the crazed priest to flee, and Stomald felt only a distant sympathy for him. This was more than any warrior could be asked to face. These were the demons of the Valley of the Damned, come to snatch away the demon his traitor heart had longed to spare, and terror filled him, but he stood his ground. He had no choice. His faltering faith brought them here. He'd failed his flock, and though his sin cost him his immortal soul, he was God's priest.

He raised the sanctified oil like a shield, dry lips whispering in prayer, and a handful of villagers stared in horror from the cover of darkness as their youthful priest advanced alone against the forces of Hell.

Sean blew the village fountain apart, but the lone madman walked through the spray and kept right on coming. Sean bared his teeth as he saw the blue and gold priestly robe, and it took all he had not to turn the rifle upon him, yet he didn't. Somehow, he didn't. Tamman splintered a half-meter trench across the square, and the priest halted for a moment. Then he resumed his advance, stepping over the shattered cobbles like a sleepwalker, and Sean swore as Sandy went to meet him.

Stomald faltered as the smallest demon walked straight at him. The silhouetted figure entered the spill of light from the flambeaux, and, for the first time, he truly saw one of them.

His prayer rose higher at the blasphemy before him, for this demon, too, wore the semblance of a woman in the holiest of raiment. Torchlight fumed in her eyes and glittered from the gold of her profaned vestments, the fires of Hell roared behind her, and she came on as if his exorcism was but words. Terror strangled his voice, yet the holy oil he bore was more potent than any exorcism, and he sent up a silent prayer for strength, unworthy though he'd proved himself. She stopped five paces away, and there was no fear in her face—not of the frightened priest, not of the blessed weapon he bore . . . not even of God Himself.

Sandy swallowed rage as she looked past the priest at Harriet, chained amid her waiting pyre. But then she saw his terrified face, and she felt a grudging admiration for the courage—or the faith—that held him here.

He stared at her, eyes filled with fear, and then his hands lashed. Something leapt from the beaker he held, but reflex activated her implant force field. Thick, iridescent oil sluiced down it, caught millimeters from her skin, and the priest's mouth moved.

"Begone!" he shouted, and she twitched, for she understood him. His voice was high and cracked with terror but determined, and he spoke the debased Universal of the Church. "Begone, Demon! Unclean and accursed, I cast you out in the Name of the Most Holy!"

Stomald shouted the exorcism with all the faith in him as the shining oil coated the demon. She paused—perhaps she even gave back a step—and hope flamed in his heart. But then hope turned to even greater horror, for the demon neither vanished in a flash of lightning nor fled in terror. Instead she came a step closer . . . and she smiled.

"Begone yourself, wretched and miserable one!" He reeled, stunned by the terrible thunder of that demonic voice, and his brain gibbered. No demon could speak the Holy Tongue! He retreated a faltering step, hand rising in a warding sign, and the demon laughed. *She laughed!* "I have come for my friend," she thundered, "and woe be unto you if you have harmed her!"

Crashing peals of laughter ripped through him like

echoes from Hell, and then she reached out to the nearest torch. The holy oil sprang alight with a seething hiss, clothing her in a fierce corona, and her voice boomed out of the roaring flames.

"Begone lest you die, sinful man!" she commanded terribly, and the furnace heat of her faceless, fiery figure came for him.

Sean watched Sandy confront the priest. Her implant-amplified voice made *his* head hurt—God only knew how it must have sounded to the priest! Yet the man had stood his ground until she touched the oil to flame. That was too much, and he took to his heels at last, stumbling, falling, leaping back to his feet and running for the imagined sanctuary of his church while Sandy's bellowing laughter pursued him.

Yet there was no time to admire her tactics, and he slung his grav rifle and charged across the square. Tamman's energy gun splintered more cobbles, driving the villagers still further back, but Sean hardly noticed. He scattered heavy faggots like tumbleweeds, and his face was a murderous mask as he gripped the chain about Harriet's body and twisted the links like taffy. They snapped, and he hurled them aside and caught at the manacles. His back straightened with a grunt. Anchoring bolts screamed and sheared like paper, and if she was still breathing as her limp body slid into his arms, he was close enough to read her implants directly at last. He paled. The damage was at least as bad as Brashan had said, and he cradled her like a child as he turned and ran like a madman for the cutter.

Stomald cowered in the nave of the broken church, rocking on his knees and praying with all his strength amid lumps of stone blown from the vault above him. He clung to sanity with bleeding fingernails, then cringed in fresh terror as something flashed into the very heavens beyond the village. A howling streak of light exploded across the stars in an echoing peal of thunder, and a hot breath of air rolled down through the church's cracked roof on the shrieking wind of its passage as it screamed low over Cragsend.

Then it was gone, and he buried his face in his hands and moaned.

Chapter Twenty-Two

Father Stomald stared at the garments on his vicarage table while wagons creaked beyond his windows. Nioharqs dragged loads of rubble down Cragsend's streets, drovers shouted, and repair crew foremen bawled orders, but the men laboring within the church itself only whispered.

The youthful priest felt their fear, for their terror was graven in his mind, as well, and with it an even greater horror.

Mother Church had failed them. *He* had failed them, and he steeled his nerve and touched the bloodstained fabric once more. He was but the vicar of a small mountain village, but he'd made his pilgrimage to the Temple and served at the Command Hatch as High Priest Vroxhan intoned mass. He'd seen the Temple's magnificence and the Sanctum that housed God's Own Voice and marveled at the high priest's exquisite vestments, at their splendid fabric and shining gold braid, the glitter of their buttons. . . .

And all that splendor paled beside *these* bloodied garments, like a child's clumsy copy of reality.

He made himself lift the tunic, and its gleaming buttons flashed under the window's sunlight, trapping the sun's heart within the crowned glory of God's holy Starburst. But his breath hissed as he looked closer, for a strange, winged creature—a magnificent beast whose like he'd never imagined—erupted from the Star's heart to claim God's Crown . . . even as the demon had erupted from the flames as she advanced upon him.

He fought a hysterical urge to fling the garment away.

Blasphemy! Blasphemy to deface those holiest of symbols! Yet that beast, that winged beast, like the winged badge of a Temple courier and yet unlike . . .

He forced calm upon his mind and examined the garment once more. Splendid as the buttons were, they were but ornaments, unlike those of High Priest Vroxhan's vestments. A quivering fingertip traced the invisible seal which had actually closed the tunic, and even now he could see no sign of how it worked.

When they'd first tried to strip the profaned fabric from the . . . the woman, the heretic or . . . or demon, or *whatever* she'd been . . .

His shoulders tensed, and he made them relax. When they'd tried to strip it from—her—they'd found no fastenings, and it had laughed at their sharpest blades. But then, with no real hope, he'd tugged—thus.

The cloth opened, and he licked his lips. It was uncanny. Impossible. Yet he held it in his hands. It was as real as his own flesh, and yet—

He opened the tunic wide once more, caressing the union of sleeve and shoulder, and bit his lip. He'd watched his own mother sew and done sewing enough of his own at seminary to know what he should find, yet there was no seam. The tunic was a single whole, perfect and indivisible, as if it had been woven in a single sitting and not pieced together, its only flaws the holes punched in it by musket balls. . . .

He went to his knees, folding his hands in prayer. Not even the fabled looms of Eswyn could have woven that fabric. Not the Temple's finest tailor could have formed it without thread or seam. No human hand could have wrought that magic closure.

They *must* have been demons. He told himself that fiercely, quivering with remembered terror before the thunder of the demon's voice. Yet there was an even greater terror at his heart, for the rolling majesty of that voice had crashed over him with the words of the Holy Tongue itself!

He moaned to the empty room, and the forbidden

thought returned. He fought to reject it, but it hung in the corners of his mind, and he squeezed his eyes so tightly closed they ached as it whispered in the silence.

They'd come from the Valley of the Damned, and lightning had wracked the cloudless heavens above the Valley. They'd smitten Cragsend with fire and thunder. One of them, alone, had ripped the entire roof from his church. Another had shattered three heavy wagons. A third had blazed alive in the flames of Mother Church's holiest oils and laughed—*laughed!* And when the smoke had wisped away, Stomald had stared at bubbled sheets of glass, flashing like gems under the morning sun, where the smithy had burned to less than ash.

Yet with all that inconceivable power, they'd killed no one. *No one.* Not a man, woman, or child. Not even an *animal!* Not even the men who'd wounded and captured their fellow and intended to burn her alive. . . .

The Church taught love for one's fellows, but demons should have slain—not simply frightened helpless mortals from their paths! And no demon could endure the Holy Tongue, far less speak it with its own mouth!

He opened his eyes, stroking the tunic once more, recalling the beauty of the woman who'd worn it, and faced the thought he'd fought. They had not—could not—have been mortals, and that should have made them demons. But demons couldn't have spoken the Holy Tongue, and demons *wouldn't* have spared where they might have slain. And if no woman might wear the vestments of Mother Church, these were *not* those of Mother Church, but finer and more mystical than anything Man might make even for the glory of God.

He closed his eyes and trembled with a different fear, like sunshine after the tempest, mingling with his terror in glory-shot wonder. No woman might wear Mother Church's raiment, no, but there were other beings who might. Beings of supernal beauty who might enter even that accursed valley and smite its demonic powers with thunder more deadly than that of Hell itself. Beings who *could* speak the Holy Tongue . . . and would not speak another.

"Forgive me, Lord," he whispered into the sunlight streaming through his window. His eyes sparkled as he raised his hands to the light, and he stood, opening his arms to embrace its radiance.

"Forgive my ignorance, Lord! Let not Your wrath fall upon my flock, for it was my blindness, not theirs. They saw only with their fear, but I—I should have seen with my heart and understood!"

Harriet MacIntyre opened her eyes and winced as dim light burned into her brain. There was no pain, but she'd never felt so weak. Her sluggish thoughts were blurred, and vertigo and nausea washed through her.

She moaned, trying to move, and quivered with terror when she could not. A shape bent over her, and she blinked. Half her vision was a terrible boil of featureless glare and the other half wavered, like heat shimmer or light through a sheet of water. Tears of frustration trickled as she fought in vain to focus and felt the world slipping away once more.

"Harry?" A hand touched hers, lifted it. "Harry, can you hear me?"

Sean's rough-edged voice was raw with pain and worry. Worry for her, she realized muzzily, and her heart twisted at the exhaustion that filled it.

"Can you hear me?" he repeated gently, and she summoned all her strength to squeeze his hand. Once that grip would have crumpled steel; now her fingers barely twitched, but his hand tightened as he felt them move.

"You're in sickbay, Harry." His blurred shape came closer as he knelt by her bed, and a gentle hand touched her forehead. She felt his fingers tremble, and his voice fogged. "I know you can't move, sweetheart, but that's because the med section has your implants shut down. You're going to be all right." Her eyes slid shut once more, blotting out the confusion. "You're going to be all right," he repeated. "Do you understand, Harry?" The urgency in the words reached her, and she squeezed again. Her lips moved, and he leaned close, straining his enhanced hearing to the limit.

"Love . . . you . . . all. . . ."

His eyes burned as the thready whisper faded, but her breathing was slow and regular. He watched her for a long, silent moment, and then he laid her hand beside her, patted it once, and sank back in his chair.

There were other moments of vague awareness over the next few days, periods of drifting disorientation which would have terrified her had her thoughts been even a little clearer. Harriet had been seriously injured once before—a grav-cycle accident that broke both legs and an arm before she'd been fully enhanced—and Imperial medicine had put her back on her feet in a week. Now whole days passed before she could hang onto consciousness for more than a minute, and that said horrifying volumes about her injuries. Worse, she couldn't remember what had happened. She didn't have the least idea *how* she'd been hurt, but she clung to Sean's promise. She was all right. She was going to be all right if she just held on. . . .

And then, at last, she woke and the bed beneath her was still, and the vertigo and nausea had vanished. Her lips were dry, and she licked them, staring up into near total darkness.

"Harriet?" It was Brashan this time, and she turned her head slowly, heart leaping as muscles obeyed her once more. She blinked, trying to focus on his face, and her forehead furrowed as she failed. Try as she might, half her field of vision was a gyrating electrical storm wrapped in a blazing fog.

"B-Brash?" Her voice was husky. She tried to clear her throat, then gasped as a six-fingered alien hand slipped under her. It cradled the back of her head, easing her up while the mattress rose behind her, and another hand held a glass. Her lips fumbled with the straw, and then she sighed as ice-cold water filled her mouth. The desiccated tissues seemed to suck it up instantly, yet nothing had ever tasted half so wonderful.

He let her drink a moment more, then set the glass aside and settled her back against the pillow. She closed her right eye, and sighed again as the tormenting glare vanished. Her left eye obeyed her, focusing on his saurian, long-snouted face and noting the half-flattened concern of his crest.

"Brash," she repeated. Her hand rose, and his took it.

"Doctor Brash, please," he said with a Narhani's curled-lip smile.

"Should've guessed." She smiled back, and if her voice was weak, it sounded like hers once more. "You always were better with the med computers."

"Fortunately," another voice said, and she turned her head as Sandy appeared on her other side. Her friend smiled, but her eyes glistened as she sank into the chair and took her free hand.

"Oh, Harry," she whispered. Tears welled, and she brushed at them almost viciously. "You scared us, honey. God, how you scared us!"

Harriet's hand tightened, and Sandy bent to lay her cheek against it. She stayed there for a moment, brown hair falling in a short, silky cloud about a too-thin wrist, and then she drew a deep breath and straightened.

"Sorry," she said. "Didn't mean to go all mushy on you. But 'Doctor Brashan' damn well saved your life. I—" her voice wavered again before she got it back under control "—I didn't think he was going to be able to."

"Hush," Harriet soothed. "Hush, Sandy. I'm all right." She smiled a bit tremulously. "I know I am—Sean promised me."

"Yes. Yes, he did." Sandy produced a tissue and blew her nose, then managed a watery grin. "In fact, he's gonna be ticked he wasn't here when you woke up, but Brashan and I chased him back into bed less than an hour ago."

"Is everyone else all right?"

"We're fine, Harry. Fine. Sean's got some damage to his left arm—he drove himself too hard—but it's minor, and Tam's fine. Just exhausted. With you out, Brashan stuck here in sickbay, and Sean ready to kill anybody who suggested he leave you, poor Tam's been carrying most of the load."

"Tam and *you*, you mean," Harriet said, seeing the weariness in her face.

"Oh, maybe." Sandy shrugged. "But I haven't left the ship—Tam was the one who did all the traveling back and forth with the computer."

"Computer?" Harriet said blankly. "What computer?"

"The computer we—" Sandy started in a surprised voice, then stopped. "Oh. What's the last thing you remember?"

"We were . . . going to the valley?" Harriet said uncertainly. "There was some sort of . . . of defensive system, I think. Did I—" She released Brashan's hand to cover her right eye. "Is that what happened to me?"

"No." Sandy patted the hand she held. "That happened later. We'll tell you all about it, but what matters is we found a personal computer and brought it back. It's in miserable shape, but Tam's managed to recover some of it, and it looks like some kind of journal. I think—" she smiled fondly "—he's been concentrating on it to keep his mind off worrying about you."

"A journal?" Harriet rubbed her closed eye harder, and her open eye brightened. "That sounds good, Sandy. I just wish I—"

"Harriet." Brashan interrupted quietly, and his hand closed on her right wrist, stilling the fingers on her eye. "Why are you rubbing your eye?"

"I— Oh, it's probably nothing," she said, and heard the strangeness in her voice. Denial, she thought.

"Tell me," he commanded.

"I—" She swallowed. "I just can't get it to focus."

"I think it's more than that." His voice accepted no evasion, and she felt her lips quiver. She stilled them and turned to face him squarely.

"I think it's gone blind," she said, and heard Sandy's soft gasp beside her. "All I get is a . . . a blur and a glare."

"Is it bothering you now?"

"No." She drew a deep breath, curiously relieved to have admitted there was something wrong. "Not as long as it's closed."

"Open it." She obeyed, then squeezed it instantly back shut. The glare was worse than ever, jagged with pain even her implants couldn't damp.

"I . . . I can't." She licked her lips. "It hurts."

"I see," he said, and she felt her nerve steady under his composed voice. "I feared you might have difficulties, but when you said nothing—" His crest flipped a Narhani shrug.

"What's wrong?" She was pleased by how nearly normal she sounded.

"Nothing irreparable, I assure you. But as you know, *Israel's* sickbay, while capable of bone and tissue repair and implant *adjustment*, was never intended for enhancement or major implant *repair*. Her designers—" he smiled a wry, Narhani smile "—assumed injuries such as that would be treated aboard her mother ship, which, alas, is beyond our reach."

He paused, and she nodded for him to continue.

"You were struck in the right temple, left shoulder, and right lung by heavy projectiles," the centauroid explained gently. "Despite the crudity of the weapons used, they had sufficient power at such short range to shatter even enhanced human bone, but the one which struck your head fortunately impacted at an angle and your skull sufficed to turn it."

She breathed a bit harder as he cataloged her wounds but nodded for him to continue, and his eyes approved her courage.

"Your implants sealed the blood loss from the wounds to your shoulder and lung. There was considerable damage to the lung, but those injuries are healing satisfactorily. The head wound resulted in intracranial bleeding and tissue damage"—she tensed, but he continued calmly—"yet I see no sign of motor skill damage, though there may be some permanent memory loss. Your vision problem, however, stems not from tissue damage but from damage to your implant hardware. Fragments of bone were driven into the brain and also forward, piercing the eye socket. The injuries to the eye structures are responding to therapy, and the optic nerve was untouched, but an implant, unlike the body, cannot be regenerated. I knew it was damaged, but I'd hoped the impairment would be less severe than you describe."

"It's only in the hardware?" Relief washed through her at his nod, but then she frowned. "Why not just shut it down through the overrides?"

"The damage is too extensive for me to access it. Short of removing it entirely—a task for a fully qualified neurosurgeon which I would hesitate to attempt and which would, at best, leave you effectively blind until we can obtain proper medical assistance, anyway—I can do nothing with it."

"Well, you're going to have to do *something*. I know you've got the lights way down in here, but I can't even keep it open!"

"I know. Yet, as you point out, as long as no light reaches it you experience no discomfort. Rather than risk damaging your presently unscathed optic nerve, I would prefer simply to cover it."

"An eye patch?" Despite herself, her lips twitched at the absurdity of such an archaic approach. Sandy actually chuckled.

"Yo, ho, ho and a bottle of rum!" she murmured. Harriet gave her a one-eyed glare, but she only grinned, too relieved to hear the damage wasn't permanent to be deflated so easily.

"Indeed." Brashan gave Sandy a moderately severe glance, then looked back down at Harriet. "Given the unimpaired enhancement of your left eye, you should be able to adjust once the distraction is suppressed."

"An eye patch." Harriet sighed. "God, I hope you get

holos of this, Sandy. I know you'll just die if you miss the opportunity!"

"Damn straight," Sandy said, and smoothed hair from Harry's forehead.

"But you must report it, Father!" Tibold Rarikson stared at the priest in disbelief, yet Stomald's smile was serene.

"Tibold, I *will* report it, but not yet." The Guard captain started to protest, but Stomald shushed him with a gesture. "I will," he repeated, "but only when I'm certain precisely what I'm to report."

"What you're to *report*?" Tibold's eyes bugged, but he gripped his innate respect for the cloth in both hands and drew a deep breath. "Father, with all due respect, I don't see what the problem is. Cragsend was attacked by demons who burned the fifth part of the village to the ground!"

"Indeed?" Stomald smiled and took a turn around the room, feeling the other's eyes on his back. If there was one man with whom he wished to share his wondering joy, Tibold was that man. Hard-bitten warrior that he was, he was a kindly man whose sense of pity not even war could quench. And despite his Guard rank and the traditional Malagoran resentment of outside control, he stood almost as high in Cragsend's estimation as Stomald himself. But for all his desire, how did Stomald bring the other to see what he himself now saw so clearly?

He drew a deep breath and turned back to the Guardsman.

"My friend," he said gently, "I want you to listen to me carefully. A great thing has happened here in our tiny town—a greater thing than you may believe possible. I know you're afraid, and I know why, but there are some points about the 'demons' you should consider. For example . . ."

Chapter Twenty-Three

Sean tried not to hover as Harriet walked unaided to the astrogator's couch. She was still shaky, and her missing memories refused to return, yet she had to smile at his expression. Tamman sat beside her and slipped an arm about her, and she leaned against him, wishing she knew how to thank them for her life.

But, of course, there was no need.

"Well!" Sean flopped into his couch with customary inelegance. "Looks like your body-and-fender shop does good work, Brashan."

"True," the Narhani replied with one of his clogged-drain chuckles. "And while I regret my inability to repair your implant, Harry, I must say your patch gives you a certain—" He paused, seeking the proper word.

"Raffishness?" Sean suggested, his smile almost back to normal.

"Thank you, kind sir." Harriet stroked the black patch and grinned. "I glanced in the mirror and thought I was looking at Anne Bonny!"

"Who?" Brashan's crest perked, but she only shook her head.

"Look her up in the computer, Twinkle Hooves."

"I shall. You humans have such *interesting* historical figures," he said, and her laughter lifted the last shadow from Sean's heart.

"I'm really glad to see you up again, Harry, and I'm sorry you can't remember what happened. The rest of us'll put together a combined implant download later, but for now let's turn our attention to what we got out of it. Aside, of course, from the reincarnation of Captain Bonny."

His wave gave Sandy the floor, and she stood.

"Speaking for myself, Harry, I'm *delighted* you're back. Tam's been doing his best, but he'll never make an analyst." Tamman made a pained sound, and Harriet poked him in the ribs.

"However," Sandy went on with a grin, "our hamhanded Marine and I have recovered a fair amount from our purloined computer, and our original hypothesis was correct. It *was* a journal. This man's."

Sean gazed at the image in the command deck display, mentally turning the hair white and the skin to parchment, and recognized the lonely, mummified body from the tower bedroom.

"This is—or was—an engineer named Kahtar. Much of his journal's unrecoverable, and he didn't mention the planet's name in the portions we've been able to read, so we still don't know what it was called originally. But I've been able to piece together what happened."

She looked around, satisfied by the hush about her. Even Tamman knew only fragments of what she was about to say, and she wondered if the others would react as she had . . . and if they'd have the same nightmares.

"Apparently," she began, "the planetary governor closed down the mat-trans at the first hypercom warning, then began immediate construction of a quarantine system under the direction of his chief engineer. Who," she added wryly, "was obviously a real whiz.

"Things weren't too bad at the start. There was some panic, and a few disturbances from people afraid they hadn't gotten quarantined soon enough, but nothing they couldn't handle . . . at first." She paused, and her eyes darkened.

"They might have made it, if they'd just shut down their hypercom. Their defenses destroyed over a dozen incoming refugee ships, but I think they could have lived even with that . . . if the hypercom hadn't still been up.

"It was like a com link to Hell." Her voice was quiet. "It was such a slow, agonizing process. Other worlds thought *they* were safe, too, but they weren't, and, one by one, the plague killed them all. It took years—years of desperate, dwindling messages from infected planets while their entire universe died."

Icy silence hovered on the command deck, and she blinked misty eyes.

"It . . . got to them. Not at once. But when the last hypercom went silent, when there was no one else left— no one at all—the horror was too much. The whole planet went mad."

"Mad?" Brashan's voice was soft, and she nodded.

"They knew what had happened, you see. They knew they'd done it to themselves. That it had all been a mistake—a technological accident on a cosmic scale. So they decided to insure there would never be another one. Technology had killed the Empire . . . so they killed technology."

"They what?" Sean jerked up, and she nodded. "But . . . but they had a high-tech population. How did they expect to *feed* it without technology?"

"They didn't care," Sandy said sadly. "The psychic wounds were too deep. That's what happened to their tech base: they smashed it themselves."

"Surely not all of them agreed," Harriet half-whispered.

"No." Sandy was grim. "There were some sane ones left—like Kahtar—but not enough. They fought a war here like you wouldn't believe. A high-tech war *intended* to destroy its own culture . . . and anyone who tried to stop them. Harry, they threw people into bonfires for trying to hide *books*."

Harriet covered her mouth, trembling with a personal terror they all understood too well, and Tamman hugged her.

"Sorry," Sandy said gently, and Harriet nodded jerkily. "Anyway, they didn't quite get all of it. The Valley of the Damned was a sort of high-tech redoubt. There'd been others, but the mobs rolled over them—sometimes they used human wave attacks and literally ran the defenses out of ammunition with their own bodies. Only the valley held. Their energy guns didn't need ammo, and they threw back over thirty attacks in barely ten years. The last one was made by a mob on foot, in the middle of a mountain winter, armed with spears and a handful of surviving Imperial weapons."

She fell silent once more, and they waited, sharing her horror, until she inhaled and went on in a flat voice.

"The attacks on the valley finally ended because the others *had* managed to destroy their technology, and, with it, their agriculture, their transport system, their medical structure—everything. Starvation, disease, exposure, even cannibalism . . . within a generation, they were down to a population they could support with an almost neolithic culture. Kahtar estimated that over a billion people died in less than ten years.

"But—" her voice sharpened and she leaned forward "—there was, obviously, one other high-tech center left: the quarantine HQ. Even the most frenzied mob knew that was all that stood between them and any possible refugee ship, however slight the chance one might arrive, and the HQ staff rigged up a ground defense element in the quarantine system itself. It's nowhere near as powerful as the space defenses, but it's designed to smash anyone or anything using Imperial weapons within a hundred klicks of the HQ."

"Oh, *crap*," Sean breathed, and she smiled tightly.

"You got it. And there's worse. You see, the command staff may have set things up to keep the mobs from smashing the HQ, but they agreed with the need to destroy all *other* technology."

"I don't think I'm going to like this," Tamman muttered.

"You're not. They moved out of those ruins near the Temple, put the HQ computer on voice access, set the shipyard up to handle all maintenance on an automated basis, and manufactured a religion."

"Oh, Jesus!" Sean moaned.

"According to Kahtar, who was pretty much running the valley by then, the port admiral had some sort of vision that turned the bio-weapon into the Flood and

Pardal into Noah's Ark. But *this* Flood was a punishment for the sin of technological pride into which the 'Great Demons' had seduced mankind, and the 'Ark' was a refuge to which God had guided the handful of faithful who had resisted the demons' temptation. The survivors were the seed corn of the New Zion, selected by God to create a society without the 'evils' of technology."

"But if that's true," Brashan said, "why didn't they destroy the valley? If they had the capability to set up ground defenses, surely they had the capability to strike Kahtar's people."

"There was no need. There were never more than a hundred people in the valley, and it was a vacation resort before they forted up, without any real industrial base. They were trapped inside it, with too little genetic material to sustain a viable population, and the new religion had a use for them—one so important it didn't even pull the plug on their power supply."

"Demons," Harriet murmured.

"Or, more precisely, a nest of 'lesser demons' and their worshipers. The valley gave their religion a 'threat' that might last for centuries to help it get its feet under it. What we walked into was Hell itself as far as the Church is concerned, and that's why anyone who has anything to do with it *must* be exterminated."

"Merciful God." Sean looked as sick as he felt. The warped logic and cold-blooded calculation that left those poor, damned souls penned up in their valley as the very embodiment of evil twisted his guts. He tried to imagine how it must have felt to know every other human on the planet was waiting, literally praying for the chance to murder you, and wanted to vomit.

"I think Kahtar went mad himself, at the end. Some of the others walked out of the valley when the despair finally got to be too much—walked out *knowing* what would happen. Others suicided. None of them were interested in having children. What future would children have had on a planet of homemade barbarians itching to torture them to death?

"But Kahtar had to find something to believe in, and he did—something that kept him alive to the very end, after all the others were gone. He decided, against all evidence and sanity, that at least one other world had to have survived. That's why he wired his journal into the main computers. He left it there for us, or someone like us, so we'd know what had happened. And that's why he included something very important for us to know."

"What?" Sean asked.

"The last of the original HQ crew didn't just put the computer on voice access, Sean. They knew there were still at least some enhanced people in the valley. People who could have ordered the Voice to denounce their precious religion if they'd been able to get close enough to access the computer, because they could have overridden voice commands through their implants once the last of the original 'priests' were gone. So they disengaged the neural feeds. The *only* way in is by voice, and they had an entire damned army sitting on top of it to keep everyone but the priesthood out of voice access range. With the quarantine system set up to wax anybody who tried to use Imperial weapons to shoot their way in, there was no way a handful of old, tired Imperials could get to them."

She paused and met their horrified gazes.

"Which means, of course, that *we* can't get to them, either."

Sean sat in the cutter bay hatch, high on *Israel*'s flank, and gazed sightlessly out through the wavering distortion of her stealth field. They were still making progress on their linguistic programs, helped by the fact that they were no longer afraid to use their remotes at full range as long as they stayed outside the Temple's hundred-kilometer kill zone, yet two weeks had passed since Sandy's bombshell, and none of them had the least idea what to do next. The only good thing was that Harriet was completely back on her feet now—she was even jogging on *Israel*'s treadmill again.

He sighed and tugged on his nose, looking very like an oversized, black-haired version of his father as he contemplated the problem. He'd expected difficulties getting into the Temple, but he'd never anticipated that they wouldn't even be able to use Imperial small arms! Hell, they might not even be able to use their own *implants*, so how did four humans—and one Narhani, who'd be mobbed on sight as an incontrovertible "demon"—break into the most strongly guarded fortress on the entire goddamned planet?

There was, of course, one very simple answer, but he couldn't do it. He couldn't even think of it without nausea. Kahtar's journal indicated "the Sanctum" was heavily armored and deeply dug in, but they could always take the place out with a gravitonic warhead, and *Israel* could launch hyper weapons from atmosphere. They could hit the Temple before the quarantine system even began to react, and if the computer went down, so did the entire system. Unfortunately, they also killed everyone in Pardal's largest city—almost two million people, by Sandy's estimate.

He squeezed his nose harder. His clever stratagem to get them down had worked, all right, and he'd poked their collective heads right into a trap. They couldn't take off—assuming they'd had anywhere to go—without the quarantine system killing them for trying to leave the planet, but there wasn't any way to shut the system off *from* the planet!

"Sean?" He looked up at Sandy's voice. She was standing at the far end of the bay, waving at him. "Come on! You've gotta see this!"

"See what?" he asked, climbing to his feet with a puzzled frown.

"It's too good to spoil by telling you." Her expression was strange, and she sounded amused, frightened, excited, and surprised, all in one.

"At least give me a clue!"

"All right." She eyed him with an odd, lurking smile. "I didn't have anything else to do, so I sent a remote back to take a peek at the village we pulled Harry out of, and you won't *believe* what's going on!"

"Well, Father," Tibold closed the spyglass with a click and grimaced at Stomald, "it seems His Grace was unimpressed."

Stomald nodded, shading his eyes with his hand, and tried not to show his own despair. He hadn't expected Bishop Frenaur to accept his unsupported word without question, but he certainly hadn't counted on *this*.

Mother Church's blood-red standards advanced up the twisting valley, blue and gold cantons glittering, and metal gleamed behind them: pikeheads and muskets, armor, and the dully-flashing barrels of artillery.

"How many, do you think?" he asked quietly.

"Enough." The Guard captain squinted into the sun, frowning. "More than I expected, really. I'd say that's most of the Malagoran Temple Guard out there, Father. Call it twenty thousand men."

Stomald nodded again, grateful Tibold hadn't said, "I told you so." The Guard captain had argued against sending the good word to the Temple. Unlike Stomald, Tibold wasn't a native-born Malagoran, but he knew the Temple regarded Malagor as a hotbed of sedition, and seeing that armed, advancing host, Stomald was just as glad he'd at least agreed to send his news by semaphore rather than taking it in person.

He shook that thought off and pressed his lips together. Surely God had sent His angels to Cragsend for a purpose. He didn't promise His servants would always be bright enough to *see* His purpose, but He always had one. Of course, sometimes it wasn't a very safe one. . . .

"What do you advise?"

"Running away?" Tibold suggested with a smile, and Stomald surprised himself with a chuckle.

"I don't think God would like that. Besides, where would we run to? We're backed up against the mountains, Tibold."

"Just like a kinokha in a trap," the Guard captain

agreed, wondering why he wasn't more frightened. He'd thought his young priest was mad at first, but something about him had been convincing. Certainly, Tibold told himself yet again, those *hadn't* been demons. He'd seen too much of what men, touched with God's immortal spirit, were capable of in time of war. No, if they'd been demons, Cragsend would be a smoking ruin peopled only by the dead.

And, like Father Stomald, he could think of only one other thing they could have been, though he did wish they'd been a bit less ambiguous in their message. Still, he supposed that was *his* fault. He was the damn-fool idiot who'd shot the first of them down. Even an angel might forget her message with a bullet in her head, and the others had seemed more intent on getting her back than dropping off any letters.

He snorted. The other local villages and towns—even Cragwall, the largest town in the Shalokar Range—had sent their priests to stare at the wreckage and hear Father Stomald's tale. Tibold had never realized just how powerful a preacher Stomald was until he heard him speaking to those visitors, bringing forward other villagers to bear witness, describing the angel who'd spoken in the Holy Tongue even while the sanctified oil blazed upon her. It was a pity he couldn't have a word or two with the commander of that army, for he'd brought everyone else around. Of course, his audience had been Malagorans, with all a Malagoran's resentment of foreign domination, and Tibold knew better than most how jealous the Temple was of its secular power. Whoever was in command down there had his orders from the Circle; he was hardly likely to forget them on the say-so of a village under-priest, however eloquent.

Tibold reopened his glass to study the standards once more. Columns of smoke rose behind them—columns which had once been farmsteads and small villages. The people who'd lived there had either come to join the "heresy" or fled to escape it, and he was grateful they had, for the smoke told him what the Guard's orders were. Mother Church had decided to make an example of the "rebels" and declared Holy War, and her Guard would take no prisoners.

"Well, Father," he said at last, "I don't see much choice. I've got five hundred musketeers, a thousand pikemen, and four thousand with nothing but their bare hands. Even with God on our side, that's not a lot."

"No," Stomald sighed. "I wish I could say God will save us, but sometimes we can meet our Trial only by dying for what we know to be right."

"Agreed. But I'm a soldier, Father, and, if it's all the same to you, I'd like to die as one—without making it any easier for them than I have to."

"I don't know of any Writ that says you should," Stomald said with a sad smile.

"Then we'll fall back to Tilbor Pass. It's less than four hundred paces across, and it'll take even this lot a few days to dig us out of that." Stomald nodded, and the Guardsman smiled crookedly. "And in the meantime, Father, I won't take it a bit amiss if you ask God to help us out of the mess we've landed ourselves in!"

"You're joking!" Sean stared at the images from the remote. "*Angels?*"

"Yep." Sandy's eyes sparkled. "Wild, isn't it?"

"My God." Sean sank onto his couch. All the others were gazing as fixedly as he at the display.

"Actually, it's not as crazy as it sounds," Harriet mused. "I mean, we obviously weren't mortals—not with bio-enhancement, grav guns, and plasma grenades—and if you aren't mortal, you're either a demon or an angel. And I've been back over your reports." Her voice wavered, for the others had prepared their promised implant download. She still had no memory of the event, but the download had shown it all to her through her friends' eyes. She shivered as her mind replayed the image of her own bloody body, awaiting the torch, then shook herself. "It looks like the only two they saw clearly were Sandy and me."

"That's what I gather from what this Father Stomald is saying." Sandy switched to an image of the priest and smiled wryly as she recalled the last time she'd seen the broad-shouldered, curly-haired young man with the neatly trimmed beard. He looked far more composed now as he stood talking to the hard-faced soldier at his side.

"He's kind of cute, isn't he?" Harriet murmured, then blushed as Sean gave her a very speaking look and she remembered what that cute young man had almost done to her. She rubbed her eye patch and gave herself another shake.

"Anyway, if we're the only ones he saw, it all makes sense. Their church is patriarchal—well, for that matter, most of Pardal is. Malagor's sort of radical in that respect; they actually let women own property. The thought of a woman in the priesthood is anathema, but there Sandy and I were in Battle Fleet uniform . . . which just happens to be what their bishops wear for their holiest church feasts. Add the fact that this patriarchal outfit has decided, for reasons best known to themselves, that angels are female—"

"And beautiful," Tamman inserted.

"As I say, angels are female," Harriet went on repressively. "They're also immortal, but not invulnerable, which explains how I could have been injured, and this Stomald seems to realize you three deliberately didn't kill anyone when you came in like gangbusters. Given all that, there's actually a weird sort of logic to the whole thing."

"Yeah," Sean said more soberly, and changed the display himself. The marching columns of armed men sent a visible chill through *Israel*'s crew, and he sighed. "We may not have killed anyone, but it looks like maybe we *should* have. At least then we would have been 'demons' instead of some kind of divine messengers that're going to get *all* of them massacred."

"Maybe . . . and maybe not. . . ." Sandy was gazing at the advancing Temple Guard, and the light in her eyes worried Sean.

"What d'you mean?" he demanded, and she gave him a beatific smile.

"I mean we just found the key to the Temple's front door."

"Huh?" her lover said sapiently, and her smile became a grin.

"We don't want all those people slaughtered for something we started, however unintentionally, do we?" Four heads shook, and she shrugged. "In that case, we've got to rescue them."

"And how do you propose to do that?"

"Oh, that's the easy part. Those guys are a heck of a lot more than a hundred kilometers from the Temple."

"Hold on there!" Sean protested. "I don't want to see Stomald and his fellow nuts massacred, but I don't want to massacre anyone else, either!"

"No need," she assured him. "We can probably scare the poo out of them with a few holo projections without even a demonstration of firepower."

"Hum." Sean looked at the others, and his eyes began to dance. "Yeah, I suppose we could. Might even be fun."

"Don't get too carried away," Sandy said, "because what happens *after* we scare 'em is what really matters."

"What are you talking about?" Tamman sounded puzzled.

"I mean that whether we like it or not, the fat's in the fire. Either we let the Church massacre these people, or we rescue them. If we rescue them, do you think the Temple's just going to say, 'Gosh! Looks like we better leave those nasty demon-worshiping heretics alone'? And *they're* not going to go home like nothing happened, either, because if we save them, we reconfirm their belief in divine intervention."

"Great," Sean sighed.

"Maybe it is." He looked up in surprise, and she shrugged. "We didn't do it on purpose, but we can't *un*do it. So if the Temple wants a crusade, why not give it one?"

"Are you saying we should instigate a religious war?!"

Harriet stared at her in horror, and Sandy shrugged again.

"I'm saying we already have," she said more soberly. "That gives us a responsibility to end it, one way or another, and we're not going to be able to do that without getting our hands bloody. I don't like that any more than you do, Harry, but we don't have a choice—unless we want to sit back and watch Stomald and his people go down.

"So if we have to get involved, let's go whole hog. The Church is too big, too static. Even the secular lords are lap dogs for it. But the only way Stomald's going to survive is to take out the Inner Circle . . . and that just happens to be what *we* need to do to get into the Sanctum."

"I don't know. . . ." Harriet said slowly, but Sean was staring at Sandy in admiration.

"My God, Sandy—that's brilliant!"

"Well, pretty darn smart, anyway," she agreed. Then she laughed. "Anyway, we're certainly the right people for the job!" Sean looked blank, and her grin seemed to split her face. "Of course we are, Sean! After all, we *are* the Lost Children of *Israel*, aren't we?"

Chapter Twenty-Four

Sean grimaced as his stealthed fighter, one of only three *Israel* carried, hovered above the twisting gorge. It was sheer, deep, and dizzy, with vertical walls that narrowed to less than two hundred meters where they'd been closed with earthworks, and he saw why the "heretics" had retreated into it, but such tight quarters made maneuvering for the shot a bitch.

He checked his scanners. The cutter Sandy, Harriet, and Brashan rode was as invisible as the fighter, but their synchronized stealth fields made it clear to his own instruments while they ran their final checks.

He wished there'd been time to test their jury-rigged holo projector properly. It would have been nice to have had more planning time, too. Building a strategy in less than ten hours offered little scope for careful consideration, though he had to admit Sandy seemed to have answered his major objections.

The hardest part, in many ways, was the limits on what they could offer these people. It would take a "miracle" to save them this time, but it was the only miracle *Israel*'s crew could work. They dared not use Imperial technology within a hundred klicks of the Temple, yet if they used it up to that point and then stopped, the result would be disastrous. Not only would it offer the Temple fresh hope, but the sudden cessation would fill the "heretics" with dismay. It might well convince them they *were* heretics, that the "false angels" dared not confront the Temple on its own ground, and that limitation was going to make even more problems than Harriet's monkey wrench.

He puffed his lips and wished his twin were just a little less principled. Her insistence that they never claim divine status was going to make things difficult—and probably wouldn't be believed anyway. Yet she was right. They'd done enough damage, and, assuming they won the war they'd provoked, they'd eventually have to convince their "allies" they weren't really angels. Besides, demanding their worship would have made him feel unclean.

He turned his attention to the army of the Church. Those earthworks looked almost impregnable, but the valley formed a funnel to them, and the Temple Guard was busy deploying field guns under cover of darkness. With the dawn, dozens of them would be able to open fire across a wide arc. They didn't look very heavy—they might throw five or six-kilo shot—but there were a lot of them, and he didn't see any in the heretics' camp.

"Wish Sandy's dad was here," he muttered.

"Or *my* dad," Tamman grunted. "Better yet, Mom!"

"I'd settle for any of 'em, but Uncle Hector's the history nut. I don't know crap about black powder and pikes."

"We'll just have to pick up on-the-job training. And at least we've got the right accouterments." Tamman grinned and rapped his soot-black breastplate. Sean wore a matching breast and backplate with mail sleeves. The armor, like the swords racked behind their flight couches, came from *Israel*'s machine shops, and the materials of which they were made would have raised more than a few eyebrows in either of the camps below.

"Easy for you to say," Sean grunted. "You were the big wheel on the fencing team—I'm likely to cut my own damn head off!"

"These guys are more into broadsword tactics," Tamman pointed out. "I don't know how much fencing's going to help against that. But we've both got enhanced reaction speeds, and none—"

"Sean, it's show time." Sandy's quiet transmission cut Tamman off.

✧ ✧ ✧

Tibold Rarikson stood behind the parapet, straining his eyes into the night, and rubbed his aching back. It had been years since last he'd plied a mattock, but most of his "troops" were only local militia. They had yet to learn a shovel was as much a weapon as any sword . . . and it seemed unlikely they'd have time to digest the lesson. He couldn't see it in the dark, but he knew they were bringing up the guns, and Mother Church's edict against secular artillery heavier than chagors gave the Guard a monopoly on the heavier arlak. Of course, *he* didn't even have any chagors, though his malagors might come as a nasty surprise. Except that he faced Guards who'd spent most of their enlistments in Malagor, so they knew all about the heavy-bore musket that was the princedom's national trademark. . . .

He shook himself. His wandering thoughts were wearing ruts, and it wasn't as if any of it really mattered. There were more than enough Guardsmen to soak up all the musket balls he had and close with cold steel, which meant—

His thoughts broke off as a dim pool of light glowed suddenly into existence between him and the Guard's pickets. He rubbed his eyes and blinked hard, but the wan radiance refused to vanish, and he poked the nearest sentry.

"Here, you! Go get Father Stomald!"

"Captain Ithun! Look!"

Under-Captain Ithun jumped and smothered a curse as heated wine spilled down his front. The Guard officer—one of the very few native Malagorans in the Temple's detachment to the restive province—mopped at his breastplate, muttering to himself, and stalked towards the picket who'd shouted.

"Look at what, Surgam?" he demanded irritably. "I don't—"

His voice died. An amorphous cloud of light hovered five hundred paces away, almost at the edge of the ditch footing the heretic's earthen rampart. It seethed and wavered, growing brighter as he watched, and his hair tried to stand on end under his helmet. The incredible tales told by the handful of heretics they'd so far captured poured through his mind, and his mouth was dust-dry as the eerie luminescence flowed towards him.

He swallowed. If the heretics were meddling with the Valley of the Damned, then that might be a—

He stopped himself before he thought the word.

"Get Father Uriad!" he snapped, and Private Surgam raced off into the dark with rather more than normal speediness.

"What is it, Tibold?" Stomald had finally managed to fall asleep, and his mind was still logy as he panted from his hasty run.

"Look for yourself, Father," Tibold said tautly, and Stomald's mouth fell open. The ball of light was taller than three men and growing taller.

"I— How long has that been there?!"

"No more than five minutes, but—" Tibold's explanation broke off, and the Guardsman swallowed so hard Stomald heard it plainly even as he fell to his own knees in awe.

The pearly light had suddenly darkened, rearing to a far greater height, and he groped for his starburst as it coalesced into a mighty figure.

"Saint Yorda preserve us!" someone cried, and Stomald's thoughts echoed the unseen sentry as the blue and gold shape towered in the night, lit by fearsome inner light. Her back was to him, and she might be twenty times taller than the last time he'd seen her, but he recognized that short hair, cut like a helmet of curly silk, and his lips shaped a soft, fervent prayer as he recalled a thundering voice from a mass of flames.

"Dear God!" Under-Captain Ithun whispered.

The light streaming from the unearthly figure washed the gorge walls in rippling waves of blue and gold, and its brown eyes glowed like beacons. He fought his panic, locking trembling sinews against the urge to fall to his knees, and cries of terror rose from his men. A demon, he told himself. It had to be a demon! But there was something in that stern face. Something in the set of that firm mouth. Could it be the heretics were—?

He slashed the thought off, wavering on the brink of flight. If he so much as stepped back his company would vanish, but he was only a man! How—?

"God preserve us!"

He wheeled at the whispered prayer and gasped in relief. He reached out, heedless of discourtesy in his fear, and shook Father Uriad.

"What is it, Father?" he demanded. "In the name of God, *what is it?*"

"I—" Uriad began, and then the apparition spoke.

"Warriors of Mother Church!"

Stomald gasped, for the rolling thunder of that voice was ten times louder than in Cragsend—a hundred times! All about him men fell to their knees, clapping their hands over their ears as its majesty crashed through them. Surely the very cliffs themselves must fall before its power!

"Warriors of Mother Church," the angel cried, "turn from this madness! These are not your enemies—they are your brothers! Has Pardal not seen enough blood? Must you turn against the innocent to shed still more?"

The giant figure took one stride forward—a single stride that covered twenty mortal paces—and bent towards the terrified Temple Guard. Sadness touched those stern features, and one huge hand rose pleadingly.

"Look into your hearts, warriors of Mother Church," the sweet voice thundered. "Look into your souls. Will you stain your hands before man and God with the blood of innocent babes and women?"

"Demon!" Father Uriad cried as men turned to him in terror. "I tell you, it's a demon!"

"But—" someone began, and the priest rounded on him in a frenzy.

"Fool! Will you lose your own soul, as well? This is no angel! It is a demon from Hell itself!"

The Guardsmen wavered, and Uriad snatched a musket from a sentry. The man gawked at him, and he charged forward, evading the hands that clutched at him, to face the monster shape alone.

"Demon!" His shrill cry sounded thin and thready after that majestic voice. "Damned and accursed devil! Foul, unclean destroyer of innocence! I cast you out! Begone to the Hell from whence you came!"

The Temple Guard gaped, appalled yet mesmerized by his courage, and the towering shape looked down at him.

"Would you slay your own flock, Priest?" The vast voice was gentle, and clergymen in both armies gasped as it spoke the Holy Tongue. But Uriad was a man above himself, and he threw the musket to his shoulder.

"Begone, curse you!" he screamed, and the musket cracked and flashed.

"That tears it," Sean muttered, jockeying the fighter as Sandy's holo image straightened. "Why the hell couldn't they just *run?* Got lock, Tam?"

"Yeah. Jesus, I hope that idiot isn't as close as I think he is!"

"Priest," the contralto voice rolled like stern, sweet thunder, "you will not lead these men to their own damnation."

Upper-Priest Uriad stared up, clutching his musket. Powder smoke clawed at his nostrils, but the ball had left its target unmarked and terror pierced the armor of his rage. He trembled, yet if he fled his entire army would do the same, and he pried one clawed hand from the musket stock. He scrabbled at his breast, raising his starburst, and it flashed in his hand, lit by the radiance streaming from the apparition as her own hand pointed at the earth before her.

"These innocents are under my protection, Priest. I

have no wish for any to die, but if die someone must, it will not be they!"

A brilliant ray of light speared from her massive finger.

Tamman tightened as the fighter's main battery locked onto the laser designator within that beam. He took one more second, making himself double-check his readings. God, it was going to be close. They'd never counted on some idiot being gutsy enough to come to *meet* Sandy's holo image!

The ray of light touched the ground, and twenty thousand voices cried out in terror as a massive trench scored itself across the valley, wider than a tall man's height and thrice as deep. Dirt and dust vomited upward as the very bedrock exploded, and Father Uriad flew backward like a toy.

The raw smell of rock dust choked nose and throat, and it was too much. The Guardsmen screamed and turned as one. Sentries cast aside weapons. Artillerists abandoned their guns. Cooks threw down their ladles. Anything that might slow a man was hurled away, and the Temple Guard of Malagor stampeded into the night in howling madness.

The ray of light died, and the blue-and-gold shape turned from the shattered hosts of Mother Church to face Father Stomald's people.

The young priest drove himself to his feet, standing atop the rampart to face the angel he'd tried to slay, and the burning splendor of her eyes swept over him. He felt his followers' fear against his back, yet awe and reverence held them in their places, and the angel smiled gently.

"I will come among you," she told them, "in a form less frightening. Await me."

And the majestic shape of light and glory vanished.

Chapter Twenty-Five

Father Stomald sat down to the supper on the camp table with a groan. He hadn't expected to be alive to eat it, and he was tired enough to wonder if it was worth the bother. Just organizing the unexpected booty abandoned by the Guard had been exhausting, yet Tibold was right. The dispersal of one army was no guarantee of victory, and those weapons were priceless. Besides, the Guard might regain enough courage to reclaim them if they weren't collected.

But at least deciding what to do with pikes and muskets was fairly simple. Other problems were less so—like the more than four thousand Guardsmen who'd trickled back and begged to join "the Angels' Army" as wonder overcame terror. Stomald had welcomed them, but Tibold insisted no newcomer, however welcome, be accepted unquestioningly. It was only a matter of time before the Church attempted to infiltrate spies in the guise of converts, and he preferred to establish the rules now.

Stomald saw his point, but discussing what to do had taken hours. For now, Tibold had four thousand new laborers; as they proved their sincerity, they would be integrated into his units—with, Tibold had observed dryly, non-Guardsmen on either side to help suppress any temptation to treason.

Yet all such questions, while important and real, had been secondary to most of Stomald's people. God's own messengers had intervened for them, and if Malagorans were too pragmatic to let joy interfere with tasks they knew must be performed, they went about those tasks with spontaneous hymns. And Stomald, as shepherd of a vaster flock than he'd ever anticipated, had been deeply involved in planning and leading the solemn services of thanksgiving which had both begun and closed this long, exhausting day.

All of which meant he'd had little enough time to breathe, much less eat.

Now he mopped up the last of the shemaq stew and slumped on his camp stool with a sigh. He could hear the noises of the camp, but his tent stood on a small rise, isolated from the others by the traditional privacy of the clergy. That isolation bothered him, yet the ability to think and pray uninterrupted was a priceless treasure whose value to a leader he was coming to appreciate.

He raised his head, gazing past the tied-back flap at the staff-hung lantern just outside. More lanterns and torches twinkled in the narrow valley below him, and he heard the lowing of the hundreds of nioharqs the Guard had abandoned. There were fewer branahlks—the speedy saddle beasts had been in high demand as the Church's warriors fled—but the nioharqs, more than man-high at the shoulder, would be invaluable when it came to moving their camp. And—

His thoughts chopped off, and he lunged to his feet as the air before him suddenly wavered like heat above a flame. Then it solidified, and he gazed upon the angel who had saved his people.

Sean and Tamman waited outside the tent inside their portable stealth fields. The trip across the camp had been . . . interesting, since people don't avoid things they can't see. Sandy had almost been squashed by a freight wagon, and her expression as she nipped aside had been priceless.

Sean had planned to get this over with last night, but the totality of the Guard's rout—and the treasure-trove of its abandoned camp—had changed his schedule. One thing Stomald hadn't needed while he organized that windfall was the intrusion of still more miracles. Besides, the delay had given Sean time to watch the "heretics" work, and he'd been deeply impressed by Stomald's military commander. That man was a professional to his toenails, and a soldier of his caliber was going to be invaluable.

But that was for the future, and right now he tried not to laugh at the priest's expression when Sandy suddenly materialized in front of him.

Stomald's jaw dropped, and then he fell to his knees before the angel. He signed God's starburst while his own inadequacy suffused him, coupled with a soaring joy that, inadequate as he was, God had seen fit to touch him with His Finger, and held his breath as he awaited some sign of her will.

"Stand up, Stomald," a soft voice said in the Holy Tongue. He stared at the floor of his tent, then rose tremblingly. "Look at me," the angel said, and he raised his eyes to her face. "That's better."

The angel crossed his tent and sat in one of his camp chairs, and he watched her in silence. She moved with easy grace, and she was even smaller than he'd thought on that terrible night. Her head was little higher than his shoulder when she stood, but there was nothing fragile about her tiny form.

Brown hair gleamed under the lantern light, cut short as a man's but in an indefinably feminine style. Her clean-cut mouth was firm, yet he felt oddly certain those lips were meant to smile. Her triangular face was built of huge eyes, high cheekbones, and a determined chin that lacked the beauty of the angel Tibold's huntsmen had wounded yet radiated strength and purpose.

She returned his gaze calmly, and he cleared his throat and fiddled with his starburst, trying to think. But what did a man *say* to God's messenger? Good evening? How are you? Do you think it will rain?

He had no idea, and the angel's eyes twinkled. Yet it was a kindly twinkle, and she took pity on his tongue-tied silence.

"I said I would visit you." Her voice was deep for a woman's, but without the thunder of her wrath it was sweet and soft, and his pulse slowed.

"You honor us, Holiness," he managed, and the angel shook her head.

" 'Holiness' is a priestly title, and I am but a visitor from a distant land."

"Then . . . then by what title shall I address you?"

"None," she said simply, "but my name is Sandy."

Stomald's heart leapt as she bestowed her name upon him, for it was a new name, unlike any he'd ever heard.

"As you command," he murmured with a bow, and she frowned.

"I'm not here to command you, Stomald." He flinched, afraid he'd angered her, and she shook her head as she saw his fear.

"Things have gone awry," she told him. "It was no part of our purpose to embroil your people in holy war against the Church. It was ill-done of us to endanger your land and lives."

Stomald bit down on a need to reject her self-accusation. She was God's envoy; she could not do ill. Yet, he reminded himself, angels were but God's servants, not gods themselves, and so, perhaps, they *could* err. The novel thought was disturbing, but her tone told him it was true.

"We did more ill than you," he said humbly. "We wounded your fellow angel and laid impious, violent hands upon her. That God should send you to us once more to save us from His own Church when we have done such wrong is a greater mercy than any mortals can deserve, O Sandy."

Sandy grimaced. She'd intended to leave angels entirely out of this if she could, but Pardalians, like Terrans, had more than one word for "angel." *Sha'hia*, the most common, was derived from the Imperial Universal for "messenger," just as the English word descended from the Greek for the same thing. Unfortunately, there was another, derived from the word for "visitor"—from,

in fact, *erathiu*, the very word she'd just let herself use—
and her slip hadn't escaped Stomald. He had been using
sha'hia; now he was using *erathu*, and if she corrected
him, he would only assume he'd mispronounced it.
Explaining what *she* meant by "visitor" would get into
areas so far beyond his worldview that any attempt to
discuss them was guaranteed to produce a crisis of conscience, and she bit her lip, then shrugged. Harry was
right about the care they had to take, but Harry was just
going to have to accept the best she could do.

"You did only what you thought was required," she said
carefully, "and neither I nor Harry herself hold it against
you."

"Then . . . then she lived?" Stomald's face blossomed
in relief, and Sandy reminded herself that Pardalian
angels could be killed.

"She did. Yet what brings me here is the danger in
which your people stand, Stomald. We have our own purpose to achieve, but in seeking to achieve it we put you
in peril of your lives. If we could, we would undo what
we've done, yet that lies beyond our power."

Stomald nodded. Holy Writ said angels were powerful beings, but Man had free will. His actions could set
even an angel's purpose at naught, and he flushed in
shame as he realized his flock had done just that. Yet the
Angel Sandy wasn't enraged; she'd saved them, and the
genuine concern in her soft voice filled his heart with
gratitude.

"Because we can't undo it," Sandy continued, "we must
begin from what has happened. It may be we can com-
bine our purpose with our responsibility to save your
people from the consequences of our own errors, yet
there are limits to what we may do. Last night, we had
no choice but to intervene as we did, but we can't do
so again. Our purpose forbids it."

Stomald swallowed. With Mother Church against
them, how could they hope to survive without such aid?
She saw his fear and smiled gently.

"I didn't say we can't intervene at all, Stomald—only

that there are limits on how we may do so. We will aid you, but you must know that the Inner Circle will never rest until you've been destroyed. You threaten both their beliefs and their secular power over Malagor, and your threat is greater, not less, now, for word of what happened last night will spread on talmahk wings.

"Because of that, fresh armies will soon move against you, and I tell you that our purpose is not to see you die. We seek no martyrs. Death comes to all men, but we believe the purpose of Man is to help his fellows, not to kill them in God's name. Do you understand that?"

"I do," Stomald whispered. That was all he'd ever asked to do, and to be told by an angel that it was God's will—!

"Good," the angel murmured, then straightened in her chair, and her mouth turned firmer, her eyes darker. "Yet when others attack you, you have every right to fight back, and in this we will help you, if you wish. The choice is yours. We won't force you to accept our aid or our advice."

"Please." Stomald's hands half-rose, and he fought an urge to throw himself back to his knees. "Please, aid my people, I beg you."

"There is no need to beg." The angel regarded him sternly. "What we can do, we will do, but as friends and allies, not dictators."

"I—" Stomald swallowed again. "Forgive me, O Sandy. I am only a simple under-priest, unused to any of the things happening to me." His lips quirked despite his tension, for it was hard not to smile when her eyes were so understanding. "I doubt even High Priest Vroxhan would know what to say or do when confronted by an angel in his tent!" he heard himself say, and quailed, but the angel only smiled. She had dimples, he noted, and his spirits rose before her humor.

"No, I doubt he would," she agreed, a gurgle of laughter hovering in her soft voice, and then she shook herself.

"Very well, Stomald. Simply understand that we neither

desire nor need your worship. Ask what you will of us, as you might ask any other man. If we can do it, we will; if we can't, we'll tell you so, and we won't hold your asking against you. Can you do that?"

"I can try," he agreed with greater confidence. It was hard to be frightened of one who so obviously meant him and his people well.

"Then let me tell you what we can do, since I've told you what we cannot. We can aid and advise you, and there are many things we can teach you. We can tell you much of what passes elsewhere, though not all, and while we can't slay your enemies with our own weapons, we can help you fight for your lives with your own if you choose to do so. Do you so choose?"

"We do." Stomald straightened. "We did no wrong, yet Mother Church came against us in Holy War. If such is her decision, we will defend ourselves against her as we must."

"Even knowing both you and the Inner Circle cannot survive? One of you must fall, Stomald. Are you prepared to assume that responsibility?"

"I am," he said even more firmly. "A shepherd may die for his flock, but his duty is to preserve that flock, not slay it. Mother Church herself teaches that. If the Inner Circle has forgotten, it must be taught anew."

"I think you are as wise as you are courageous, Stomald of Cragsend," she said, "and since you will protect your people, I bring you those to help you fight." She raised her hand, and Stomald gasped as the air shimmered once more and two more strangers appeared out of it.

One was scarcely taller than Stomald himself, square-shouldered and muscular in his night-black armor. His hair and eyes were as brown as the angel's, though his skin was much darker, and his hair was even shorter. A high-combed helmet rode in his bent elbow, and a long, slender sword hung at his side. He looked tough and competent, yet he might have been any mortal man.

But the other! This was a giant, towering above Stomald and his own companion. He wore matching armor and carried the same slender sword, but his eyes were black as midnight and his hair was darker still. He was far from handsome—indeed, his prominent nose and ears were almost ugly—but he met the priest's eyes with neither arrogance nor inner doubt . . . much, Stomald thought, as Tibold might have but for his automatic deference to the cloth.

"Stomald, these are my champions," the angel said quietly. "This—" she touched the shorter man's shoulder "—is Tamman Tammanson, and this—" she touched the towering giant, and her eyes seemed to soften for a moment "—is Sean Colinson. Will you have them as war captains?"

"I . . . would be honored," Stomald said, grappling with a fresh sense of awe. They weren't angels, for they were male, but something about them, something more even than their sudden appearance, whispered they were more than mortal, like the legendary heroes of the old tales.

"I thank you for your trust," Sean Colinson—and what sort of name was that?—said. His voice was deep, but he spoke accented Pardalian, not the Holy Tongue, as he offered a huge right hand. "As Sandy says, your destiny is your own, but your danger is none of your making. If I can help, I will."

"And I." Tamman Tammanson stood a half-pace behind his companion, like a shieldman or an under-captain, but his voice was equally firm.

"And now, Stomald," the Angel Sandy said in the Holy Tongue, "it may be time to summon Tibold. We have much to discuss."

Tibold Rarikson sat in his camp chair and felt his head turning back and forth like an untutored yokel. He'd found his eyes had a distinct tendency to jerk away from the Angel Harry's beautiful face whenever she glanced his way, and it shamed him. She hadn't said a word to condemn him for shooting her down, and he was grateful for her understanding, yet somehow he suspected he would have felt better if she'd been less so.

But it wasn't just guilt which kept pulling his gaze from her, for he'd never imagined meeting with such a group. The man the angels called Sean was a giant among men, and the one called Tamman had skin the color of old jelath wood, yet the angels automatically drew the eye from their champions. The Angel Harry might be shorter than Lord Sean, but she was a head taller than most men, and despite her blind eye, she seemed to look deep inside a man's soul every time her remaining eye met his. Yet for all that, it seemed odd to see her in trousers, even those of the priestly raiment she wore. She should have been in the long, bright skirts of a Malagoran woman, not men's garb, for despite her height and seeming youth, she radiated a gentle compassion which made one trust her instantly.

And then there was the Angel Sandy. Even on this short an acquaintance, Tibold suspected no one was likely to imagine *her* in skirts! Her brown eyes glowed with the resolution of a seasoned war captain, her words were crisp and incisive, and *she* radiated the barely leashed energy of a hunting seldahk.

". . . so as you and the Angel Sandy say—" Stomald was saying in response to Lord Sean's last comment when the angel leaned forward with a frown.

"Don't call us that," she said. Tibold had spent enough years in the Temple's service to gain a rough understanding of the Holy Tongue, but he'd never heard an accent quite like hers. Not that he needed to have heard it before to recognize its note of command.

Stomald sat back in his own chair with a puzzled expression, looking at Tibold, then turned back to the angel. His confusion was evident, and it showed in his voice when he spoke again.

"I meant no offense," he said humbly, and the angel bit her lip. She glanced at the Angel Harry, whose single good eye returned her look levelly, almost as if in command, then sighed.

"I'm not offended, Stomald," she said carefully, "but there are . . . reasons Harry and I wish you would avoid that title."

"Reasons?" Stomald repeated hesitantly, and she shook her head.

"In time, you'll understand them, Stomald. I promise. But for now, please humor us in this."

"As you comm—" Stomald began, then stopped and corrected himself. "As you wish, Lady Sandy," he said, and glanced at Tibold once more. The ex-Guardsman shrugged slightly. As far as he was concerned, an angel could be called whatever she wished. Labels meant nothing, and any village idiot could tell what the angels *were*, however they cared to be *addressed*.

"As *Lady* Sandy says," Stomald continued after a moment, "the first step must be to consolidate our own position. The weapons the Guard abandoned will help there—" he glanced at Tibold, who nodded vigorously "—but you're correct, Lord Sean. We cannot stand passively on the defensive. I am no war captain, yet it seems to me that we must secure control of the Keldark Valley as soon as possible."

"Exactly," Lord Sean said in his deep, accented voice. "There are a lot of things Tamman and I can teach your army, Tibold, but we can't make the Temple stand still while we do it. We've got to secure control of the valley—and the Thirgan Gap—quickly enough to discourage the Guard from anything adventurous."

"Agreed, Lord Sean," Tibold said. "If the An—" He paused with a blush. "If *Lady* Sandy and Lady Harry can provide us with the information on enemy movements you've described, we'll have a tremendous advantage, but too many of our men have little or no experience. They'll need good, hard drilling, and if we can do it in a strong enough defensive position, the Guard may leave us alone long enough to do some good."

"Very well, then," Stomald said firmly. "We will be guided by you and the An—you and the Lady Sandy and Lady Harry, Lord Sean. Tomorrow morning, Tibold and I will introduce you to our army as its new commander, and we will act as you direct."

✧   ✧   ✧

High Priest Vroxhan sat behind his desk and glared at Bishop Frenaur and Lord Marshal Rokas. Neither quite met his fiery eyes, and he growled something under his breath, then inhaled deeply and managed—somehow, out of a lifetime of clerical discipline—to still his need to curse at them.

"Very well," he grated, placing one hand on the message upon his blotter, "I want to know how this happened."

Frenaur cleared his throat. He hadn't visited Malagor in half a year, but he'd read the semaphore messages to Vroxhan and additional, personal ones from Under-Bishop Shendar in Malgos, the Malagoran capital. He wasn't certain he believed what they reported, but if even a tenth of them were true. . . .

"Holiness, I'm not certain," he said at last. "Father Uriad led the Guard against the heretics as the Circle directed, and for almost a moon he met with total success. There was no resistance until they reached the northern Shalokars and the heretics fortified a pass. He moved against them and—" He broke off and shrugged helplessly. "Holiness, the Guardsmen who fled all insist they saw *something*, and their descriptions certainly tally with the heretic Stomald's descriptions of his 'angels.' "

"*Angels?*" Vroxhan spat. "*Angels* who kill a consecrated priest?"

"I didn't say it *was* an angel, Holiness." Frenaur managed not to retreat. "I said it matched Stomald's descriptions. And whatever it was, it protected the heretics with powers which were far more than mortal."

"Assuming the cowards who fled aren't lying in fear of Mother Church's wrath," Vroxhan snarled, and Marshal Rokas stirred at Frenaur's side.

"Holiness," the grizzled veteran's rough voice was deferential but unafraid, "Captain-General Yorkan reports the same thing. I know Yorkan. I would know if his report was an attempt to cover himself." The grim old warrior met his master's eyes, and Vroxhan glowered for a moment, then sighed.

"Very well," he said heavily, "I must accept their story when all of them agree. But whatever that . . . *thing* was, it was no angel! We didn't come through the Trial only to have angels suddenly appear to tell us we all stand in doctrinal error! If that were the case, the Voice wouldn't have saved us."

Frenaur bit his tongue. Wisdom suggested this was no time to mention the irregularity of the Trial's liturgy. And, he thought unhappily, far less was it a time to point out that Stomald had never claimed his "angels" had said anything at all, much less condemned the Church for error. Besides, the mere fact that they'd had dealings with the Valley of the Damned proved they couldn't be angels . . . didn't it?

"Yet whatever happened, it's deprived us of over twenty thousand Guardsmen," Vroxhan continued grimly.

"It has, Holiness," Rokas agreed. "Worse, we've lost their equipment, as well. The heretics have gained their weapons, including their entire artillery train . . . and their position divides our strength."

Vroxhan looked like a man drinking sour milk, but he nodded. There might even have been a glimmer of respect in his eyes for Rokas' unflinching admission, and he pinched the bridge of his nose while he thought.

"In that case, Marshal," he said finally, "we shall just have to call forth a greater host. There can be no compromise with the heretical—especially not when they now possess such strength of arms." He turned cold eyes upon Frenaur. "How widely has this heresy spread?"

"Widely," Frenaur confessed. "Before . . . whatever happened, there were only some few thousand, mostly peasant villagers from the Shalokars. Now word of the 'miracle' is spreading like wildfire. It's even reached beyond the Thirgan Gap to Vral. God only knows how many people have flocked to Stomald's standard by now, but the signs are bad. Messages indicate entire villages are streaming north to join 'the Army of the Angels.' "

Vroxhan scowled at him for a moment, then shrugged. "I know it's not your fault." He sighed, and the bishop relaxed. "You're simply in range of my ill humor and fear." His mouth tightened. "And I *am* afraid, Brothers. Malagor has always been prone to schism, and this comes too close upon the Trial. The vile powers of the valley have awakened to the defeat of the Greater Demons. Perhaps still more of the unclean star spawn wait to smite us—the Writ says there are many Demons—and they use these lesser evil spirits to divide us before they assail us yet again."

He brooded down at his desk, then straightened his shoulders.

"Lord Marshal, you will summon the Great Host of Mother Church to Holy War." Rokas bowed, and Frenaur bit his lip. The full Host had not been summoned since the Schismatic Wars themselves. "But we must prepare our men to withstand demonic deceit before we offer battle," Vroxhan continued heavily, "and I fear much of Malagor will go over to the heretics before we are ready."

He looked up at Frenaur's unhappy face, and his angry eyes softened.

"The same would be true anywhere, Frenaur. The common folk are ill-equipped to judge such matters, and when their own priests lead them astray it's hardly their fault that they believe. Yet be that as it may, those who embrace heresy must pay heresy's price." He returned his eyes to the marshal. "I do not yet wish to summon the secular lords to your banner, Rokas, but even if we rely solely on the Guard, we must first send priests among them, preaching the truth of what's happened lest we lose still more troops to panic and spiritual seduction. Do you agree?"

"I do, Holiness, but I must urge caution lest we delay overlong."

"What do you mean, 'overlong'?"

"Holiness, Malagor has always been difficult to invade, and its position divides our forces. Worse, my own reports indicate the heretics are as inflamed by what they see as foreign control as by whatever other seeds the demons may have sown."

Rokas watched Vroxhan with care and was relieved

when the high priest gave a slow nod. Before the Schismatic Wars, Malagor had been strong enough to give even Mother Church pause. Indeed, the traditional Malagoran restlessness under the Tenets' restrictions had helped fuel the Great Schism, and the Inner Circle of the time, already engaged upon a life-or-death struggle with the Schismatics, had used the wars to break the princedom. Prince Uroba, Malagor's present "ruler," was the Temple's pensioner—a drunkard sustained in power not by birth or merit but by the pikes of the Guard—and his people knew it.

"Our forces west of Malagor are weak," Rokas went on. "We have perhaps forty thousand Guardsmen in Doras, Kyhyra, Cherist, and Showmah, but less than five thousand in Sardua and Thirgan, and the heresy has spread more quickly to the west than to the east. Indeed, I fear the Guard's strength may be hard pressed to prevent more of the common folk from joining the heresy in those regions. More, the semaphore chains across Malagor will soon fall into heretic hands, depriving us of direct communications. We will have to send messages by semaphore to Arwah and thence by ship to Darwan for relay through Alwa via the Qwelth Gap chain. Such a delay will make it all but impossible to coordinate closely between our forces east and west of Malagor."

He paused until Vroxhan nodded once more, then went on in measured tones.

"The Guard's total strength west of Malagor is, as I say, perhaps forty-five to fifty thousand. Here in the east, the Temple can summon five times that many Guardsmen if we strip our garrisons to the bone. For more than that, we would require a general levy, yet, as you, I prefer not to rely upon the secular lords' troops—not, at least, until we've won at least one victory and so proved these 'angels' are, in fact, demons."

He paused again, and again Vroxhan nodded, this time impatiently.

"The only practical routes for armies into or out of Malagor are the Thirgan Gap and the Keldark Valley. The gap is broader, but its approaches are dotted with powerful fortresses which the heretics may well secure before we can move. Given those facts and our weakness in the west, I would recommend massing the western Guard south of the Cherist Mountains around Vral. In that position, they can both seal the Thirgan Gap and maintain civil control."

Rokas began to pace, tugging at his jaw as he marshaled words like companies of pikes.

"Our major strength lies in the east, and with the gap secured we may concentrate in Keldark, using the Guardsmen of Keldark to block the valley against heretical sorties until we're ready. The valley is bad terrain and even narrower than the gap, but most of its fortresses were razed after the Schismatic Wars. There are perhaps three places the heretics might choose to stand: Yortown, Erastor, and Baricon. All are powerful defensive positions; the cost of taking any of them will be high."

He made a wry face. "There won't be much strategy involved until we actually break into Malagor, Holiness, not with such limited approach routes, but the same applies to the heretics. And, unlike us, they must equip and train their forces. If we strike quickly, we may well clear the entire valley before they can prepare."

"I agree," Vroxhan said after a moment's thought. "And it will, indeed, be best to move from the east. If they *can* strike before we prepare, they'll move east, directly for the Temple."

"That was my own thought," Rokas agreed.

"In the meantime," Vroxhan returned to Frenaur, "I see no choice but to place Malagor under Interdict. Please see to the proclamation."

"I will," Frenaur agreed unhappily. What must be must be.

"Understand me, Brothers," Vroxhan said very quietly. "There will be no compromise with heresy. Mother Church's sword has been drawn; it will not be sheathed while a single heretic lives."

Chapter Twenty-Six

Robert Stevens—no longer "the Reverend"—watched the broadcast with hating eyes. Bishop Francine Hilgemann stared out over her congregation from a carven pulpit, and her soft, clear voice was passionate.

"Brothers and sisters, violence is no answer to fear. Perhaps some souls *are* mistaken, but the Church cannot and will not condone those who defy a loving God's will by striking out in unreasoning hatred. God's people do not stain their hands with blood, nor is it fitting that the death of any human should be wreaked in anger. Those who style themselves 'The Sword of God' are not His servants, but destroyers of all He teaches, and their—"

Stevens snarled and killed the HD, sickened that he'd once respected that . . . that— He couldn't think of a foul enough word.

He paced slowly, and his eyes warmed with an ugly light. Disgust and revulsion had driven him from the Church, but Hilgemann and those like her could never weaken God's Sword. Their corruption only filled the true faithful with determination, and the Sword struck deeper every day.

As he had struck. The most terrifying—and satisfying—day of his life had been the one in which he realized why his cell had been sent against Vincente Cruz. The deaths of Cruz's wife and children had bothered some of his people, yet God's work required sacrifices, and if innocents perished, God would receive them as the martyrs they'd become. But that he had been the instrument which destroyed the heirs—heirs so corrupt

they'd claimed a Narhani as a *friend*—had filled Stevens
with exaltation.

There'd been other missions, but none so satisfying as
that . . . or as the one he now looked forward to. It was
time Francine Hilgemann learned God's true chosen
rejected her self-damning compromises with the Anti-
Christ.

Sergeant Graywolf was calm-eyed and relaxed, for he
knew how to wait. Especially when he awaited something
so satisfying.

He didn't know how the analysts had developed the
intel. From the briefing, he suspected they'd intercepted
a courier, but all that mattered was that they knew. With
luck, they might even take one of the bastards alive.
Daniel Graywolf was a professional, and he knew how
valuable that could be . . . yet deep down inside, he
hoped they wouldn't be quite *that* lucky.

Stevens gave thanks for the rainy night. Its wet blackness wouldn't bother Imperial surveillance systems, but
the people behind those systems were only human. The
dreary winter rain would have its effect where it mattered, dulling and slowing their minds.

Alice Hughes and Tom Mason walked arm-in-arm
behind him like lovers, weapons hidden by their rain-
coats. Stevens carried his own weapon in a shoulder holster: an old-style automatic with ten-millimeter "slugs"
of the same explosive used in grav guns. He didn't see
Yance or Pete, but they'd close in at the proper moment.
He knew that, just as he knew Wanda Curry would bring
their escape flyer in at precisely the right second. They'd
practiced the operation for days, and their timing was
exact.

His pulse ticked faster as he reached the high-rise. It
was of Pre-Siege construction, but it had been modern-
ized, and he paused under the force field roof protecting
the front entrance. He wiped rain from his face with just
the right gratitude for the respite while Alice and Tom

closed up on his heels, and the corner of his eye saw
Yance and Pete arriving from the opposite direction. The
five of them came together by obvious coincidence, and
then all of them turned and stepped through the
entrance as one.

There were no security personnel in the lobby, only
the automated systems he'd been briefed upon, and he
paused in the entry, head bent to hide his features,
shielding Yance and Pete as they reached under their
coats. Then he stepped aside, and their suppressors rose
with practiced precision and burned each scan point into
useless junk with pulses of focused energy.

Stevens grunted, jerked the ski mask over his face, and
snatched out his own weapon, and the well-drilled quin-
tet raced for the transit shafts.

Graywolf stiffened at the implant signal. Clumsy, he
thought with a hungry smile. Obviously their information had been less complete than they'd thought, for
they'd missed three separate sensors.

Nine more Security Ministry agents stood as one
behind nine closed doors as Graywolf cradled his hyper
rifle and moved to the window.

Stevens led his followers from the transit shaft, and
they spread out behind him, hugging the walls, weapons poised. His own eyes were fixed on the door at the
end of the corridor, yet his attention roamed all about
him, acute as a panther's after so many months at the
guerrilla's trade.

They were half way down the hall when nine doors
opened as one.

"Lay down your weapons!" a voice shouted. "You're
all under arr—"

Stevens spun like a cat. He heard Yance's enraged
bellow even as he tried to line up on the uniformed
woman in the doorway, but his people's reactions didn't
match their murderousness, for none were enhanced. His
barking automatic blasted a chunk from the wall beside

the door, and then a hurricane of grav gun darts blew all five terrorists into bloody meat.

Graywolf heard the thunder and shrugged. They'd had their chance.

He held his own position and watched the getaway flyer slide to a neat halt. It was right on the tick, and he aligned his hyper rifle on the drive housing before he triggered his com.

"Land and step out of the flyer!" he told the pilot.

There was a split-second pause, and then the flyer leapt ahead with blinding acceleration. But unlike Stevens' killers, Graywolf *was* fully enhanced, and the exploding flyer gouged a fifty-meter trench in the street below as its drive unit vanished into hyper-space.

Lawrence Jefferson completed his report with profound satisfaction.

He'd never really been happy about penetrating security on Birhat. The distance was too great, and any communication with agents there was vulnerable to interception. But that was no longer necessary; his plans had matured to a point at which it no longer mattered what the military did, and he controlled *Earth's* security forces from his own office.

His lips pursed as he considered his intertwining strategies. His latest ploy should remove Francine from any suspicion. She'd openly become the Church of the Armageddon's leader, but as one who denounced the Sword of God's fanaticism. Her masterful pleas for nonviolence only underscored the Sword's growing ferocity, yet *she* was emerging as a moderate, and Horus and Ninhursag were obligingly accepting his own "astonished" conclusion that she was someone they could work with against the radicals.

Now his security forces' defeat of the Sword's attempt on her life would make her whiter than snow. He'd wondered if he was being too clever, for it would never have done for any of Stevens' people to be taken alive and disclose the truth about *Imperial Terra*, but he'd chosen his agents with care. All were utterly loyal to the Imperium . . . but each had lost friends or family to the Sword. He was certain they'd tried to take the terrorists alive—and equally certain they hadn't tried any harder than they had to. And, of course, he'd known he could trust Stevens' fanatics to resist.

He was just as happy to have that loose end tied, for Ninhursag's decision to flood Earth with ONI agents worried him, especially since he didn't know why she was doing it. Her official explanation *might* be the truth, for reinforcing Earth Security and opening a double offensive against the Sword made sense. He didn't like it, but it did make sense. Yet he wasn't quite convinced that was her real motive. At first he'd been afraid she was somehow onto him, but five months had passed since she'd started, and if he had, indeed, been her objective, he'd be in custody by now.

Whatever she was up to, it enforced greater circumspection upon him. Since taking over from Gus, Jefferson had found it expedient to make adjustments in certain background investigations, culling his own cadre of fully-enhanced personnel from the Ministry of Security itself. It was so convenient to have the government enhance his people for him, but Ninhursag's swarm of busybodies had forced a temporary shutdown in such activities.

Not that it worried him too much. His plans were in place, centered upon the crown jewels of his subversions: Brigadier Alex Jourdain and Lieutenant Carl Bergren. Jourdain's high position in Earth Security made him invaluable as Jefferson's senior field man and cutout, but Bergren was even more important. That lowly officer was the key, for he was a greedy young man with expensive habits. How Battle Fleet had ever let him into uniform, much less placed him in such a sensitive position, passed Jefferson's understanding, but he supposed even the best screening processes had to fail occasionally. He himself had stumbled upon Bergren almost by accident, and he'd taken pains to conceal Bergren's . . . indiscretions, for thanks to Lieutenant Bergren, Admiral Ninhursag Mac-Mahan had just over five months to do whatever she was doing before she died.

Senior Fleet Captain Antonio Tattiaglia looked up in surprise, trowel in hand and his newest rose bush half-planted, as Brigadier Hofstader entered his atrium. Hofstader was a small, severe woman, always immaculate in her black-and-silver Marine uniform, and this hasty intrusion was most unlike her.

"Yes, Erika?"

"Sorry to bother you, Sir, but something's come up."

Tattiaglia hid a sigh. Hofstader had commanded *Lancelot*'s Marines for over a year, and she still sounded as if she were on a parade ground. The woman was almost oppressively competent, but he couldn't warm to her.

"What is it?"

"I believe we've just detected a Sword of God strike force en route to its target, Sir," she said crisply, and he forgot all about her manner.

"Are you *serious?*"

"Yes, Sir. The scanner tech of the watch—Scan Tech Bateman—decided to run an atmospheric-target tracking exercise, in the course of which she detected three commercial conveyors with inoperable transponders executing a nape-of-the-earth approach to the Shenandoah Power Reception Facility."

Hofstader had her expression well in hand, but excitement was burning through her professionalism for the first time since he'd known her.

"Have you alerted Earth Security?" he demanded, already trotting towards the transit shaft.

"No, Sir. Fleet Captain Reynaud informed ONI." She moved briskly at his side, and her smile was cold. "ONI has requested that *we* investigate."

"Hot damn," Tattiaglia whispered. They stepped into the shaft and it hurled them towards *Lancelot*'s bridge. "Do we have something in position?"

"Sir, I alerted my ready duty platoon as soon as Bateman reported the conveyors. They'll enter atmosphere in approximately—" she paused to consult her internal chronometer "—seventy-eight seconds."

"Good work, Brigadier. Very good work!" The shaft deposited them outside the planetoid's bridge, and Tattiaglia rubbed his mental hands in glee as he raced for the command hatch.

"Thank you, Sir."

Captain Tattiaglia arrived on his bridge just as Hofstader's assault shuttle entered atmosphere at eleven times the speed of sound. A corner of the command deck display altered silently, showing them what the shuttle pilot was seeing, and the captain dropped into his command couch with hungry eyes.

"Listen up, people," Lieutenant Prescott said as his shuttle hurtled downward. "We don't *know* these're terrorists, so we ground, watch 'em, and get ready to move if they are, but nobody does squat unless I say so. Got it?" A chorus of assents came back. "Good. Now, if they *are* bad guys, ONI wants prisoners. We take some of 'em alive if we can—everybody got *that?*"

The fresh affirmatives were a bit disappointed, but he had other things to worry about as the shuttle grounded to disgorge his Marines, then swooshed back into the heavens in stealth to give air support if it was needed. Prescott didn't even watch it go; he was already maneuvering his troops into the hastily chosen positions he'd selected on the way in.

Three big conveyors ghosted to a landing in a patch of woods, and forty heavily armed people filed out with military precision. The raiders moved quietly towards the floodlit grounds of the Shenandoah Valley Power Receptor, then split, diverging towards two different security gates.

The commander of one attack party studied a passive scanner as he neared the perimeter fence, hunting security systems their briefing might have missed, then stiffened. He whirled, and his jaw dropped as his eyes confirmed his instrument's findings.

Well, they sure as hell aren't picnickers, Prescott thought as his armor scanners confirmed the intruders' heavy load of weapons, *and— Oh shit! So much for surprise!*

"Take 'em!"

The terrorist leader saw the armored shapes and tried to scream a warning, but a burst of fire splattered him across his troops halfway through the first syllable.

His followers gaped at the Marines, but they had weapons of their own and two of them were fully enhanced, and a Marine blew apart as the night exploded in a vicious firefight. An energy gun killed a second trooper, the whiplash of grav gun darts crackled everywhere, and a third Marine went down—wounded, not dead—but the Marines had combat armor, and the terrorists didn't.

Forty-one seconds after the first shot, three Marines were dead and five were wounded; none of the four terrorist survivors was unhurt.

Prescott waved his medics towards the casualties, then turned as the parked conveyors screamed upwards. They were still climbing frantically when *Lancelot*'s assault shuttle blew them apart from stealth.

Funny, I could've sworn I told Owens to challenge 'em before she shot. Prescott ran back over his conversation with his pilot. *Oops, guess not.*

"Friend," Fleet Lieutenant Esther Steinberg said, "I don't really care whether you talk to me or not. We've got three of your buddies, too, and one of you is going to tell me what I want to know."

"*Never!*" The young man cuffed to the chair under the lie detector looked far less defiant than he tried to sound. "None of us have anything to say to servants of the Anti-Christ!"

You're talking too much, friend. Got a little case of nerves here, do we? Good. Sweat, *you bastard!*

"Think not?" She crossed her arms. "Let me explain something. We caught you in the act, and you killed three Fleet Marines. Know what that means?" Her prisoner stared at her, sullen eyes frightened, and she smiled. "That means there's not gonna be any fooling around. You're gonna be tried and convicted so fast your head swims." The young man swallowed audibly. "I don't imagine your mama and papa'll be real pleased to see their itty-bitty son shot—and they will, 'cause every data channel's gonna carry it live. I'd guess you've seen one or two people catch it with grav guns, haven't you? Kinda messy, isn't it? I figure a half second burst ought to just about saw you in two, friend. Think your folks'll like that?"

"*You bitch!*" the prisoner screamed, and she smiled again—coldly.

"Sticks and stones, friend. Sticks and stones. I'll make sure I've got some spare time to watch, too."

"You—you—!" The prisoner writhed against his restraints, wounds forgotten, eyes mad, and Steinberg's laugh was a douche of ice-water.

"You seem a mite upset, friend. Too bad." She turned towards the hatch, then paused, listening to his incoherent, terrified rage and gauging his mood. *This boy's just about ripe.*

"Just one thing." He froze, glaring at her. "Talk to me, and ONI'll recommend leniency. You still won't like what happens, but you'll be alive." She smiled like a shark. "Only catch is, we only make the deal with *one* of you— and you've got ten seconds to decide if you're the lucky one."

"That," Fleet Captain Reynaud observed, "is one *nasty* lieutenant."

"She is, indeed," Tattiaglia murmured, watching the holo of the "interview" with his exec as the terrorist began to spill his guts, then glanced up at the captain from ONI. "I'm not going to shed any tears for the prisoners, but will any of this stand up in court?"

"Not in a *civilian* court, but it won't have to. His Majesty's invoked the Defense of the Imperium Act, and that gives military courts jurisdiction over prisoners captured by the military. Besides," the captain's grin was as sharklike as his lieutenant's, "we don't *need* any of it. Your boys and girls caught these jokers with enough physical evidence to shoot them all."

"Then what's the point?"

"The point, Captain Tattiaglia," the ONI officer said, switching off the holo and turning to *Lancelot's* CO, "is that I've got another little job for you. Among the other tidbits our gallant fanatic let slip is the location of his own cell's HQ—and Esther set a new personal record breaking that little prick. If we get a move on, we can hit them before they figure out their raiders aren't coming back."

"You mean—?"

"I mean, Captain, that twenty more terrorists are just sitting there waiting for you to drop a few Marines down their chimney."

"Oh boy," Tattiaglia whispered. "Oh boy, oh boy, oh *boy!* Now I *know* there's a God."

Fleet Admiral MacMahan's smile was wolfish as she studied the report. *That Lieutenant Steinberg is one sharp cookie. Have to do something nice for her in the next promotion list. And Tattiaglia's people deserve one hell of a pat on the back, too.*

She finished the report with a sigh of satisfaction. *Nice. Very nice. Jefferson's people swat an assassination attempt Tuesday, and we pick off an entire cell Thursday. Not a good week for the Sword of God.*

Of course, it hadn't gotten them any closer to Mister X, but she wasn't complaining. She punched up the holo record of the terrorist hideout and studied it. Steinberg had accompanied the Marines in and gotten every bit of the raid and its aftermath for her report, and Ninhursag whistled at the size of the terrorists' arsenal. There was a lot of Imperial weaponry in it, and she made a mental note to ask about the serial numbers. They hadn't had a lot of luck in that regard from Jefferson's occasional successes, but they had a lot more hardware this time, and all they really needed was one hard lead.

The holo record shifted to a view of the terrorist's main planning area. They seemed to have been well equipped with maps, too, and she frowned as she saw the precision with which some were marked. They even had a trophy room, she noted, grimacing at the wall-mounted displays. Stupid bastards. They'd collected bits and pieces from past raids as if they were counting coup! Well, it might help her people figure out which attacks this bunch had been responsible for, and—

Ninhursag MacMahan slammed the hold button and stood slowly, face pale as death, and walked into the holo to peer at one particular trophy. She licked her lips, trying to tell herself she was wrong, but she wasn't, and she whispered a soft, frightened prayer as she stared at her worst nightmare: a second-stage initiator from Tsien Tao-ling's super bomb.

The council room was quiet. Colin and Jiltanith sat between Gerald Hatcher and Tsien Tao-ling, and their faces were as pale as Ninhursag's own.

"Sweet Jesu," Jiltanith murmured at last. "Thy news is worse than e'er I durst let myself believe, 'Hursag, yet 'tis God's Own grace thou'st beagled out this threat."

"Amen to that." Colin frowned down at the tabletop. "Does this suggest a link between the Sword and Mister X?"

"I don't think so," Ninhursag said. "None of the survivors can tell us where that particular 'trophy' came from, but they're all souvenirs of attacks their cell carried out. I wish we *did* know where they got it; at least then we'd have some idea where to look for whoever has the thing. It's possible the Sword hit them before they finished it, but it wouldn't mean much if they did.

Whoever's behind this must've made more than one copy of the plans. Losing one construction team might slow them down; it wouldn't stop them."

"Lord." Colin pulled on his nose, and Ninhursag saw the lines months of worry had carved in his face. "Gerald? Tao-ling?"

" 'Hursag is correct," Tsien said. Hatcher only nodded, and Colin sighed.

"Okay, 'Hursag. Where do we go from here?"

"We start from a worst-case assumption. First, the thing's been built. Second, the people who *probably* have it killed eighty thousand people just to get the twins. Third—and scariest of all—the Sword may have captured it." A visible shudder ran through her audience at that thought.

"I think we're still fairly safe in assuming Earth isn't the target. I'm not going to cast that in stone, but I simply cannot conceive of anyone wanting to destroy the bulk of the human race. Certainly the Sword wouldn't; their whole purpose is to save the rest of humanity from us back-sliders and the Narhani. And there's not too much doubt Mister X is operating from Earth, which means he'd be blowing up his own base."

"Agreed." Colin pulled on his nose again, then looked at Hatcher. "Get hold of Adrienne, Hector, and Amanda. I want an evacuation plan for Birhat yesterday. We can't rehearse it without risking warning Mister X that we know he's got this thing, but we can at least get organized for it. I'll warn Brashieel's people personally. There's not much chance of a leak at their end, and there's still few enough Narhani we can pull them all out by mattrans if we have to."

The admiral nodded, and he turned back to Ninhursag, nodding for her to continue.

"While they do that," she said, "I intend to start an immediate high-priority search of Narhan and Birhat. Maker knows that bomb's a damnably small target, but Battle Fleet can carry out centimeter-by-centimeter scans without tipping Mister X. It'll take time, especially under a security blackout, but if it's out there, Gerald's and my people will find it."

She paused, and her dark eyes met her Emperor's.

"I only pray we find it in time," she said softly.

Chapter Twenty-Seven

Tibold Rarikson lay beside Lord Sean atop the cliff and watched his youthful commander pretend to use a spyglass.

The ex-Guardsman's bushy mustache hid his smile as the black-haired giant made a great show of adjusting the glass. Tibold didn't know why the Captain-General tried to hide his more-than-human abilities, but he was willing to play along, even though Lord Sean and Lord Tamman were probably the only people who thought they were fooling anyone.

In all his years, Tibold had never met anyone like these two. They were young; he'd seen enough hot-blooded young kinokha in his career to know that, and Lord Tamman was as impulsive as he was young. But Lord Sean . . . There was a youthful recklessness in his eyes, and a matching abundance of ideas behind them, but there was also discipline, and Tibold had known gray-bearded marshals less willing to listen to suggestions. And though he tried to hide it, Tibold had seen how his strange, black eyes warmed whenever the Angel Sandy was about. He treated her with the utmost respect, yet Tibold had the odd suspicion that was more for the army's benefit than for the angel's. Indeed, the angel seemed to watch for Lord Sean's reaction to whatever she might be saying even as she said it.

Tibold hadn't figured out why an angel should—well, defer wasn't quite the word, though it came close—even to Lord Sean's opinion, but there was no denying Lord Sean and Lord Tamman were uncanny. They might have keener eyes and greater strength than other men, and they certainly knew things Tibold hadn't, yet there were peculiar holes in their knowledge. For instance, Lord Tamman had actually expected nioharqs to slow infantry, and Lord Sean had let slip a puzzling reference to "heavy cavalry," a manifest contradiction in terms. Branahlks were fleet, but they had trouble carrying an *un*armored man.

Yet neither seemed upset when he corrected them. Indeed, Lord Sean had spent hours picking his brain, combining Tibold's experience with things he *did* know to create the army they now led, and he'd been delighted by Tibold's insistence upon remorseless drill—one more thing whose importance young officers frequently failed to appreciate.

And if their ignorance in some matters was surprising, their knowledge in others was amazing! He'd thought them mad to emphasize firearms over polearms. A joharn-armed musketeer did well to fire thirty shots an hour, while the heavier malagor could manage little more than twenty. There was simply no way musketeers could break a determined charge . . . until Lord Sean opened his bag of tricks. And, of course, until the angels intervened.

Even Tibold had felt . . . unsettled . . . when the Angel Sandy had Father Stomald stack a thousand joharns in a small, blind valley and leave them there overnight. Indeed, he'd crept back—strictly against Father Stomald's orders—late that night . . . and crept away again much more quietly than he'd come when he found all thousand of them had disappeared!

But they'd been back by morning, and Tibold hadn't argued when the Angel Sandy had him pile *two* thousand in the same valley the next night. Not after he'd seen what had happened to the first lot.

Changing wooden ramrods for iron had been but the first step, and Lord Sean had accompanied it by introducing paper cartridges to replace the wooden tubes hung from a musketeer's bandoleer. A man could carry far more of them, and all he had to do was bite off the end, pour the powder down the barrel, and spit in his ball. The paper wrapper even served as a wad!

The thing Lord Sean called a "ring bayonet" was another deceptively simple innovation. Hard-pressed musketeers often shoved the hafts of knives into their weapons' muzzles to turn them into crude spears as the pikes closed in, yet that was always a council of desperation, since it meant they could no longer fire. But they *could* fire with the mounting rings clamped *around* their weapons' barrels, and Tibold looked forward to the first time some Guard captain assumed musketeers with fixed bayonets couldn't shoot him.

Then there was the gunlock. No one had ever thought of widening the barrel end of the touch-hole into a funnel, but that simple alteration meant it was no longer necessary to prime the lock. Just turning the musket on its side and rapping it smartly shook powder from the main charge into the pan.

Yet the most wonderful change of all was simpler yet. Rifles had been a Malagoran invention (well, Cherist made the same claim, but Tibold knew who *he* believed), yet it took so long to hammer balls down their barrels—the only way to force them into the rifling—that they fired even more slowly than malagors. While prized by hunters and useful for skirmishers, the rifle was all but useless once the close-range exchange of volleys began.

No longer. Every altered joharn—and malagor—had returned rifled, and the angels had provided molds for a new bullet, as well. Not a ball, but a hollow-based cylinder that slid easily down the barrel. Tibold had doubted the rifling grooves could spin a bullet with that much windage, but Lord Sean had insisted the exploding powder would spread the base into them, and the results were phenomenal. Suddenly a rifle was as easy to load as a smoothbore—and able to fire far more rapidly than anyone had ever been able to shoot before! Tibold couldn't see why Lord Sean had been so surprised to find the weapons were . . . "bore-standardized," he called them (it only made sense to issue everyone the same size balls, didn't it?), but the Captain-General had been delighted by how easy that made it to produce the new bullets for them.

Nor had he ignored the artillery. Mother Church restricted secular armies to the lighter chagon, and the Guard's arlaks threw shot twice as heavy, even if their shorter barrels didn't give them much more range. But Lord Sean's gunners were supplied with cloth bags of powder instead of clumsy loading-ladles of loose powder. And for close-range firing there were "fixed rounds"—thin-walled, powder-filled wooden tubes with grape or case shot wired to one end. A good crew could fire three of those in a minute.

And when all those changes were added together, the Angels' Army could produce a weight of fire no experienced commander would have believed possible. Instead of once every five minutes, its artillerists fired three times in two minutes—even faster, using the "fixed rounds" at close range. Instead of thirty rounds an hour, its musketeers—no, its *rifle*men—could fire three or even four *a minute* and hit targets they could hardly even see! Tibold still wasn't certain fire alone could break a phalanx, but *he* wouldn't care to charge against such weapons.

Perhaps even better, there were maps. Wonderful maps, with every feature to scale and none left out. It was kind of the angels to try to make them look like those he'd always used, and he lacked the heart to tell them they'd failed when they seemed so pleased by their efforts, but no mortal cartographer could have produced them. Some of his militiamen hadn't realized how valuable they were, but he'd worn his voice hoarse until they did. To know exactly how the ground looked, where the best march routes lay, and precisely where the enemy might be hidden—and where your own troops could be best deployed—was truly a gift worthy of angels.

Best of all, the angels always knew what was happening elsewhere. The big map in the command tent showed every hostile army's exact position, and the angels updated it regularly. The sheer luxury of it was addictive. He was glad Lord Sean continued to emphasize scouting, but knowing where and how strong every major enemy force was made things so much simpler . . . especially when the enemy *didn't* know those things about you.

Still, he reminded himself, the odds were formidable. None of Malagor had remained loyal to the Church, but the "heretics" had far too few weapons for their manpower, and garrisoning the Thirgan Gap fortresses had drawn off over half of their strength, while the Temple had over two hundred thousand Guardsmen in eastern North Hylar, not even counting any of the secular armies.

Yet Tibold no longer doubted God was on their side, and while he knew too much of war to expect His direct intervention, Lord Sean and Lord Tamman were certainly the next best thing.

Sean closed the spyglass and rolled onto his back to stare up into the sky. Lord God, he was tired! He hadn't expected it to be easy—indeed, he'd feared the Pardalians would resist his innovations, and the eagerness with which they'd accepted them instead was a tremendous relief—but even so, he'd underestimated the sheer, grinding labor of it all, and he'd expected to get more advantage from *Israel's* machine shops. To be sure, Sandy's stealthed flights to shuttle muskets back and forth for rifling had been an enormous help, but this was Sean's first personal contact with the reality of military logistics, and he'd been horrified by the voracious appetite of even a small, primitively-armed army. Brashan and his computer-driven minions had been able to modify existing weapons at a gratifying rate, but *producing* large numbers of even unsophisticated weapons would quickly have devoured *Israel's* resources.

Not that Sean intended to complain. His troops were incomparably better armed (those who were armed at all!) than anything they were likely to face, and if he'd been disappointed in *Israel's* productivity, he'd been amazed by how quickly the Malagoran guilds had begun producing new weapons from the prototypes "the angels" had provided.

He'd been totally unprepared for the hordes of skilled artisans who'd popped up out of the ground, but he'd forgotten that Earth's own industrial revolution had begun with waterwheels. Pardal—and especially Malagor—had developed its own version of the assembly line, despite its limitation to wind, water, or muscle power, and that required a *lot* of craftsmen. Most had declared for "the angels"—as much, Sean suspected, from frustration at the Church's tech limitations as in response to any miracles "the angels" had wrought—but even with their tireless enthusiasm, there were never enough hours in the day.

Nor did the long year Pardal's huge orbital radius produced ease things. On a planet where spring lasted for five standard months and summer for ten, the campaigning seasons of Terra's preindustrial armies were a useless meterstick. Sean was devoutly thankful the Temple had seen fit to postpone operations for over two months while it indoctrinated its troops, but a delay which would have meant having to hold the Temple off only until the weather closed in on Terra meant nothing of the sort here. He faced an immediate, decisive campaign, and the sheer size of Pardalian armies appalled him. There were over a hundred thousand men headed up the Keldark Valley, and by tomorrow—the day after at latest—a lot of people were going to die.

Too many people, whichever side they're on, but there's not a damned thing I can do about that.

He clapped Tibold on the shoulder, and, despite everything, his heart rose at the older man's confident grin as they headed for their branahlks.

Stomald rose as the Angel Harry entered the command tent to update the "situation map." She smiled, and he knew she was chiding him for his display of respect, but he couldn't help it. And, he reminded himself, he

had finally managed to stop addressing her and the Angel
Sandy as "angels," even if he didn't understand why they
were so adamant about that. But, then, there were a lot
of things he didn't understand. He'd expected the angels
to be angry when the army's mood began to shift, yet
they were actually *pleased* to see the troops becoming
Malagoran nationalists rather than religious heretics.

He watched her work. She was a head taller than he,
and even more beautiful (and younger) than he'd remembered, now that her face was alive with thought and
humor, and he chided himself—again—as he thought of
the body hidden by her raiment. She might not use his
people with the authority which was her right, but she
was an angel.

She cocked her head to check her work with her
remaining eye, and he bit his lip in familiar anguish. Her
other terrible wounds had healed with angelic speed, but
that black eye patch twisted his heart each time he saw
it. Yet despite all Cragsend had done to her, there was
no hate in the Angel Harry. Stomald didn't believe she
could hate, not after the gentleness with which she always
spoke to him, the man who'd almost burned her alive.

She turned from the map, and amusement deepened
her smile as he blushed under her regard. But it didn't
embarrass him further. Instead, he felt himself smiling
back.

"Sandy will have a fresh update in a few hours," she
said in the Holy Tongue. "We're keeping a closer eye on
them now that they're approaching."

"I'm no soldier—or," he corrected himself wryly, "I *was*
no soldier—but that seems wise to me."

"Don't belittle yourself. You're fortunate to have a captain like Tibold—and Sean and Tamman, of course—but
you've got a good eye for these things yourself."

He bent his head, basking in her praise, but before
he could say anything more Lord Sean walked in, followed by Tibold.

Lord Sean touched his breastplate in respectful salute,
and the angel acknowledged it gravely, yet Stomald noted

the twinkle in her eye. For just an instant, he resented it, and then shame buried his pique. She was an *angel*, and Lord Sean was the Angel Sandy's chosen champion.

"Is that the latest update?" Lord Sean's Pardalian had developed a distinct Malagoran accent in the past five days, and he smiled as the angel nodded. He moved closer to the map and leaned forward beside her to study it.

Tibold grinned at Stomald behind their backs, and the priest smiled back despite another tiny stab of envy. It was easier for Tibold, for whatever else he was, Lord Sean was a born soldier. Tibold took paternal pride in him, and Lord Sean seemed to return his regard. He certainly listened attentively to anything Tibold had to say.

Lord Sean was murmuring to the Angel Harry in that other odd-sounding language they often spoke. Stomald suspected they sometimes forgot no one else understood it (Lord Sean always fell back into Pardalian whenever he remembered others were present), and the young war captain's ability to speak it awed the heretic priest. To be so close to the angels he spoke their own tongue almost unthinkingly must be wondrous, indeed.

Lord Sean stood back from the map at last, and his eyes were pensive. "Tibold, I think they'll hit our forward pickets this afternoon. Do you agree?"

Tibold studied the map a moment and nodded.

"Then it's time," Lord Sean sighed. "I'll speak to Tamman again, but you have a word with the under-captains. Make sure they keep their heads. We're fighting for survival, not honor, and we don't want any wasted lives."

"I will, Lord Sean," Tibold promised, obviously pleased by the Captain-General's concern for his men, and Lord Sean turned to Stomald.

"I expect to hold them, Father, but are we ready if we can't?"

"We are, Lord Sean. I've sent the last of the women back to safety, and the nioharqs will be in the traces by dawn, ready to advance or retreat."

Lord Sean nodded in satisfaction, then nodded again

as the Angel Harry murmured something too soft for any other ears to hear.

"Father, Captain Tibold and I will be unable to release the troops for services this evening with the enemy so near at hand, but if you'd care to send the chaplains forward—?"

"Thank you," Stomald said. Lord Sean was always careful about such things, yet the priest wondered why neither he nor Lord Tamman nor even the angels attended the services. Of course, such as they had their own links to God, but it was almost as if they stood aside intentionally.

"In that case, I think I'll go find lunch. Will you join me?"

Stomald nodded, and noted the amusement in the Angel Harry's eye. She smiled on the captain, and a surprising thought flickered in Stomald's mind. Lord Sean was as homely as the Angel Harry was beautiful, and the angel, for all her height, seemed tiny beside him, yet there was something . . .

It was the eyes, he thought. Why had he never noticed before? Lord Sean's strange, black eyes, darker than night, were exactly the same shade. And the hair, so black it was almost blue. That, too, was the same. Why, aside from Lord Sean's homeliness, they might have been brother and sister!

Like everyone else, Stomald knew Lord Sean and Lord Tamman were more than human—one had only to watch their blinding reflexes or see them occasionally forget to hide their incredible strength to know that—but it hadn't occurred to him they might share the angels' *blood!*

The thought was somehow chilling. Lord Sean and Lord Tamman were mortal. They both insisted on that, and Stomald believed them, and that meant they *couldn't* be related to angels. Besides, Holy Writ said all angels were female, and how could mortal blood mingle with divine? And yet . . . what if—?

He thrust the idea aside. It was disrespectful at best, and, a hidden part of him knew guiltily, it sprang from an unforgivable yearning that would have appalled him had he faced it squarely.

Tamman leaned against the thyru tree, watching the road to the east, then glanced back up at the man perched in the branches with his mirror. Pardalian armies had surprisingly sophisticated signal systems, but both mirrors and flags were "daylight-only," and the afternoon was passing.

He wanted to pace, but that would never do for an angelically chosen war captain. Besides, he was out here instead of Sean expressly to win his men's confidence, which might be important tomorrow, so he contented himself with crushing dried thyru husks under his heel. The thyru resembled an enormous acorn, but its soft, inner tissues produced an oil which filled much the same niche as Terra's olive oil, and he wondered how the Pardalians dealt with its thick shell. Now *there* was a messy thought!

He realized his mind was straying and tinkered with his adrenaline levels. He didn't really know why he was watching the road so hard. Unlike his scouts, he had a direct link to *Israel's* scanner arrays via Sandy's cutter. He *knew* where the enemy was, and glaring at an empty piece of road wasn't going to get them here a moment sooner.

He gave himself a shake and moved along the line, patting shoulders and exchanging smiles. Pardalian armies knew about mounted firearms—indeed, most Pardalian cavalry were dragoons—but they'd never been a real threat. While handy for scouting and harassment, dragoons could wear only light armor, their shorter muskets had neither the range nor rate of fire to stand off pikemen, and you couldn't put pikes on branahlks. But *these* dragoons were something new, for their joharns were rifled. Not, he reminded himself, that this was the time to show the Holy Host all they could do. That would come tomorrow.

He reached the end of the line and strolled back to

his tree, then rechecked his uplink. *Well, how about that? Looks like I spent just about exactly the right time with the troops.*

"Rethvan?" He glanced up at the signaler once more.

"Yes, Captain?"

"I expect their point to round the bend in about five minutes. Get ready to pass the signal."

"At once, Lord Tamman." Rethvan couldn't see around that bend, but he sounded so confident Tamman grinned. *Now all we have to do is never ever make a mistake—'cause if we do, that confidence could turn around and bite us right on the ass.*

The westering sunlight turned steadily redder, and a corner of his mind looked down through the scanner arrays. *Just . . . about . . . now.*

The first mounted scout rounded the bend exactly on cue.

"Send it, Rethvan." He was pleased by how calm he sounded.

"Yes, Captain."

The flashing mirror alerted the outposts to the west, and Tamman heard branahlks whistle behind his hill as their holders got them ready, but it was only a distant background. His attention was on the advancing company of Temple Guard cavalry, and his eyes slipped into telescopic mode.

They looked tired, and little wonder. Lord Marshal Rokas had moved fast once he started. The logistic capabilities of Pardalian armies amazed Tamman; he'd expected something like Earth's pike-and-musket era, but Pardal had nioharqs. The huge, tusked critters—they reminded him of elephant-sized hogs—could eat almost anything, which made forage far less of a problem than it had been for horse-powered armies, and their sustained speed was astonishing. True, their low *top* speed made them useless as cavalry, but they let Pardalians move artillery, rations, tents, portable forges, and mobile kitchens at a rate which would have turned Gustavus Adolphus green with envy.

Even so, Rokas' troops had to be feeling the pace. Sean had sealed the borders, and the Temple didn't know diddly about their deployment—their remotes couldn't penetrate the Temple itself, but they'd eavesdropped on enough of Rokas' field conferences to prove that. Yet the lord marshal had made a pretty fair estimate of their maximum possible strength, and he wasn't worrying about subtle maneuvers. He was going to throw enough bodies at them to plow them under and bull right through . . . he thought.

Tamman's smile was evil as he watched the scouts advance. They might be tired, but they seemed alert. Unfortunately for them, however, they were watching for threats inside the range they "knew" Pardalian weapons had.

"Let's get ready, boys," he said quietly as the first branahlk passed the four-hundred-meter range stakes. A soft chorus of responses came back, and his hundred dragoons settled down in their paired-off positions. He watched them sighting across fallen trees and logs as Rokas' scouts closed to just over two hundred meters. That was still far beyond aimed smoothbore range, but some of them were beginning to look more speculatively his way than he liked.

"Fire!" he barked, and fifty rifled joharns cracked as one. The muzzle flashes were bright in the shadows of the grove, and powder smoke stung his nose, but his attention was on the scouts. Thirty or more went down—many, he was sure, dismounted rather than hit; branahlks were bigger targets than men—and the others gaped at the smoke cloud rising from the trees. Tamman grinned at their stunned reaction, counting under his breath while the first firers reloaded. The second half of each team waited until his partner was half-reloaded, then fired, and more riders went down. The survivors wheeled and spurred frantically back towards the bend, dismounted men racing after them on foot, but individual shots barked at their heels, and most of them were picked off before they could get out of range.

"Okay, boys, saddle up," Tamman said, and grinning dragoons filtered back towards their mounts. Their commander waited a moment longer, and his own grin faded as he watched the road. A handful of wounded crawled along it, their agony plain to his enhanced eyes, while others writhed where they'd fallen, and even unenhanced ears could have heard their screams and sobs.

He shivered and turned away, hating himself just a little because not even his horror made him feel one bit less satisfied.

Lord Marshal Rokas glowered at the map in the lamplight, but his glare couldn't change it, and the reports were just as disturbing now as they'd been when they were fresh.

He scowled. The first ambush had cost him seventy-one men, and that at a range Under-Captain Turalk swore was two hundred paces if it was a span. The second and third had been worse. The Host's total losses were over four hundred, and they were concentrated in his cavalry—which he wasn't over-supplied with in the first place.

His scouts would be more than human if what had happened today didn't make them cautious tomorrow, which was bad enough, but how had the heretics done it? Where had they gotten that many dragoons? Or hidden them? He wouldn't have believed more than a hundred men could be concealed in any of those ambush sites, but his casualties argued for three or four times that many—with malagors, at that—in each.

He poured a goblet of wine and sank into a folding chair. How they'd done it mattered less than that they had, but ambushes wouldn't save them. Unless they wanted to lose any chance to bottle him up in the mountains, they had to stand and fight; when they did, he would crush them.

He'd better, for two-thirds of Mother Church's own artillery and muskets and half her armor and pikeheads had come from Malagor's foundries. Rokas had never liked being so dependent on a single source, yet what they faced now was worse than his worst nightmare, for every foundry Mother Church had lost, the heretics had gained.

Rokas knew to the last pike and pistol how many weapons had lain in the Guard's armories in Malagor. His figures were less accurate for the secular arsenals but still enough for a decent guess, and even if the heretics had them all, they could field little more than a hundred thousand men. Yet given time, Malagor's artisans could arm every man in the princedom, and if that happened, the cost of invading that mountain-guarded land would become almost unbearable.

He'd finally managed to convince the Circle of that simple, self-evident fact; if he hadn't, the prelates would have delayed the Host until first snow "strengthening their souls against heresy."

But High Priest Vroxhan had listened at last, and now Rokas brooded down at the map tokens representing a hundred and twenty thousand men—the picked flower of the Guard from eastern North Hylar. His force was really too large for the constricted terrain, but, as he'd told the high priest, strategy and maneuver were of scant use in this situation.

He stared unhappily at the blue line of the Mortan River and sipped his wine. An infant could divine his only possible path, and Tibold was no infant, curse him! He was a seldahk, with all the speed and cunning of the breed; a seldahk who'd offended a high-captain and been banished to the most miserable post that high-captain could find. Tibold would know precisely what Rokas planned . . . and how to make the most of whatever force *he* had.

The marshal chewed his mustache at the thought. Mother Church's last true challenge had been the conquest of barbarian Herdaana six generations ago, and even that had been far short of what *this* could become. If the heresy wasn't crushed soon, it might turn into another nightmare like the Schismatic Wars, which had laid half of North Hylar waste, and the thought chilled him.

Sean MacIntyre stood on the walls of the city of Yortown and stared down at the fires of his men. *His* men. The thought was terrifying, for there were fifty-eight thousand people down there, and their lives depended on him.

He folded his hands behind him and considered the odds once more. Worse than two-to-one, and they'd have been higher if the Church had chosen to squeeze more troops into the valley. He'd rather hoped they might do just that, but this Lord Marshal Rokas knew better than to crowd himself—unfortunately.

He gnawed his lip and wished he weren't so far out of his own time, or that the Academy's military history hadn't tended to emphasize strategy and skimp on the military nuts and bolts of earlier eras. Half of what they'd introduced to the Malagorans had been dredged up from remembered conversations with Uncle Hector. The rest had been extrapolated from that or gleaned from *Israel's* limited (and infuriatingly nonspecific) military history records, and he intended to have a severe talk with Aunt Adrienne about her curriculum.

He paced slowly, brooding in the night wind. The pike was the true mankiller of Pardal, and most armies had at least three of them for every musket. The Temple Guard certainly did, and Tibold had explained how it used its phalanx-like formations to pin an enemy under threat of attack, "prepared" him with artillery and small arms, and finally charged home with cold steel. Yet for all their horrific shock power, those massive pike blocks were unwieldy; he suspected traditional Malagoran tactics would have given Rokas problems even without the "angels" and their innovations.

The Malagorans' polearms reminded him of Earth's Swiss pikemen, but with fewer pikes and more bills which, in the absence of any heavy cavalry threat, were shorter, handier melee weapons than those of Earth.

Tactically, they were far more agile than the Guard, relying on shallower pike formations to hold an enemy in play while billmen swept out around his flanks, and Sean's modifications should make them even deadlier . . . assuming they were ready.

If only he'd had more time! He'd let Tibold handle training, and the tough old captain made Baron von Steuben look like a Cub Scout, but they'd had barely two months. Their army had incredible *esprit* and a hard core of militia (Malagor's self-governing towns and villages raised their own troops in the absence of feudal grandees), and over eight thousand Guardsmen had defected to the rebels, but fusing them into a single force and teaching them a whole new tactical doctrine in two months had been a nightmare.

Worse, none of his own training had taught him how to lead troops with so little command and control. He was used to instant, high-tech communication, and he suspected his most pessimistic estimates fell far short of just how bad *this* was going to be. His men looked good at drill, but would they hang together in battle when the whole world went crazy about them? He didn't know, but he knew too many battles in Earth's history had been lost when one side lost its cohesion and fell apart in confusion.

Still, he told himself firmly, if they *did* hold together, the Guard was in trouble. Normally, its phalanxes would have had the edge at Yortown, where flanks could be secured by terrain and mass and momentum were what counted, but that was where the contributions of *Israel*'s crew came in. They hadn't gotten the volume of their troops' fire up to anything approaching a modern level, but it was far heavier than Pardal had ever seen . . . and pike blocks made big targets. If he could get the Guard stuck, it was going to learn what the bear did to the buckwheat, and he thought—hoped—he'd found the place to bog it down. The Keldark Valley narrowed to a little more than six kilometers of open terrain at Yortown, and if Lord Rokas was as good a student of military history as Tibold said . . .

He sighed and shook free of the thoughts wearing grooves in his brain, then stretched, glanced up at the alien stars, and took himself off to bed, wondering if he'd sleep a wink.

Chapter Twenty-Eight

Lord Marshal Rokas climbed the hill and opened his spyglass with a click. The morning mist had lifted, though tendrils still clung to the line of the Mortan, and his mouth tightened as he studied the terrain. He'd expected—feared—from the start that Tibold would offer battle here, for more than one invading army had been broken against Yortown.

The town stood on the bluffs beyond the river. Its walls had been razed after the Schismatic Wars, but the heretics were building new ones. Not that they were really needed. The Mortan ran all the way to the Eastern Ocean, twisting down the Keldark Valley to escape the Shalokars, and it coiled like a hateful serpent about Yortown's feet. The river swooped from the northern edge of the valley to the southern cliffs before it turned east once more, and like many a Malagoran before him, Tibold had drawn up beyond that icy natural moat.

Rokas' glass lingered on the Yortown bridges with wistful longing, but the demolitions had been too thorough. The broken spans had been dropped into water too deep to ford even across their rubble, and he smothered a curse. If the Circle hadn't hesitated so long, he could have been past Yortown and into Malagor's heart before the heretics got themselves organized!

He turned further south. No position was impregnable, but his mouth tightened anew as he considered the fords the blown bridges had made the key to this one. They lay southeast of Yortown, where the river broadened, and raw earthworks reared on the western bank. He saw the glint of pikes and gleam of artillery, and his heart sank.

Those fords were over a hundred paces wide and more than waist deep; the wounded would be doomed even without armor. With it—

He turned back to the north to glare at the dense forest which sprawled down from the valley wall almost to his hilltop vantage point. It offered his right flank a natural protection—God knew no pikeman could get through *that* tangle!—but it was a guard against nothing. The river was too deep to bridge, much less ford, north of Yortown, and no captain as canny as Tibold would put men in a trap from which they could not withdraw.

He closed his glass. No, Tibold knew what he was about . . . and so did Rokas. Too many battles had been fought at Yortown; defender and attacker alike knew all the moves, and if the cost would be high, it was one he could pay. It would trouble too many dreams in years to come, but he could pay it.

"I see no need to alter our plans," he told his officers. "Captain Vrikadan," he met the high-captain's eyes, "you will advance."

"God, look at them!" Tamman muttered over his com implant, and Sean nodded jerkily, forgetting his friend couldn't see him. No sensor image could have prepared him for seeing that army uncoiling in the flesh, and he braced himself in the tree's high fork, peering through its leaves while the Host deployed towards the fords. Musketeers screened massive columns of pikes, and nioharq-drawn artillery moved steadily between the columns. Armor flashed, pikeheads were a glittering forest above, and the marching legs below made the columns look like horrible caterpillars of steel.

"I see them," he replied after a moment, "and I wish to hell we had the Holy Hand Grenade of Antioch!"

Tamman chuckled at the feeble joke, and Sean's dry mouth quirked. He wished he—or Tibold, at least—could be at the fords with Tamman. He knew he couldn't, and he needed Tibold here in case something happened to him, but he'd felt far more confident before he saw the Host with his own eyes.

He sighed, then slithered down the tree. Tibold stood with Folmak, the miller who commanded Sean's headquarters company, and Sean met their eyes.

"They're doing it."

"I see." Tibold plucked at his lower lip. "And their scouts?"

"You were right about them, too. There's a screen of dragoons covering their right flank, but they're not getting too far out."

"Aye." Tibold nodded. "Rokas didn't become Lord Marshal by being careless even of unlikely threats. But—" his teeth flashed in a tight grin "—it seems Lord Tamman did indeed teach his men caution yesterday."

"So it seems," Sean agreed, and peered into the green shadows where twenty thousand men lay hidden amid undergrowth as dense as anything Grant had faced at The Wilderness. They wore dull green and brown, their rifle barrels had been browned to prevent any betraying gleam, and they made a sadly scruffy sight beside the crimson and steel of the Guard, but they were also almost totally invisible.

He flicked his neural feed to the stealthed cutter above the valley, exchanging a brief, wordless caress with an anxious Sandy, then plugged into Brashan's arrays through the cutter's com. The Host was closing up, packing tighter behind the assault elements. With a little luck . . .

He shifted his attention to the pontoon bridges north of Yortown, hidden behind the woods. Pontoons were new to Pardal, and they'd been trickier to erect than he'd hoped, but they seemed to be holding. He hoped so. If it all came apart, those bridges were the only way home for a third of his army.

Stomald watched the Angel Harry make another small adjustment on the situation map. She was intent upon her work, yet he saw a tiny tremble in her slender fingers and wanted to slip an arm about her to comfort her. But she was an angel, he reminded himself again, and gripped his starburst, instead, trying to share the army's mood.

The men were confident, filled with near idolatry for the angels' champions. Indeed, they were more than confident. They no longer looked to simply defending themselves, but to smashing their enemies, despite the odds, and if they'd prayed dutifully for mercy, their fervor was reserved for prayers for strength, victory, and—especially—Malagoran independence.

Now he listened to the steady cadence of the Guard's drums and sweat dotted his brow as he prayed silently—not for himself, but for the men he'd led to this. A surgeon began to hone his knives and saws, and he watched the shining steel with appalled eyes, unable to look away.

A hand touched his shoulder, startling despite its lightness, and he looked up with a gasp. The Angel Harry squeezed gently, and her remaining eye was soft and understanding. He reached up and covered her hand with his own, marveling at his own audacity in touching her holy flesh, and she smiled.

High-Captain Vrikadan's branahlk jibed and fretted as ten thousand voices rose to join the thunder of the drums, and he turned in the saddle to study his men. The mighty hymn swelled around him, strong and deep, but the leading pike companies were tight-faced as they roared the words.

Vrikadan urged the branahlk closer to a battery of arlaks, creaking along between the columns. Even the stolid nioharqs were uneasy, tossing their tusks and lowing, and a gray-bearded artillery captain looked up and met his eye with a grim smile.

Tamman stood on the fighting step and watched the juggernaut of steel and flesh roll towards him. The rumble of its singing was a morale weapon whose potency he hadn't really appreciated, but at least the Host was performing exactly as Tibold had predicted. So far.

Twenty thousand men marched towards the fords. As many more followed to exploit any success, and he felt very small and young. Worse, he sensed his men's disquiet. It wasn't even close to panic, but that hymn-roaring monster was enough to shake anyone, and he turned to his second-in-command.

"Let's have a little music of our own, Lornar," he suggested, and High-Captain Lornar grinned.

"At once, Lord Tamman!" He beckoned to a teenaged messenger, and the lad dashed back to the rear of the redoubt. There was a moment of muttered consultation, and then a high-pitched skirling. The Malagorans had invented the bagpipe, and Tamman's troops looked at one another with bared teeth as the defiant wail of the pipes rose to meet the Guard.

God, I never realized how long *it took!* Sean made himself stand still, listening to the music swelling from the redoubts to answer the Guard's singing, and felt sick and hollow, nerves stretched by the deliberation with which thousands of men marched towards death. This wasn't like *Israel*'s frantic struggle against the quarantine system. This was slow and agonizing.

The range dropped inexorably, and he bit his lip as the first gouts of smoke erupted from the redoubts. Round shot ripped through the Guard's ranks, dismembering and disemboweling, and his enhanced vision made the carnage too clear. He swallowed bile, but even as the guns fired the music of the pipes changed. It took on a new, fiercer rhythm, and he looked at Tibold.

"I haven't heard that hymn before."

"That's no hymn," Tibold said, and Sean raised an eyebrow. "That's 'Malagor the Free,' Lord Sean," the ex-Guardsman said softly.

Vrikadan heard the high, shivering seldahk's howl of

the Malagoran war cry—a terrifying sound which, like the music shrilling beneath it, had been proscribed on pain of death for almost two Pardalian centuries—but he had other things to worry about, and he fought his mount as a salvo of shot shrieked through his men. And another. *Another!* Dear God, where had they *gotten* all those guns?

A cyclone howled, and he kicked free of his stirrups as a round shot took his branahlk's head. The beast dropped and its blood fountained over him, but he rolled upright and drew his sword. The range was too great for his own guns to affect earthworks, but he grabbed at the knee of a mounted aide.

"Unlimber the guns!" he snapped. "Get them into action *now!*"

Tamman coughed, watching one of his arlak crews as the reeking smoke rolled over him. A bagged charge slid down the muzzle while the captain stopped the vent with a leather thumbstall. The eight-kilo round shot followed, and the wad, and the crew heaved the piece back to battery as the captain cocked the lock and drove a priming quill down the vent to pierce the bag. The gun vomited flame and lurched back, a dripping sponge hissed into its maw, quenching the embers of the last shot, and a fresh charge was waiting.

He turned away, dazed by the bellow and roar and insane keening of the pipes, and his hands clenched on the earthen rampart as the lines of Guard musketeers parted to reveal the pikes and their own unlimbering guns.

Lord Rokas strained to pierce the smoke. The waves of fire washing along those redoubts was impossible. No one could fit that many guns into so small a space even if they had them, and the heretics couldn't *have* that many!

But they did. Tongues of flame transfixed the pall, smashing tangles of bloody limbs through his advancing pikes. Vrikadan's men were falling too quickly and too soon, and he turned to a signaler.

"Tell High-Captain Martas to tighten the interval. Then instruct High-Captain Sertal to advance."

Signal flags snapped, and Rokas chewed his lip. He'd hoped Vrikadan would clear at least one ford, but that would take a special miracle against those guns. Yet his bleeding columns should cover Martas long enough for him to reach charge range of the river.

He raised his glass once more, cursing silently as his men entered grapeshot range and his estimate of Yortown's cost rose.

Sandy MacMahan was white, and her brain screamed for her to arm her cutter's weapons, but she couldn't. She was sickened by how glibly she'd suggested taking part in this horror, yet stubborn rationality told her she'd been right—as Sean was right now. Imperial weapons could never be used if they couldn't be used throughout, but logic and reason were cold, hateful companions as she watched the smoke and blood erupting below her.

High-Captain Vrikadan's arlaks thundered. They were too distant to penetrate the earthen ramparts, but their crews heaved them further forwards with every shot, pounding away in a desperate effort to suppress the heretic guns.

They weren't accomplishing much, Vrikadan knew, yet every little bit helped, and if they could dismount a few of those guns . . .

His northern column wavered, and Vrikadan charged through the smoke, bouncing off wounded men, beating at stragglers with the flat of his blade.

"Keep your ranks!" he bellowed. "Keep your ranks, damn you!"

A wild-eyed under-captain recognized him and wheeled on his own men, quelling their panic. Vrikadan shouldered up beside the younger man, waving his sword while the lead company of the stalled phalanx stared at him.

"*With me, lads!*" he screamed, and dashed forward like a man possessed.

Smoke blinded Tamman, and he switched his vision to thermal imaging. The image was blurry, and he could no longer see the range stakes, but a mass of men was almost to the east bank. He sent a runner forward.

Vrikadan's lips drew back in a snarl as a ray of sunlight pierced the smoke and the river glistened before him. Grapeshot heaped his men in ugly, writhing tangles, but the weight of numbers behind them was an avalanche. They couldn't stop—they couldn't *be* stopped!—and the water beckoned.

And then, just as he reached the bank, the smoke lifted on a billow of flame. There were gun pits at the feet of the redoubts! Camouflaged pits filled not with arlaks but with chagors, light guns packed hub-to-hub and spewing fire.

He had only an instant to see it before a charge of grape ripped both legs off at the hip.

Sean swallowed again, cringing inwardly as he watched through Sandy's scanners and saw the east bank of the Mortan writhe with screaming, broken bodies . . . and saw living men advancing through the horror.

God in Heaven, how could they *do* that? He knew the momentum of the men behind drove them forward, giving them no choice, but it was more than that, too. It was unreasoning, blood-mad insanity and it was courage, and there was no longer any difference between them.

They were going to reach the fords despite Tamman's guns, and he hadn't really believed they could.

The first Guardsmen splashed into the river. It ran scarlet as case shot flailed at them, but they came on. High-Captain Lornar saw Lord Tamman's slender sword rise above his head and blew his whistle, and more whistles shrilled up and down the fighting step. Three thousand rifled joharns were leveled across the rampart, and Lord Tamman's sword hissed down.

The leading pikemen were still three hundred paces away when a sheet of lead slashed through them like fiery sleet. Whole companies went down, and those following stared in horror at the writhing carpet of their companions and the isolated individuals who still stood, stunned by the density of the volley. They wavered, but High-Captain Martas' men were on their heels, driving them forward. There was nowhere to go but into those flaming muzzles, and they lowered their pikes and charged.

The first three thousand musketeers reached for cartridges and stepped down from the fighting step, and three thousand more replaced them. Ramrods clinked and jerked, whistles screamed again, and a second stupendous volley smashed out. Sergeants shouted, bellowing to control the lethal ballet, and the musketeers exchanged places again. The first group's reloaded joharns leveled, and lightning sheeted across the rampart once more.

Lord Rokas paled as the roar of massive volleys drowned even the artillery. With no way to know how quickly Tamman's men could reload, those steady, crashing discharges could only mean the heretics had far more muskets than he'd believed possible.

He couldn't see through the wall of smoke, but experience told him what had happened to Vrikadan—and that Martas was moving into the maelstrom, with High-Captain Sertal on his heels. Those fords were mincing machines, devouring his troops, yet they were also the only way into Yortown, and he banished all expression as he barked out orders to send even more of the Guard to their deaths.

✧   ✧   ✧

High-Captain Martas' men burst through the smoke. Bodies littered the riverbank, but the heretics' guns and muskets had been too busy dealing with Vrikadan's men to ravage Martas' companies. Now they lunged for the river, for their only salvation lay in reaching and silencing those redoubts.

They began to die as more volleys roared, and their fellows stumbled forward over their bodies, floundering and cursing in the shallows, wading deeper, crouching to hide as much of themselves below the water as they could.

And then the lead ranks lunged upright, screaming as the rear ranks drove them forward onto the sharpened stakes and needle-pointed caltrops hidden in the river. They thrashed and shrieked in the scarlet water, and the deadly waves of musketry ripped them to pieces.

Round shot hissed overhead or thudded into the earthwork as the Host's guns scrambled into action, and one of them slammed into the arlak beside Tamman. The barrel spun away, the carriage disintegrated, and something less than human twitched and mewled amid the wreckage. His guns were protected by the redoubt's embrasures, but they were also outnumbered. More and more of the Guard's artillery was coming into action between the bleeding infantry columns, and musketeers stood fully exposed on the flanks to fire into the smoke. They were shooting blind at extreme range, but even with their low rates of fire, an awesome number of balls buzzed overhead.

He stared down into the carnage of the ford. Pikemen and musketeers waded out into that madness, advancing until grapeshot or musket balls hammered them under, but the men behind them were stopping at last. Or were they? He strained his eyes and swallowed. They weren't stopping; they were reforming.

High-Captain Sertal's face was white under its dust and

grime, but his hoarse voice cut through the din. His forward companies absorbed the survivors of Vrikadan's and Martas's men, standing with iron discipline under the tornado of the heretics' fire. Under-captains and sergeants shouted orders. Where necessary, they kicked troopers into formation with boots caked in bloody mud, and Sertal winced as another deadly lash of grapeshot scythed through his men. He couldn't hold them here long, but he *had* to hold them long enough to reorder their ranks, and he gripped his sword and coughed on smoke, listening to the screams.

Sean checked the scanners once more as the zone south of the High Road became a solid mass of advancing Guardsmen, then nodded to Tibold.

"They're stuck in deep," he said, trying to hide his anxiety, "and Rokas is sending his reserves forward. It's time."

"Aye, Lord Sean!" Tibold began snapping orders, and twenty thousand men, without a single pike among them, rose to their feet in the "impassable" woods north of the Host.

Now!

Sertal thrust his sword at the redoubts and swept it down in command, and his men lurched into the holocaust. Tamman saw them coming and turned to shout another order to Lornar, but Lornar was down, head smashed by one of those blind-fired musket balls. He grabbed a captain's shoulder. The Malagoran's face—it was Captain Ithun, one of the ex-Guard officers—was white and strained, and he went still whiter as he realized *he* was now Tamman's senior officer in the central redoubt. Tamman saw it, but there was no time for encouragement.

"Pikes forward!" he bellowed.

The chagors in Tamman's advanced gun pits fired one last salvo, and their crews snatched for swords and pikes as the bleeding ranks of the Guard won free of the water at last. A dozen gun captains paused to light fuses before they grabbed up their own weapons, and the madmen who'd fought their way through everything the Malagorans could throw lunged towards them with a howl. Fresh concussions turned howls to screams as the crude mines seeded the river bank in fountains of flame and flying limbs, and the survivors wavered, but Sertal's men drove forward, and edged steel stabbed and cut.

Malagoran pikemen funneled through sally ports in their earthworks and foamed over the foremost Guardsmen behind the high, quavering Malagoran yell, then crashed into the ranks behind them. They thrust forward, bills rising and falling, shearing limbs and plucking heads, and hurled the Host back into the fords, but there they stopped. The hand-to-hand butchery blocked the chagors, and the arlaks were locked in a duel with the Guard's gun lines. Musketry continued to crash out above their heads, yet the Host was taking fewer fire casualties now, and the lead formations had cleared most of the obstacles with their own bodies. Thousands of Guardsmen lay dead or wounded, but more pressed forward, and sheer weight of numbers began to drive the Malagorans back.

Captain Yurkal stared south at the clouds of smoke, listening to the artillery and crashing musketry. The screams were faint with distance, a savage sound under the explosions, and he was guiltily aware of his own relief at being spared that hell. Yurkal was a son of Mother Church, but he was also grateful his dragoons had been deployed so far from the fighting, and—

He jerked in astonishment as his banner-bearer fell, clawing at his chest. There was a meaty thud as the sergeant beside him slid to the ground as well, and Yurkal whirled as the popping sounds behind him registered.

Three hundred paces away, still hidden in the edge of the forest, a green-and-brown clad marksman settled his rifled malagor into its rest and peered through his peep sight. He squeezed the trigger, and a twenty-millimeter bullet blew Captain Yurkal's heart apart.

Sean watched the snipers methodically pick off officers and noncoms while the rest of his men debouched from the forest. It wasn't chivalrous . . . but, then, neither was war.

More officers fell, and suddenly leaderless troopers began to panic. Most were already fleeing, and the pairs of malagors continued to fire, cutting down the handful of Guardsmen who stood while leather-lunged sergeants cursed their own men into formation.

Fifteen thousand men formed a three-deep battle line three kilometers long. The Malagoran yell quivered down their front, and they swept south, and five thousand more followed as a reserve.

Lord Marshal Rokas' head snapped up at the crackle of musketry. He spun to the north and gaped as a new wall of smoke billowed. Impossible!

He jerked his spyglass open, and his blood ran chill. His mounted screen had dissolved like leaves in a tempest, and even as he watched the advancing lines of muzzle flashes ripped at the fugitives' backs.

A trap. This entire position was a trap, and he'd walked right into it! Tibold had done the unthinkable, splitting his outnumbered forces, deploying those oncoming musketeers in a position from which they couldn't possibly retreat in order to hit him when he was mired in the fords!

The plan's insane audacity stunned him, but half his total force was committed to the lunge at the fords. Another quarter had been left behind, lest it constrict his movement. That left barely thirty thousand men to meet this new threat, and they were spread out behind his attacking formations.

He leapt onto his branahlk, spurring down the hill even as he began volleying orders, and signals and couriers exploded in every direction in a deadly race against that advancing horde of heretical musketeers.

✧   ✧   ✧

Another isolated company disintegrated under the rolling fire of Sean's battle-line, and his pulse pounded. His men couldn't move as quickly in line as in column, but the hours of drill were bearing fruit. Their formation was perfect, and they advanced like automatons, reloading on the move. Their fire swept the trampled crop land before them like a lethal broom, and he could see the panicky movement of Rokas' reserves ahead of them.

The carnage in the fords drove inexorably towards the redoubts, for the Guardsmen there had no way of knowing what was descending upon their flank. Sixty thousand men clawed their way forward. Only a fraction of them could reach the fords at any given moment, yet the numbers behind them seemed inexhaustible. The Malagorans fought back with equal ferocity, but they, too, were dying, and there were less of them.

The whistles shrilled again, and the Guard forged ahead with a bellow. But the Malagorans weren't breaking. They fell back, step by step, into the redoubts under cover of their musketeers, and Tamman watched anxiously.

Sean had to cross ten more kilometers of open ground to reach the fords.

Rokas' orders began to reach their destinations, and a shudder pulsed through the Host. The sudden threat to their "secure" flank mingled with the slaughter at the fords and woke a shiver of dread. Their enemies served the forces of Hell—was that how they'd managed this impossible maneuver?

But there was no time to think of such things with that battle-line sweeping down upon them. Companies wheeled, nioharq-drawn batteries lumbered to new positions, and an answering formation began to coalesce. It was shaken and uncertain, but it was there, and Rokas allowed himself to hope.

✧   ✧   ✧

Sean watched the patterns shift, and his own orders raced up and down the line. He had no artillery . . . but, then, the Guard artillerists weren't used to muskets which could kill them at eight hundred meters, either.

A forlorn hope of musketeers tried to slow him, and perhaps a hundred of his own men went down. Then the fire of his line tore the defenders apart, and the inexorable advance swept over them.

The hand-to-hand fighting reached the redoubts, and screams bubbled as Guardsmen tumbled into the ditches at their feet and died on the waiting stakes. Their fellows advanced over them, marching across their writhing bodies, too frenzied even to realize what they were doing.

The musketeers fired one last volley and fell back to clear the fighting step. Pikes and bills crossed at the ramparts, and Tamman knew he should go with the marksmen, but Lornar was dead. His men were fighting like demons, yet it all hinged on their morale, and if he seemed to waver . . .

A pikeman leapt up a pile of bodies, thrusting at him, and his left hand darted out with inhuman quickness. He caught the pike haft, enhanced muscles jerked, and the Guardsman clung in disbelief as he was wrenched in close.

A battle steel blade hissed, and a head bounded away.

Two batteries of arlaks unlimbered, and the gunners wheeled their pieces frantically into position to stem the heretics' advance. They were six hundred paces from the enemy, three times effective malagor range—and they died in deep astonishment as the crackling fire killed them anyway.

The second wave of attackers was thrown back, but a third formed and crashed forward over the bodies, and the man beside Tamman went down screaming with a pikehead in his guts. Tamman lunged at his killer, grunting as his slender sword punched through breast and backplate alike, and kicked the body aside, then grunted again as a musket ball smashed into his own breastplate. It whined aside, marking the undented Imperial composite with a long smear of lead, and he cut down two more Guardsmen. But this time the bastards were coming through, and his free hand ripped a mace from a dead man's belt as the defending line crumbled to his left.

"Follow me!" he bellowed, and sensed the rush of his men behind him as he hurtled to meet the penetration.

Sean's line swept over the guns and the bodies of their crews, and a hungry roar went up as his men saw the first pike blocks formed across their path. His own pipes screamed, wailing their fury, and his amplified voice bellowed through the din.

"Halt!"

Fifteen thousand men paused as one, and the waiting Guardsmen's pikes swung down into a leveled glitter of steel.

"Front rank, kneel!"

Five thousand men went to one knee, shouldering their muskets as the Guard's drums thundered and the charge began. Seven or eight thousand men swept forward, shrieking their battlecries, and he watched them come.

Three hundred meters. Two hundred.

"Take aim!"

One hundred. Seventy-five. Fifty.

"By ranks—*fire!*"

A sheet of flame rolled down his kneeling rank, and the front of the pike blocks collapsed in hideous ruin. Men stumbled and sprawled over the bodies of their fellows as the charge wavered, and the second rank fired. A third of the Guardsmen were down, and the charge slithered to a halt as the hurricane blast swept over them . . . and the *third* rank fired!

The surviving pikemen hurled away their weapons and fled.

Captain Ithun watched his company reel back as the Guard swept over the parapet. Its men wavered, shaken by the terror thundering about them and ready to flee, then stared in disbelief as Lord Tamman charged the enemy's flank. The fighting step was wide enough for five men abreast, but there was no one beside him, for he'd outdistanced them all . . . and it didn't matter.

Ithun gaped as the black-armored figure erupted into the Guardsmen, mace in one hand, skinny sword in the other. No Pardalian had faced a fully enhanced enemy in forty-five thousand years, and any Guardsman who'd doubted the heretics were allied to demons knew better now. Limbs and dead men exploded from Lord Tamman's path. A pike lunged at him, and metal screamed as that impossible sword sheared through the pikehead.

"Come on, Malagorans!" Ithun shrieked, and his men roared as they swept back up the fighting step in his wake.

It was over, Rokas thought remotely.

A line of fire ground down from the north in a haze of powder smoke, shattering everything in its path and crunching over the wreckage. No army in the world could advance like that, not without a single polearm, but the heretics were doing it, and his men refused to face them.

He stood numbly, watching the Host disintegrate as his men threw away their weapons and bolted, and he couldn't blame them. There was something dreadful about that deliberate, remorseless advance—something that proved the tales of demons—and all of Mother Church's exorcisms couldn't stop it.

An aide jerked at him, shouting about withdrawal, and Rokas turned like a man in a nightmare, then gasped as a fiery hammer smashed his side.

The lord marshal fell to his knees, and the tumult about him had grown suddenly faint. He rolled onto his back, staring up at his panicked aide and the smoke-streaked sky, and his dimming mind marveled that evening had come so soon.

But it wasn't evening, after all; it was night.

Chapter Twenty-Nine

The stench was enough to turn a statue's stomach.

Eleven thousand Guardsmen lay dead. Another twenty thousand wounded littered the Keldark Valley, whimpering or screaming . . . or lying silent while they waited to die. Another thirty or forty thousand (the count was far from done) huddled in shocked disbelief under the weapons of their enemies.

A miserable, battered third of the Holy Host was still running as darkness covered the horror.

And horror it was. Sean stood beside a field hospital, watching the surgeons, and only his implants held down his gorge. Pardalians had a good working knowledge of anatomy and a kitchen sink notion of sepsis, but distilled alcohol was their sole anesthetic and disinfectant. There were no medical teams to rebuild shattered limbs; amputation was the prescription, and the treatment of men's wounds was more horrifying than their infliction.

Sandy and Harry were out there in the middle of it. *Israel*'s facilities couldn't have healed a fraction of the suffering, but Brashan had sent forward every painkiller his sickbay had, and the iron-faced "angels" moved through Hell, easing its pain and following the anesthetic with broad-spectrum Imperial antibiotics. Guardsmen who cursed them as demons fell silent in confusion as they watched them heal their enemies, and hundreds who should have died would live . . . and none of it absolved *Israel*'s crew of their guilt.

Sean and Tamman had visited their own wounded—blessedly few compared to the Host's—but their responsibilities lay elsewhere, and Sean turned away to stare

out at the torches and lanterns creeping across the battlefield. He shuddered as he braced himself for another
journey into that obscenity, yet he had to go. He squared
his shoulders and started forward against the steady
stream of litter-bearers, and Tibold followed him silently.

He tried not to think, but he couldn't stop looking . . . or
smelling. The reek of blood and torn flesh mixed with the
sewer stench of riven entrails, scavengers—some of them
human—were already busy beyond the reach of the moving torches, and Pardal's small moon added its wan light to
the horror.

More people had died with *Imperial Terra* than here,
but they'd died without even knowing. These men had
died screaming, ripped apart and mutilated, and he was
the one who'd planned their murder. He knew he'd had
no choice, that less than four thousand of his own lay
dead or wounded because he'd gotten it right, but this
moonlit nightmare was too much.

His vision blurred, and he stumbled over a body. His
legs gave, and he sank to his knees before his lieutenant, trying to speak, fighting to explain his inner agony,
but no words came. Only terrible, choking sounds.

Tibold knelt beside him, brown eyes dark in the moonlight, and a hard-palmed hand touched his cheek. Sean
stared at him, twisted by shame and guilt and a wrench-
ing loss of innocence, and Tibold raised his other hand
to cradle his captain-general's head.

"I know, lad," the ex-Guardsman murmured. "I *know*.
The fools who call war 'glorious' have never seen *this*,
curse them."

"I-I—" Sean gasped and fought for breath, and Tibold's
hands slid down from his head. The older man cradled
him like a lover or a child, and Crown Prince Sean Horus
MacIntyre sobbed upon his shoulder.

Tamman huddled close to the fire with his captains as
aides came and went. Enhancement kept the outer chill
at bay, but he hugged the fire's light, refusing to think
about what lay beyond its reach. The chainmail on his

right arm was stiff with other men's dried blood, his implants were busy with half a dozen small wounds, and he'd never been so tired in his life.

Branahlks whistled as some dragoons herded in more prisoners, and a messenger came in with a report from the troops Sean had sent to watch the fleeing Guardsmen. The messenger wanted nioharqs to collect another half-dozen abandoned guns, and Tamman cudgeled his brain until he remembered who to send him to. Another messenger trotted up on a drooping branahlk to announce his men had gathered up four thousand joharns, and what should he do with them? He dealt with that, as well, then looked up as Sean and Tibold walked into the fire lit circle.

The officers raised a tired cheer, and Tamman saw Sean wince before he raised a hand to acknowledge it. His friend's face was like iron as they clasped forearms tiredly, and the two of them stared into the fire together.

Stomald closed two more dead eyes, then rose from aching knees. The captured priests and under-priests of the Temple would have nothing to do with him. They spat upon him and reviled him, but their dying soldiers saw only his vestments and heard only his comforting voice.

He closed his own eyes, swaying with fatigue, and whispered a prayer for the souls of the dead. For the many dead of both sides, and not for his own, alone. Pardal had not seen such slaughter, nor such crushing victory, in centuries, yet there was no jubilation in Stomald's heart. Thankfulness, yes, but no one could see such suffering and rejoice.

A slender arm steadied him, and he opened his eyes. The Angel Harry stood beside him. Her blue-and-gold garments were spattered with blood, and her face was drawn, her one eye shadowed, but she looked at him with concern.

"You should rest," she said, and he shook his head drunkenly.

"No." It was hard to get the word out. "I can't."

"How long since you've eaten?"

"Eaten?" Stomald blinked. "I had breakfast, I think," he said vaguely, and she clucked her tongue.

"That was eighteen hours ago." She sounded stern. "You're not going to do anyone any good when you collapse. Go get something to eat."

He gagged at the thought, and she frowned.

"I know. But you need—" She broke off and looked about until she spied the Angel Sandy. She said something in her own tongue, and the Angel Sandy replied in the same language. The laughter had leached even out of her eyes, but she held out her hand, and the Angel Harry handed over her satchel of medicines without ever removing her arm from Stomald's shoulders.

"Come with me." He started to speak, but she cut him off. "Don't argue—march," she commanded, and led him towards the distant cooking fires. He tried again to protest, then let himself slump against her strength, and she murmured something else in that strange language. He looked up at her questioningly, but she only shook her head and smiled at him—a sad, soft little smile that eased his wounded heart—and her arm tightened about him.

The Inner Circle sat in silence as High Priest Vroxhan laid the semaphore message aside. He pressed it flat with his fingers, then tucked his hands into the sleeves of his robe, hugging himself against a chill which had nothing to do with the cool night, and met their gaze. Even Bishop Corada was white-faced, and Frenaur sagged about his bones.

Lord Rokas was dead; barely forty thousand of the Host had escaped, less than half of them with weapons; and High-Captain Ortak had the Host's rearguard working with frantic speed to dig in further down the Keldark Valley. Ortak's report was short of details, yet one thing was clear. The Host hadn't been beaten. It hadn't even been routed. It had been destroyed.

"There you have it, Brothers," Vroxhan said. "We've

failed to crush the heresy, and surely the heretics will soon counterattack." He glanced at High-Captain—no, Lord Marshal—Surak, and the man who had just become the Guard's senior officer looked back with stony eyes. "Exactly how bad is the situation, Lord Marshal?"

Surak winced at his new title, then squared his shoulders.

"Even with Ortak's survivors, we have barely seventy thousand men in all of Keldark. I don't yet know how many men the heretics deployed, but from the casualties we've suffered, they must have many more than that. I would have said they could never have raised and armed them, even with demonic aid, yet that they must have is evident from the result. I've already ordered every pike in Keldark forward to Ortak, but I fear they can do little more than slow the heretics. They can't stop them if they keep coming."

A soft sigh ran around the table, but Vroxhan looked up sternly, and it faded. Surak continued in a harsh voice.

"With Your Holiness' permission, I will order Ortak to retire on Erastor until more men—and weapons—can reach him. He can fight delaying actions, but if he stands, the heretics will surely overwhelm him."

"Wait," Corada objected. "Did not Lord Rokas say that an attacker needed twice or thrice a defender's numbers?"

Surak looked to Vroxhan, who nodded for him to answer.

"He did, and he was right, Your Grace, but those calculations are for battles in which neither side has demonic aid."

"Are you suggesting God's power is less than that of demons?"

Surak was no coward, but he fought an urge to wipe his forehead.

"No, Your Grace," he replied carefully. "I think it plain the demons *did* aid the heretics, and until I have Ortak's detailed report I can't say how they did so, but that isn't what I meant. Consider, please, Your Grace. Our men have been defeated—" that pallid understatement twisted his mouth like sour wine "—and they know it. They've lost many of their weapons. Ortak may have forty thousand men, but barely twenty thousand are armed, and their morale is—must be—shaken. The heretics have all the weapons abandoned on the field to swell their original strength, and demons or no, they know they won. Their morale will be strengthened even as ours is weakened."

He paused and raised his empty hands, palms uppermost.

"If I order Ortak to stand, he will. And as surely as he does, he'll be destroyed, Your Grace. We *must* withdraw, using the strength we still possess to slow the enemy until fresh strength can be sent to join it."

"But by your estimate, Lord Marshal," Vroxhan said, "we lack the numbers to meet the heretics on equal terms." The high priest's voice was firm, but anxiety burned in its depths.

"We do, Holiness," Surak replied, "but I believe we have sufficient to hold at least the eastern end of the Keldark Valley. I would prefer to do just that and open a new offensive from the west, were our strength in Cherist and Thirgan great enough. It isn't, however, so we must fight them here. I realize that it was the Inner Circle's desire to defeat this threat solely with our own troops, Holiness, yet that's no longer possible either. Our main field army has, for all intents and purposes, been destroyed, not merely defeated, and I fear we *must* summon the secular armies of the east to Holy War. Were all their numbers gathered into a single new Host under the Temple's banner, they would—they must—suffice for victory . . . but only if we can hold the heretics in the mountains until they've mustered. For that reason, if no other, Ortak must be ordered to delay the enemy."

"I see." Vroxhan sighed. "Very well, Lord Marshal, let it be as you direct. Send your orders, and the Circle will summon the princes." Surak stooped to kiss the hem of the high priest's robe and withdrew, his urgency evident in his speed, and Vroxhan looked about the table once more.

"And as for us, Brothers, I ask you all to join me in the Sanctum that we may pray for deliverance from the ungodly."

Chapter Thirty

Sean MacIntyre stood with Sandy and frowned down at the relief map. Tibold and a dozen other officers stood around respectfully, watching him and "the Angel Sandy" study the map, and the absolute confidence in their eyes made him want to scream at them.

The Battle of Yortown lay one of the local "five-days" in the past. The Angels' Army had advanced a hundred and thirty kilometers in that time, but now High-Captain Ortak's entrenched position lay squarely in its path, and try as he might, Sean saw no way around it. In fact, he'd come to the conclusion Tibold had offered from the first: the only way around was *through*, and that was the reason for his frown.

Sean's army had every advantage in an open field battle. The Yortown loot had included twenty-six thousand joharns, enough for Sean to convert all fifty-eight thousand of his men into musketeers and send several thousand to the force covering the Thirgan Gap in the west to boot, and Brashan had shifted *Israel* to the mountains directly above Yortown to decrease cutter transit time to the battleship. The Narhani's machine shop modules had increased their modification rate to forty-five hundred rifles (with bayonet rings) a night, and the Malagoran gunsmiths were adding almost a thousand a day more on their own, now that "the angels" had taught them about rifling benches. Unfortunately, over half Sean's army had been trained as *pikemen*, and the new men were still learning which end the bullet came out of.

Even so, his troops were fleeter of foot and had incomparably more firepower than any other Pardalian army.

The new, standardized rifle regiments he and Tibold had organized could kill their enemies from five or six times smoothbore range, and the absence of polearms made them far more mobile. Even the best pikemen were less than nimble trailing five-meter pikes, and his rifle-armed infantry could dance rings around the Guard's ponderous phalanxes. Coupled with its higher rate of fire, the Angels' Army could cut four or five times its own number to pieces in a mobile engagement.

Unhappily, High-Captain Ortak knew it. He was well supplied with artillery, since Lord Marshal Rokas had known the cramped terrain at Yortown would reduce his guns' efficiency and left many of them with his rearguard, and reinforcements had come forward, but less than half his roughly eighty thousand men were actually armed. Less than twelve thousand were musketeers, and he dared not face the Angels' Army in the open. But short of arms or not, his men still outnumbered Sean's by almost forty percent, and all those unarmed men had been busy with mattocks. The earthworks he'd thrown up at Erastor closed the Keldark Valley north of the Mortan, and he clearly had no intention of venturing beyond them. Nor could any army go around them. The Mortan was unfordable for over ninety kilometers upstream or down from Erastor, and the terrain south of the river was so boggy not even nioharqs could drag artillery or wagons through it.

In many respects, Erastor was a stronger defensive position even than Yortown, and Sean and Tibold had considered meeting Rokas there. In the end, they'd decided in favor of Yortown because its terrain had let Sean set his ambush, but for a simple holding engagement, Erastor would actually have been better. There were no open flanks between the Erastor Spur and the river, which left an opponent with superior numbers—or mobility—no openings. He had to attack head-on, and if Ortak refused to come out, Sean would have to go in after him . . . which meant the Guard's outnumbered and outranged musketeers could hunker down behind their parapets until Sean's men entered *their* range. The Guard's morale had to be shaken by what had happened at Yortown, while the Angels' Army's morale had soared in inverse proportion, and Sean knew his troops could take Erastor. It was the *cost* of taking it that terrified him.

He frowned more deeply at the map and once more castigated himself for not pushing on more quickly. He'd taken five days to march a distance a Pardalian army could have done in three if it was pushed, and the consequences promised to be grim. If he'd crowded the routed Host harder, he might have bounced Ortak out of Erastor before the high-captain dug in, and telling himself his troops had been exhausted by the Yortown fighting made him feel no better. He should have gotten them on the way with the next dawn, however tired, not wasted two whole days burying the dead and collecting the Host's cast away weapons, and he swore at himself for delaying.

He wanted to swear at Tibold, as well, for letting him, but that wouldn't have been fair. The ex-Guardsman was a product of the military tradition which had evolved after the Schismatic Wars, and Pardalian wars were fought for territory. Ideally, battles were avoided in favor of efforts to outmaneuver an opponent, and campaigns were characterized by intricate, almost formal march and countermarch until they climaxed in equally formal engagements or sieges for vital fortresses. The Napoleonic doctrine of pursuing a beaten foe to annihilation was foreign to local military thought. It shouldn't have been, given the mobility nioharqs bestowed, but it was, and a crushing victory like Yortown would have brought most wars to a screeching conclusion as the defeated side treated for terms. Not this time. High Priest Vroxhan and the Inner Circle might not have the least idea what Sean and his marooned friends were truly after, but they'd realized they were fighting for their very survival. Worse, they were fighting, as they saw it, for their souls. Oh, it was obvious they'd become firmly attached to their secular power, but they also saw no distinction between "God's Will" and the Temple's domination of Pardal. Under the circumstances, there were—*could* be—no acceptable "terms" for them short of the "heretics'" utter destruction, and they were mobilizing their reserves. Within another two weeks, at most three, thousands of fresh troops would be marching into Erastor. Somehow he had to crush the Erastor position before those reinforcements arrived, and his soul cringed at the thought of the casualties his men would suffer because *he'd* screwed up.

His frown at the map became a glare. He knew, intellectually, that there wasn't always a clever answer, but he was also young. Centuries older than he'd been before Yortown, but still young enough to believe there *ought* to be an answer, if he were only smart enough to see it.

A hand touched his elbow, and he turned his head to see Sandy looking up at him. Her face was no longer the haunted mask it had been the first night after Yortown, but, as for all of *Israel*'s crew, the slaughter of that day had left its mark upon her. Her eyes had learned to twinkle once more, yet there was less brashness behind them. No less confidence, perhaps, but a deeper awareness of the horrible cost reality could exact. Now those eyes met his searchingly, the question in them plain, and he sighed.

"I don't see an answer," he said in English. "They've put in too solid a roadblock, and it's my own damned fault."

"Oh, shush!" she said in the same language, squeezing his elbow harder. "We're all getting on-the-job training, and the last thing we need is for you to kick yourself for things you can't change. Seems to me you did a pretty fair job at Yortown, and you've got a lot more to work with now."

"Sure I do." He tried to keep the bitterness from his voice. His officers might not understand English, but they could recognize emotional overtones, and there was no sense shaking *their* confidence. "Unfortunately," he went on in a determinedly lighter tone, "the bad guys have more to work with, too. Not in numbers, but in position." He waved at the fifteen kilometers of earth-works linking the stony Erastor Spur to the river. "We surprised Rokas by doing something he *knew* was impossible, but Ortak has a much better idea of our capabilities, and he's dug in to deny us all our advantages. We can take him out with a frontal assault, but we'll lose thousands, and I just can't convince myself it's worth it, Sandy. Not just so we can get hold of a computer!"

"It's *not* just to get us to the computer!" she said fiercely, then smoothed her own tone as a few officers stirred in surprise. She shook her head and went on more calmly. "It's life and death for all these people, Sean— you know that."

"Yeah? And whose fault is that?" he growled.

"Ours," she said unflinchingly. "Mine, if you want to be specific. But it's something we blundered into, not something we did on purpose, and if we started all this, then we have to *finish* it."

Sean closed his eyes and tasted the bitterness of knowing she was right. It was a conversation they'd had often enough, and rehashing it now would achieve nothing. Besides, he *liked* the Malagorans. Even if he'd borne no responsibility for their predicament, he still would have wanted to help them.

"I know," he said finally. He opened his eyes and smiled crookedly, then patted the hand on his elbow. "And it's no more your fault than it is mine or Tamman's or Brashan's—even Harry's. It's just knowing how many of them are going to get killed because I didn't push hard enough." She started to open her mouth, but he shook his head. "Oh, you're right. People make mistakes while they learn. I know that. I only wish *my* mistakes could be made somewhere that didn't get people killed."

"You can only do the best you can do." Her voice was so gentle he longed to take her in his arms, but God only knew how his officers would react if he started going around hugging an "angel"!

He actually felt his mouth quirk a smile at the thought, and he folded his hands behind him again and walked slowly around the table, studying the relief map from all angles. If only there were a way to use his mobility! Someone—he thought it had been Nathan Bedford Forrest—had once said war was a matter of "getting there firstest with the mostest," not absolute numbers, and the one true weakness of Ortak's position was its size. He had fifteen kilometers of frontage—more, with the salients built into his earthworks—and that gave him barely two thousand armed men per kilometer even if he withheld no reserve at all. Of course, he had another thirty or forty thousand he could send in to pick up the weapons of their fallen comrades, but even so he was stretched thin. If Sean could break his front anywhere, and get *behind* his works, he could sweep them like a broom. But there was no way he could—

He paused suddenly, and his eyes narrowed. He stood absolutely still, staring down at the map while his mind raced, and then he began to smile.

"Sean? *Sean?*" Sandy had to call him twice before he looked up with a jerk. "What is it?" she asked, and his smile took on a harder, fiercer cast.

"I've been going at this wrong," he said. "I've been thinking about how Ortak has us blocked, and what I *should* have been thinking about is how he's trapped himself."

"Trapped?" she asked blankly, and he waved Tibold closer and pointed at the map.

"Could infantry get through these swamps?" he asked in Pardalian, and it was the ex-Guardsman's turn to frown down at the map.

"Not pikes," he said after a moment, "but you might be able to get musketeers through." He cocked his head, comparing the exquisitely detailed map the angels had provided to all the ones he'd ever seen before, then tapped the southern edge of the swamp with a blunt forefinger. "I always thought the bad ground was wider than that down along the south face of the valley," he said slowly. "We could probably get a column across this narrow bit in, oh, ten or twelve hours. Not with guns or pikes, though, Lord Sean. There's no bottom to most of this swamp. You *might* get a few chagors through, but arlaks would sink to the axles in no time. And even after you get through the swamp, the ground's still soft enough between there and the river to slow you."

"Would Ortak expect us to try anything like that?" Sean asked, and Tibold shook his head quickly.

"He's got the same maps *we* had before you and the ang—" The ex-Guardsman bit the word off as he remembered how Lord Sean and the angels kept trying to get people not to call them that. For a moment his face felt hot, but then he grinned up at his towering young commander. "He's got the same maps we always had before. Besides, no Guard captain would even consider leaving his pikes and guns behind."

"That's what I hoped you'd say," Sean murmured, and his brain whirred as he estimated times and distances. The Mortan was the better part of three unfordable kilometers wide above and below Erastor, but it *could* be forded at Malz, a farm town ninety-odd klicks below its junction with the Erastor River. If he moved back west, out of sight of Ortak's lines, and threw together enough rafts . . . Or, for that matter, could his engineers knock together proper bridges? He considered the thought for a moment, then shook his head. No, that would take a good two or three days, and if this was going to work at all, he didn't have two or three days to waste.

"All right, Tibold," he said. "Here's what we'll do. First . . ."

High-Captain Ortak stood in his entrenchments' central bastion and stared west. Drizzling rain drew a gray veil across the Keldark Valley, limiting his vision, but he knew what was out there and breathed a silent thanks for his enemies' lack of initiative. Every day that passed without attack not only helped the morale of his battered force but brought its desperately needed relief one day closer.

He strained his eyes, trying to make out details of the

earthworks the heretics had thrown up to face his own. Part of him shuddered every time he thought of the cost of taking that position once the Holy Host had reinforced and resumed the offensive, but not even that could shake his gratitude. *He* knew how thin-stretched he was, and if the heretics had been willing to throw a column straight at him anywhere—

He shivered, and not because of the rain. He disliked having to stand with a river at his back, but the Erastor was fordable for most of its length. If he had to, he could fall back across it, though he'd have to abandon what remained of his baggage, and this was the best— probably the only—point at which to stop an army from the west. Conscripted laborers were building another position in his rear at Baricon, but Baricon was better suited to resisting attacks from the east. No, he had to hold the heretics here if he meant to keep them out of Keldark, and if they ever got loose in the duchy their freedom of maneuver would increase a hundredfold. After what they'd done to Lord Marshal Rokas at Yortown, that was enough to strike a chill in the stoutest heart.

He wrapped his cloak about himself and pursed his lips in thought. The semaphore chain across Malagor had been cut, but it continued to operate east of him, and the Temple's dispatches were less panicky than they had been. The secular lords were being slow to muster, but the Guard had stripped its garrisons throughout the eastern kingdoms to the bone, and fifty thousand men were on their way to him. Better yet, the first trains of replacement weapons had begun coming in. There were less of them than he would have liked, especially given what the heretics had captured at Yortown, but he'd already received eight thousand pikes and over five hundred joharns. If the reports from Yortown were right, the heretics had found some way to give joharns and malagors the range of rifles, which suggested final casualties would be atrocious even if the Guard managed to rearm every man, but that should be less of a factor defending entrenched positions than in the open field. They were going to have to find some reply to the heretics' weight of fire in the future, and Ortak was already considering ways to increase the ratio of firearms to pikes, but for the moment he had a stopper in the bottle and the heretics seemed unwilling to take the losses to remove it.

He sighed and shook himself. The light was going, and he had more than enough paperwork waiting to keep him up half the night. At least his quarters in Erastor were better than a tent in the field, he told himself, and smiled wryly as he turned and called for his branahlk.

Sean MacIntyre dismounted and wiped rain from his face. He could have used his implants to stay dry, but that would have felt unfair to his troops, which was probably silly but didn't change his feelings. He smiled at his own perversity and scratched his branahlk's snout, listening to its soft whistle of pleasure, and tried to hide his worry as the sodden column squelched past.

It was taking longer than planned, and the rain was heavier than *Israel*'s meteorological remotes had predicted. The cold front pushing down the valley had met a warm front out of Sanku and Keldark, and Brashan's latest forecast warned of at least twenty hours of hard rain, probably with thunderstorms. They would make the ground still softer and the going harder, and they were also going to deepen the fords at Malz, but at least it didn't look as if the Mortan would reach critical depths. Or, he thought grimly, not *yet*.

Tibold splashed up on his own branahlk and drew up beside him.

"Captain Juahl's reached the bivouac area, Lord Sean." The ex-Guardsman's tone made Sean crook an eyebrow, and Tibold sighed. "It's under a handspan of water, My Lord."

"Great." Sean closed his eyes and inhaled deeply, then flipped his fold com up to Sandy's hovering cutter. "Got a problem down here," he subvocalized. "Our bivouac site's underwater."

"Damn. Hang on a sec," she replied, and brought up her sensors, berating herself for not having checked sooner. She frowned in concentration over her neural feed as she swept the area ahead of the column, then her eyes brightened. "Okay. If you push on another six klicks, the ground rises to the south."

"Firewood?" he asked hopefully.

"'Fraid not," she replied, and he sighed.

"Thanks anyway." He turned to Tibold. "Tell Juahl he'll find higher ground if he bears a bit south and keeps moving for another hour or so."

"At once, Lord Sean." Tibold didn't even ask how his commander knew that; he simply turned his branahlk and splashed off into the gathering gloom, and Sean leaned back against his own mount and sighed.

He had twenty-five thousand men marching through mud towards fords which *ought* to be passable when they arrived, and he was beginning to wonder if he'd been so clever after all. Pardal's days were long, and on good roads (and Pardalian roads would have made any Roman emperor die of jealousy), infantry routinely made fifty kilometers a day in fair weather. Marching cross-country in the rain, even through open terrain, they were doing well to make thirty pushing hard, and they hadn't even reached the swamps yet. The men were in better spirits than he would have believed possible under the circumstances, but they'd marched for three grueling days, mostly in the rain and with no hot meals. Even for someone with full enhancement, this march was no pleasure jaunt; for the unenhanced, it was unadulterated, exhausting misery, and they were barely halfway to the fords.

He flicked his mind back over the latest reports from their stealthed remotes. Ortak was receiving fresh weapons, but any additional reinforcements were still at least twelve days away. Even allowing for his column's slower than estimated progress, Sean should be back north of the Mortan within another four days, but he was grimly aware of the risk he was running. The valley's peasants had been moved out by the Holy Host on its way in, and the Temple's troops had already accounted for everything that could be foraged from the abandoned farms. Pack nioharqs had accompanied them this far, but they'd have to be sent home once the column reached the swamp. From there, Sean's infantry would have to pack all of their supplies—including ammunition—on their backs, and that gave them no more than a week's food. Which meant that if his plan to surprise Ortak didn't work, he was going to find himself with twenty-five thousand starving men trapped between Erastor and the Guard reinforcements.

At least Ortak was cooperating so far. The high-captain "knew" the terrain south of the river was impassable, and he was too short of armed men to spare many from his prepared positions. He had pickets east of the Erastor, but they were fairly close to the bridges. It was still a bit hard to adjust to a pre-technic society's limitations, and despite everything, Sean felt vaguely exposed. His column was barely fifty air kilometers from Ortak's position, and it was hard to believe Ortak had no suspicion of what he was up to, yet the high-captain's deployments and the reports of Sandy's eavesdropping remotes all confirmed that he didn't.

The thought drew a wet chuckle from Sean. Miserable as he and his troops might be, they had the most deadly weapon known to man: surprise. And at least if he screwed up, it wouldn't be because the Guard had surprised *him*.

He gave his branahlk another scratch, then swung back into the saddle and trotted forward along the column.

Father Stomald stepped into the command tent and paused. The Angel Harry stood alone, staring down at the map and unaware of his presence, and her shoulders were tight.

The young priest hesitated. Part of him was loath to disturb her, but another part urged him to step closer. An angel needed no mortal's comfort, yet Stomald was guiltily aware that he was coming less and less to think of her as he ought.

The angels had fallen into a division of their duties which was too natural to have been planned, and the Angel Harry's share of those duties had brought her into almost constant contact with Stomald. The fighting of the war in which they were all trapped was the task of Lord Sean and Lord Tamman, but ministering to its consequences was Stomald's task. It was he who had begun it, whatever his intent, and it was he who must bear the weight of caring for its victims. He accepted that, for it was but an extension of his priestly duties, and his own faith would have driven him to shoulder that weight even if he could somehow have avoided it. But he was not alone before the harsh demands of his responsibilities, for as Lord Sean and Lord Tamman had Tibold and the Angel Sandy, Stomald had the Angel Harry. However grim the burden he faced, however terrible the cost war and its horrors exacted, she was always there, always willing to give him of her own strength and catch him when he stumbled. And that, he thought, was why he had come to feel these things he should not—*must* not—feel.

Yet knowing what he should not do and stopping himself from doing it were two very different things. She seemed so young, and she was different from the Angel Sandy. She was . . . softer, somehow. Gentler. The Angel Sandy cared deeply—no one who'd seen her face the night after Yortown could doubt that—yet she had a talmahk's fierceness the Angel Harry lacked. No one could ever call either angel weak, but the Angel Sandy and Lord Sean were kindred souls who threw off uncertainty like a too-small garment whenever it touched them. Their eyes were always on the next battle, the next challenge, yet it was the Angel Harry to whom those in trouble instinctively turned, as if they, as Stomald, sensed the compassion at her heart. Any angel must, of course, be special, but Stomald had seen how even the most hardened trooper's eyes followed the Angel Harry. The army would have followed Lord Sean or the Angel Sandy or

Lord Tamman against Hell itself, but the Angel Harry owned their hearts.

As she did Stomald's, and yet . . .

The priest sighed, and his eyes darkened as he admitted the truth. His love for the Angel Harry was wrong, for it was not what a man should dare to feel for one of God's holy messengers.

She heard his soft exhalation and turned, and he was shocked by the tears in her one good eye. She wiped them as quickly as she'd turned, but he'd seen them, and before he remembered what she was, he reached out to her.

He froze, hand extended, shocked by his own temerity. What was he *thinking*? She was an *angel*, not simply the beautiful young woman she appeared. Had he not learned to rely upon her strength? To turn to *her* for comfort when his own weariness and the sorrow of so much death pressed upon him? How dared he reach out to comfort *her*?

But he saw no anger in her eye, and his heart soared with curiously aching joy as she took his hand. She squeezed it and turned her head to look back down at the map table, and Stomald stood there, holding her hand, and confused emotions washed through him. It felt so right, so natural, to stand with her, as if this were the place he was meant to be, yet guilt flawed his contentment. He was aware of her beauty, of her wonderful blend of strength and gentleness, and he longed, more than he'd ever longed for anything other than to serve God Himself, for this moment to last forever.

"What is it?" he asked finally, and the depth of concern in his voice surprised even him.

"I'm just—" She paused, then gave her head a little shake. "I'm just worried about Sean," she said softly. "The way the river's rising, how far they still have to go, the odds when they get there . . ." She drew a deep breath and looked at him with a wan smile. "Silly of me, isn't it?"

"Not silly," Stomald disagreed. "You worry because you care."

"Maybe." She still held his hand, but her other hand ran a finger down the line of Lord Sean's march, and her voice was low. "I feel so guilty sometimes, Stomald. Guilty for worrying so much more about Sean than anyone else, and for having caused all this. It's my fault, you know."

Stomald flinched, and self-loathing filled him as he recognized his own jealousy. He was *jealous* of her concern for Lord Sean! The sheer impiety of his emotions frightened him, but then the rest of what she'd said penetrated, and he shook off his preoccupation with his own feelings.

"You didn't cause this. It was our fault for laying impious hands upon you." He hung his head. "It was *my* fault, not yours, My Lady."

"No it wasn't!" she said so sharply he looked up, dismayed by her anger. Her single eye bored into him, and she shook her head fiercely. "Don't ever think that, Stomald! You did what your Church had taught you to do, and —" She paused again, biting her lip, then nodded to herself. "And there's more happening here than you know even yet," she added with quiet bitterness.

Stomald blinked at her, touched to the heart once more by her readiness to forgive the man who'd almost burned her alive, yet confused by her words. She was an angel, with an angel's ability to know things no mortal could, yet her voice suggested she'd meant more than that. Perplexity filled him, and he reached for the first thing that crossed his mind.

"You care deeply for Lord Sean, don't you, My Lady?" he asked, and could have bitten off his tongue in the instant. The question cut too close to his own forbidden longings, and he waited for her anger, but she only nodded.

"Yes," she said softly. "I care for them all, but especially for Sean."

"I see," he said, and the dagger turning in his heart betrayed him. He heard the pain in his own voice and tried to turn and flee, but her fingers tightened about his, stronger than steel yet gentle, trapping him without harming him, and against his will, his gaze met hers.

"Stomald, I—" she said, then shook her head and said something else. She spoke to herself, in her own language, the one she spoke to the Angel Sandy and their champions. Stomald couldn't understand her words, but he recognized a curious finality, an edge of decision, and his heart hammered as she drew him over to a stool. He sat upon it at her gesture, uncomfortable, as always, at sitting in her presence, and she drew a deep, deep breath.

"I *do* care for Sean, very much," she told him. "He's my brother."

"Your—?" Stomald gaped at her, trying to understand, but his mind refused to work. He'd speculated, dreamed, hoped, yet he'd never quite dared *believe*. Lord Sean was mortal, however he might have been touched by God, yet if he was her brother, if mortal blood *could* mingle with the angels', then—

"It's time you knew the truth," she said quietly.

"The . . . the truth?" he repeated, and she nodded.

"There's a reason Sandy and I have tried to insist that you not treat us as angels, Stomald. You see, we aren't."

"Aren't?" he parroted numbly. "Aren't . . . aren't *what*, My Lady?"

"Angels." She sighed, and her expression shocked him. She was staring at him, her remaining eye soft, as if she feared his reaction, but he could only stare back. Not angels? That was . . . it was preposterous! Of *course* they were angels! That was why he'd preached their message to his people and the reason Mother Church had loosed Holy War upon them! They *had* to be angels!

"But—" The word came out hoarse and shaking, and he wrapped his arms about himself as if against a freezing wind. "But you *are* angels. The miracles you've worked to save us, your raiment—the things we've all seen Lord Sean and Lord Tamman do at your bidding—!"

"Aren't miracles at all," she said in that same soft voice, as if pleading for *his* understanding. "They're—oh, how can I make you understand?" She turned away, folding her arms below her breasts, and her spine was ramrod stiff. "We . . . can do many things you can't," she said finally, "but we're mortal, Stomald. All of us. We simply have tools, skills, you don't, yet if you had those tools, you could do anything you've seen us do and more."

"You're . . . mortal?" he whispered, and even through the whirlwind confusion uprooting all his certainty, he felt a sudden, soaring joy.

"Yes," she said softly. "Forgive me, please. I . . . I never meant to deceive you, never meant—" She broke off, shoulders shaking, and his heart twisted as he realized she was weeping. "We never wanted any of this to happen, Stomald." Her lovely voice was choked and thick. "We only . . . we only wanted to get home, and then I ran into Tibold, and he shot me and brought me back to Cragsend, and somehow it all—"

She shook her head fiercely, and turned back to face him.

"*Please*, Stomald. Please believe we never, ever, meant to hurt anyone. Not you, not your people, not even the Inner Circle. It just . . . happened, and we couldn't let the Church destroy you for something *we'd* caused!"

"Get home?" Stomald rose from the stool and crossed to stand directly before her, staring into her tear-streaked face, and she nodded. "Home . . . where?" he asked hesitantly.

"Out there." She pointed at the sky invisible beyond the roof of the tent, and for just an instant sheer horror filled the priest. The stars! She *was* from the stars, and the Writ said only the demons who had cast Man from the firmament—

Sick panic choked him. Had he done the very thing the Inner Circle charged him with? *Had* he given his allegiance to the Great Demons who sought only the destruction of all God's works?

But then, as quickly as it had come, the terror passed, for it was madness. Whatever else she might be, the Angel Harry—or whoever she truly was—was no demon.

He'd seen too much of her pain among the wounded and dying, too much gentleness and compassion, to believe that. And the Writ itself said no demon, greater or lesser, could speak the Holy Tongue, yet she spoke it to him every day! All his life, Stomald had been taught the inviolability of the Writ, but now he faced a truth almost more terrifying than the possibility that she might actually be a demon, for if she came from the stars, the Writ said she *must* be a demon, and yet the Writ also proved she *couldn't* be one.

He felt the cornerstone of his life turning under his feet like wet, treacherous sand, and fear washed through him. But even as that fear sought to suck him under, he clung to his faith in her. Angel or no, he *trusted* her. More than trusted, he admitted to himself. He loved her.

"Tell me," he begged, and she stepped forward. She rested her hands on his shoulders and gazed into his face, and he felt his fear ease as her fingers squeezed gently.

"I will. I'll tell you everything. Some of it will be hard to understand, maybe even impossible—at first, at least—but I swear it's true, Stomald. Will you trust me enough to believe me?"

"Of course," he said simply, and the absolute certainty in his tone was distantly surprising even to him.

"Thank you," she said softly, then drew a deep breath. "The first thing you have to understand," she said more briskly, "is what happened—not just here on Pardal, but out there, as well—" her head jerked at the tent roof once more "sixteen thousand of your years ago."

It took hours. Stomald lost count of how many times he had to stop her for fuller explanation, and his brain spun at the tale she told him. It was madness, impossible, anathema to everything he'd ever been taught . . . and he believed every word. He had no choice, and a raging sense of wonder mingled with shock and the agonizing destruction of so much certainty.

". . . so that's the size of it, Stomald," she said finally. They sat on facing stools, and the candles had burned low in the lanterns set about the tent. "We never meant to harm anyone, never meant to deceive anyone. We *tried* to tell you Sandy and I weren't angels, but none of you seemed able to believe it, and if we'd insisted and shattered your cohesion when the Church was determined to kill you all because of something *we'd* started—" She shrugged unhappily, and he nodded slowly.

"Yes, I can see that." He rubbed his thighs, then licked his lips and managed a strained smile. "I always wondered why you and the An—why you and *Sandy* insisted that we not call you 'angel' when we spoke to you."

"Can . . . can you forgive us?" she asked quietly. "We never wanted to insult your beliefs or use your faith against you. Truly we didn't."

"Forgive you?" He smiled more naturally and shook his head. "There's nothing to forgive, My Lady. You are who you are and the truth is the truth, and if the Writ is wrong, perhaps you *are* God's messengers. From what you say, this world has spent thousands upon thousands of years blind to the truth and living in fear of an evil that no longer exists, and surely God can send whomever He wishes to show us the truth!"

"Then . . . you're not angry with us?"

"Angry, My Lady?" He shook his head harder. "There are many parts of your tale I don't understand, but Lady Sandy was right. Once events had been set in motion, I and all who followed me would have been destroyed by Mother Church without your aid. How could I be angry at you for saving my people? And if the Writ *is* wrong, then the bishops and high-priests must learn to accept that, as well. No, Lady Harry. I don't say all our people could accept what you've told me. But the day will come when they can, and will, know the truth, and when they are once more free to travel the stars without fear of demons and damnation, they will no more be angry with you than *I* could ever be."

"Stomald," she said softly, "you're a remarkable man."

"I'm only a village under-priest," he objected, uncomfortable and yet filled with joy by the glow in her eye.

"Beside you, I'm an ignorant child playing in the mud on the bank of a tiny stream."

"No, you're not. The only difference between us is education and access to knowledge your world denied you, and I grew up with those things. You didn't, and if our positions were reversed, I doubt I could have accepted the truth the way you have."

"Accepted, My Lady?" He laughed. "I'm still trying to believe this isn't all a dream!"

"No, you're not," she repeated with a smile, "and that's what makes you so remarkable." Her smile turned suddenly into a grin. "I always wondered how Dad really felt when Dahak started explaining the truth about human history to him. Now I know how Dahak must've felt making the explanation!"

"I should like to meet this 'Dahak' one day," Stomald said wistfully.

"You will," she assured him. "I can hardly wait to take you home and introduce you to Mom and Dad, as well!"

"Take . . . ?" He blinked at her, then stiffened as she reached out and cupped the side of his face in those steel-strong, moth-gentle fingers.

"Of course, Stomald," she said very, very softly. "Why do you think I wanted to tell you the truth?"

He stared at her in disbelief, and then she leaned forward and kissed him.

Chapter Thirty-One

Tamman stood sipping a steaming mug of tea and tried not to yawn. Brashan's predicted thunderstorms had rolled up the valley yesterday, and the entire camp was ankle-deep in mud. Pardalian field sanitation was far better than that of most preindustrial armies, and he and Sean had improved on that basic platform, but it was simply impossible to put forty or fifty thousand human beings into an encampment without consequences. Coupled with decent diet, the latrines were holding things like dysentery within limits, yet the ground had been churned into sticky soup and everyone was thoroughly wet and miserable.

He stretched, then lifted his face gratefully to the morning sun. The rain had moved further up the valley, and it was still raising the level of the Mortan, but sunlight poured down over him, and he felt his spirits rise even as concern over Sean's slow progress simmered in the back of his brain.

Feet sucked through the mud towards him, and he turned and saw Harriet and Stomald. High-Captain Ithun had mentioned that the priest and "Ang—*Lady* Harry" had spent hours in the command tent last night, and he'd wondered why Harry hadn't mentioned it to him herself. Now he detected a subtle change in their body language as they approached him, and his eyebrows rose.

"Tamman." Harriet nodded as he touched his breastplate in the gesture of respect he and Sean always gave "the angels," but there was something different about *that* as well, and he wondered just what the hell she and Stomald had been discussing last night. Surely she hadn't—?

The question must have showed on his face, for she met his gaze unflinchingly and nodded. His eyes widened, and he looked around quickly.

"Would you and the boys pardon us a moment, Ithun?" he asked.

"Of course, Lord Tamman." The man who'd become his exec after the Battle of Yortown nodded and waved to the rest of his staff. They waded away from the campfire through the morning mist, and Tamman turned back to Harriet.

A moment of silence stretched out between them, and Stomald's expression confirmed his worst suspicions. The man knew. It showed in his wary eyes . . . and how close he stood to Harriet. Tamman felt his lips quirk, and he snorted. He'd seen this coming weeks ago, and it wasn't as if he'd expected Harry to be his love forever. Neither of them was—no, he corrected himself, neither of them *had been*—ready to settle down like Sean and Sandy, and he'd told himself he was mature enough to handle it. Well, perhaps he was, but it still stung. Not that he could blame Stomald. The priest was a good man, even if his first meeting with Harry *had* been an attempt at judicial murder, and he shared the same compassion which was so much a part of Harry.

None of which changed the fact that she hadn't so much as discussed her decision to tell him the truth! The possible repercussions of that little revelation in the middle of a holy war hardly bore thinking on, and her defiant expression showed she knew it. He considered half a dozen cutting remarks, then made himself set them all aside, uncertain how many of them stemmed from legitimate concern and how many from bruised male ego.

"Well," he said finally, in Pardalian, "you look like you have something to tell me."

"Lord Tamman," Stomald replied before Harriet could, "Lady Harry told me the truth last night." Tamman eyed him wordlessly, and the priest returned his gaze steadily. "I have told no one else, and I have no intention of telling anyone until the Inner Circle is defeated and you and your companions have gained access to this . . . computer." His tongue stumbled over the unfamiliar word, but Tamman felt his own shoulders relax. His worst fear had been Stomald's invincible integrity; if the priest had decided *Israel*'s crew had defiled his religion, the results could have been unmitigated disaster.

"I see," Tamman said slowly, then pursed his lips. "May I ask why not, Father?"

"Because Lady Sandy was right," Stomald said simply. "We're trapped in a war, and if I was wrong to think Lady Harry and Lady Sandy angels, the Inner Circle is even more wrong in what *it* believes. There will be time to sort things out once the Guard is no longer trying to kill us all, My Lord."

The priest smiled wryly, and Tamman smiled back. Damned if *he* could have taken the complete destruction of his worldview as calmly as Stomald seemed to be taking it!

"At the same time, My Lord," Stomald went on a bit more hesitantly, "Lady Harry told me of her relationship with you." Tamman stiffened. Pardalian notions of morality were more flexible than he'd expected. Unmarried sex wasn't a mortal sin on Pardal, but it *was* something the Church frowned upon, yet Stomald's tone was that of a wary young man, not an irate priest.

"Yes?" he said in his most conversational tone.

"My Lord," Stomald met his eyes squarely, "I love Lady Harry with all my heart. I don't pretend to be her equal, or worthy of her," Harriet made a sound of disagreement, but he ignored her to hold Tamman's eyes, "yet I love her anyway, and she loves me. I . . . do not wish for you to think either of us has betrayed you or attempted to deceive you."

Tamman gazed back for several seconds while he wrestled with his own emotions. Damn it, he *had* seen this coming, and Harry had been his friend long before she'd become his lover! They'd both known the forced intimacy of their battleship-lifeboat was what had made them lovers, and he'd known it was going to end *someday*, yet for just an instant he felt a terrible, burning envy of Sean and Sandy.

But then he shook himself and drew a deep breath.

"I see," he said again, holding out his hand, and Stomald took it with only the briefest hesitation. "I won't pretend it does great things for my self-image, Stomald, but Harry's always been her own person. And, much as it might pain me to admit it, you're a pretty decent fellow yourself." The priest smiled hesitantly, and Tamman chuckled. "It's not as if I haven't seen it coming, either," he said more cheerfully. "Of course, she couldn't tell *you* what she felt, but the way she's talked about you to the *rest* of us—!"

"Tamman!" Harriet protested with a gurgle of laughter, and Stomald turned bright red for just an instant before he laughed.

"She's been watching you like a kinokha stalking a shemaq for weeks," Tamman said wickedly, and watched *both* of them blush, amazed that he could feel such genuinely unbitter pleasure in teasing Harriet.

"You're riding for a fall, Tamman!" she warned, shaking a fist at him, and he laughed. Then she lowered her fist and stepped closer. She put her arms around him and hugged him tightly. "But you're a pretty decent fellow yourself," she whispered in his ear.

"Of course I am," he agreed, and put his own arm around her, then looked back at Stomald. "You don't need them, but you have my blessings, Stomald. And if you need a groomsman—?"

"I—" Stomald began, then stopped, blushed even brighter, and looked at Harriet appealingly.

"I think you're getting a bit ahead of yourself," she told Tamman, "but assuming we all get out of this in one piece and I get him home to Mom and Dad, we might just take you up on that."

"Shit!"

No one understood the English expletive, but Sean's

officers understood the tone. All of them were splashed from head to toe in mud, and Sean stood in cold, thigh-deep water that rose nearly to the Pardalians' waists. The rain had stopped, but the air was almost unbearably humid, and swarms of what passed for gnats whined about their ears. The column stretched out behind them, for Sean was leading the way now, since his implant sensors made it far easier for him to pick a route through the swamp—or would have if there'd *been* a way through it, he thought savagely.

He inhaled and made himself calm down before he opened his mouth again, then turned to his staff.

"We'll have to backtrack," he said grimly. "The bottom drops off ahead, and there's some kind of quicksand to the right. We'll have to cut further north."

Tibold said nothing, but his mouth tightened, and Sean understood. Their original plans had called for passing the column's head through the swamp in ten or twelve hours, and so far they'd been slogging around in it for over twenty. What had seemed a relatively simple, if unpleasant, task on the map had become something very different, and it was all his own fault. He had the best reconnaissance capabilities on the planet, and he should have scouted their route better than this. If he had, he would have known the foot of the valley's northern wall was lined with underground springs. The narrowest part of the swamp was also one of the least passable, and his stupid oversight had mired his entire corps down in it.

"All right," he said finally, sighing. "We won't get anywhere standing here looking at the mud." He thought for a few moments, calling up the map he'd stored in his implant computers on the way through, then nodded sharply. "Remember where we stopped for lunch?" he asked Tibold.

"Yes, My Lord."

"All right. There was a spit of solider ground running northeast from there. If there's a way through this glop at all, we'll have to go that way. Turn the column around and stop its head there. While you're doing that, I'll see if Lady Sandy can pick a better path than I can."

"At once, My Lord," Tibold agreed, and turned to slosh back along the halted column while Sean activated his com.

"Sandy?" he subvocalized.

"Yes, Sean?" She was trying to hide her own anxiety, he thought, and made his own tone lighter.

"We're gonna have to backtrack, kid."

"I know. I had a remote tuned in."

"In that case, you know where we're headed, and I'm one dumb asshole not to have had you checking route for us already." He sighed. "Tune up your sensors and see if you can map us a way through this slop."

"I'm already working on it," she said, "but, Sean, I don't see a *fast* way through it."

"How bad is it?"

"From what I can see, it's going to take at least another full day and a half," she said in a small, most un-Sandy-like voice.

"Great. Just fucking great!" Sean felt her flinch and shook his head quickly, knowing she was watching him through her remotes. "Sorry," he said penitently. "I'm not pissed at *you*; I'm pissed at *me*. There's no excuse for this kind of screwup."

"No one else thought of it, either, Sean," she pointed out in his defense, and he snorted.

"Doesn't make me feel any better," he growled, then sighed. "Well, I guess standing around pissing and moaning won't make it any better, either. Let's get this show back on the road—such as it is!"

He turned to slog off in Tibold's wake, and the swarming clouds of gnats whined about his ears.

Even Sandy's estimate turned out to have been overly optimistic. What Sean and Tibold had envisioned as a twelve-hour maneuver consumed over three of Pardal's twenty-nine-hour days, and it was an exhausted, sodden, mud-spattered column of infantry that finally crawled out of the swamp proper into the merely "soft" ground south of it. Thank God Tibold had warned him against even trying to bring artillery through that muck, Sean thought wearily. Their five hundred dragoons had lost a quarter of their branahlks, and Lord only knew what would have happened to nioharqs. Given his druthers, he decided, he'd take Hannibal's elephants and the Alps over a Pardalian swamp and *anything*.

Under the circumstances, he'd eased the "no miracles" rule, and Sandy and Harry had been busy using cutters to bring in fresh food. The cargo remotes had stacked it neatly to await his column's arrival, and the troops gave a weary cheer as they saw it. There was even a little wood for fires, and the company cooks quickly got down to business.

"Sean?"

He turned and flashed a mud-spattered smile as Sandy walked out of the gathering evening. His officers and men saw her as well, and she waved to them as a soft, wordless murmur of thanks rose from them. She made a shooing gesture at the waiting rations, and the troops grinned and returned to their tasks as she crossed to Sean. Unlike her towering lover, she was spotless. Not even her boots were muddy, and he shook his head.

" 'Ow can you tell she's an angel?" he murmured. " 'Cause she's not covered wi' shit loike the rest of us!" he answered himself.

"Very funny." She smiled dutifully, but her eyes were worried, and he raised an eyebrow.

"The reinforcing column got on the road a day sooner than Ortak expected," she said softly in English, "and it's moving faster than *we* expected. They'll reach Malz within four or five days."

"Wi—?" Sean stared at her, then clamped his teeth hard. "And just why," he asked after a moment, "is this the first *I'm* hearing of this?"

"It wouldn't have done a bit of good to worry you with it while you were mucking around in the swamp," she replied more tartly. "You were already going as fast as you could. All you could have done was fret."

"But—" He started to speak sharply, then made himself stop. She was right, but she was also wrong, and he controlled his tone very carefully when he went on. "Sandy, don't *ever* hold things back on me again, please? There may not have been anything I could have done, but as long as I'm in command, I need *all* the information we've got, as soon as we get it. Is that understood?"

He held her eyes sternly, and her nostrils flared with answering anger. But then she bit her lower lip and nodded.

"Understood," she said in a low voice. "I just—" She looked down at her hands and sighed. "I just didn't want you to worry, Sean."

"I know." He reached out to capture one of her hands and squeezed it tightly until she looked up. "I *know*," he said more softly. "It's just that this isn't the time for it, okay?"

"Okay," she agreed, and then her brown eyes suddenly gleamed. "But if you really want to know *everything*, then I suppose I should tell you what Harry's been up to, too."

"What *Harry's* been up to?" Sean looked speculatively down at her, then raised his head as Tibold called his name. The ex-Guardsman pointed to the meal preparations, and Sean waved for the others to go ahead without him and returned his attention to Sandy. "And just what," he asked in a deliberately ominous voice, "has my horrid twin done now?"

"Well, it turned out fine, but she decided to tell Stomald the truth."

"My God! I turn my back for an instant, and *all* of you run amok!"

"Oh, no! Not us—*you're* the one who's been running around in the muck!" Sandy gurgled with laughter as he winced, then sobered—a little. "Besides, Harry had an excuse. She's in love."

"Think I hadn't figured that out weeks ago? How'd Tamman take it?"

"Quite well, actually," Sandy said wickedly. "I wouldn't say he's completely over it, but I *did* overhear a couple of the Malagoran girls sighing over how handsome 'Lord Tamman' is."

"Handsome? *Tam?*" Sean cocked his head, then chuckled. "Well, compared to me, I guess he is. You mean he's, um, encouraging their interest?"

"Let's just say he isn't *dis*couraging it." Sandy grinned.

"Well, in that case, I suppose you'd better catch me up on all the gossip before I join the others for supper."

"Why? I could brief you while you eat, Sean. None of them understand English."

"I know that," Sean said. He picked out a relatively dry spot, spread his Malagoran-style poncho over it, and waved her to a seat upon it. "The problem, dear, is that I can't eat very well while I'm laughing. Now give."

Chapter Thirty-Two

"All right, then. Everybody clear on his orders?"

Sean looked around the circle of faces in the late afternoon light. He and Tibold had spent weeks convincing their officers to ask questions whenever there was *anything* they didn't understand, but, one by one, each captain nodded soberly.

"Good!" He folded the map with deliberate briskness, then turned and gazed northeast to the screen of dragoons deployed across his line of advance. Beyond them, he could just see a village that was supposed to have been totally evacuated . . . and hadn't been.

Sandy's warning that there were still people about had come in time—he hoped. He'd sent flanking columns of dragoons forward, then had them curl back in from the east, and they seemed to have caught all the villagers before anyone got away to Malz.

It was the ninth day since he'd set out for Erastor. By his original estimate, he should already have been in striking distance of Ortak's rear; as it was, he was still south of the Mortan, the weather was going bad on him again, and the head of the Guard relief column should reach the Malz turn-off within four days. His time margin had become knife-thin, and if any of those peasants *had* fled with word of his presence, he was in a world of trouble.

Well, Sandy's stealthed spies would warn him if the bad guys *did* figure out he was coming. Which, unfortunately, wasn't going to help him a lot if they figured it out after he'd crossed the river and trapped himself between Ortak and High-Captain Terrahk's relief force.

He shook off his worry and nodded to his officers.

"Let's get this show on the road, then," he said, and they slapped their breastplates in salute and dashed off.

Considering the unexpected rigors of the swamp crossing, the men were in excellent shape, Sean thought. Tired, but far from exhausted, and their morale was better than he would have dared hope. They'd *hated* the swamps, but despite the delays, their confidence was unshaken. Which was good, because they had another ten kilometers to cover this day, and Malz was tied into the semaphore chain which connected Erastor to points east. Each semaphore station was a looming, gantry-like structure which let its crew see for kilometers in every direction and turned it into a watch tower. That meant the chain had to be cut in darkness, before any warning could be sent in either direction, and defined not only when Sean had to reach and secure Malz, but when he had to get his troops across the river to the Baricon-Erastor high road, as well.

He called for his own branahlk and trotted back towards his infantry. Part of him longed to go with the dragoons in person, but Sandy's stealthed cutter hovered above them. She'd tell him if anything went wrong, and he needed to be with his main body, ready to respond to any warning she might send.

He turned in the saddle to watch Captain Juahl lead the dragoons east. Juahl was a good man, he told himself, and he understood the plan. That was just going to have to be enough.

It was almost midnight, local time, when Sean's lead rifle regiments reached Malz. Bonfires encircled the town, and parties of dragoons picketed its unprepossessing walls. It wasn't a large town—no more than eight thousand even in normal times, and its population had declined drastically when the Holy Host came through en route to Yortown—but enough people remained inside those walls to stand off dragoons. Worse, there were plenty of potential messengers to warn Ortak what was happening, which was the reason for those pickets and bonfires.

A mounted messenger trotted up to him and saluted.

"Captain Juahl sent me to report, Lord Sean," the exhausted young officer said. "We haven't secured the Malz tower yet—they got the town gates shut and we didn't have the strength to force them—but Captain Juahl and Under-Captain Hahna secured the fords and both towers between here and the crossroads. Hahna's company is posted just east of the crossroads, and we got both towers intact. Captain Juahl said to tell you our men are ready to pass messages both ways, My Lord."

"Good!" Sean slapped the messenger's shoulder, and the young man grinned at him. "Are you up to riding back to Captain Juahl?"

"Yes, My Lord!"

"In that case go tell him I'm delighted with his news. Ask him to thank all of his officers and men for me, as well, and tell him I'll get infantry support up as fast as I can."

"Yes, My Lord!" The messenger saluted again and vanished into the darkness, and Sean turned to Tibold.

"Thank God for that!" he said softly, and the ex-Guardsman nodded. Most of the men who'd managed the Temple's semaphore chain across Malagor had fled the heresy, but enough had joined it to give Sean the personnel to man the towers he'd hoped to capture. Now *he* controlled High-Captain Ortak's mail . . . and the information flowing east to the oncoming relief column, as well.

"I want you to help handle the negotiations here," he went on after a moment, waving at the closed gates. "We haven't had any massacres yet, and I'd sooner not start now because someone makes a mistake." He tugged on his nose. "Let's send Folmak's brigade up to Juahl. He's level-headed enough to handle anything that comes at him unexpectedly. Make sure he's got a copy of our message notes, and tell him I'll join him in person as soon as possible."

"At once, Lord Sean." Tibold turned his branahlk and trotted off with a briskness Sean knew he didn't feel.

Today's long march had been worse even than the swamp, and Tibold had spent part of it marching with each regiment. He insisted it was good for morale, and Sean believed him. It also meant "Lord Sean" had to stump along with the troops, too, but he was thirty-five years younger than Tibold and enhanced, to boot. He was undoubtedly the freshest man in the entire column, and all he wanted to do was sleep for a week.

Well, if Tibold could manage to look sharp and fresh, then so could Sean, and he'd damned well better do just that!

He grinned and dismounted, tossed his reins to one of his aides, and felt a spasm of pity for the townsfolk of Malz as he walked towards their closed gates. They had to know he could burn their town around their ears, and given the Inner Circle's propaganda, they probably expected him to do just that so their children would be nicely browned when he sat down to eat them! Convincing the poor bastards to open up was going to be a pain, but he needed to get it done before somebody did something stupid. Between them, Stomald and "the angels"— with a little help from the bloodthirsty field regulations of a certain Captain-General Lord Sean—had created a remarkably well-behaved army. The fact that it regarded itself as an elite force and confidently expected to kick the butt of a much larger army in a few days also helped by giving it a certain image to live up to, but Sean knew most of its restraint stemmed from the Holy Host's failure to reach Malagor. The Malagoran Temple Guard had done its share of village-burning on its abortive march to Cragsend, but half the men who'd done that were now members in good standing of the Angels' Army, and they'd done their very best to make amends. Yortown and the seizure of the Thirgan Gap had precluded the other atrocities religious wars routinely spawned, and the men felt little need for vengeance. Sean intended to keep it that way, but a handful of panicky townsmen who took it into their heads to "resist heresy" or simply thought they were defending their families could easily provoke a fire fight that might well expand into a full-blown massacre.

But that wasn't going to happen, he told himself firmly. He was a golden-tongued devil, and Tibold was going to advise him, and between them, they were going to talk those townsfolk into opening their gates without a shot being fired.

He stopped well out of aimed smoothbore range to wait for Tibold, and began to consider just how to accomplish that ambition.

"They've got Malz, and nobody got hurt on either side!" Harriet said as she entered the command tent, and her relief was so obvious Tamman refrained from observing that a lot of somebodies were going to get hurt at Erastor in a few days. Harry was too much like her dad and, appearance aside, not enough like her mom, he thought sadly.

"That's wonderful news," Stomald said, and Tamman nodded. It *was* wonderful news, too, he thought. At least Sean was finally out of those godawful swamps! None of them had expected him to lose that much time crossing them, and the entire operation was badly behind schedule, but it looked like they were going to make it after all . . . assuming the weather held.

"How are the fords?" he asked, gazing at the map and trying to hide a grin as Harriet stepped up beside Stomald and each of them tucked an arm around the other. So far they'd remembered not to do that in front of anyone but him or Sandy, and he didn't really want to find out how the troops would react if they slipped up and did it in public, but there was something incredibly touching about the shared tenderness in their eyes.

"Um?" Harriet looked up, then gave her head a shake. "Sorry, Tam. Sean says the fords are deeper than expected, but manageable if he takes it easy. The dragoons got across without losses, and the engineers are rigging guide ropes for the rest of the column. Tibold figures it'll take about five hours to get them all across once they start, but Sean's taking Folmak's brigade up to the crossroads tonight still. Well, this morning, I guess."

"So we've cut the semaphore chain, and it *looks* like no one knows we have," Tamman mused, plucking at his lip and gazing sightlessly at the map.

"Sandy and Brashan—" Harriet glanced at Stomald "—are monitoring their remotes in Erastor and tracking the relief column. So far, nobody in either place *does* know we're there."

"Yeah." Tamman nodded, then shrugged. "I know we've got them wired for sound, but I can't help worrying until we link back up with Sean." He studied the map a moment longer, then straightened. "I think I'll have a word with Ithun. If something does tip the bad guys, Ortak'll have to pull strength from our side of his position to do anything about it, and that might just let us slip an assault column through on him after all."

"Don't do anything rash without discussing it with Sean, Tam!"

"I won't get creative on you," he replied with a smile, "but Tibold's rubbing off on both of us. Like he says, 'Improvised responses work best when you've planned them well in advance!' "

" 'Bout time *someone* convinced you two of that," Harriet sniffed, and his smile turned into a broad grin.

"We're maturing, we are," he asserted virtuously. "And, ah, I'll see that no one disturbs you two while you 'confer,' too," he added wickedly as he opened the tent flap.

Sean looked up as Tibold's branahlk trotted up to the semaphore tower. The ex-Guardsman had gotten a whole three hours' sleep, and it was almost revolting how much that had restored him. He was soaked to the waist from fording the Mortan, but he waved cheerfully.

"The rearguard should be crossing just about now, Lord Sean," he said. "The lead brigade should arrive within the hour."

"Banners ready?" Sean asked.

"Aye, My Lord." Tibold grinned. The suggestion had come from Sandy, but he approved of it wholeheartedly. They'd captured more than enough Guard standards at Yortown to distribute among their regiments, and Sean had already sent Ortak a message from 'High-Captain Terrahk' to report he was further along than expected. With the banners for cover and the semaphore crews *expecting* to see Terrahk, any towers further up the chain that saw them coming should report them to Erastor as Ortak's expected relief.

Now Sean nodded to Tibold and turned back to the man who would command this semaphore garrison.

"Keep a sharp eye out, Yuthan," he said—for, he estimated, the sixth time, but Yuthan only nodded soberly. "You're doing an important job, but not important enough to risk getting cut off. If High-Captain Terrahk turns up, burn the tower and clear out."

"Aye, Lord Sean. Don't worry. None of us wants to get killed, My Lord, but we'll keep 'em confident until we do clear out."

"Good man." Sean squeezed the Malagoran's shoulder, then mounted his own branahlk and turned back to Tibold.

"I sent one of Folmak's regiments a little way west with a company of Juahl's dragoons, just to be on the safe side," he said, urging his mount to a trot. "They've got orders to stay out of sight from the next tower, but they're our front door. They've already hauled in about thirty people."

"That many?" Tibold was surprised. "I wouldn't have expected Ortak to allow that much traffic out of Erastor."

"Most of them seem to be trying to get as far from Erastor as they can," Sean snorted, "and I sort of doubt Ortak even knows they're doing it. Two-thirds of them are deserters, as a matter of fact."

"There are always some," Tibold said with a curled lip. "I imagine there's even more temptation than usual if you believe you're up against demons. On the other hand, they might just think they could convince Ortak not to shoot them if they hustled back to tell him we're coming. Once the main body gets up here, have them sent back to Malz and kept there till Yuthan and his boys pull out. After that, they can do whatever they want."

"I don't envy them," Tibold said, almost against his will. "With Terrahk coming up the road, the best they can hope for is to take to the hills before he gets his hands on them."

"That's their problem, I'm happy to say," Sean grunted back. "I'll settle for making sure Terrahk doesn't get his hands on *us*."

High-Captain Ortak reread the message with enormous relief. Terrahk had set a new record for the march from Kelthar, the capital of Keldark, if he was already at Malz! He'd shaved another three days off his estimated arrival, and Ortak wondered how he'd done it. Not that he intended to complain. With those fifty thousand well-armed and (hopefully) unshaken men to reinforce it, Erastor would become impregnable. Better yet, Terrahk outranked him. Ortak could turn the responsibility over to him, and he was guiltily aware of how terribly he wanted to do just that.

"Any reply, Sir?" his aide asked, and Ortak leaned back in his chair, then shook his head.

"None. They're obviously already moving as fast as they can. Let's not make them think we're *too* nervous."

"No, My Lord," the aide agreed with a smile, and Ortak waved him out of the room and bent back to his paperwork. Three more days. All the heretics had to do was hold off for three more days, and their best chance to smash their way out of Malagor would be gone forever.

For all its self-inflicted technical wounds, Pardal was an ancient and surprisingly sophisticated world, Sean reflected, and its road network reflected it. He'd wondered, when they first spotted the Temple from orbit, how a preindustrial society could transport sufficient food for a city that size even with the canal network to help, but that was before he knew about nioharqs or how good their roads were. They'd developed some impressive engineers over the millennia, and most of them seemed to have spent their entire careers building either temples or roads. Even here in the mountains, the high road was over twenty meters wide, and its hard-paved smoothness rivaled any of Terra's pre-Imperial superhighways.

He drew up and watched his men march past. Like the Roman Empire, Pardalian states relied on infantry, and the excellence of their roads stemmed from the same need to move troops quickly. Of course, come to think of it, the same considerations had created the German autobahns and the United States interstate highway system, hadn't they? Some things never seemed to change.

Whatever their reasoning, he was profoundly grateful to the engineers who'd built *this* road. After their nightmare cross-country journey, the men moved out with a will, relieved to be out of the mud and muck, and they'd made over thirty kilometers today despite the hours spent crossing the Malz fords.

They'd also nabbed three more semaphore towers without raising any alarms. He was a bit surprised by how smoothly that part had gone, but Juahl had devised a system that seemed to work perfectly. He sent an officer and a couple of dozen men on ahead of the main body in captured Guard uniforms, and they simply rode straight up to each tower and asked the station commander to assemble his men. The semaphore crews belonged to the civil service, not the army. None of them were going to argue with Guard dragoons, and as soon as the Malagorans had them out in the open, they suddenly found themselves looking down the business ends of a dozen rifled joharns at very short range. Since the signal arms were controlled from the ground, it didn't even matter if the men manning the tower platforms realized what was happening. They couldn't tell anyone, and so far none of them had been inclined to argue when the rest of Juahl's men arrived and invited them to come down.

In the meantime, neither Ortak nor Terrahk seemed to harbor any suspicion an entire heretic army corps had nipped in between them. The towers Sean now controlled relayed all normal message traffic without alterations, but they were intercepting every dispatch either Guard officer sent the other. It was almost more delicious than what Sandy's and Brashan's stealthed remotes could tell him, for he was actually reading his enemies' mail, then dictating the responses *he* wanted them to receive. It looked like it was already having an effect, as well. Sandy reported that Terrahk had slowed his headlong pace just a bit thanks to the more confident tenor Sean had been giving Ortak's messages. But, of course, Ortak didn't know that, now did he?

Sean grinned wickedly, but then he looked up at the sky and his grin faded. The sun was sinking steadily in the west, and it was about time to bivouac, but what worried him was the growing humidity. Another front was coming through, and Brashan was still figuring out Pardal's weather patterns. The mountains made prediction even harder, and Sean suspected the front was moving faster than expected. But they should still have enough time, he told himself as he urged his branahlk back into motion. All he needed was two more of Pardal's twenty-nine-hour days.

"Two more days," Tamman murmured. He leaned back in a camp chair in his tent, eyes closed while his neural feed linked him to *Israel* and Sandy's remotes through the com in the stealthed cutter permanently parked in hover above "the Angel Harry's" commodious tent. He replayed the day's scan records at high speed and watched mentally as Sean's column sped up the high road towards Erastor. They were really moving, and they were still a good four days in front of High-Captain Terrahk. The way the relief column was easing up would open the gap a bit further, but sometime the day after tomorrow the Guardsmen were going to reach Malz and find out what had *actually* been happening.

They'd have no way to warn Ortak, and he wondered what Terrahk would do. Would he hustle on forward as fast as he could? If he knew how many men Sean had, the high-captain might figure he could take him in the open, but he'd be too far behind to overtake before Sean reached Erastor, and he'd know it. Just as he'd know that if Sean blew Ortak out of the way, his own column would be hopelessly inadequate to face the two hundred thousand screaming heretics the Temple now assumed the Angels' Army had.

It all came down to a guess, Tamman mused. Unlike Sean and himself, Terrahk was totally reliant on mounted scouts, and with the towers between him and Erastor in Malagoran hands, he'd have no way to know what was happening ahead of him. All he'd know was that if Ortak had somehow figured out what was coming at him and managed to throw up any sort of an east-facing defense, he'd need all the help Terrahk could send him to hold it. Or, conversely, that if Ortak had already been waxed, the only chance for his own troops' survival would be to run as hard as they could in the other direction.

Under the circumstances, Tamman suspected Terrahk would retreat. Abandoning Ortak might cost the Guard seventy or eighty thousand men, but if he lost his own command throwing good money after bad, the Temple would also lose its last field force. It was a pity Sean couldn't ambush Terrahk first and *then* take on Ortak, but too many things could go wrong, including the possibility that Sean would find himself trapped between enemies who outnumbered him by more than five to one. With room to maneuver and unlimited ammunition, odds like that might be workable; trapped between the Mortan and the valley's northern rim and with only the ammo his troops could carry, the situation would have all the ingredients for a MacIntyre's Last Stand.

Nope. The best outcome would probably be for

Terrahk to keep coming and arrive a couple of days after he and Sean had crushed Ortak. If they could reunite their own army, they'd make mincemeat out of Terrahk—assuming they could catch him. At the very least, they should be able to stay close enough on his heels to keep him from settling into the prepared positions around Baricon. But Terrahk would know that as well as they did, which was why Tamman expected the Guardsman to fall back the instant he figured out what was happening.

He straightened and opened his eyes. One thing was certain, whatever Terrahk did, he reminded himself. Before he and Sean could get back into contact, they had to take Erastor, and he shoved up out of his chair. There was just enough light left for him and Ithun to make a last recon of Ortak's lines before darkness fell, and if it turned out that they had to storm those entrenchments to save Sean's posterior, he wanted all of his officers to know everything they could about their target.

More rain swept up the Keldark Valley, and High-Captain Ortak glared sourly at the clouds. The valley was always damp, of course. It was the only real opening in the Shalokar Range, and wet air from the east poured through it like a funnel as it swept up towards the Malagor Plateau. Some of the Temple's experts argued that as the air moved higher and grew thinner, the moisture fell out of its own weight. Ortak didn't fully understand the theory behind it, but all he really needed to know was that it rained in the valley—a lot—and that it was starting to do it again.

He growled a soft curse, then shrugged. Rain was his friend, not the heretics'. Their musketeers outnumbered his tremendously, and if God was kind enough to soak their priming powder for them, Ortak had no intention of complaining. Let them come in and take him on with cold steel!

"How long is this going to last?" Sean asked fretfully.

He and Sandy stood fifty meters from the nearest Malagoran and conferred over their coms with Brashan.

"At least another two days," the Narhani said soberly. He sat alone on *Israel*'s command deck, and his long-snouted, saurian face was grave. "I am sorry, Sean. We thought—"

"Not your fault," Sean interrupted. "We all knew it was coming. We just expected it to hold off longer, and then we lost all that time in the swamps. Our window should have been big enough, Twinkle Hooves."

"True, but it's not only coming in faster, it's going to rain harder than we'd predicted." The Narhani sounded worried. Sean was less than one day's march from Erastor, and the rain—only a drizzle now—would be a downpour by evening. What that would do to flintlock rifles hardly bore thinking on.

"Can we hold off till it clears?" Sandy gazed up at Sean, and her voice was anxious.

"'Fraid not." Sean sighed. "Ortak expects his 'reinforcements' by nightfall. If we suddenly stop moving, he's going to wonder why and send someone to find out. And if he does that—" He shrugged.

"But you can't fight him without your rifles!" Sandy protested. "You don't have any pikes at all!"

"No, but we do still have surprise."

"Surprise! Are you out of your mind?! There are *eighty thousand* men up there, Sean! There's no *way* you can take their position away from them before they figure out what's happening!"

"Maybe yes, and maybe no," Sean said stubbornly. "Don't forget the confusion factor. The rain's going to cut visibility. We should be able to get a lot closer before they figure out we aren't really Guardsmen, and there's a good chance they'll panic when their 'reinforcements' suddenly attack them. They don't have the kind of communication net a modern army would have, either. It's going to be mighty hard for them to get themselves sorted out when they have to rely on messengers to carry orders."

"You're crazy!" she hissed. "Tamman, Harry—tell him!"

"I think Sandy's right, Sean," Harriet said quietly. "It's too risky. Besides, even if he does figure out what's happening, Terrahk's already falling back on Baricon. Wait till the rain stops. Ortak's not going anywhere, and maybe he'll surrender when he realizes he's trapped between you and Tam."

"Wrong answer, Harry," Tamman put in unhappily. "Ortak's not the surrendering kind, or he wouldn't have stopped at Erastor."

"What else *can* he do?" Harriet demanded hotly.

"He can come out after us," Sean answered. "He knows as well as we do that it's our rifles that give us the edge. You think he wouldn't take his chances on hitting us in the open if the rain knocks them out of the equation?"

Sandy started to snap back, then stopped and bit her lip. She hugged herself and turned her back on Sean for a long, taut moment, then sighed.

"No," she said finally, her voice low. "That's exactly what he'll do if he figures out what's happening."

"You got it," Sean said, equally quietly, and kicked his toe into the mud beside the raised roadbed. "Any way you cut it, we've got to carry through with my marvelous plan."

Chapter Thirty-Three

"All right, boys—you heard Lord Sean. Now let's go kick the bastards' asses!"

The officers of the First Brigade growled in agreement, and Folmak Folmakson grinned fiercely. He was a long, long way from Cragsend and anxious days waiting for the Church to condemn him for error just for searching for ways to make his mill a bit more efficient, and he was passionately grateful for it. Folmak loved God as much as the next man, but Malagor had been a captive province for twenty generations, and like many Malagorans, he'd harbored a festering resentment against the Inner Circle and their absentee bishops. Father Stomald, now. *He* was what a priest was supposed to be, and if the rest of the Temple had been like him . . .

But it wasn't. Folmak settled into the saddle and checked all four pistols before he tucked them away in his boots and under his captured Guard cloak. The rain was falling harder, as Lord Sean had warned, and he'd ordered his sergeants to check each individual pan to be sure it was securely shut until it was needed. They were still going to have an appalling number of misfires, but he'd done all he could to minimize them.

He put away the last pistol and looked over his shoulder for the signal to advance. Lord Sean stood surrounded by aides, speaking quietly and urgently to Tibold, hands moving in quick, incisive gestures, and Folmak remembered his look of surprise when the men had cheered his orders.

Folmak hadn't been surprised, but Lord Sean had actually apologized to them, as if it were *his* fault they couldn't just stand around and wait till the rain stopped. That sort of concern made the army love Lord Sean, but it knew what it was about. Especially Folmak's men. His was the First Brigade, already called "the Old Brigade," composed of men who'd followed Father Stomald from the very beginning. They regarded themselves as the elite of Lord Sean's army, though the Second and Third Brigades were every bit as old—and, Folmak admitted grudgingly, as good—and they understood what was forcing Lord Sean's hand. Every man in the column knew they'd taken far longer than expected getting to Erastor, yet they also knew only Lord Sean and the Angel Sandy could have gotten them here at all. And the angels' message—that men should be free to shape their own lives and their own understanding of God's will—had ignited a furnace in the Malagorans' stubborn hearts. If Lord Sean needed them now, they were proud to be here, and if he decided to fix bayonets and charge a hurricane, they'd follow with a cheer.

The regimental pipers formed in the intervals in the brigade's column, and Lord Sean nodded to his aides. They spurred up and down the entire length of the corps, and Folmak waved to his unit commanders.

"Move out!" he barked, and the Angels' Army slogged through blowing sheets of rain towards Erastor.

Sean watched his men move forward and tried to look confident. Every man in Folmak's brigade had been issued a Guard cloak, and his vanguard looked as much like Terrahk's relief force as he could make them, but the rest of his men wore Malagoran ponchos. One look at *them* would tell the dullest picket what they were. The rain wasn't falling as hard as he'd feared—yet—but it was getting worse, and only First Brigade marched with slung weapons. The rest of his men carried their bayoneted rifles under their arms like hunters to shield the priming with their bodies and ponchos and keep rain from running down the muzzles. It was awkward and it looked like hell, but it was the best he could do to insure their ability to fire.

He and Tibold had reorganized the army into six-hundred-man regiments, three to the brigade, and despite the rain and the slaughter to which he'd led them, each regiment cheered as it passed him. He slapped his streaming breastplate in answering salute, and his emotions were a welter of confusion. Shame for the mistakes which sent them into battle under such a hideous handicap. Pride in how they'd responded. Dread of the butcher's bill they were going to pay, a sense of awe that they were willing to pay it for him, and a strange, shivering eagerness. He'd seen battle and its aftermath now. He *knew* how horrible it was, how ugly and vile and brutal, yet part of him was actually eager to begin. Not glad, but . . . impatient. Anticipating.

He shook his head, angry with himself. He couldn't think of the word, and he was ashamed of feeling whatever it was, but that didn't change it. He spurred ahead to overtake Folmak's brigade, and as he splashed along the road, he wished he could ride away from his own complex feelings as easily.

Under-Captain Mathan stood under the lean-to and gazed out into the rain. It was barely midafternoon, yet it looked like late evening as charcoal clouds billowed overhead. His dragoons were glad to be spared the lot of the men manning the half-flooded entrenchments facing the heretics, but that didn't make their own duty pleasant. Like most of the Host, they'd lost all their baggage at Yortown, and they'd had to cobble up whatever they could to replace their Guard-issue tents. Mathan doubted the foraging parties had left an intact roof for miles around Erastor, but the valley's frequent rains soaked them to the skin anyway, whatever they did, and he was heartily sick of it.

He spoke to himself sternly. He should be down on his knees thanking God for sparing him the slaughter the demon-worshipers had wreaked on the rest of the Host, not complaining because of a little rain! He'd certainly told his troopers that often enough!

He turned to pace briskly. He could only go a few strides in either direction and stay under the roof, but the rain had chilled the mountain air, and the activity warmed his blood.

Perhaps he'd feel happier if his present assignment had some point. With the heretics blocked west of the Erastor Spur, the pickets east of the main position were little more than an afterthought. They were out here getting soaked simply because the field manuals said all approaches, however unlikely, should be covered, and like most soldiers, they resented being made miserable just because some headquarters type wanted to be neat and tidy.

A branahlk splashed up to the shelter, and Sergeant Kithar saluted.

"We've sighted the head of the column, Sir. Should reach the pickets in about another twenty minutes."

"Thank you, Sergeant. That's good news." Mathan returned Kithar's salute, then pointed at the smoky fire crackling under another crude awning. "Warm yourself and dry off a bit before you head back."

"Thank you, Sir."

The sergeant hurried towards the fire, and Mathan folded his hands behind him with a sigh of relief. High-Captain Ortak had sworn the Temple would reinforce them, but after Yortown it had been hard for many of his men—including, Mathan admitted, himself—to believe it would happen in time. Now it had, and he breathed a silent prayer of thanks.

Captain Folmak trotted at the head of his brigade, and his belly was a hard, singing knot. He could see the first dragoons now, and they looked as miserable as Lord Sean had predicted. They were waving, and he heard a few cheers, but they also weren't budging out from under the crude lean-tos they'd erected in a vain effort to stay dry.

"You know what to do, boys," he told his grim-faced riflemen. "No shooting if you can help it, but be damned sure none of them get away!"

✧   ✧   ✧

"Sight for sore eyes, aren't they?" Shaldan Morahkson demanded. "I *told* you Lord Marshal Surak would reinforce us!"

"Sure you did," one of his companions jeered. "Between pissing and moaning about the rain, your saddle sores, and how fucked up the whole war's been, you told us all about your personal friend the Lord Marshal!"

The others laughed, and Shaldan made a rude gesture as the lead ranks of the relief column squelched past. The incoming Guardsmen looked almost as shabby and sodden as Shaldan and his fellows after their hard march, and he turned his back on the others to wave and shout at the newcomers, then paused.

"That's funny."

"What?" his critic demanded. "Your buddy Lord Marshal Surak screw up somehow?"

"They're all musketeers," Shaldan said. "Look." He pointed as far down the column as they could see in the blowing rain. "There must be a thousand, fifteen hundred of them, and not a pike among 'em!"

"What?" The other dragoon turned to peer in the direction of Shaldan's pointing finger.

"And another thing. I've never seen bayonets like those. Have you?"

"I—"

Shaldan never found out what his fellow meant to say, for even as they stared at the column, it suddenly broke apart.

"Take them!" Under-Captain Lerhak shouted, and his men swarmed out across the picket. There were cries of alarm from the watching dragoons, and two or three turned to race for tethered branahlks, but surprise was total. Musket butts and bayonets did their lethal work, and within ten minutes, every man of High Captain Ortak's easternmost picket was dead or a prisoner.

✧   ✧   ✧

Under-Captain Mathan stretched and called for his mount. He'd already sent a messenger ahead to Erastor, and if Sergeant Kithar was right, the column should have reached his forward position by now. Little though a ride in the rain appealed to him, he'd best go up to greet them like a properly industrious junior officer, and he trotted away from the lean-to with regret. He was riding directly into the wind, and the water running into his eyes made it hard to see where he was going. His branahlk tossed its head and jibed under him, whistling mournfully to voice its own verdict on the weather, and he tightened his knees to remind it who was in charge.

He looked back up and blinked on rain as mounted men in the soaked crimson cloaks of the Guard loomed out of the dimness. One of them waved, and Mathan started to wave back, then paused.

He stared at them, watching them ride closer, unable to believe his eyes. Their saddles and tack were mismatched, not standard Guard issue, and aside from their cloaks, they weren't even in uniform. Two of them actually wore what looked like farmer's boots, not jackboots. But that was impossible. They *had* to be Guardsmen! No one else could get at Erastor from the east! Not unless the demons had—

He jerked out of his shock and wheeled his mount. The branahlk squealed in protest as his spurs went home, then bounded forward with a teeth-rattling jerk. He had to warn High-Captain Ortak! He—

Something cracked behind him, and he didn't even have time to scream as the rifled pistol bullet smashed him from the saddle.

"Sir, the relief column's been sighted."

High-Captain Ortak looked up and smiled at his aide's report.

"Well, thank God for that! Call for my branahlk. High-Captain Terrahk deserves to be met in person."

✧　　　✧　　　✧

"Did you hear something?" Sergeant Kithar raised his head, ears cocked, and glanced at the man beside him.

"In this rain?" The trooper gestured at the water drumming from the eaves of their rough roof.

"It sounded like a shot. . . ."

"You're joking, Sarge! It'd take a special miracle to get a joharn to fire in this stuff!"

"I know, but—"

Kithar was still gazing out into the rain when Folmak's lead company stormed into the picket's rear area.

"Folmak's taken out the picket."

Sean nodded as his com implant carried him Sandy's voice.

"Anyone get away?" he subvocalized back.

"I don't think so. It's hard to be sure with so many people moving around in the rain, but I don't see anyone headed away from the picket."

"What's Folmak doing?"

"Rounding up POWs and shifting into assault column to hit the bridge. Don't worry, Sean. He knows what he's doing."

"So far, so good," Folmak murmured, then raised his voice. "This is what we came for, boys! Follow me, and from here on out, make all the racket you can. Let's make these bastards think the 'Cragsend Demons' are here to eat 'em all! First Brigade, *are you with me?*"

"Aye!" The roar almost blew him from the saddle.

High-Captain Ortak dismounted, handed his reins to an orderly, and tried not to scurry as he hurried for the shelter of the bridge tollhouse. The under-captain commanding the bridge traffic control detachment jumped up and saluted, but Ortak waved him back into his chair.

"Sit down, sit down!"

"Thank you, Sir, but I prefer to stand." The bridge commander was a very junior officer, but he knew better than to sit in the presence of a high-captain, whatever the high-captain in question said.

"Suit yourself, Captain." Ortak stood in the doorway, peering into the gloomy afternoon. He could just make out the head of Terrahk's column at the far end of the bridge, and he wondered why they'd stopped in the rain. Were they dressing ranks for some sort of parade?

He frowned. The rain and the rush of river water around the bridge pilings filled his ears, but that didn't keep him from hearing the cheer. What in the world—? Were they *that* happy to be here?

And then, suddenly, the relief column lunged forward onto the bridge, and High-Captain Ortak stared in horror as it swept over the half-dozen men watching the far end of the span. Bayonets flashed in the rain, musket butts struck viciously, and the high-captain went white, for he could hear the voices clearly, now.

"*Malagor and Lord Sean!*" they howled, and twenty-five thousand men stormed into the Guard's undefended rear behind their screaming war pipes.

"That's it!" Tamman snapped to High-Captain Ithun. "They're hitting the bridges now. Get the columns formed!"

"At once, Lord Tamman!"

Ithun dashed off, and Tamman's enhanced eyes swept the entrenchments facing his position. There was no movement over there yet, but there would be soon. Now if only they'd pull enough off the parapets to give him an opening!

For the Yortown survivors, it was a hideous, recurring nightmare. They'd seen their formations smashed at Yortown, watched that wall of fire and smoke grinding down from the north behind the terrifying Malagoran yell, and known—not thought; *known*—they'd faced demons, but somehow they'd escaped. They'd fallen back, dug in, waited for the demon-worshipers to sweep over them, and as the weeks passed, they'd come, slowly, first to hope and finally to believe it wouldn't happen after all. They'd stopped the heretics, held them, and at least their rear was secure if they were forced to retreat again.

But now their rear *wasn't* secure. They'd spent days preparing bivouac areas for High-Captain Terrahk's column, chattered in their relief, swapped lies and rumors about what would happen next, only to see the forces of Hell do it to them again. Some evil sorcery had transformed their reinforcements into rampaging demons that stormed into their positions in a solid, deadly mass of bristling bayonets and the terrible, shrieking war pipes of Malagor.

Surprise was total, High-Captain Ortak was nowhere to be found, and officers floundered in shock as the first, incredible intimations of disaster reached them. Folmak's brigade slammed over the bridges and butchered its way across the closest encampment. Guardsmen looked up from routine camp tasks to see eighteen hundred screaming maniacs scythe into their position, and panic was a deadlier weapon than any bayonet. Cooks and drovers scattered, half-naked men erupted from tents and lean-tos and fled into the rain, officers shouted in vain for their men to rally, and Folmak's riflemen swarmed forward like some dark, unstoppable tide.

Here and there a handful *did* rally around an officer or a noncom, but there were too few of them, and they were too stunned to be effective. The tiny knots of resistance vanished into the oncoming First Brigade's bayonet-fanged maw, and Folmak slammed a full kilometer forward before his initial charge even slowed. Behind him, more men thundered across the Erastor, fanning out to secure the bridgehead, and behind *them* the weight of Sean's entire corps swept forward in double time.

"They're hitting us in the *rear*, I tell you! My God, there're *thousands* of them!"

High-Captain Marhn stared at the gasping, half-coherent officer. Impossible! It was *impossible!* Poison-raw terror quivered deep inside, yet he'd been a soldier for over thirty Terran years. He didn't know what had happened to High-Captain Ortak, and he couldn't even begin to guess how the heretics could be *behind* Erastor in strength or what had happened to High-Captain Terrahk, but he knew what would happen if this attack wasn't crushed.

"They've already got the bridges!" The officer was still babbling his terrified message. "We're trapped, Sir! They're going to—"

"They're going to *die*, Captain!" Marhn barked so sharply the officer's mouth snapped shut in pure reflex. "We've got eighty thousand men in this position, so stop howling like an old woman and *use* them, curse you!"

"But—"

Marhn whirled away with a snarl of disgust just as Captain Urthank, his own second-in-command charged up, still buckling his armor.

"What—?" Urthank started, but Marhn cut him off with a savage wave.

"Somehow the demon-worshipers got 'round behind us. They've taken the bridges, and they're advancing fast." Urthank paled, and Marhn shook his head. "Get back there. Send in the Ninth and Eighteenth Pikes. You won't be able to hold, but slow them up enough to buy me some time!"

"Yes, Sir!" Urthank saluted and disappeared, and Marhn began bellowing orders to a flock of messengers.

The Ninth Pikes thudded through the mud towards the clamor in their rear, and their eyes were wild. There'd been no time for their officers to explain fully, but the Ninth were veterans. They knew what would happen if the heretics weren't stopped.

The Eighteenth turned up on their left, and whistles shrilled as their officers brought them to a slithering, panting halt. A forest of five-meter pikes snapped into fighting position, and eight thousand men settled into formation as the wailing Malagoran pipes swept down upon them.

✧   ✧   ✧

Folmak reined in so violently his branahlk skidded on its haunches as the Guard phalanx materialized out of the rain. Lord Sean had warned him the surprise wouldn't last, and he'd managed—somehow—to keep his men together as they swept across the Guard's rear areas. The clutter of tents and wagons and lean-tos had made it hard, yet he'd kept his brigade in hand, and he felt a stab of thankfulness that he had.

But he was also well out in front, and half his third regiment had been left behind to hold the bridges. He had little more than fifteen hundred men, barely a sixth of the numbers suddenly drawn up across his front, and not a single pike among them.

That phalanx wouldn't stop the regiments coming up behind him, but he couldn't let them stop *him*, either. If the Guard realized how outnumbered its attackers were and won time to recover, it had more than enough power to crush Lord Sean's entire force.

"First Battalion—action front!" he screamed, and whistles shrilled.

His men responded instantly. First Battalion of Second Regiment, his leading formation, deployed into firing line on the run, and the officer commanding the Guard pikes hesitated. All he knew was that his position was under attack, and the visibility was so bad he couldn't begin to estimate Folmak's numbers. Rather than charge forward in ignorance, he paused, trying to get some idea of what he was up against, and that hesitation gave First Battalion time to deploy in a two-deep firing line and the rest of Folmak's men time to tighten their own formation behind them. It was still looser than it should have been, but Folmak sensed the firming resolution of his opponents. There was no time for further adjustment.

"Fire!" he bellowed.

Almost a third of the First's rifles misfired, but there were three hundred of them. Two hundred-plus rifles blazed at less than a hundred meters' range, and the Guardsmen recoiled in shock as, for the first time in

Pardalian history, men with fixed bayonets poured fire into their opponents.

"At 'em, Malagorans!" Folmak howled. *"Chaaaarge!"*

The Guard formation wavered as the bullets slammed home. At such short range, a rifled joharn would penetrate five inches of solid wood, and a single shot could kill or maim two or even three men. The shock of receiving that fire was made even worse by the fact that it came from bayoneted weapons, and then, against every rule of warfare, musketeers actually *charged* pikemen!

The Guardsmen couldn't believe it. Musketeers ran *away* from pikes—everyone knew that! But these musketeers were different. The column behind exploded through the firing line and hit the Eighteenth Pikes like a tidal bore. Dozens, scores of them, died on the bitter pikeheads, but while the Guardsmen were killing them, their companions hurled themselves in among the pikes, and the Guard discovered a lethal truth. Once a phalanx's front was broken, once the Malagorans could get inside the pikes' longer reach, bayoneted rifles were deadly melee weapons. They were shorter, lighter, faster, and these men knew how to use them to terrible effect.

"Drive 'em!" Folmak shrieked. *"Drive 'em!"* and First Brigade drove them. The Malagoran yell and the howl of their pipes carried them onward, and once they'd closed, they were more than a match for any pikemen.

Bayonets stabbed, men screamed and cursed and died, and mud-caked boots trod them into the mire. Folmak's men stormed forward with a determination that had to be killed to be stopped, and the Guardsmen—shaken, confused, stunned by the impossibility of what was happening—were no match for them.

The Eighteenth broke. Those of its men who tried to stand paid for their discipline, for they couldn't break free, couldn't get far enough away to use their longer weapons effectively, and First Brigade swarmed them under like seldahks. Six minutes after that first volley had exploded in their faces, the Eighteenth Pikes were a shattered, fleeing wreck, and Folmak swung in on the flank of the Ninth.

Even now, he was outnumbered by better than two-to-one, and the melee with the Eighteenth had disordered his ranks. Worse, the Ninth was made of sterner stuff, and its commander had managed to change front while the Eighteenth was dying. His men were still off balance, but they howled their own war cries and lunged forward, slamming into Folmak's brigade like a hammer, and this time they hadn't been shaken by a pointblank volley.

Folmak's lead battalion had already been more than decimated. Now it reeled back, fighting stubbornly but driven by the longer, heavier weapons of its foes, and the officers of both sides lost control. It was one howling vortex, sucking in men and spitting out corpses, and then, suddenly, Sean's Sixth Brigade slammed into the Ninth from the *other* side.

It was too much, and the Guardsmen came apart. Unit organization disintegrated. Half the Ninth simply disappeared, killed or routed, and the other half found itself surrounded by twice its own number of Malagorans. They tried to fight their way out, then tried to form a defensive hedgehog, but it was useless. Despite the rain, scores of riflemen still managed to reload and fire into them, and even as they died, more Malagoran regiments rushed past. They weren't even slowing the enemy down, and their surviving officers ordered them to throw down their weapons to save as many of their men as they could.

High-Captain Marhn's face was iron as more and more reports of disaster came in. The heretics had swept over the entire bivouac area, then paused to reorganize and fanned out in half a dozen columns, each storming forward towards the rear of the entrenchments. A third of his men had already been broken, and the panicky wreckage of shattered formations boiled in confusion, hampering their fellows far more than their enemies. The last light was going, and the Host's entire encampment had disintegrated into a rain-soaked, mud-caked madness no man could control.

He had no idea how many men the heretics had. From the terrified reports, they might have had a million. Worse, the units they were hitting were his worst-armed, weakest ones, the men who'd been reformed out of the ruin of Yortown. They'd been placed in reserve because their officers were still trying to rebuild them into effective fighting forces, and the demon-worshipers were cutting through them like an ax, not a knife.

He clenched his jaw and turned his back, shutting out the confused reports while he tried to find an answer. But there was only one, and it might already be too late for it to work.

"Start pulling men out of the redoubts," he grated. Someone gasped, and he stabbed a finger at a map. "Form a new line here!" he snapped, jabbing a line across the map less than four thousand paces behind the earthworks.

"But, Sir—" someone else began.

"*Do it!*" Marhn snarled, and tried to pretend he didn't know that even if he succeeded, it could stave off disaster for no more than a few more hours.

"They're moving men from the trenches, Sean!" Sandy shouted over the com.

"Good—I think!" Even with Sandy's reports and his own implant link to her sensors, Sean had only the vaguest notion what was happening. This was nothing like Yortown. It was an insane explosion of violence, skidding like a ground car on ice. His men were moving towards their objectives in what *looked* like a carefully controlled maneuver, but it was nothing of the sort. No one *could* control it; it was all up to his junior officers and their men, and he could hardly believe how well they were carrying out their mission.

Even in the madness and confusion, he felt a deep,

vaulting pride in his army—*his* army!—as his out-numbered men cut through their enemies. He was losing people—hundreds of them, probably more—and he knew how sick and empty he'd feel when he counted the dead, but he had no time for that now. A desperate counterattack by the broken remnants of several Guard pike units had taken his HQ group by surprise and smashed deep into it before a reserve battalion could deal with it, and only Sean's enhancement had kept him alive. His armor had turned two pikeheads, and his enhanced reactions had been enough to save his eye, but a dripping sword cut had opened his right cheek from chin to temple, and Tibold limped heavily from a gash in his left thigh.

Now he waved his battered aides to a halt, and the reserve battalion—whose commander had made himself Sean's chief bodyguard without orders—fanned out in a wary perimeter.

"How much movement?" he asked Sandy in English, speaking aloud and ignoring the looks his men gave him.

"A lot, all up and down the center of his lines."

"Tam?"

"I see it, Sean. We're moving now."

"Give 'em time to pull back! Don't let them catch you in the open!"

"Suck eggs! You just keep pushing 'em hard."

"Hard, the man says!" Sean rolled his eyes heavenward and turned to Tibold. "They're pulling men out of the trenches to stop us, and Tamman and Ithun are moving up to hit them in the rear."

"Then we have to push them even harder," Tibold said decisively.

"If we can!" Sean shook his head, then grabbed an aide. "Find Captain Folmak. If he's still alive, tell him to bear right. You!" he jabbed a finger at another messenger. "Find Fourth Brigade. It's over that way, to the right. Tell Captain Herth to curl in to the left to meet Folmak. I want both of them to hammer straight for their reserve artillery park."

The aides repeated their orders and ran off into the maelstrom, and Sean grimaced at Tibold.

"If this is a successful battle, God save me from an *un*successful one!"

"Sir!" Marhn looked up as a gasping, mud-spattered messenger lurched into his command post. "High-Captain! The heretics are coming from the west, as well!" The messenger swayed, and Marhn realized the young officer was wounded. "Captain Rukhan needs more men. Can't . . . can't hold without them, Sir!"

Marhn stared at the young man for one terrible, endless moment. Then his shoulders slumped, and his watching staff saw hope run out of his eyes like water.

"Sound parley," he said. Urthank stared at him, and Marhn snarled at him. "Sound parley, damn you!"

"But . . . but, Sir, the Circle! High Priest Vroxhan! We can't—"

"*We* aren't; *I* am!" Marhn spat. His hand bit into Urthank's biceps like a claw. "We've lost, Urthank. That attack from the rear blew the guts out of us, and now they've broken our *front* as well. How many more of our men have to die for a position we can't hold?"

"But if you surrender, the Circle will—" Urthank began in a quieter, more anxious voice, and Marhn shook his head again.

"I've served the Temple since I was a boy. If the Circle wants my life for saving the lives of my men, they can have it. Now, sound parley!"

"Yes, Sir." Urthank looked into Marhn's face for a moment, then turned away. "You heard the High-Captain! Sound parley!" he barked, and another officer fled to pass the order.

"Here, boy!" Marhn said gruffly, catching Rukhan's wounded messenger as he began to collapse. He took the young man's weight in his arms and eased him down into a camp chair, then looked back up at Urthank. "Call the healers and have this man seen to," he said.

Chapter Thirty-Four

Lieutenant Carl Bergren was grateful for his bio-enhancement. Without it, he'd have been sweating so hard the security pukes would have arrested him the moment he reported for duty tonight.

His adrenaline tried to spike again, but he pushed it back down and told himself (again) the risk was acceptable. If it all blew up on him, he could find himself facing charges for willful destruction of private property and end up dishonorably discharged with five or ten years in prison, which was hardly an attractive proposition. On the other hand, it wasn't as if anyone were going to be hurt—in fact, he was going to have to separate any passengers from the freight—and it wasn't every night a mere Battle Fleet lieutenant earned eight million credits. That payoff was sufficient compensation for any risks which might come his way. He told himself that firmly enough to manage a natural smile as he walked into the control room and nodded to Lieutenant Deng.

"You're early tonight, Carl." Deng had learned his English before he was enhanced, and its stubbornly persistent British accent always seemed odd to Bergren coming from a Chinese.

"Only a couple of minutes," he replied. "Commander Jackson's on Birhat, and I stole her parking spot."

"A court-martial offense if ever I heard one." Deng chuckled, and rose to stretch. "Very well, Leftenant, your throne awaits."

"Some throne!" Bergren snorted. He dropped into the control chair and flipped his feed into the computers, scanning the evening's traffic. "Not much business tonight."

"Not yet, but there's something special coming through from Narhan."

"Special? Special how?" Bergren's tone was a bit too casual, but Deng failed to notice.

"Some sort of high-priority freight for the Palace." He shrugged. "I don't know what, but the mass readings are quite high, so you might want to watch the gamma bank capacitors. We're getting a drop at peak loads, and Maintenance hasn't found the problem yet."

"No?" Bergren checked the files in case Deng was watching, but he already knew all about the power fluctuation. He didn't know how it had been arranged, but he knew why, and he damped another adrenaline surge at the thought. "You're right," he observed aloud. "Thanks. I'll keep an eye on them."

"Good." Deng gathered up his personal gear and cocked his head. "Everything else green?"

"Looks that way," Bergren agreed. "You're relieved."

"Thanks. See you tomorrow!"

Deng wandered out, and Bergren leaned back in his chair. He was alone now, and he allowed a small smile to hover on his lips. He had no idea who his mysterious patron was, nor had he cared . . . until tonight. Whoever it was paid well enough to support his taste for fast flyers and faster women, and that had been enough for him. But the services he'd performed so far had all been small potatoes beside tonight, and his smile became a thoughtful frown.

He hadn't realized, until he received his latest orders, how powerful his unknown employer must be, but pulling *this* off required more than mere wealth. No, whoever could arrange something like this had to have access not simply to highly restricted technology but to Shepherd Center's security at the very highest levels. There couldn't be many people who had both those things, and the lieutenant had already opened a mental file of possible candidates. After all, if whoever it was had paid so well for relatively minor services in the past, he'd pay still better in the future for Bergren's silence.

A soft tone sounded, and he shrugged his thoughts aside to concentrate on his duties. He plugged into the computer net and checked the passenger manifest against the people actually boarding the mat-trans. Two of them were technically overweight for their baggage, but it was well within the system's max load parameters, and he decided to let it pass. He made the necessary adjustments to field strength and checked his figures twice, then sent the hypercom transit warning to Birhat. An answering hypercom pulse told him Birhat was up and ready, awaiting reception of the controlled hyper-space anomaly he was about to create, and he sent the transit computer the release code. The control room's soundproofing was excellent, but he still heard the whine of the charging capacitors, and then his readouts peaked as the transmitter kicked over. Another clutch of bureaucrats, temporarily converted into something they were no doubt just as happy they couldn't understand, disappeared into a massive, artificially induced "fold" in hyper-space. The waiting Birhat station couldn't "see" them coming, but, alerted by Bergren's hypercom signal, its receivers formed a vast, funnel-shaped trap in hyper-space. At eight hundred-plus light-years, even the vastest funnel was an impossibly tiny target, but Bergren's calculations flicked the disembodied bureaucrats expertly into its bell-shaped mouth. In his mind's eye, the lieutenant always pictured his passengers rattling and bouncing as they zinged down the funnel and then—instantaneously, as far as they could tell, but 8.5 seconds later by the clocks of the rest of the universe—blinked back into existence on distant Birhat.

Now he sat waiting, then nodded to himself as Birhat's hypercommed receipt tone sounded seventeen seconds later. He noted the routine transit in his log and checked the schedule. Traffic really was light tonight, and it was getting lighter as the hour got later. Shepherd Center Station was only one of six mat-trans stations Earth now boasted, and it handled mostly North American traffic, though it also caught a heavier percentage of the through-traffic from Narhan to Birhat and vice versa. The receiving platforms were far busier than the outbound stations, but, then, it was midmorning in Phoenix on Birhat and only early evening in Andhurkahn on Narhan. He had a good five minutes before his next scheduled transmission, and he returned once more to his speculations.

Lawrence Jefferson sat in his private office at home. His split-image com screen linked him to another mat-trans half a planet from Bergren's—half showing the installation's control room; the other half a huge, tarpaulin-covered shape waiting on the transmission platform— and he poured more sherry into his glass as he watched both images. No one at the other end knew he was observing them, and he supposed his high-tech spyhole was a bit risky, but he had no choice, and at least the Lieutenant Governor of Earth had access to the best technology available. His link had been established using a high security fold-space com that bounced its hyper frequency on a randomized pattern twice a second. That made simply detecting it all but impossible and, coupled with the physical relays through which it also bounced, meant tapping or tracing it *was* impossible. Besides, anyone who happened to spot it would report it to the Minister of Planetary Security, now wouldn't they?

He chuckled at the thought and sipped sherry as he watched the purposeful activity in the control room. No one—aside from the men and women who'd built and staffed it for him—even knew it existed, and all but three of them were on duty tonight. The three absent faces had been killed in a tragic flyer accident almost two years previously, and though their deaths had been a blow, their fellows had taken up the slack without difficulty. Now his carefully chosen techs checked their equipment with absolute concentration, for the upcoming transmission— the one and only transmission the installation would ever make—had to be executed perfectly.

It would never have done for Jefferson to admit he was nervous. Nor would it have been true, for "nervous" fell far short of what he felt tonight. This was the absolutely critical phase, the one which would make him Emperor of Humanity—if it worked—and anxiety mingled with a fierce expectation. He'd worked over a decade—more than twenty-five years, if he counted from his first contact with Anu—for this moment, and even as a part of him feared it would fail, the gambler part of him could hardly wait to throw the dice.

It was odd, but, in a way, he'd actually be sorry if it worked. Not because he didn't want the crown, and certainly not because he regretted what he had to do to get it, but because the game would be over. He would have carried out the most audacious coup in the history of mankind, but all the daring, the concentration and subtle manipulation, would be a thing of the past, and he could never share the true magnitude of his accomplishment with anyone else.

He shook his head at his own perversity, and a small smile flickered. The curse of his own makeup, he chided himself, was that he could never be entirely content, however well things went. He always wanted more, but there were limits, and he supposed he'd just have to settle for absolute power.

Bergren straightened in his chair as five Narhani entered the outbound terminal with a huge, tarpaulin-draped object on a counter-grav dolly. The centaurs fussed with their burden, placing it carefully on the platform and taking their places about it in a protective circle, and, despite all his implants could do, the lieutenant swallowed nervously as he flashed a mental command to the power sub-net. It was a routine testing order, but tonight it had another effect, and he winced as the induced surge flashed through the gamma bank of capacitors and an audio alarm shrilled.

The Narhani on the platform looked up, long-snouted heads twisting around in confusion as the high-pitched warble hurt their ears, and Bergren sent quick, fresh commands to his computer to shut it down. Then he leaned forward and keyed a microphone.

"Sorry, gentlemen," he told the Narhani over the speakers in the terminal area. "We've just lost one of our main capacitor banks. Until we get it back, our transmission capacity's down to eighty percent of max."

"What does that mean?" the senior Narhani asked, and Bergren shrugged for the benefit of the control room security recorders.

"I'm afraid it means you're over the limits for our available power, sir," he replied smoothly.

"May we shift to another platform?"

"I'm afraid it wouldn't matter, sir. As you know, this system is very energy intensive. For this much mass, any of the platforms would draw on the same capacitor reserve, so you might as well stay where you are."

"But did you not say you cannot send us?" The Narhani sounded confused, and Bergren hid a smile.

"No, sir. I just can't transmit the entire load at once. I'll have to send your freight through in one transmission, then send you and the other members of your party through in a second, that's all."

"I see." The Narhani spokesman and his companions spoke softly and quickly in their own language. Bergren didn't know what the object they were accompanying was, but he knew they were a security detachment, and he forced himself to sit calmly, hiding any trace of anxiety over what they might decide. After a moment, the spokesman looked back up and raised the volume of his vocoder.

"Can we not send at least one of our number through with our freight?"

"I'm afraid not, sir. We'll be right at the limits of our available power, and Regs prohibit me from sending passengers under those conditions."

"Is there risk to our freight?" The question was sharp for a Narhani.

"No, sir," Bergren soothed. "Not if it's not alive. The

regulations are so specific because a power fluctuation that won't harm inanimate objects can cause serious neural damage in living passengers. It's just a precaution."

"I see." The spokesman looked back at his companions for a moment, then twitched his crest in the Narhani equivalent of a shrug. "We would prefer to wait until your power systems have been repaired," he told Bergren, "but our schedule is very tight. Can you assure us our freight will arrive undamaged?"

"Yes, sir," Bergren said confidently.

"Very well," the Narhani sighed. He spoke to his companions in their own language again, and all five of them stepped off the platform and moved back behind the safety line.

"Thank you, sir," Bergren said, and his fold-com implant sent a brief, prerecorded burst transmission to a waiting relay as he began to prep for transmission.

"Alert signal," a woman said quietly in the control room on Jefferson's screen. The two men at the main console nodded acknowledgment without ever opening their eyes, and one of them activated the stealthed sensor arrays watching Shepherd Center from orbit.

"Good signal," his companion announced in the toneless voice of a man concentrating on his neural feed. "We've got their field strength. Coming up nicely now."

"Synchronizer on-line," the third tech said. "Power up and nominal. Switching to auto sequence."

Carl Bergren watched his readouts through his feeds. This was the tricky part that was going to earn him that big stack of credits. The settings had to be *almost* right, and he straightened his mouth as he felt it trying to curl in a grin of tension. The power levels were already off the optimum curve, thanks to the failure of the gamma bank, and he very carefully cut back the charge on the delta bank. Not by much. Only by a tiny, virtually undetectable fraction. But it would be enough—if whoever was in charge of the other part of the operation got *his* numbers right—and he sent the alert signal to Birhat and waited for the response.

Lawrence Jefferson leaned towards his com, clutching his wineglass, and his heart pounded. This was the moment, he thought. The instant towards which he'd worked so long.

"Their field's building now," the sensor tech murmured. "Looking good . . . looking good . . . stand by . . . stand by . . . coming up to peak . . . *now!*"

Carl Bergren sent the release code, and the capacitors screamed. The shrouded object on the platform vanished as the mat-trans sent a mighty pulse of power into hyper-space, and he held his breath. The transmission he'd sent out was almost precisely four millionths of a percent too weak to reach Birhat. It would waste its power twenty light-minutes short of the funnel waiting to catch it for the reception units, but no one would ever know if—

The control room on Lawrence Jefferson's com screen was silent, its personnel frozen. Not even a mat-trans was truly instantaneous over an eight-hundred-light-year range, and Jefferson held his breath while he waited.

A soft tone beeped, and Carl Bergren let out a whooshing breath as the Birhat mat-trans operator acknowledged receipt. He'd done it! The person at the other end of the hypercom link didn't realize someone else had invaded the system. He thought he'd just received Bergren's transmission!

The lieutenant suppressed an urge to wipe his forehead. Deep inside, he hadn't really believed his employer could pull it off, and it was hard to keep his elation out of his voice as he activated his mike.

"Birhat has confirmed reception, sir," he told the Narhani spokesman. "If you'd step onto the platform, I can send you through now, as well."

✧   ✧   ✧

"We did it!" someone shouted gleefully. "They accepted the transmission!"

The staff of Jefferson's illicit mat-trans whistled and clapped, and the Lieutenant Governor checked the computer tied into his com. Good. The exact readouts of the transmission, which just happened to carry the same identifier code as Lieutenant Bergren's system, had been properly stored. He'd have to wait until the regular Shepherd Center data collection upload late next week to exchange them for Bergren's actual log of the transmission, but that part of the pipeline had already been tested and proved secure. It was inconvenient, since he would have preferred to make the switch sooner, yet there was nothing he could do about it. The mass readings of the transit would prove the statue Birhat had just received had not, in fact, been the solid block of marble Bergren had just destroyed, and for his Reichstag fire to work, it was vital that Battle Fleet itself discover that fact when the time came.

He smiled at the thought, then looked back at his link to the hidden control room and its celebrating personnel. Two of them had cracked bottles of champagne, and he watched them pouring their glasses full while they chattered and laughed with the release of long-held tension. They'd worked hard for this moment—and, of course, for the huge pile of credits they'd been promised—and the Lieutenant Governor leaned back in his chair with a sigh of matching relief. They deserved their moment of triumph, and he let them celebrate it for another few minutes, then pressed a button.

Half a world away, the explosive charges three long-dead technicians had installed at his orders detonated. One of the control room personnel had time for a single scream of terror before the plunging roof of the subterranean installation turned him and all his fellows into mangled gruel.

Carl Bergren dutifully logged a full report on the capacitor bank failure and completed his shift without further incident. He turned over to his relief at shift change and signed out through the security checkpoints, then walked slowly to his parked flyer while he pondered the entire operation. Whoever had arranged it, he thought, had to have incredible reach and command equally incredible resources. He'd had to gain access to the routing schedules weeks in advance to be sure Bergren would be on duty when the transmission came through. Then he'd had to get someone in to sabotage the capacitors, and he'd had to make sure the sabotage was untraceable. *And* he'd had to have the resources to build his own mat-trans *and* find a way to monitor the Shepherd Center system precisely enough to time his own transmission perfectly.

It was big, Bergren told himself as he unlocked his flyer, climbed in, and settled into the flight couch. It was really big, and there couldn't be more than a dozen people—probably less—who could have put it all together. Now it was just a matter of figuring out which of those dozen or so it had really been, and little Carl Bergren would live high on the hog for the rest of his natural life.

He smiled and activated his flyer's drive, and the resultant explosion blew two entire levels of the parking garage and thirty-six innocent bystanders into very tiny pieces. Forty minutes later, an anonymous spokesman for the Sword of the Lord claimed responsibility for the blast.

Chapter Thirty-Five

The last reeking powder smoke drifted away, and Sean MacIntyre surveyed a scene that had become too familiar. The only thing that had changed were the colors the dead wore, he thought bitterly, for the eastern Temple Guard had been reduced to barely forty thousand men, and they were being held back to cover the Temple itself. He was fighting the secular lords' armies now, and he shuddered as he watched the "merely" wounded writhe among the corpses.

His army was out of the Keldark Valley at last and, as he'd known it would, marching circles about its opponents. High-Captain Terrahk had fallen back on Baricon, but he'd lacked the men to hold an attack from the west. There were too many avenues of approach, and when Tamman blasted his way through a gap with fifteen thousand men and got around his flank, Terrahk had retreated desperately. His attempt to stand had cost him his entire rearguard—another eight thousand men (most, Sean was thankful, captured and not killed)—and Sean had broken out into the rolling hills of the Duchy of Keldark.

The more open terrain offered vastly improved scope for maneuver, but every step he advanced also drew him further from the valley and exposed his supply route to counterattack. At the moment, the Temple was too hard pressed to think about cutting his communications, and he kept reminding himself they didn't really have "cavalry" in the classic Terran sense, but he also kept thinking about what a Pardalian Bedford Forrest or Phil Sheridan could do if it ever got loose in his rear. His edge in reconnaissance would make it hard for them to get past him, but he simply didn't have the men to garrison his supply line properly. He could have freed them up, but only by reducing his field army, which, in turn, would have reduced his ability to keep advancing.

He sighed and sent his branahlk mincing forward. The beast whistled unhappily at the battlefield stench, and Sean shared its distaste. Whoever had commanded the Temple's forces in this last battle should be shot, he thought grimly, assuming one of his riflemen hadn't already taken care of that. He supposed it was a sign of the Temple's desperation, but ordering forty-five thousand pikemen and only ten thousand musketeers to face him in the open had been the same as sending them straight to the executioner.

Had Sean armed his men in the classic Pardalian proportion of pikes to firearms, he could have fielded close to the quarter-million men the Temple credited him with. They had all the weapons they'd captured from the Malagoran Guard plus, effectively, all the weapons of Lord Marshal Rokas' Holy Host, including its entire artillery park, but he'd opted to call forward only enough reinforcements—and replacements, he thought bitterly, recalling the five thousand casualties Erastor had cost—to put sixty thousand infantry and dragoons and two hundred guns in the field. Two hundred battalions of rifles, most veterans of Yortown, Erastor, and Baricon, supported by a hundred and fifty arlaks and fifty chagors, had been more than enough to slaughter the secular levies of Keldark, Camathan, Sanku, and Walak. He controlled all of northeastern North Hylar, now, from the Shalokars to the sea, and he wondered dismally how many more men were going to die before the Temple agreed to negotiate. God knew he and Stomald had been asking—almost *begging*—it to ever since the fall of Erastor! Couldn't the Inner Circle understand they didn't *want* to kill its troops? Brashan still couldn't get any of his remotes inside the hundred-kilometer zone around the Temple, so they couldn't know what was passing in Vroxhan's council meetings, but the prelates seemed willing to send every fighting man in North Hylar to his death before they'd even talk to "demon-worshipers"!

The litter-bearers were already busy. Theirs was the most horrible duty of all, yet they went about it with a compassion which still surprised him. The Angels' Army recognized its tactical superiority as well as its commander did, and, like Sean, most of its troops knew the men littering the field had been utterly outclassed. His own casualties, dead and wounded alike, had been under a thousand, and most of his men had come, in their own ways, to share his sickness at slaughtering their foes. It was too one-sided, and the men they were killing weren't the ones they wanted. With every battle, every army they smashed, their hatred of the Inner Circle grew, yet it wasn't a religious hatred. "The Angels" had always been careful not to deliver an actual religious message—other than backing the Malagoran hankering for freedom of conscience—and since Harry's revelation of the truth, Stomald had begun stressing the Temple's political tyranny and enormous, self-serving wealth far more strongly. The Angels' Army longed to settle accounts once and for all with the old men in Aris who kept sending other people out to die, but more even than that, it wanted simply to be rid of them.

Sean drew rein and watched a group of litter-bearers troop past with their pitiful, broken burdens. Walking wounded limped and staggered back with them, and at least Harry, coached by Brashan and *Israel's* med computers, had been teaching the Malagoran surgeons things they'd never dreamed were possible. The introduction of ether, alone, had revolutionized Pardalian medicine, and Sean had sworn a solemn oath that the first thing he would have sent to Pardal from Birhat would be medical teams with proper regeneration gear. He couldn't breathe life back into the dead, but he *could*, by God, give the maimed, whichever side they'd fought upon, *their* lives back!

His lip curled as he wondered how much of that fierce determination was an effort to assuage his own guilt.

With today's body count, the war he and his friends had inadvertently started had cost over a hundred thousand *battlefield* deaths. He had no idea how many more had perished of the diseases that always ravaged nonindustrial armies, and he was terrified of what the number would finally be. He could trace every step of the journey which had led them to this, and given their options as they took each of those steps, he still saw no other course they might have chosen, yet all this death and brutal agony seemed an obscene price to buy five marooned people a ticket home.

He drew a deep breath. It seemed an obscene price because it *was*, and he would pay no more of it than he must. The Temple had ignored his semaphore offers to parley and refused to receive his "demon-worshiping" messengers, but he had one last shot to try.

High Priest Vroxhan sat in his high seat, and his lips worked as if to spit upon the men who faced him. High-Captain Ortak, High-Captain Marhn, High-Captain Sertal . . . the list went on and on. Over *fifty* senior officers stood before him, the surviving commanders of the armies the demon-worshipers had smashed in such merciless succession, and he longed to fling the entire feckless lot to the Inquisitors as their failure deserved.

But much as he wished to, and however richly they'd earned it, he couldn't. The morale of his remaining troops was too precarious, and if wholesale executions might stiffen the spines of the weak, it also might convince them the Temple was lashing out in blind desperation. Besides, Lord Marshal Surak had spoken in their defense. He needed their firsthand observations if he was to understand the terrible changes the accursed demon-worshipers had wrought in the art of war.

Or, at least, he says *he does.* Vroxhan closed his eyes and clenched his fists on the arms of his chair. *A bad sign, this suspicion of* everyone. *Does it mean I am desperate?* He clutched his faith to him and made himself open his eyes once more.

"Very well, Ortak," he growled, unable to make himself give the failure the honor of his rank. "Tell us of these demon-lovers and their *terms*."

Ortak winced, though it was hard to tell—his face was as heavily bandaged as the stump of his right arm—and reached for very careful words.

"Holiness, their leaders bade me say they ask only for you to speak with them. And—" he drew a deep breath "—Lord Sean said to tell you you may speak to him now, or amid the ruins of this city, but that you *will* speak to him at last."

"Blasphemy!" old Bishop Corada cried. "This is *God's* city! No one who traffics with the powers of Hell will ever take it!"

"Your Grace, I tell you only what Lord Sean said, not what he can accomplish," Ortak replied, but his tone said he *did* think the heretics could take even the Temple, and Vroxhan's hand ached to strike him.

"Peace, Corada," he grated instead, and smoothed the written message Ortak had brought across his lap as the bishop retreated into sullen silence. His eyes burned down at it for a moment, then rose to Ortak once more. "Tell me more of this Lord Sean and the other heretic leaders."

"Holiness, I've never seen their like," Ortak said frankly, and the other returned prisoners nodded agreement. "The man they call Lord Sean is a giant, head and shoulders taller than any man I've ever seen, with eyes and hair blacker than night. The one they call Lord Tamman is shorter and looks less strange, but for the darkness of his skin, yet all of us have heard stories—from our own men who have seen them in battle, not just the heretics—of the miraculous strength both share."

" 'Sean,' 'Tamman,' " Vroxhan snorted. "What names are these?"

"I don't know, Holiness. Their men say—" Ortak bit his lip.

"*What* do 'their men say'?" Bishop Surmal purred, and Ortak swallowed at the look in the High Inquisitor's eyes.

"Your Grace, I repeat only what the heretics claim," he said, and paused. Pregnant silence shivered until High Priest Vroxhan broke it.

"We understand," he said coldly. "We will not hold you responsible for lies others may tell." He didn't, Ortak noted sinkingly, say what else the Circle *would* hold him responsible for, but at this point he was willing to settle for whatever mercy he could get.

"Thank you, Holiness," he said, and drew a deep breath. "The heretics say these men are warriors from a land beyond our knowledge, chosen by . . . by the so-called 'angels' as their champions. They say all of their new weapons and tactics were given to them by Lord Sean and Lord Tamman. That the two of them are God-touched and can never be defeated."

A savage hiss ran through the assembled prelates, and Ortak felt sweat slick his face under its bandages. He made himself stand as straight as his wounds allowed, meeting High Priest Vroxhan's burning eyes, and prayed Vroxhan had meant his promise not to hold him responsible.

"So," the high priest said at last, his voice an icicle. "I note, Ortak, that you have not yet mentioned these so-called 'angels.' " Ortak dared not reply, and Vroxhan smiled a thin, dangerous smile. "I know you've seen them. Tell us of them."

"Holiness, I *have* seen them," Ortak admitted, "but what they actually are, I cannot say."

"What do they *appear* to be, then?" Surmal snapped.

"Your Grace, they wear the seeming of women. There are two of them, the 'Angel Harry' and the 'Angel Sandy.' " A fresh stir at the outlandish names swept the Circle, and the high-captain went on doggedly now that he'd begun. "The one they call Sandy is smaller, with short hair. From all I could learn, it was she who routed the Guard units initially sent to crush the heresy, and she and Lord Sean appear to be the heretics' true war leaders. The one they call Harry is taller than most men, and—forgive me, Your Grace, but you asked—of surpassing beauty, yet wears an eye patch. From what the heretics told us, it was she who was wounded and captured by the villagers of Cragsend and the one they call Sandy who led the demons to her rescue."

"And did they tell *you* they were God's messengers?" Surmal demanded.

"No, Your Grace," Ortak said cautiously.

"*What?*" Vroxhan snapped to his feet and glared at the high-captain. "I warn you, Ortak! We have the written messages of the traitor Stomald himself to claim they are!"

"I realize that, Holiness," Ortak's mouth was dust dry, yet he made his voice come out level, "but Bishop Surmal asked what *they* say. I did not myself speak with them, yet their own followers seem perplexed by their insistence that they *not* be called 'angel.' The heretics do so anyway, but only among themselves, never to the ang— To the so-called angels themselves."

"But—" Corada started, then shook his head and went on almost plaintively. "But we have reports they wear holy vestments at all times! Why would they do that if they don't claim to be angels? And why would even heretics follow those who claim to be mere mortal women yet profane the cloth? What do these madmen *want* of us?"

"Your Grace," Ortak said, frightened and yet secretly grateful for the opening, "I can't tell you why they wear the garb they choose or why the heretics follow them, but Lord Sean himself has told me they seek only to defend themselves. That he and his companions came to the aid of the heretics only because Mother Church had proclaimed Holy War against them."

"Lies!" Surmal thundered. "*We* are Mother Church, God's chosen shepherds for His people! When heresy stirs, it must be crushed, root and branch, lest the whole body of God's people be poisoned and their souls lost to damnation forever! He who defies us in this defies God Himself, and whatever this 'Lord Sean' claims, he and his fellows are—must be!—demons sent to destroy us all!"

"Your Grace," Ortak said quietly, "I wasn't called to the priesthood, but to serve God as a soldier, in accordance with the commands of the Temple. It may be that I've failed in that service, despite all I could do, yet a soldier is all I know how to be. I tell you not what I believe, but what I was told by Lord Sean. Whether or not and how he may have lied is for you to judge, Your Grace; I only answer your questions as best I may."

Vroxhan raised his hand, cutting off Surmal's fresh, angry retort, and his hooded eyes were thoughtful. Fresh silence lingered for over a minute before he cleared his throat.

"Very well, Ortak—speak as a 'soldier' then. What is your estimate of this Lord Sean *as* a soldier?"

Ortak gazed back up at the high priest, and then Vroxhan frowned in surprise as he slowly and painfully lowered himself to his knees. High-Captain Marhn dared the assembled prelates' wrath by assisting his wounded commander, but Ortak never took his eyes from Vroxhan's.

"Holiness, heretic or no, demon-worshiper or demonspawn as he may be, I tell you that not once in a hundred generations has Pardal seen this man's equal as a war captain. Wherever he may spring from, whatever the source of his knowledge, he is a master of his trade, and the men he commands will follow where he leads against any foe."

"Even against God Himself?" Vroxhan asked very softly.

"Against *any* foe, Holiness," Ortak repeated, and closed his eyes at last. "Holiness, my life is forfeit, if you choose to claim it. I gave of my very best for God and the Temple, yet I speak not in any effort to excuse my failure or save myself when I tell you no Guard captain is this man's equal. His army is far smaller than any of us believed possible, yet no captain has held a single field against him. As a soldier I know only the art of battle, Holiness, but that I *do* know. Do with me as you will, yet for the sake of Mother Church and the Faith, I beg you to heed me in this. *Do not take this man lightly*. Were every Guardsman in both Hylars, Herdaana, and Ishar gathered in one place, *still* I fear he would defeat them. Demon or devil he may be, but as a war captain he is without peer on all Pardal."

The kneeling high-captain bent his head, and shocked silence filled the chamber.

"So at last the enemy has a face and a name," Vroxhan said softly. He and the Inner Circle had withdrawn to their council chamber, accompanied only by Lord Marshal Surak.

"For all the good it does us," Corada replied heavily. "If Ortak is correct—"

"He *isn't* correct!" Surmal snapped, and turned to Vroxhan. "I claim Ortak for the Holy Inquisition, Holiness! Whatever else he may or may not have done, he has fallen into damnation by the respect he grants this demon. For the sake of Mother Church and his own soul, he must answer to the Inquisitors!"

Surak stirred, and Vroxhan looked up at him.

"You disagree, Lord Marshal?" he asked in a dangerous voice.

"Holiness, I serve the Temple. If the Circle judges that Ortak must answer, then answer he must, but before you decide, I beg you to weigh his words most carefully."

"You *agree* with him?" Corada gasped, but Surak shook his head.

"I didn't say that, Your Grace. What I said is that his words must be weighed. Mistaken or not, Ortak is the most experienced officer to have met the demon-worshipers and survived, and he *has* spoken to them. Perhaps this has corrupted his soul and led him into damnation, yet his information is our *only* firsthand report of the heretics' leadership. And," Surak looked at Surmal, "with all due respect, Your Grace, punishing him will not make any truth he may have uttered untrue."

"Truth? What *truth*?" Vroxhan demanded before Surmal could respond.

"'The truth that the demon-worshipers have defeated every army sent against them . . . and that we have no more armies to send, Holiness." Deathly silence fell, and Surak went on in a grim, hard voice. "I have forty thousand Guardsmen to garrison the Temple itself. Aside from them, there are less than ten thousand of the Guard in all eastern North Hylar. The secular lords of the north have been defeated—no, My Lords, *crushed*—as completely as Lord Marshal Rokas and High-Captain Ortak, and the better part of the levies of Telis, Eswyn, and Tarnahk with them. We have fifty thousand of the Guard west of the Thirgan Gap and another seventy thousand in South Hylar, yet they can reach us here only by ship, and it will take many five-days to bring any sizable portion of that force to bear. The secular levies of the remaining eastern lands amount to no more than sixty thousand. They, and the men I have here to guard the Temple, are *all* we can throw against the heretics, and every officer who returned with Ortak reports the same of the demon-worshipers' army. It is far smaller than our original estimates, yet every man in it appears to be armed with a rifle which fires *more* rapidly than a joharn, not less."

"Which means?" Vroxhan prompted when the lord marshal paused.

"Which means, Holiness, that I can't stop them," Surak admitted in a voice like crushed gravel. The prelates stared at him in horror, and he squared his shoulders. "My Lords, I am your chief captain. My responsibility to you before God Himself is to tell you the truth, and the truth is that somehow—I do not pretend to know the manner of it—this 'Lord Sean' has built an army which can crush any force on Pardal."

"But we're *God's* warriors!" Corada cried. "He won't *let* them defeat us!"

"He has so far, Your Grace," Surak replied flatly. "Why He should let this happen I can't say, but to pretend otherwise would violate my sworn oath to serve God and the Temple to the best of my ability. I've searched for an answer, My Lords, in prayer and meditation as well as in my map rooms and with my officers, without finding one. At present, the heretics are less than three five-day's march from the Temple itself, and the last army in their path has been destroyed. If you command it, I will gather every man in the Temple and every man the remaining secular levies can send me and meet the heretics in battle, and my men and officers will do all that mortal men can do. Yet it is my duty to tell you our numbers may actually be lower than the heretics', and I fear our defeat will be complete unless God Himself intervenes."

"He will! *He will!*" Corada cried almost desperately.

Surak said nothing, only looked at Vroxhan, and the high priest's hands clenched under the council table. He could almost smell the panic Surak's words had produced, yet even in his own fear, he knew the lord marshal had spoken only the truth. Why? Why was God letting this *happen?* The thought battered in his brain, but God sent no answer, and the silence after Corada's outburst stretched his nerves like an Inquisitor's rack.

"Are you telling us, Lord Marshal," he said at last, in a carefully controlled voice, "that the Temple of God has no *choice* but to surrender to the forces of Hell?"

Surak flinched ever so slightly, but his eyes were level.

"I am telling you, Holiness, that with the forces available to me, all I and my men can do is die in the Faith's defense as our oaths require us to. We will honor those oaths if no other answer can be found, yet I beg you, My Lords, to search your own hearts and prayers, for whatever answer God demands of us, I do not believe it lies upon the field of battle."

"What if . . . what if we accept the heretics' offer to parley?" Bishop Frenaur said hesitantly. The entire Circle turned on him in horror, but the Bishop of fallen Malagor met their eyes with a strength he hadn't displayed since Yortown. "I don't mean we should accept their terms," he said more sharply, "but the Lord Marshal tells us his forces are too weak to defeat them in battle. If we *pretend* to negotiate with them, could we not demand a cease-fire while we do so? At the least, that would win time for our forces in western North Hylar and our other lands to reach us!"

"*Negotiate* with the powers of Hell?" Surmal cried, but to Vroxhan's surprise, old Corada straightened in his chair with suddenly hopeful eyes. "Our very souls would—" Surmal went on wildly, but Corada raised his hand.

"Wait, brother. Perhaps Frenaur has a point." The High Inquisitor gaped at him, and the old man went on in a thoughtful voice. "God knows the peril we face. Would He not expect us to do anything that we can, even to pretending to treat with demons, to buy time to crush them in the end?"

"Your Grace," Surak said gently, "I doubt the heretics would fall into such a trap. Whatever the source of their intelligence, it's fiendishly accurate. They would know we were bringing up additional forces and act before we could do so, and—forgive me, My Lords, but I must repeat this once more—even if we brought up *all* of our strength, I fear their army could defeat us if we took the field against them."

"Wait. Wait, Lord Marshal," Vroxhan murmured, and his brain raced. "Perhaps this *is* God's answer to our prayers," he said slowly, intently, and his eyes snapped back into focus and settled on Surak's face. "You say we cannot defeat this 'Lord Sean' in the field, Lord Marshal?"

"No, Holiness," the soldier said heavily.

"Then perhaps the answer is not to meet him there," Vroxhan said softly, and his smile was cold.

Chapter Thirty-Six

"It sounds too good to be true." Sandy paced up and down the command tent, hands folded behind her, and her face was troubled.

"Why?" Tamman retorted. "Because it's what we've asked them to do for weeks?"

"Because it doesn't fit with anything *else* they've done since this whole thing started!" she shot back sharply.

"Perhaps not, My Lady," Stomald said, "but it *does* accord with the orders they've sent their commanders. Perhaps Lord Sean's messengers have finally convinced Vroxhan to see reason."

"Um." Sandy's grunt was unhappy, and Sean sat back in his camp chair. He shared her wariness, but Stomald was right; their remotes had snooped on the Temple's orders to all its commanders to stand fast until instructed otherwise. Lord Marshal Surak had, in effect, frozen every force outside Aris itself, in sharp reversal of his efforts to funnel every available man to the front.

He reached out a long arm to lift the Temple's illuminated letter from the table and reread it carefully.

"I have to agree with Stomald and Tam," he said finally. "It *sounds* genuine, and everything we've observed indicates they mean it."

"Maybe, but we haven't observed *everything*, now have we?" Sandy shot back. Her eyes flicked to Tibold, the only person in the tent who didn't know the truth about their origins—and the reason they couldn't snoop on the Temple directly—and Sean nodded unhappily. But, damn it, it *did* all hang together, and he was sick unto death of slaughtering armies of pawns!

"Tibold?" He glanced at the ex-Guardsman. "You're the only one who's lived in the Temple or seen their high command firsthand. What do you think?"

"I don't know, My Lord," Tibold replied frankly. "Like Lady Sandy, I can't help thinking it sounds too good to be true, yet they've followed all the proper forms. Promises of safe passage. An offer of hostages for the safety of our negotiators. They've even agreed to let us march our entire army to the walls of the Temple itself!"

"Why not?" Sandy demanded. "We've proven we can march anywhere we want and defeat any army they can field, but they know we don't have a siege train. The risk we could storm the Temple's walls is minimal, so why *not* invite us to come ahead when they can't stop us anyway? Can you think of a better way to make us over-confident?"

"And the hostages?" Harriet asked. "They're offering to send us a third of the Guard's senior officers, a hundred upper-priests, twenty bishops, *and* a member of the Circle itself! Would they do that if they weren't serious? And doesn't it make sense for them to at least try to find out what we want?"

"If they wanted to know that, all they had to do was ask us months ago!" Sandy objected.

"That's true enough," Sean agreed. "On the other hand, months ago they thought they could wipe us out. Now they know they can't." He shook his head. "The situation's changed too much to be certain of anything, Sandy— aside from the fact that they've finally agreed to parley."

"I don't like it," she said unhappily. "I don't like it at all. And I especially don't like the fact that they didn't ask for Stomald to attend but *did* ask for both you and Tam." She glared at him. "If they get you two, they cut off the army's head," she added in English, but Sean shook his head.

"By this time you and Harry could lead the troops as well as Tam and I," he said in English.

"Maybe so, but do *they* know that?" she shot back. Sean started to reply, then settled for shaking his head once more, and Stomald eased cautiously into the conversation.

"I understand your concern, My Lady, but I must be the man they most hate in all the world," he pointed out. "If there's one man they would do anything to keep beyond the precincts of the Temple, that man is me." He, too, shook his head. "No, My Lady. Lord Sean and Lord Tamman are our war leaders. If they prefer—as it would seem from their language that they do—to keep any parley on a purely military level, leaving any doctrinal questions untouched for the moment, then my exclusion makes perfect sense."

"Father Stomald's right, My Lady," Tibold said. "And the oaths of good faith they've offered to swear upon God and their own souls are not such as any priest would lightly break."

Sandy tossed her head unhappily and paced faster for several minutes, then sank into another camp chair and rubbed her temples tiredly.

"I don't like it," she repeated. "It looks good, and there's a logical—or at least plausible—answer to every objection I can raise, but they've turned reasonable too fast, Sean. I *know* they're up to something."

"Maybe so," he said gently, "but I don't see any choice but to find out what it is. We're killing people, Sandy— thousands and thousands of them. If there's any hope at all of stopping the fighting, then I think we have to explore it. We owe that to these people."

She sat rigid for a moment, and then her shoulders slumped.

"I guess you're right," she said, and her low voice was weary.

"They've accepted, Holiness," Lord Marshal Surak said.

He looked less than pleased, but Vroxhan was God's chosen shepherd. It was his overriding duty to defeat the forces of Hell and preserve the power of God's Church, and nothing he did in such a cause could be "wrong," whatever Surak thought. He stood at the council chamber window, watching distant, jewel-bright talmahks drift lazily above the cursed ruins of the Old Ones beyond the wall, and said a silent prayer for all of God's martyrs, then turned back to the Guard's commander.

"Very well, Lord Marshal. I shall draft our formal response to their acceptance while you see to the details."

"As you command, Holiness," Surak said, and bent to kiss the hem of the high priest's robe before he withdrew.

The city Pardalians called the Temple was an impressive sight as the Angels' Army halted just beyond cannon shot of its walls. The broken towers of a ruined Imperial city rose behind it, the shortest of the shattered stubs still three times the walls' height, and a single structure dominated its center. Most of the Temple was built of native stone, exquisitely dressed and finished with mosaic frescoes exalting the glory of God (and His Church), but the Sanctum was a massive bunker of white, glittering ceramacrete, untouched by any adornment. It clashed wildly with the spires and minarets about it, yet there was a strange harmony to it, as if the rest of the city had been deliberately planned and built to complement the Sanctum by its very contrast.

Sean stood on a small hill while the command tent went up behind him, and clouds of dust drifted across a cloudless blue sky as the army prepared its camp. Promise of truce or no, he and Tibold were taking no chances, and each brigade kept one regiment under arms while the other two collected their mattocks and shovels. By the time night fell, the entire army would be covered by earthworks which would have made a Roman general proud, and they outnumbered the city's garrisoning Guardsmen by fifty percent. Whatever else might happen, he was confident no surprise attack would overwhelm his men.

He frowned and tugged on his nose as a familiar mental itch stirred anew. He wasn't about to admit that part of him shared Sandy's misgivings. If he told her that, she'd be quite capable of singlehandedly turning the whole damned army around and marching back north, so he had no intention of breathing a word of it, but it was one reason he approved of the army's readiness to dig itself in. His troops were as hopeful as he that the fighting might end, yet they were wary and alert, as well, and that was good.

He sighed. They couldn't operate remotes in the Temple, and Brashan's orbital arrays were restricted to pure optical mode lest active systems set off the automated defenses, but those arrays had reported zero movement of troops into the area, exactly as High Priest Vroxhan had promised, and the Guardsmen actually inside the walls seemed to be going about routine duties and drill. There were some signs of heightened readiness, but that was inevitable with the dreaded demon-worshipers encamped just outside the Temple's North Gate.

No, he told himself again, everything they could see looked perfect. The parley might achieve nothing, but at least the Temple seemed ready to negotiate in good faith, and that was a priceless opportunity.

He turned from the walls. The hostages were due to arrive early tomorrow, and he wanted another word with Tibold. The last thing they needed was for some hothead on *their* side to wreck things by abusing one of the hostages!

High Priest Vroxhan stood on the walls and watched the fires of the heretic host glitter against the night. He knew the demon-worshipers were less numerous than that seeming galaxy of fires might suggest, yet his heart was heavy at the thought of allowing such blasphemers so close to God's own city. And, he admitted, at the price of his own plan to break them for all time.

He turned his head as a foot sounded on the wall's stone. Bishop Corada stood beside him, gazing out over their enemies while the night breeze ruffled his fringe of white hair, and his face was far calmer than Vroxhan felt.

"Corada—" he began, but the old man shook his head serenely.

"No, Holiness. If it's God's will that I die in His service, well, I've had a long life, and the risk is necessary. We both know that, Holiness."

Vroxhan rested a hand on the bishop's shoulder and squeezed, unable to find the words to express the emotions in his heart. The suggestion had been Corada's own, yet that made it no easier, and the old man's courage shamed him. Corada smiled at him and reached up to pat the hand on his shoulder gently.

"We've come a long way together, you and I, Holiness," he said. "I know you used to think me a blustering old bag of piss and wind—" Vroxhan started to interrupt, but Corada shook his head. "Oh, come now, Holiness! Of course you did—just as I used to think old Bishop Kithmar, when I was your age. And, truth to tell, I suppose in many ways I *am* an old bag of piss and wind. We tend to get that way as we grow older, I think. Still," he gazed back out over the forest of campfires, "sometimes old dodderers like me can see a bit more clearly than those of you with your lives still before you, and there's something I want to say to you before . . . well—" He shrugged.

"What?" The hoarseness of Vroxhan's own voice surprised him, and Corada sighed.

"Just this, Holiness: perhaps not all the demon-worshipers have said should be disregarded."

"*What?*" Vroxhan stared at the old man, the staunchest defender of the Faith of them all after High Inquisitor Surmal himself, in shock.

"Oh, not this nonsense about 'angels'! But the very thing that made it possible for them to come this far is the kernel of truth amid their lies. We know we serve God, for His Voice would tell us if it were otherwise, yet Mother Church has grown too distant from her flock, Holiness. Stomald is a damnable, heretical traitor, yet his lies could never have succeeded did the people of Pardal truly see us as their shepherds. I know Malagor has always been restive, but have you not heard reports of the heretics' denunciations of the Temple? Of its wealth? Of its secular power and the arrogance of Mother Church's bishops?"

The old man turned earnestly to his high priest and reached out to rest both hands on Vroxhan's shoulders.

"Holiness, this business of bishops who see their flocks but twice a year, of temples gilded with gold squeezed from the faithful, of princes who rule only on Mother Church's sufferance—these things must change, or what we face today will not end tomorrow. Mother Church must rededicate herself to winning her flock's love and devotion or, in time, other heretics will arise, and we will lose not simply our people's obedience, but their souls, as well. I'm an old man, Holiness. Even without the risk I run tomorrow, the problems I foresee wouldn't come to pass before I was safely buried, but I tell you now that we *have* become corrupt. We have tasted the power of princes, not just of priests, and that power will destroy all Mother Church stands for if we allow it. In my heart, I've come to believe that is God's purpose in allowing the demon-worshipers to come so near to success. To warn us that we—that *you*—must make changes to see that it never happens again."

Vroxhan stared at the simple-hearted old man, tasting the iron tang of Corada's sincerity, and his heart went out to him. The purity of his faith was wonderful to behold, yet even as tears stung Vroxhan's eyes, he knew Corada was wrong. The authority of Mother Church was God's authority, hard won after centuries of struggle. To return to the old ways when the cold steel of power had not underlain her decrees was to court the madness of the Schismatic Wars and permit the very lies and heresies which had spawned the army beyond the Temple's walls to flourish unchecked. No, God's work was too vital to entrust to the simple-minded, pastoral bishops Corada's tired old heart longed for, yet Vroxhan could never say that to him. Could never explain why he was wrong, why his beautiful dream could be no more than a dream, forever. Not when Corada had so willingly accepted his own fate to preserve Mother Church and the sanctity of the Faith. And because he could never tell Corada those things, High Priest Vroxhan smiled and touched the old man's cheek with gentle fingers.

"I shall think upon what you've said, Corada," he lied softly, "and what I can do, I will. I promise you."

"Thank you, Holiness," Corada said even more softly. He gave the high priest's shoulders one last squeeze and raised his head. His nostrils flared as he inhaled the cool sweetness of the night's air, and then he released the high priest, bowed once to him, and walked slowly away into the darkness.

"Well, here they come," Sean muttered to Tamman.

"Yeah. Hard to believe we may actually have made it."

The two of them stood together, flanked by their senior captains, and watched the column emerge from the city gates. A score of Guard dragoons led the way, joharns peace-bonded into their saddle scabbards with elaborate twists of scarlet cord. Twice as many infantry followed under the snapping crimson banners of the Church, and behind them came the mounted officers of the Guard and the clerics the Circle had designated as hostages. A hundred priests and twenty bishops in the full blue-and-gold glory of their vestments surrounded a litter of state, and Sean's enhanced vision zoomed in on the litter. Bishop Corada, fourth in seniority in the Inner Circle, sat amid its cushions, and Sean sighed in relief. Corada's presence as a hostage for the safety of the Angels' Army's negotiators had been the crowning proof of the Circle's sincerity, and he was vastly relieved to see him at last.

"Looks like they're serious after all, Sandy," he subvocalized over his com.

"We'll see." Her response was so grim he winced, and he wished with all his heart that she could be here this morning. But that was impossible. The Temple would neither meet with nor even acknowledge "the angels'" existence, and Sandy and Harriet had taken themselves elsewhere with the dawn.

He brushed the thought aside as the head of the column reached him. The escorting honor guards tried to hide their anxiety behind professional smartness, but their nervously roving eyes betrayed them, and Sean couldn't blame them. They were pure window dressing, a sop to the importance of the hostages. If anything went wrong, the "heretical" force about them would crush them like gnats and never even notice it had done so.

A white-haired, magnificently uniformed officer with the heavy golden chain of a high-captain dismounted and advanced on the waiting Malagorans. He'd obviously been briefed on who to look for, and Sean wasn't exactly hard to spot as he towered over the Pardalians about him.

"Lord Sean," the Guardsman touched his breastplate in formal salute, "I am High-Captain Kerist, second-in-command to Lord Marshal Surak."

"High-Captain Kerist." Sean returned the salute, then nodded to the pavilions which had been erected near at hand. "As you see, High-Captain, we've prepared a place for you and our other visitors"—Kerist's eyes glittered with wintry amusement at Sean's choice of nouns—"to await our return. I trust you'll all be comfortable, and please inform one of my aides if you have any needs we've failed to anticipate."

"Thank you," Kerist said. He gave quiet orders to the escort, and the hostages moved towards the pavilions. Sean watched them go and felt a small temptation to go over and introduce himself to Corada, but only a small one. The Circle's decision to meet in the Church Chancery rather than the Sanctum signaled its intent to keep this a matter between soldiers, at least initially, and there was no point risking misunderstandings.

"This is Captain Harkah, my nephew," Kerist said, indicating a much younger officer who'd dismounted beside him. "He'll be your guide to the parley site."

"Thank you, High-Captain. In that case, Lord Tamman

and I should be going. I hope to have the chance to speak further with you when I return."

"As God wills, Lord Sean," Kerist said politely, and Sean hid a smile as they exchanged salutes once more and the high-captain moved away to join the other hostages. An entire regiment of riflemen stood sentry duty around the pavilions, both to insure their privacy and to keep them out of mischief, and Sean glanced at Tamman.

"Let's do it," he said shortly in English.

"May the Force be with us," Tamman replied solemnly in the same language, and despite his tension, Sean grinned, then turned to Tibold.

"I wish you were coming along," he said with quiet sincerity, "but with me and Tam both in the city, I need you here."

"Understood, Lord Sean." Tibold spoke calmly, but there was a parental anxiety in his eyes as he faced his towering young commander. "You be careful in there."

"I will. And you stay ready out here."

"We will."

"Good."

Sean squeezed the ex-Guardsman's hand firmly, then mounted his own branahlk. He would vastly prefer to have met the Temple's representatives in some neutral spot well away from either army, but things didn't work that way here. The Inner Circle would treat with the heretics only from within the walls of its city, and Pardalian negotiating tradition supported its position. As part of its offer to parley, the Circle had extended the traditional invitation for Sean and Tamman to bring along a powerful bodyguard, as well as providing hostages for their safety. At Tibold's insistence, Sean had held out for the biggest security force he could get, and a full brigade would accompany them into the city. Neither he nor Tibold expected eighteen hundred men to make much difference if things went sour, but they should at least be a pointed warning to any fanatic tempted to disagree with the Circle's decision to negotiate.

The rest of the Angels' Army was at instant readiness

for combat. They hadn't been blatant about it, but they hadn't hidden it, either. In fact, they *wanted* the Temple to know their guard was up.

Sean drew rein beside Tamman and Captain Harkah and nodded to High-Captain Folmak. The miller-turned-brigadier and his First Brigade deserved to be here for this moment, and he smiled hugely.

"Ready to proceed, Lord Sean!" he barked.

"Then let's," Sean replied, and the pipes began to drone as the column moved off.

Chapter Thirty-Seven

Sean, Tamman, and Captain Harkah followed the vanguard as First Brigade marched down the North Way, one of the four principal avenues that converged on the Sanctum itself, and Sean marveled at the city's size and beauty. The Church had lavished Pardalian centuries of wealth and artistry upon its capital, and it showed. Yet for all the Temple's beauty, Sean sensed an underlying arrogance in its spacious buildings and broad streets. This was more than a city of religion; it was an imperial capital, mistress of its entire world, exulting as much in its secular power as in the glory of God. It made him uncomfortable, and he wondered how much of that stemmed from distaste and how much from knowing the trap this city could become if something went wrong.

He watched the Guard pikemen who lined the street as an honor guard. They were only a single rank deep, too spread out to pose any threat, but he noted the wary eye Folmak's officers kept upon them. Tibold had insisted that the negotiators' "bodyguards" should march with loaded weapons, and Sean hadn't argued. Now he wondered if he should have. If someone thought he saw a threatening movement and opened up . . .

He snorted at his own ability to find things to worry about and reminded himself every man in Folmak's brigade was a veteran. Poised on a hair trigger or no, they knew better than to fire without orders—unless, of course, some maniac was crazy enough actually to attack them!

He turned his head and smiled at Tamman, hoping he looked as calm as his friend, and made himself relax.

✧   ✧   ✧

High Priest Vroxhan stood on the Chancery roof and gazed impatiently up the ax-straight North Way. He'd chosen this spot for the parley because it stood on the south side of the Temple's largest square, the Place of Martyrs, and despite his tension he smiled grimly at the aptness of that name.

The van of the heretic column came into sight, and the high priest's hard eyes blazed. *Soon,* he thought. *Very soon, now.*

"*Sean!*"

Sean's head snapped up as Sandy screamed his name. Not over the com—in person!

He whipped around in the saddle, and his face twisted in mingled disbelief and fury as a very small figure in the breastplate and body armor of an officer spurred her branahlk forward.

"What the *hell* do you think—?" he began in English, but then her expression registered.

"Sean, it's a trap!" she shouted in the same language. "*What?*"

Her branahlk sent the last few men scampering aside as she forced it up beside him.

"Aren't you using your implants?!"

"Of course not! If the computer picked them up—"

"Damn it, there's no time for that! Kick them up—*now!*"

He stared at her, then brought up his implanted sensors, and his face went pale as they picked up the solid blocks of armed men closing in down the side streets which paralleled the North Way.

For one terrible moment, his brain completely froze. They were ten kilometers from the gates, halfway to the city's center. If he tried to turn around, those flanking pikes would close in through every intersection and cut his column to pieces. But if he *didn't* retreat—

He jerked his mind back to life, and his thoughts flashed like lightning. The column was still moving forward, unaware of the trap into which he'd led it, and so were the Guard formations closing in upon it. They were almost into a huge, paved square—it was over a kilometer and a half across, and he could see the enormous fountains at its center splashing merrily in the sunlight—and the Temple's intention was obvious. Once his men were out into the open, the ambushers would close in from all directions and crush them. But no attackers were following *behind* them, so if the Guard wanted to hit them—

"Warn Harry and Stomald!" he snapped, and turned in the saddle. "Folmak!"

"Lord Sean?" Folmak's face was perplexed. He couldn't understand English, but he'd recognized their tones, and his combat instincts had quivered instantly to life.

"It's a trap—they're going to ambush us when we hit that square up ahead." The captain paled, but Sean went on urgently. "We can't go back. Our only chance is to go ahead and hope they don't guess we know what's coming. Drop back and pass the word. They're still several streets over, keeping out of sight, and they'll probably wait to close in until most of the column's into the square, so here's what we're going to do—"

"*A trap?*" Tibold Rarikson stared at the Angel Harry in horror. She couldn't be serious! But her strained face and the fear in her single eye told him differently. He stared at her for one more moment, then wheeled away, shouting for his officers.

High Priest Vroxhan smiled triumphantly as the heretics began entering the Place of Martyrs. He could just see the first Guardsmen moving into position, and other troops, invisible to him here, had closed the North Way far behind the demon-worshipers. So "Lord Sean" was a war captain without peer, was he? Vroxhan barked a laugh as he recalled Ortak's whining warning.

If the heretics believe "Lord Sean" and "Lord Tamman" unbeatable, they're about to learn differently! And let us see how their morale responds when we drag their accursed "angels'" champions to the Inquisition in chains!

His smile grew cruel as the heretics continued into the square. In just minutes, Lord Marshal Surak's handpicked commanders would send their men forward and—

His smile died. The infidels had stopped advancing! They were— What *were* they doing?

"Form square! *Form square!*"

Under-Captain Harkah twisted around in disbelief as Sean's amplified voice bellowed the command and whistles shrilled. Two companies of Folmak's lead battalion—primed by quiet warnings from their officers—faced instantly to the left and right and marched directly away from one another. The rest of the regiment advanced another fifty meters, then spread across the growing space between them in a two-deep firing line. It wasn't a proper square—more of a three-sided, hollow rectangle, short sides anchored on the north side of the Place of Martyrs—and it grew steadily as more men double-timed out of the North Way and slotted into position.

"Lord Sean!" the Guardsman cried. "What do you think—?!"

His question died as he suddenly found himself looking down the muzzle of Sean's pistol at a range of fifteen centimeters.

"In about ten minutes," Sean said in a deadly voice, "the Temple Guard is going to attack us. Are you trying to tell me you didn't know?"

"*Attack—?*" Harkah stared at Sean in disbelief. "You're mad!" he whispered. "High Priest Vroxhan himself swore to receive you as envoys!"

"Did he?" The muzzle of Sean's pistol twitched like a pointer. "Is that his negotiating team?" he grated.

Harkah whipped around in the indicated direction, and his face went bone-white as the leading ranks of Guard pike companies suddenly appeared, filling every opening on the east, west, and south sides of the Place of

Martyrs. There were thousands of them, and even as he watched, they flowed forward and fell into fighting formation.

"Lord Sean, I—" he began, then swallowed. "My God! The *hostages!* Bishop Corada! *Uncle Kerist!*"

"You mean you *didn't* know?" Despite his fury, Sean found himself tempted to believe Harkah's surprise—and fear for his uncle—were genuine.

"This is madness!" Harkah whipped back to Sean. "*Madness!* Even if it succeeds, it will do nothing to the *rest* of your army!"

"Maybe High Priest Vroxhan disagrees with you," Sean said grimly.

"It can't be His Holiness! He swore upon his very soul to protect you as his own people!"

"Well, *someone* wasn't listening to him." Sean's voice was harsh, and he nodded to one of Folmak's aides. The Malagoran rode up beside Harkah, and the Guard captain didn't even turn his head as his pistols and sword were taken. "For the moment, Captain Harkah, I'll assume you *didn't* know this was coming," Sean said flatly. "Don't do anything to make me change my mind."

Harkah only stared sickly at him, and Sean turned his branahlk and trotted into the center of his shallow square. He was too outnumbered to hold back a reserve; aside from individual squads to cover the smaller streets opening onto the Place of Martyrs in his rear, all three regiments of the First Brigade were in firing line, and the Guardsmen had paused. Even from here he could see their surprise at the speed with which the Malagorans had fallen into formation, and he swept his eyes over his own men.

"All right, boys! We're in the shit, and the only way out is through those bastards over there! Are you with me?"

"*Aye!*" The answer was a hard, angry bellow, and he grinned fiercely.

"Fix bayonets!" Metal clicked all about him as bayonets glittered in the morning light. "No one fires until

I give the word!" he shouted, and drew his sword. "Pipers, give 'em a tune!"

Vroxhan cursed in fury as the heretics snapped from an extended, vulnerable column into a compact, bayonet-bristling square in what seemed a single heartbeat. He'd seen the Guard at drill enough to recognize the lethal speed with which the demon-worshipers had reacted, and he snarled another curse at his own commanders for their hesitation. Why weren't they charging? Why weren't they *closing* with the heretics to finish them before they got set?

And then, clear in the stillness, he heard their accursed bagpipes wailing the song which had been banned since the Schismatic Wars, and swore more vilely yet as he recognized the wild, defiant music of "Malagor the Free."

"Here they come!" Sean shouted as the Guard pikes swept down. "Wait for the word!"

"*God wills it!*"

The deep, bass thunder of the Guard's battle cry roared its challenge, and the phalanx lunged forward in a column eighty men across and a hundred men deep. That formation wasn't even a hammer; it was an unstoppable battering ram, hurled straight at the heart of Sean's square in a forest of bitter pikeheads driven by the mass of eight thousand charging bodies. Something primitive and terrified gibbered deep within him with the sure and certain knowledge that it couldn't be stopped, that it *had* to break through, shatter the formation that spelled survival, and he felt the pound of his heart and the fountains' spray on his cheek as his eyes darted to where Sandy sat taut and silent on her own branahlk at his side. A terrible spasm of fear for the woman he loved twisted him, but he drove it down. He couldn't afford it, and his eyes hardened and moved back to the oncoming enemy.

"All right, boys!" He raised his voice but kept it calm, almost conversational. "Let 'em get a little closer. Wait for it. Wait for it! Wait—" His brain whirred like a computer as the range dropped to two hundred meters, and then he rose in his stirrups and his sword slashed down.

"By platoons—*fire!*"

The sudden, stupendous concussion rocked the Temple, and a pall of smoke choked the morning. First Brigade had sixteen hundred men, a total of eighty platoons, in a line four hundred meters long and two ranks deep, and the standard reload time for Sean's riflemen was seventeen seconds. But that was the *minimum* the drill sergeants demanded; an experienced man could do it in less under the right conditions of weather and motivation, and today, Folmak's brigade did it in twelve. The fire and smoke started at the line's extreme left and rolled down its face like the wrath of God, each platoon firing its own volley on the heels of its neighbor to the left; by the time the rolling explosion reached the line's right end, the left end had already reloaded and the lethal ballet began afresh.

One hundred and twenty shots crashed out each second—all aimed at a target only eighty men wide. Only superbly trained troops with iron discipline could have done it, but First Brigade was the *Old* Brigade. It had the training and discipline, and cringing ears heard nothing but the thunder, not even the wail of the pipes or the screams as whole ranks of Guardsmen went down in writhing tangles. Sheer weight of numbers kept the men behind them coming, but the shattering volleys were one smashing, unending drumroll. Waves of flame blasted out from the square like a hurricane, and the Guard had never experienced anything like it. The shock value of such massed, continuous, rifle fire was unspeakable, and the Guard's charge came apart in panic and dead men.

High-Captain Kerist's head whipped up. The whiplash crack of massed volleys was faint with distance, but he'd seen too many battlefields to mistake it. He jerked up out of his camp chair, wine goblet spilling from his fingers, and twisted around to stare in horror at the Temple's walls.

He was still staring when another sound, lower but much closer to hand, snapped his eyes back to his immediate surroundings, and he paled. The sound had been the cocking of gunlocks as an entire regiment of heretics appeared out of the very ground, and he looked straight into the muzzles of their bayoneted weapons.

The honor guard froze, and sweat beaded Kerist's brow. Horrified gasps went up from the priests and bishops, but the Guard officers among the hostages stood as frozen as Kerist, and unbearable tension hovered as a Malagoran officer stepped forward.

"Drop your weapons!" The honor guard hesitated, and the Malagoran snarled. "Drop them or die!" he barked.

The guards' commander turned to Kerist in raw appeal, and the high-captain swallowed.

"Obey," he rasped, and watched the Malagoran riflemen tautly as his men dropped their weapons.

"Move away from them," the Malagoran officer said harshly, and the Guardsmen backed up. "Any man who's still armed, step forward and drop your weapons. If we find them on you later, we'll kill you where you stand!"

Kerist squared his shoulders and moved forward. His sword was peace-bonded into its sheath, and he slipped the baldric over his head and bent to lay it with the discarded pikes and joharns, then turned to his officers.

"You heard the order!" His own voice was as harsh as the Malagoran's, and he breathed a silent prayer of thanks as the senior Guardsmen walked slowly forward to obey and no shots were fired. The Malagoran waited until every sword had been surrendered, then raised his voice once more.

"Now, all of you, back to the central pavilion!" The hostages and their disarmed guards obeyed, stumbling in fear and confusion. Only Kerist held his position, and the Malagoran officer's lip curled dangerously. He advanced on the high-captain with sword in one hand and pistol in the other. "Perhaps you didn't hear me." His voice was cold, and metal clicked as he cocked the pistol and aimed it squarely between Kerist's eyes.

"I heard, and I will obey," Kerist said as levelly as he could, "but I ask what you intend to do with us?"

A faint flicker of respect glimmered in the Malagoran's eyes. He lowered his pistol, but his face was hard and hating.

"For now, nothing," he grated. "But if Lord Sean and Lord Tamman are killed, you'll all answer with your lives for your treachery."

"Captain," Kerist said quietly over the distant musketry, "I swear to you that I know nothing of what's happening. Lord Marshal Surak himself assured me your envoys would be safe."

"Then he lied to you!" the Malagoran spat. "Now go with the others!"

Kerist held the other man's eyes a moment longer, then turned away. He marched back to the huddled, frightened hostages, his spine straight as a sword, and men scattered aside as he made his way directly to Bishop Corada. He could smell the terror about him, yet there was no terror, not even any fear, in Corada's eyes, and somehow that was the most terrifying thing of all.

"Your Grace?" The high-captain's voice was flat, its very lack of emphasis a demand for an explanation, and Corada smiled sadly at him.

"Forgive us, Kerist, but it was necessary."

"His Holiness *lied*?" Even now Kerist couldn't—wouldn't—believe God's own shepherd would perjure his very soul, but Corada only nodded.

"We are all in God's hands now, my son," he said softly.

The shattering roar of massed musketry faded into a terrible chorus of screams and moans as the last Guardsman reeled back, and Sean coughed on reeking smoke. He hadn't really thought they could do it, but the First had held. The closest Guardsmen were heaped less than twenty meters from his line, but none had been able to break through that withering curtain of fire. *Thank God*

I listened to Uncle Hector explain how the Brits broke Napoleon's columns! This was the first time he'd actually tried the tactic, and sheer surprise had done almost as much as the weight of fire itself to break the Guardsmen.

Which means the bastards won't be as easy to break next time, but—

"Lord Sean!" He turned in surprise as Captain Harkah approached him. The Guardsman was pale as he stared out at the carnage, but his mouth was firm.

"What?" Sean asked shortly, his mind already trying to grapple with what to do next.

"Lord Sean, this *has* to be some madman's work. Lord Marshal Surak personally assured my uncle you and Lord Tamman would be safe, and—"

"Time, Captain! I don't have *time* for this!"

"I—" Harkah closed his mouth with a click. "You're right, Lord Sean. But the last thing my uncle told me to do was guide you safely to the Chancery. Whatever's happening here, those are *my* orders—to see to your safety. And because they are, you have to know that the Guard maintains an artillery park only ten blocks in that direction." He pointed east, and Sean's eyebrows rose in surprise, for he was telling the truth. Brashan's orbital arrays had mapped the city well enough for Sean to know that.

"And?" he said impatiently.

"And if they bring up guns, not even your fire can save you," Harkah said urgently. "You can't make a stand here, My Lord—not for long. You *must* move on, quickly!"

Sean frowned. Improbable as it seemed, perhaps the young man was telling the truth about his own ignorance. And perhaps it wasn't so improbable after all. Harkah and, for that matter, *all* the hostages, could have been sacrificial lambs, sent to the slaughter themselves to lead *him* to it.

But whatever the truth of that, Harkah was right. He might be able to hold off pikes here—as long as his ammunition lasted—but it was a killing ground for artillery.

"Thank you for the warning," he said more courteously to the captain, then waved him back and brought up his com. "Harry?"

"*Sean!* You're alive!" his twin gasped.

"For now," he said flatly.

"How bad—?"

"We're intact and, so far, we haven't lost anyone, but we can't stay here. We have to move. Are you in touch with Brashan?"

"Yes!"

"What's our rear look like?"

"Not good, Sean." It was Brashan's voice, and the Narhani sounded grim. "It looks like they've got at least ten thousand pikemen filling in to cut you off from the gates. You'll never be able to cut your way through them."

Sean grunted, and his brain raced. Brashan was right. A street fight would cramp his formations, preventing him from bringing enough fire to bear to blast a path, and once it got down to an unbroken pike wall against bayoneted rifles his men would melt like snow in a furnace. But if he couldn't retreat and he couldn't stay here, either, then what—?

"What's Tibold doing, Harry?"

"We're going to storm the gates," Harriet said flatly, and Sean winced. the Temple's curtain wall was ten meters thick at the base, and the tunnel through it was closed by three consecutive portcullis-covered gates and pierced with murder holes for boiling oil. He shuddered, but at least he hadn't smelled any smoke when he came through. If Tibold moved fast, he *might* get through and take the gatehouses before the defenders got set.

Might.

He bit his lip, weighing his own fear and desire to live against the terrible casualties Tibold might suffer, then drew a deep breath.

"All right, Harry, listen to me. Tell Tibold he can go ahead, but he is not—I repeat, he is *not*—to throw away lives trying to get us out if he can't break in quickly!"

"But, Sean—"

"*Listen* to me!" he barked. "So far only one brigade's in trouble; don't let him break the entire army trying to save us. We're not worth it."

"You are! *You are!*" she protested frantically.

"No, we're not," he said more gently. He heard her weeping over the com and cleared his throat. "And another thing," he said softly. "*You* stay out of the fighting, whatever happens."

"I'm coming in after you!"

"No, you're not!" He closed his eyes. "Sandy and Tam are both in here with me. If we don't make it, you and Brashan are all that's left, and *you're* the only one who can talk to the army. Brash sure can't! If they get you, too, the bastards win!"

"Oh, Sean," she whispered, and her pain cut him like a knife.

"I know, Harry. I know." He smiled sadly. "Don't worry. I've got good people here; if anyone can make it, we can. But if we don't—" He drew a deep breath. "If we don't, I love you. Take Stomald home to Mom and Dad, Harry."

He cut the com link and turned back to Tamman, Sandy, and Folmak.

"Tibold's going to try to storm the gates." Folmak didn't ask how he knew that, and the other two simply nodded. "If he makes it in, he may be able to fight his way through to us, but in the meantime, we've got to fort up. There's a Guard artillery depot to the east. If they bring the guns up, we're in trouble, and it's as good a place as any to head for for now. Tam, you know the spot?" Tamman nodded. "Good. Folmak, give Lord Tamman your lead regiment. He'll seize the depot, and the rest of us will cover his back. Clear?"

"Clear, Lord Sean," the Malagoran said grimly.

"Then let's move out before they come at us again."

Chapter Thirty-Eight

"Get those guns up! Move! *Move*, damn you!"

Tibold Rarikson raged back and forth, eyes blazing, as the Angels' Army swarmed like an angry hive. It was insane to launch a major assault with no preplanning, yet he forced his fear aside and drove his men like one of the demons the Temple claimed they worshiped. He knew Lord Sean had beaten off the first attack, but he also knew his commander was trapped inside a city of two million enemies.

A stream of arlaks rumbled past him, nioharqs lowing, and he gripped his hands together behind him. The top of the Temple's wall mounted its own guns, but it was far narrower than its base, which limited recoil space. The Guard could put nothing heavier than arlaks up there, and he had room to deploy far more pieces than they could bring to bear. Unfortunately, *their* guns were protected by stone battlements, whereas his people lacked even the time to dig gun pits. Spurts of smoky thunder already crowned the wall, yet he had no choice but to send his own artillery forward. The North Gate had slammed shut in his face; without scaling ladders, his only hope was to batter it down, and he already knew how hideous his losses were going to be.

Regiments ran to join the assault column, but there was no time to insure proper organization. It was all going to be up to the battalion and company commanders, and Tibold breathed a prayer of thanks for the months of combat experience those men had gained.

"Tibold!"

He turned in surprise as the Angel Harry grabbed his

447

right arm. Before he could speak, she'd yanked it out and strapped something around it.

"My Lady?" He peered at the strange bracelet in confusion. It was made of some material he'd never seen before, with a small grill of some sort and two lights that blazed bright green even in full sunlight.

"This is called a 'com,' Tibold. Speak into this—" the angel tapped the grill "—and Sean and I will be able to hear you. Hold it close to your ear, and you'll be able to hear us, as well." Tibold gawked at her, then closed his mouth and nodded. "I'll try to tell you what's happening in the city as you advance," she went on urgently, her beautiful face strained, "but there're so many buildings the information I can give you may be limited. I'll do my best, and at least you can talk to Sean this way."

"Thank you, My Lady!" Tibold gazed into her single anxious eye for a moment, then surprised himself by throwing his arms around her. He hugged her tightly, and his voice was low. "We'll get them out, My Lady. I swear it."

"I know you will," she whispered, hugging him back, and his eyes widened as she kissed his whiskered cheek. "Now go, Tibold. And take care of yourself. We all need you."

He nodded again and turned to run for the head of the column.

His guns were unlimbering in a solid line, sixty arlaks hub-to-hub in a shallow curve before the gate. Defending guns lashed at them, but even at this short range and packed so tightly, an individual arlak was a small target for the best gunner. Their crews were another matter. He heard men scream as round shot tore them apart, but like his infantry, these men had learned their horrible trade well. Fresh gunners stepped forward to take the places of the dead as gun captains primed and cocked their locks, and Tibold raised the strange bracelet—the "com"—to his mouth.

"Lord Sean?"

"Tibold? Is that you?" Lord Sean sounded surprised,

and the Angel Harry's voice came over the link, speaking the angels' language.

"I gave him a security com, Sean. If the computer hasn't reacted to your implants or our com traffic—"

"Good girl!" Sean said quickly, and shifted to Pardalian. "What is it, Tibold?"

"We're ready to come after you. Where are you?"

"We've occupied a Guard ordnance depot near the Place of Martyrs." Despite his obvious tension, Lord Sean managed a chuckle. "Good thing the First has ex-Guard joharns. There must be a million rounds of smoothbore ammo in the place when the rifle bullets run out!"

"Hold on, Lord Sean! We'll get you out."

"We'll be here, Tibold. Be careful."

Tibold lowered the com and turned to his artillery commander.

"Fire!"

High Priest Vroxhan stormed into the conference room Lord Marshal Surak had converted into a command post, and his face was livid. Guns thudded in the background from the direction of North Gate, but the furious high priest ignored them as he bore down on Surak.

"Well, Lord Marshal?" he snapped. "What do you have to say for yourself? What went wrong?"

"Holiness," Surak held his temper only with difficulty, despite Vroxhan's rank, "I told you this would be difficult. Most of my men knew no more of what we intended than the heretics did—or High-Captain Kerist." His voice was sharp, and Vroxhan blinked as the lord marshal's eyes blazed angrily into his. "You insisted on 'surprise,' Holiness, and you got it—for everyone!"

The high priest began a hot reply, then strangled it stillborn. He could deal with Surak's insolence later; for now, he needed this man.

"Very well, I stand rebuked. But what happened to the attack in the Place of Martyrs?"

"Somehow the heretics realized what was coming. Something must have warned them only after they entered the city, or they simply wouldn't have come, but they guessed in time to form battle-lines before our pikes could hit them. As for what happened then, you saw as well as I, I'm sure, Holiness. No other army on Pardal could have produced that much fire; our men never expected anything like it, and they broke. I estimate," he added bitterly, "that close to half of them were killed or wounded first."

"And now?"

"Now we have them penned up in the Tanners Street ordnance depot." The lord marshal grimaced. "That, unfortunately, means they now have plenty of ammunition when their own runs out, but we control all the streets between them and the gates. Their musketry won't help them much in a street fight, and we can starve them out, if we must. Assuming we have time."

"Time?" Vroxhan repeated sharply, and Surak nodded grimly.

"The rest of their army's about to assault North Gate, Holiness, and at your orders, we didn't tell the men on the wall what we intended, either."

"You mean they may actually break into the Temple?!" Vroxhan gasped.

"I mean, Holiness, that our guns are manned and we're rushing in more infantry, but if they hit fast enough, they may get through the tunnel before we can ready the oil. If that happens, then, yes, they *can* break in."

"Dear God!" Vroxhan whispered, and it was the lord marshal's turn to smile. It was a grim smile, but it wasn't defeated.

"Holiness, I would never have chosen to fight them here, but it may actually work in our favor." Vroxhan looked at him in disbelief, and the lord marshal made an impatient gesture. "Holiness, I've told you again and again: it's their range and firepower that makes them so dangerous in the field. Well, there's no open terrain in the Temple. The streets will break up their firing lines, every building will become a strong point, and they'll have to come at us head-on, with bayonets against our pikes. This may be the best chance we'll ever have to crush their main field army, and if we do, we can capture their weapons and find out how they've improved their range and rates of fire."

Vroxhan blinked, and then his face smoothed as understanding struck.

"Exactly, Holiness. If we hold them here, smash this army, copy their weapons, and then concentrate our own strength from other areas, we can win this war after all."

"I—" Vroxhan began, then stiffened at the sudden, brazen bellow of far more artillery than North Gate's defenders could bring to bear.

A wall of smoke spewed upward as the arlaks recoiled, and splinters flew as their shot smashed into the city gates. Scores of holes appeared in the stout timbers, but they held, and the gunners sprang into the deadly ballet Lord Sean and Lord Tamman had taught them. Sponges hissed down bores, bagged charges and fresh shot followed, and the guns roared again.

The defending artillery fired in desperate counterbattery, but fewer guns could be crammed in along the walls, they couldn't match the Malagorans' rate of fire, and the wind carried the thick clouds of smoke up towards them in a solid, blinding bank. The Guard's guns could kill and maim Tibold's gunners, but they couldn't silence his pieces, and the gates sagged as hurricanes of eight-kilo shot smashed them. The outermost portcullis and gate went down in ruins, but the gunners went on firing, pouring a maelstrom of shot down the narrow gullet of the gate tunnel. Tibold could no more see what was happening to the second and third gates than the next man, but that massive barrage had to be ripping them apart in turn.

He paced back and forth, gnawing his lip and trying to gauge his moment. If he waited too long, the defenders would be ready to deluge his men with oil; if he committed his column too soon, it would find itself halted by intact gates, and aside from hastily impressed wagon tongues, it had no battering rams. The losses he was going to take from the wall's artillery as he charged would be terrible; if his men had to retreat under fire from a gate they couldn't breach, they would also be useless.

Another salvo rolled out from his gun line, and another. Another. He paced harder, hovering on the brink of committing himself and then dragging himself back. He had to wait. Wait as long as he dared to be sure—

He jerked in pain as the "com" on his wrist suddenly bit him. He snatched his hand up in front of him, staring at the bracelet, and the Angel Harry's taut voice came from it.

"The middle gate must be down, Tibold! We can see shot coming through the innermost ones, and they're hanging by a thread!"

See them? How could even an angel see—? He bit off the extraneous question and held the com to his lips.

"What else can you see, Lady Harry?" he demanded.

"They've got a line of infantry waiting for you." Harriet deliberately spoke in a flat, clear voice despite her fear for Sean while she relayed the reports from Brashan's hastily redeployed orbital arrays. "It looks like two or three thousand pikes, but only a few hundred musketeers. They've brought up a battery—we can't tell if they're chagors or arlaks—in support. That's all so far, but more guns and men will be there within twenty minutes. If you're going, you have to go now, Tibold!"

The head of Tibold's column was the Twelfth Brigade. Its men stood two hundred meters behind their own guns, and they were white-faced and taut, for they understood the carnage waiting in and beyond that narrow tunnel. There were none of the usual jokes and anxious banter men used to hide their fear from one another. This time they stood silent, each man isolated in his own small world of gnawing tension despite the men standing at his shoulders. The thunder of their own guns pulsed in their blood like the beating of someone else's heart, and already they had over a hundred dead and wounded from the arlaks on the Temple's wall. They were too far out for grapeshot, and the defenders had been concentrating on efforts to silence Tibold's artillery, but that was going to change the instant the infantry started forward.

Their heads jerked up as High-Captain Tibold appeared before them. He faced them with blazing eyes, and his leather-lunged bellow cut through even the thunder of the guns.

"*Malagorans!*" he shouted. "You know all Lord Sean and the angels have done for us; now he, Lord Tamman, and the Angel Sandy have been betrayed! Unless we cut our way to them, they, and all our comrades with them, will die! Men of the Twelfth, *will you let that happen?*"

"*NOOO!*" the Twelfth roared, and Tibold drew his sword.

"Then let's go get them out! Twelfth Brigade, at a walk, *advance!*"

Whistles shrilled, pipes began to wail, and the men of the Twelfth gripped their rifles in sweat-slick hands and moved forward.

The artillerists on the walls didn't notice them at first. Smoke clogged visibility, and the thunder of their own guns covered the whistles and the drone of the pipes. But the Malagoran arlaks had to check fire as the advancing infantry masked their fire, and the Guard knew then. Powder-grimed gunners relaid their pieces, grapeshot replaced round, and they waited for the smoke to lift and give them a target.

"*Double time!*" the Twelfth's officers screamed, and the column picked up speed. They had six hundred paces to go, and they moved forward at a hundred and thirty paces a minute as the wind parted the smoke.

The defenders watched them come, and musketeers dashed along the wall, spreading out between the guns. The Guard didn't have many of them left, but four hundred settled into firing position and checked their priming as the Twelfth's advance accelerated. Six hundred paces. Five hundred. Four.

"*Malagor and Lord Sean!*" the Twelfth's commander bellowed, and his men howled the high, terrible Malagoran yell and sprang into a full run.

A curtain of flame blasted out from the wall, twenty guns spewing grapeshot into a packed formation at a range of barely three hundred meters. Hundreds of men went down as quarter-kilo buckshot smashed through them, but other men hurdled their shattered bodies at a dead run, and their speed took them in under the artillery's maximum depression before the gunners could reload. Guard musketeers leaned out over the parapet, exposing themselves to fire straight down into them as they reached the base of the wall, and the artillery poured fresh fire into the men behind them, but six full regiments of riflemen laced the battlements with suppressive fire. Scores of Guard musketeers died, and artillerists began to fall, as well, as bullets swept their embrasures. Fresh smoke turned morning into Hell's own twilight, men screamed and cursed and died, and the Twelfth Brigade's bleeding battalions slammed into the shot-riddled outer gate.

Massive, broken timbers collapsed under the impact of hurtling bodies and plunged downward, crushing dozens of men and pinning others, but the Twelfth lunged onward. There was no blazing oil from the murder holes, but Guardsmen fired joharns and pistols through them into the reeking, smoke-filled horror of the tunnel. The second gate still stood precariously, too riddled to last but enough to slow the Twelfth's headlong pace for just a moment, and another ninety men were piled dead before it when it finally went down.

The Twelfth drove onward, carried by a blood-mad fury beyond sanity and driven by the weight of numbers behind them, and a storm of musket fire met them as they slammed through the third and final gate at last. Arlaks bellowed, blasting them with case shot at less than sixty meters, and men slipped and fell on blood-slick stone as the brigade broke out into the open. Men fired their rifles on the run, still charging forward, and slammed into the waiting pikes like a bleeding, dying hammer.

The impact staggered the Guardsmen. Their longer weapons gave them a tremendous advantage in this headlong clash, but the Malagorans rammed onward, and more and more of them swept out of the tunnel. They overwhelmed the front ranks of pikes, burying them under their own bodies, and the Guard gave back—first one step, then another—before the stunning ferocity of that charge. They weren't fighting men; they were fighting an elemental force. For every Malagoran they killed, two more surged forward, and every one of those charging maniacs fired at pointblank range before he closed with the bayonet. Behind them, other men with lengths of burning slow match lit fuses, and powder-filled, iron hand grenades arced through the smoky air to burst amid the Guard's ranks. Here and there, their front broke, and Malagorans funneled forward into the holes, bayonets stabbing, taking men in the flank even as the Guard's charging reserve cut them down in turn. There was no *end* to the flood of howling heretics, and Guardsmen began to look over their shoulders for the reinforcements they'd been promised.

More Malagorans charged through the gate tunnel, and still more. The space between the wall and the pikes was a solid mass of men, each fighting to get forward to kill at least one Guardsman before he died. The casualty count was overwhelmingly in the Guard's favor, but the Malagorans seemed willing to take *any* losses, and at last, slowly, the pikes began to crumble. Here a man went down screaming; there another began to edge back; to one side, another dropped his pike and turned to run; and the Malagorans drove forward with renewed ferocity as they sensed the shifting tide.

The Guard's officers did everything mortal men could do, but mortal men couldn't stop that frenzied charge, and what had begun slowly spread and accelerated. A stubborn withdrawal became first a retreat, then a rout, and the Malagorans swarmed over any man who tried to stand while others fought their way meter by bloody meter up the stairs on the wall's inner face. The last of the pikemen, abandoned by their fellows, turned to run, and the baying Malagoran army swept into the city.

Two hundred of the Twelfth Brigade were still on their feet to join it.

"We're through the gate, Lord Sean!" Tibold shouted into the com. "We're through the gate!"

"I know, Tibold." Sean closed his eyes, and tears streaked his face, for he was tied into Brashan's orbital arrays. The smoke and chaos made it impossible to sort out details from orbit, even for Imperial optics, but he didn't need details to know thousands of his men lay dead or wounded.

"Watch it, Tibold!" Harriet's voice cut into the circuit. "The men you routed just ran into their reinforcements. You've got ten or twenty thousand fresh troops coming at you, and the survivors from the gates are rallying behind them!"

"Let them come!" the ex-Guardsman exulted. "We hold the gate now. They can't keep us out, and I'll take them in a straight fight any day, Lady Harry!"

"Sean, you've got more men coming at you, too," Harriet warned.

"I see 'em, Harry."

"Hang on, Lord Sean!" Tibold said urgently.

"We will," Sean promised grimly, and opened his eyes. "Pass the word, Folmak. They're coming in from the east and west."

"What's happening, Lord Marshal?" Vroxhan demanded edgily as a panting messenger handed Surak a message. The lord marshal scanned it, then crumpled it in his fist.

"The heretics have carried the gates, Holiness."

"God will strengthen our men," Vroxhan promised.

"I hope you're right, Holiness," Surak said grimly.

"High-Captain Therah reports the heretics took at least two thousand casualties, and they're still driving forward, not even pausing to regroup. It would seem," he faced the high priest squarely, "their outrage at our treachery is even greater than I'd feared."

"We acted in the name of God, Lord Marshal!" Vroxhan snapped. "Do not dare presume to question God's will!"

"I didn't question *His* will," Surak said with dangerous emphasis. "I only observe that men enraged by betrayal can accomplish things other men cannot. Our losses will be heavy, Holiness."

"Then they'll be heavy!" Vroxhan glared at him, then slammed his fist on a map of the Temple with a snarl. "What of the heretic leaders?"

"A fresh attack is going in now, Holiness."

The ordnance depot's stone wall was for security, not serious defense. Two wide gateways pierced it to north and south, but Folmak's men had loopholed the wall, barricaded the gates with paving stones and artillery limbers, and wheeled captured arlaks into place to fire out them. It wasn't much of a fort, but it was infinitely preferable to trying to stand in the streets or squares of the city.

The surviving Guardsmen of the original ambush surrounded the depot, reinforced by several thousand more men and four batteries of arlaks. Now their guns moved up along side streets that couldn't be engaged from the gateways. The Guard's gunners had learned what happened to artillerists who unlimbered in range of rifles, and they dragged their batteries into the warehouses that flanked the depot. Hammers and axes smashed crude gunports in warehouse walls, and arlak muzzles thrust out through them.

Sean saw it coming, but there was nothing he could do to prevent it. Ammunition parties had hauled cases of Guard musket balls out of the depot and issued them to his men, who had orders to use the smoothbore ammunition for close range fighting and conserve their rifle ammunition, and he stood in a window of the depot commander's office and watched stone dust and wooden splinters fly from the warehouse walls as picked marksmen fired on the small targets the improvised gunports offered. Some of their shots were going home, and no doubt at least a few were actually hitting someone, but not enough to stop the enemy's preparations.

And then the arlaks began to bark.

Eight-kilo balls fired at less than sixty meters slammed into the depot wall, and it had never been meant to resist artillery. Lumps of rock flew, and he clenched his jaw.

"They're going to blow breaches, then put in the pikes," he told Folmak harshly. "Start a couple of companies building barricades behind the wall. Use whatever they can find, and see about parking some more arlaks among them. We'll let them blow their breach, then open up when they come through."

"At once, Lord Sean!" Folmak slapped his breastplate and vanished, and Sandy crossed to Sean.

"I wish to hell you hadn't come," he rasped. "Goddamn it, what did you think you were *doing?*"

"Saving your butt, among other things!" she shot back, but her words lacked their usual tartness, and she touched his elbow. "How bad is it, Sean?" she asked in a softer voice. "*Can* we hold?"

"No," he said flatly. "They'll just keep throwing men at us—or stand back and batter us with artillery. Sooner or later, the First is going down."

"Unless Tibold gets here first," she said through the thunder of the guns.

"Unless Tibold gets here first," he agreed grimly.

Chapter Thirty-Nine

Case shot screamed down the street as the Malagoran chagors recoiled, and High-Captain Therah winced as it scythed through his men. Teams of heretic infantry had hauled the light guns forward, and if their shot was only half as heavy as the Guard's arlaks threw, the smaller, lighter chagors were also far more maneuverable. Worse, the heretics could fire with impossible speed—faster than a Guard musketeer!—and the deadly guns had cost Therah's men dearly.

He still didn't know what had happened, but the heretics' conviction that any treachery had been the Temple's lent them a furious, driving power Therah had never faced in seven long Pardalian years as a soldier. Half of them were screaming "Lord Sean and no quarter!" as they charged, and *all* of them were fighting like the very demons they worshiped. By his most optimistic estimate, the Guard had already lost six or seven thousand men, and there was no end in sight. But the heretics were paying, too, for their fury drove them into headlong, battering attacks.

Which didn't mean they weren't winning. His men knew the city better than they, yet somehow they spotted every major flanking move. Smaller parties seemed able to evade their attention and hit their flanks out of alleys and side streets, yet such piecemeal attacks could only slow them, and the hordes of terrified civilians choking the streets shackled his own movements.

But he was learning, too, he thought grimly. His musketeers were no match for heretic riflemen in the open, so every precious musket was dug into the taller buildings

along the heretics' line of advance. Their slower-firing
smoothbores were just as deadly at close range, and their
firing positions at second- and third-story loopholes
shielded them from return fire. Therah was positive the
heretics' losses were far higher than his own, yet *still* they
drove forward, flowing down every side street, spreading out at every intersection. They bored ever deeper into
the Temple, like a holocaust, and as the conflict spread,
it grew harder and harder to control it or even grasp what
was going on.

The chagors fired another salvo, and then the heretic infantry charged with their terrible, baying war cry.
Their accursed pipes shrilled like damned souls, and their
bayonets cut through the staggered ranks of his surviving
pikemen. The heretics howled in triumph—and then
their howls were drowned by the roar of arlaks. The pikes
had held just long enough for the artillerists behind them
to complete their chest-high barricade of paving stones,
and the guns spewed flame through gaps in the crude
barrier. Grape shot splashed walls and pavement with
blood, and not even demon-worshipers could stand that
fire. They fell back, running for their own guns, and a
bitter duel sprang up between their chagors and the
Guard arlaks. Field pieces thundered at one another at
a range of no more than eighty paces, straight down the
broad avenue of the North Way, and Therah turned away
from the window to glare down at his map.

The heretic point was halfway to the Place of Martyrs,
but he could hold. He *knew* he could. Their casualties
were even greater than his, and, aside from the North
Way itself, he'd stopped their advance along most of the
main avenues within three or four thousand paces of
North Gate. Now his guns were dug in across the North
Way, and if he didn't expect them to hold for long, suc-
cessive positions were being built behind them. He could
bleed the heretics to death as they battered their way
through one strongpoint after another, but only if he had
more men!

It was the side streets. His strength was being eaten

up in scores of small blocking forces, racing to cut off each new penetration. Every man he committed to holding them there was one less to cover the main thoroughfares, but if he *didn't* block the side routes, the heretics filtered forward—taking their accursed chagors with them—and cut in behind his main positions. He needed more men, yet Lord Marshal Surak refused to release them. A full third of the available Guard was still hammering away at the heretics' leaders or covering routes they might use to join their fellows if they somehow broke out of the artillery depot. The men Therah did have were fighting like heroes, but something was going to break if he couldn't convince Surak to reinforce him.

"Signalman!" He didn't even look up as a signals officer materialized beside him. "Signal to Lord Marshal Surak: 'I must have more men. We hold the main approaches, but the demon-worshipers are breaking through the side streets. Losses are heavy. Unless reinforced, I cannot be responsible for the consequences.'" He paused, wondering if he'd been too direct, then shrugged. "Send it."

He looked back out the window just as a ball from a heretic chagor struck an arlak on the muzzle. The gun tube leapt into the air like a clumsy talmahk, then crashed back down to crush half a dozen men, and he swore. His gunners were killing the heretic artillerists, but despite their barricade, they were being ground away by the demon-worshipers' greater rate of fire.

"Message to Under-Captain Reskah! He's to move his battery up to Saint Halmath Street. Have him deploy to take the heretics in flank as they advance on the Street of Lamps position. Then get another messenger to Under-Captain Gartha. He's to bring his pikes—"

High-Captain Therah went on barking orders even as his staff began to gather up their maps in preparation to fall back yet again.

Sean crouched behind his own rock pile with Sandy as the latest assault fell back into the smoke. The depot wall had become little more than a tumbled heap of broken stone, but his men were dug in behind it, and dead and dying Guardsmen littered the approaches. The wooden warehouses to the east were a roaring mass of flames, but the ones on the west side were stone, and the Guard arlaks in them were still in action.

Folmak crawled up beside him, keeping low as musket balls whined and skipped from the crude breastwork. The ex-miller's breastplate was dented, and his left arm hung in a bloody sling, but he carried a smoking pistol in his right hand. He flopped down beside Sean and passed the weapon back to his orderly to reload before he tugged a replacement from his sash.

"We're down to about nine hundred effectives, My Lord." The Malagoran coughed on the smoke. "I make it three hundred dead and six hundred wounded, and the surgeons are out of dressings." He turned his head to watch Sandy rip open an iron-strapped crate of musket ammunition with one bio-enhanced hand and managed a grim smile. "At least we've still got plenty of ammunition."

"Glad something's going right," Sean grunted, and rose cautiously to fire at a Guardsman. The man threw up his arms and sprawled forward, and Sean dropped back beside Folmak as answering fire cracked and whined about his ears.

He rolled on his back to reload the pistol, and his thoughts were grim. The Guard was coming at them only from the west now, but it was still coming. As Lee had proven at Cold Harbor and Petersburg, dug in riflemen could hold against many times their own numbers, but each assault crashed a little closer to success, like waves devouring a beach, and his line was a little thinner as each fell back. Another two or three hours, he thought.

He drew the hammer to the half-cocked safety position and primed the pistol while he stared up into the smoke-sick afternoon sky. He could hear the thunder of battle from the north in the rare intervals when the firing here slowed, and he was still tied into Brashan's arrays. The satellites could see less and less as smoke and the spreading fires blinded their passive sensors, but he was still in touch with Tibold and Harriet, as well. The ex-Guardsman had battered his way halfway to the Place of Martyrs, but at horrible cost. No one could be certain, and he knew people tended to assume the worst while the dying was still happening, but even allowing for that, Harriet estimated Tibold had lost over a sixth of his men. The Angels' Army was being ground away, and there was nothing he could do about it. Even if the army had tried, it was in too deep to disengage, and he knew Tibold would refuse to so much as make the attempt as long as he, Tamman, or Sandy were still alive.

Which they wouldn't be for too very much longer, he thought bitterly.

"Sean! Movement to the north!"

He rolled onto his side and rose on an elbow, peering to his right as Tamman's warning came over the com, but not even enhanced eyes could see anything from here.

"What kind of movement?" he asked, and there was a moment of silence before Tamman replied slowly.

"Dunno, Sean. Looks like . . . By God, it *is!* They're moving back!"

"Moving *back*?" Sean looked at Sandy. Her smoke-grimed face was drawn, but she shrugged her own puzzlement. "Are they shifting west, Tam?"

"No way. They're pulling straight back. Just a sec." There was another pause as Tamman crawled through the rubble to a better vantage point. "Okay. I can see 'em better now. Sean, the bastards are forming a route column! They're moving straight towards the Place of Martyrs!"

Sean was about to reply when a junior officer flung himself on his belly behind the rock pile. The young man was breathing hard and filthy from head to toe, but he slapped his breastplate in a sort of abbreviated salute.

"Lord Sean! They're moving back on the south side."

"How far back?"

"Their musketeers are still in the buildings, but their pikemen are falling clear back behind them, My Lord."

Sean stared at him and forced his cringing brain to work. The Guard had to know it was grinding the First away, so why fall back now? It couldn't be simply to reorganize, not if Tamman was right about the column marching north for the Place of Martyrs. But if not that, then—

"They're reinforcing against Tibold," he said softly. Folmak looked at him for a moment, then nodded.

"They must be," he agreed, and Sean looked at the under-captain.

"How many pikes did they pull off the south side?"

"I'm not certain, My Lord—" the Malagoran began, and Sean shook his head.

"Best guess. How many?"

"At least five thousand."

"Tam? How many from your side?"

"I make it what's left of seven or eight thousand pikes. They've left musketeers to keep us busy, but I'd guess there's no more than a thousand pikemen to support them."

Sean frowned, then switched to Tibold's com frequency.

"Tibold, they're pulling men away from us. We're guessing it at ten to twelve thousand pikes."

"Away from you?" The ex-Guardsman was hoarse and rasping from hours of bellowing orders, but there was nothing wrong with his brain. "Then they're sending them here."

"Agreed. What will that do to you?"

"It won't be good, Lord Sean," Tibold said grimly. "My lead brigades are down to battalion strength by now. We're still moving forward, but it's by finger spans. If they bring that many fresh men into action—" He broke off, and Sean could almost see his shrug.

"How long for them to get to you?"

"Under these conditions? At least an hour."

"All right, Tibold. I'll get back to you."

"Sean?" He looked up as Sandy said his name, and her eyes bored into his.

"Give me a minute." He turned to Folmak and pointed to the gaunt, fortress-like main arsenal building which sheltered their wounded.

"How many men do you need to garrison the arsenal?"

"Just the arsenal?" Sean nodded, and the Malagoran rubbed his filthy face with his good hand. "Three hundred to cover all four walls and give me some snipers upstairs."

"Only three hundred?" Sean pressed, and Folmak smiled grimly.

"We've already prepared it for our last stand, Lord Sean, and we've got half a dozen of their arlaks on each wall at ground level. I've got a couple of hundred wounded who can still shoot, and a hundred more who can still load for men who aren't hurt, and we've got plenty of rifles no one needs any more. I can hold it with three hundred, My Lord. Not forever, but for a couple of hours, at least."

"Make it four hundred."

"Yes, My Lord." Folmak nodded but never looked away from his commander. "Why, My Lord?" he asked bluntly.

"Because I'm taking the rest of your people on a little trip, Folmak." Sean bared his teeth at the Malagoran's expression. "No, I'm not crazy. The Guard wants us, Folmak. They wouldn't ease up on us if they had any choice, so if they're pulling men from here to throw at Tibold, they've probably already pulled in everyone they can scrape up from anywhere else."

"And?" Folmak asked repressively.

"And everyone they've got left is almost certainly between us and Tibold. If I can break out to the south while they're all going north, I may just be able to pay a little visit to High Priest Vroxhan in person and, ah, *convince* him to call this whole thing off."

"You're mad, My Lord. High-Captain Tibold would

have my guts for tent ropes if I let you try something like that!"

"We'll all have to be alive for that to happen, and you and I *won't* be unless I can at least distract them from reinforcing against Tibold. Think about it, Folmak. If I break out in their rear, headed away from them, they're bound to turn at least some of their men around to nail me, and we can raise all kinds of hell before they catch up to us. While we're doing that, Tibold may actually manage to break through."

"You're mad," Folmak repeated. He locked stares with Sean, but it was the ex-miller whose eyes finally fell. "You *are* mad," he said sighing, "but you're also in command. I'll give you what's left of the Second Regiment."

"Thank you." Sean gripped the Malagoran's shoulder hard for a moment. "In that case, you'd better go start getting things organized."

"Which way will you go?"

"We'll start out to the east. The fires have them disorganized on that side."

"Very well. I'll see about getting some guns into position to lay down fire before you go. At least—" the First's commander summoned a smile "—there's no wall to block our fire any longer!"

He turned to crawl away, shouting for his surviving messengers, and a small, dirty hand gripped Sean's elbow.

"He's right, you're out of your damned mind!" Sandy hissed. "You'll never get past their perimeter, and even if you do, you don't even know where to *find* Vroxhan in all this!" She waved her other hand blindly at the smoke, and the gesture was taut with anger.

"No, I don't," Sean agreed quietly, "but I know where the *Sanctum* is."

"The—?" Sandy froze, staring into his eyes, and he nodded.

"If Tam and I get into the Sanctum—and we might just pull it off while everybody's fighting on the north side of town—we can take over the computer. And if we shut down the inner defense net, then Brash and Harry can get fighters in here and knock the guts out of the Guard."

"You'll never make it," she whispered, her face ashen under its grime, but her voice was already defeated by the knowledge that he had to try.

"Maybe not, but we can sure as hell *worry* the bastards!" he said with a savage grin.

"Then I'm coming with you," she said flatly.

"*No!* If we break out, most of them'll come after us. There won't be enough to take Folmak out, and I want you here where it's safe!"

"Fuck you, Sean MacIntyre!" she shouted in sudden fury. "Goddamn it to hell, do you think I want to be *safe* while you're out *there* somewhere?" She jabbed a hand at the billowing smoke, and he watched in amazement as tears cut clean, white tracks down her filthy face. "Well, the hell with you, *Your Highness!* I'm an officer, too, not a goddamned 'angel'! And I *am* coming with you! If something happens to you and Tam, maybe *I* can get to the computer!"

"I—" Sean started to snap back, then closed his eyes and bent his head to stare down at his clenched fists. She was right, he thought drearily. He wanted—*God*, how he wanted!—to make her stay behind, but that was because he loved her, and it didn't change the fact that she was right.

"All right," he whispered finally, and looked up, blinking on his own tears. He reached out to cup the side of her face and managed a wan smile. "All right, you insubordinate little bitch." She caught his wrist, pressing her cheek tightly into his palm for just a moment, then released him and rolled to her knees.

"You tell Harry and Tibold what we're up to. I'll go help Tam get things organized."

Chapter Forty

The firing eased as most of the attacking infantry marched away from the shattered ordnance depot. Three thousand men still surrounded it, but their orders now were to hold the heretics, not crush them. Their musketeers were conserving ammunition, and their artillery caissons were almost empty. Fresh ammunition wagons were on their way, but for now the Guardsmen concentrated on simply keeping the Malagorans pinned down.

Sean breathed a silent thanks for the lighter fire, but this was going to be tricky, and all of Folmak's regimental commanders and four of his six battalion COs were casualties. Losses among junior officers had been equally heavy, and getting the men sorted out took time. If the bad guys guessed what was coming and threw in an attack at just the wrong moment . . .

Folmak would retain what remained of his Third Regiment and half the First; the rest of the First would reinforce the Second for the breakout. The choice of units had been dictated by where the men were. The Third held what was left of the western wall, and they'd fall back to the main arsenal, covered by a hundred or so men already in the building, when Sean attacked to the east.

It was taking too long, he thought, but his people were moving as fast as humanly possible and then some. He crouched behind another pile of stone—this one had once been a workshop—and watched men filter into position around him. What had been regiments were now battalions, and battalions had become companies, but, one by one, officers raised their arms to indicate their readiness, and he drew a deep breath.

A dozen arlaks, double-shotted and loaded with grape for good measure, had been dragged into position under cover of the smoke. One man crouched behind each gun, watching Sean with intent eyes, and he slashed his arm downward.

A lethal blast screamed down the only eastbound street not blocked by flames as the gunners jerked their lanyards, then snatched up their own rifles. Shrieks of agony answered the unexpected salvo, and the torn, filthy survivors of B Company, Third Battalion, Second Regiment, First Brigade, lunged over the ruin of the depot wall with the high, shrill Malagoran yell.

The rest of the Second Regiment foamed in their wake, and Sean yanked Sandy to her feet and vaulted over the wall with the second wave. Tamman was ahead of them, leading B Company down the narrow street between two infernos which had once been warehouses, and rifles and muskets cracked in the hellish glare. The Malagorans charged through a cinder-raining furnace to strike the defenders before they recovered from the unexpected bombardment, and bayonets and pikes flashed in the bloody light of the flames.

Tamman crashed into the Guardsmen at B Company's head. A pike lunged at him, and he smashed it aside with a bio-enhanced arm and snatched the luckless pikemen bodily off his feet. The Guardsman wailed in terror, and Tamman hurled him away. More pikemen flew as the improvised projectile bowled them over, and Company B closed for the kill, firing as they came. A quarter of them went down, but the others carried through, and the blocking Guard infantry disintegrated before their bayonets.

"We're through, Sean!" Tamman yelled over the com. "Don't stop to celebrate! Keep moving!"

The Second Regiment broke out of the fire-fringed street into the open on the heels of their foes. A reserve of two or three hundred Guardsmen looked up in astonishment as the ragged apparitions materialized, then took to its own heels in panic as the bayonets swept down upon it. Sean's column burst through the perimeter around the depot and vanished into the burning city, and Folmak Folmakson, listening to the fading sound of combat to the east as the last of his own men dashed into the arsenal, whispered a prayer for its safety.

Harriet MacIntyre stood at the rear of the army's encampment, white-faced and clinging to Stomald's hand as she watched mountains of smoke rise from the Temple. Her com was tied to Sean's, following her twin and her friends through the bedlam of the city's streets, and she longed with all her heart to be with them. But she couldn't be. She had to wait here, praying that they reached their objective. One hundred and ten kilometers further north, Brashan had abandoned his post aboard *Israel* and rode the cockpit of an Imperial fighter, poised just outside the computer's kill zone with a second fighter slaved to his controls. If Sean and the others could shut down the computer, he and Harriet could end the fighting in minutes . . . *if* they could shut down the computer.

Tibold Rarikson swore vilely as fresh combat roared on his right. He didn't fully understand what Lord Sean and the angels intended, and he was aghast at the risk his commander was running, but he was a soldier. He'd accepted his orders, yet he bitterly regretted the loss of intelligence from the Angel Harry. Her reports had become increasingly general as the confusion and smoke spread, but they'd given him a priceless edge. Now she could no longer provide them, and the Guard had finally gotten around his flank.

His men gave ground stubbornly, fighting every span of the way, but the Guard pikes ground forward. He sent three relatively fresh regiments racing west from his reserve and hoped it would be enough.

"What—?"
High Priest Vroxhan whirled towards the window as

shots sounded right outside the Chancery, and his jaw dropped as bullets spun men around in the Place of Martyrs. A heretic attack *here*? It couldn't be!

But it was happening. Even as he watched, ragged, battle-stained men erupted into the open, fell into line, and poured a devastating, steadily mounting fire into the single understrength Guard company in the square. He stared at the carnage, unable to believe what he was seeing, then looked up as he sensed a presence at his side.

"Lord Marshal!" he gasped. "Have they broken through Therah?"

"Impossible!" Surak jerked a spyglass open and raised it to his eye, then swore and closed it with a snap. "They're from the depot, Holiness. No one else could have gotten here, and there's a man out there who's so tall he *has* to be 'Lord Sean.'"

"What are they doing out *here*?"

"Trying to escape . . . or to divert reinforcements from the North Gate. Either way, there's not enough of them to be a threat."

"*Can* they escape?"

"It's possible, Holiness. Not likely, but possible, especially if they go south instead of trying to link up with Tibold."

"Stop them! *Stop them!*" Vroxhan shouted.

"With what, Holiness? Aside from your personal guard, my headquarters troop, and the detachment at the Sanctum, every man I have is headed for North Gate."

Vroxhan started to speak once more, then closed his mouth and watched the heretics finish routing the hapless Guard company and reform into column. As Surak had predicted, they headed south, and the high priest clenched his fists in sullen hate. They were getting away. The leaders of this damnable heresy were *escaping* him, and as soon as they were safe, the rest of their army would break off its attack. Bile rose in his throat, and he raised his eyes from the vanishing demon-worshipers to the huge, white block of the Sanctum. *Why?* he demanded of God. *Why are You letting this* happen? *Why—*

And then his thoughts froze in a sudden flash of terrified intuition. Escape? They weren't trying to *escape*! As if God Himself had whispered it in his ear, Vroxhan knew where they were headed, and his blood ran chill.

"The Sanctum!" he gasped. The lord marshal looked at him blankly, and Vroxhan grabbed him and shook him. "They're headed for the Sanctum itself!"

"The— Why should they be, Holiness?"

"Because they're *demon-worshipers!*" Vroxhan half-screamed. "My God, man! They serve the powers of Hell—what if their masters have given them some means to destroy the *Voice*? If we lose its protection, how will we stop the *next* wave of demons from the stars?"

"But—"

"There's no *time*, Lord Marshal! Signal the Sanctum detachment now! Tell them they *must* keep the heretics from entering, then send every man you can find after them!"

"But there's only your own guard, Holiness, and—"

"Send them! *Send them!*" Vroxhan shook the lord marshal again. "No! I'll take them myself!" he cried wildly, and whirled away from Surak.

Tamman led the way. His men didn't like it, and they kept trying to get past him, to put themselves between him and any possible enemies, but he waved them sharply back whenever they did. He wasn't being heroic; he needed to be up front to scout their path with his implants.

The chaos in the streets was even worse than he'd feared. There were few Guardsmen about, but thousands of civilians had fled the fighting, and most of them seemed to be headed for the Sanctum to pray for deliverance. In fairness, they had the sense to scatter the instant they saw armed men coming up behind them, but even with panic to spur them on, they took time to get out of his way. Worse, with so many civilians moving around, it was hard to spot any Guard formations he might encounter.

The column moved quickly, when it could move at all, but its progress was a series of breathless dashes separated by slow, wading progress through the noncombatants, and Tamman was sorely tempted to order his men to open fire to chase the crowds off faster. He couldn't, but he was tempted.

He crossed a small square and looked up. The huge block of the Sanctum loomed ahead of him. Fifteen more minutes, he thought; possibly twenty.

"Faster! Faster!" Vroxhan shouted.

"Holiness, we can go no faster!" Captain Farnah, his personal guard's commander protested, waving at the civilians who clogged their path. "The people—"

"What do the *people* matter when demon-worshipers go to profane the very Sanctum of God?!" Vroxhan snapped, and his eyes were mad. He'd lost sight of the heretics while his guards mustered; they were up ahead somewhere, headed for the Sanctum. That was all he knew . . . and all he *needed* to know. "Clear the path, Captain! You have pikes; now *clear the path!*"

Farnah stared at him, as if unable to believe his orders, but Vroxhan snarled at him, and the Guardsman turned away. He shouted orders of his own, and within seconds Vroxhan heard the screams as the leading pikemen lowered their weapons, faces set like iron, and swept ahead. Men, women, even children were smashed aside or died, and the seven hundred men of Vroxhan's personal guard marched over their bodies.

The fighting on Tibold's right rose to a crescendo as the Guard threw his flank back eight hundred paces in a driving, brutal attack. But then the charging pikemen ran into pointblank, massed chagor fire, and the regiments Tibold had sent from the reserve crashed into them. It was the Guard's turn to reel back, yet they retreated only half the distance they'd come, then held sullenly, and now more Guard reinforcements were hammering his left.

He swore again, more vilely than ever. He was losing his momentum. He could feel the army's advance grinding to a halt amid the blazing ruins.

"Watch the wall! *Men on the wall!*" Tamman shouted as fifty musketeers suddenly rose over the parapet of the ornamental wall about the Sanctum. The square outside it was packed with civilians who screamed in terror as the Guardsmen leveled their muskets to pour fire into B Company's skirmish line, but Tamman's warning had come before they were in position. A withering blast of rifle fire met them, and, more horribly, the civilians between the two forces soaked up much of their own fire. Despite the cover of the waist-high parapet, they took heavier losses than the skirmishers, and then the rest of B Company came up with C Company in support, and their fire swept the wall clear.

Shrieking civilians stampeded madly, trampling one another in their terror, and Second Regiment drove across the blood-slick pavement for the gates. They were locked, but their delicate ivory panels and gold filigree were no match for the rifle butts of desperate men, and Second Regiment smashed its way through their priceless artistry like a ram.

Thirty or forty pikemen were trying to form up before the Sanctum's huge doors when the gates went down. They saw the "heretics" coming and fought to get set, but the Malagorans spread back out into a ragged firing line without orders. A sharp, deadly volley crashed out, and half the Guardsmen went down. The survivors fell back into the Sanctum itself, and Tamman started to lead his men after them, then skidded to a halt as Sean came up over his com.

"Trouble behind us, Tam! Five or six hundred men coming up fast!"

"I'm at the entry now," Tamman replied. "What do I do?"

"Secure the doors and put the rest of your men on the wall. We're going to have to detach a rearguard to keep these bastards off us."

"On it," Tamman agreed, and started shouting fresh orders.

"Holiness! The heretics!"

Vroxhan looked up at Farnah's shout, and then the first crackling musket fire rolled back from ahead. A bend in the street blocked his view, but he saw clouds of powder smoke and heard the screams of the wounded. Almost half his guard were musketeers, and they scattered into doorways and shop fronts, diving for cover to return fire while the pikemen jerked back around the corner to get out of range.

"Keep moving!" he snapped, but Farnah shook his head sharply.

"We can't, Holiness. They're inside the Sanctum's wall, and there must be three or four hundred of them with their damned rifles. We can't advance across the square against their fire. It's suicide."

"What do our lives matter compared to our *souls?*" Vroxhan raged.

"Holiness, if we advance, we die, and if we die, we can accomplish nothing to save the Sanctum," Farnah grated in a voice of iron.

"Damn you!" Vroxhan's hand slashed across the captain's face. "*Damn you!* Don't you *dare* tell me—"

He cocked his arm to swing again, but then he paused. He froze, oblivious to the naked fury on Farnah's reddened, swelling face, then grabbed the captain's arm.

"Wait! *Let* them hold the walls!"

"What do you mean?" Farnah half-snarled, but Vroxhan was already turning away.

"Bring half your men and follow me!"

Sean looked back as the rifles began to crack. He hated himself for leaving those men to hold that wall without him, yet he had no choice. They could hold it as well without him as with him, but only he, Sandy, or Tamman could access the computer.

They had only thirty men with them, the survivors of B and C Companies' original two hundred, as they clattered into the Sanctum. The original command bunker had been encircled, over the centuries, with chapels and secondary cathedrals, libraries and art galleries. It was a crazed rabbit warren of gorgeous tapestries and priceless artwork, and bloody boots thudded on rich carpet and floors of patterned marble as they pounded through it.

"Left, left, left," Sean muttered to himself as he felt the energy flows of the ancient command complex through his implants. "It has to be to the *left*, damn it, but where—"

"Got it, Sean!" Tamman shouted. "This way!"

Tamman swung sharply left down a stairway, and Sean caught Sandy's hand and half-dragged her after their friend, eyes gleaming as walls of marble and paneled wood gave way to bare ceramacrete. The command center was buried beneath the bunker, and boots and combat gear clattered in the deep well of the stairs. Here and there a man lost his footing and fell, but someone always dragged him back up, and the gasping urgency of their mission drove them on.

"Hatch!" Tamman yelled, and the men behind him suddenly slowed as they beheld the great, gleaming portal of Imperial battle steel. The Sanctum's guardians had ordered the computer to close the hatch, and for just an instant, religious dread held the Malagorans, but Tamman was oblivious to it as his implants sought the access software, and he grunted in triumph.

"No ID code," he muttered in English as Sean and Sandy pushed up beside him. "Guess the guys who set up this crazy religion figured the priesthood might forget it. Let me—ahh!"

His neural feed found the interface, and the Malagorans sighed as the huge hatch slid silently aside. They stared into the holiest of Pardalian holies, and their eyes were awed as they gazed at the man who'd opened the way.

"Come on!" Sean drew two pistols and shouldered past Tamman.

"*Blasphemer!*" someone screamed, and a sledgehammer punched into his breastplate as a musket roared, but the tough Imperial composites held. One of his pistols cracked viciously, and High Inquisitor Surmal's head exploded. His corpse tumbled back into the depths of the main display, blood pooling under the glitter of holographic stars, and Sean looked around quickly. None of the equipment was proper military design, and the Pardalians hadn't helped by covering the walls with Mother Church's trophies. Banners and weapons from the Schismatic Wars were everywhere, making it almost impossible to pick out details, and he snarled. Damn it, where the hell had they hidden—?

"There, Sean!" Sandy pointed, and Sean swallowed a curse as he saw the console. The bastards hadn't just switched the neural interfacing off; they'd physically disconnected it from the computer core.

"Tam, you're our best techie. Go! Get that thing back on-line!"

"Gotcha!" Tamman dashed across the command center, and Sean turned back to the men crowding through the hatch behind him. "In the meantime, let's get some security set up here. We need to—"

"*Sean!*" Sandy screamed, and he whirled just as a tapestry on the opposite wall was ripped aside and a musket flashed fire through the sudden opening. The ball whizzed past his head by no more than a centimeter, and he saw more men filling a five-meter-wide arch.

A tunnel! A goddamned tunnel *into the command center!*

Even as the thought flashed through his mind, he had time to wonder whether the original architect had installed it, or if it had been added by the Church's founders . . . and to realize it didn't really matter.

"Take 'em!" he bellowed. "Keep them off Tamman's back!"

His men answered with a snarl, and rifles barked like

the hammer of God. Choking smoke filled the command center's vaulted chamber as muskets blazed back, yet for the first few seconds it all went the Malagorans' way, despite the surprise of their enemies' sudden arrival. They were spread out, able to pour more rounds into the arch than the Guardsmen could fire back, but three hundred men crowded the tunnel, pressing forward with fanatic devotion, and there was no time to reload.

"Hit 'em! Bottle 'em up!" Sean roared, and charged as the first Guardsmen broke out into the open.

His Malagorans charged at his heels, but the Guardsmen were charging, too. They'd left their pikes behind, unable to get through the tunnel with them, but their pikemen carried swords, maces, and battle-axes, and their musketeers hurled themselves forward with clubbed weapons.

"Malagor and Lord Sean!" someone howled.

"Holy God and no quarter!" the Guard bellowed back, and the two forces slammed together in a smoke-choked nightmare of hand-to-hand combat.

Sean rampaged at the head of his men, and his slender sword carved an arc of death before him. No unenhanced human could enter its reach and live, and he hacked his way towards the arch. If he could reach it, bottle them up inside it . . . But his men weren't enhanced. They couldn't match his strength and speed, and too many Guardsmen had gotten into the control center. They swirled about him, and he grunted in anguish as something slammed into his thigh from behind. His enhanced muscle and bone held, but blood oozed down his leg, and unenhanced or not, if they swarmed him under—

He fell back, cursing, strangling an enemy with his left hand even as he cut down two more with his sword, and someone swung a mace two-handed. It clanged into his breastplate and rebounded, staggering him despite his enhancement, but once more the Imperial composite held. Steel clashed and grated all about him, men screamed and died, and a Guardsman loomed suddenly before him, sword thrusting for his throat, and there was no time to dodge.

He saw the point coming, and then a battle-ax split his killer from crown to navel. Blood fountained over him, and he gasped in surprise as Sandy bounded past him. The ax she'd snatched from the trophies on the wall was as tall as she was, and she shrieked like a Valkyrie as she swung. She'd lost her helmet, and her brown eyes flashed fire as she cut a second man cleanly in half, and another voice screamed in horror.

"Demon! *Demon!*" it wailed as they realized she was a woman.

Guardsmen who'd been howling, fanatical warriors the instant before shrank from her in terror, and she snarled.

"*Come on, then, you bastards!*" she yelled in Imperial Universal, and a fresh wail of terror went up as the Guardsmen recognized the Holy Tongue in the mouth of a demon. She cut down another man, and for just a moment, Sean thought she was going to pull it off. But the men still in the tunnel couldn't see her. Ignorance immunized them against the terror of her presence, and the weight of their bodies drove the others forward.

Fresh pressure pushed the Malagorans back, and Sean and Sandy with them. Their infantry formed a wedge behind them, fighting to cover Lord Sean's and the Angel Sandy's backs, and they lunged forward once more while bodies flew away from them. Under any other circumstances, the Guardsmen probably would have fled from their "superhuman" foes, but the tunnel behind them was packed solid. They had to fight or die, and so they fought, and the howling bedlam of combat filled the command center.

Behind his friends, Tamman worked frantically, hands flying as he fought to reconnect the neural interface. He'd never seen one quite like this, and he was working as much by guess as by knowledge. Despite his total concentration on his task, he knew the Guardsmen were grinding forward. Sean and Sandy were worth fifty unenhanced men when it came to offense, but there were only two of them. Some of the Guardsmen were slipping past them, circling around to get at the merely mortal Malagorans behind them, and despite the reach advantage of the Malagorans' bayoneted rifles, they were going down. So far none of the attackers seemed to have noticed Tamman, but it was only a matter of time before one of them—

There! He made the last connection, flipped his neural feed into the console, and demanded access. There was a moment of utter silence, and then an utterly emotionless contralto spoke.

"ID code required for implant access. Please enter code," it said, and he stared at the console in horror.

· Sean gasped as another mace crunched into his left arm. The mail sleeve held and his implants overrode the pain and shock, but the blow had hurt him badly and he knew it. He staggered back, and Sandy whirled around him, graceful as a dancer as she swung her huge ax with dreadful precision. Sean's attacker went down without a scream, and he lashed out with his sword and killed another man before he could hit Sandy from behind.

"Sean! Sean, it's ID-coded!" He heard the voice, but it made no sense, and he hacked down another enemy. "Goddamn it, Sean, *it's ID-coded!*" Tamman bellowed, and this time he understood.

He turned his head just as Tamman hurtled past him. His friend's sword went before him, and Sean and Sandy followed. They forged forward, killing as they went, and this time there were three of them. Tamman took point, with Sean and Sandy covering his flanks, leaving a carpet of bodies in their wake, and at last, the Guardsmen began to yield. The sight of three demons—and they *must* be demons to wreak such carnage—coming straight for them was too much. They scattered out of their way, and Tamman reached the archway. His sword wove a deadly pattern before him, building a barricade of bodies to block the arch with the dead, and even with the weight of numbers pressing them forward, no man could break past him.

"Watch his back, Sandy!" Sean gasped, and turned back to the combat still raging in the command center. Only ten of his men still stood, but they'd formed a tight, desperate defensive knot in the center of the huge chamber, and he flung himself into the rear of their attackers.

The Guardsmen saw him coming and screamed in fear. They backed away, unwilling to face the demon, and their eyes darted to the arch by which they'd entered. Two more demons blocked it, cutting them off from their companions, but the main hatch was open, and they took to their heels, trampling one another in their desperate haste to escape with their souls.

The sounds of combat died. The tunnel was so choked with bodies no one could get to Tamman to engage him, even assuming they'd had the courage to try, and Sean leaned on his sword gasping for breath while the cold, hideous knowledge of failure filled him.

They'd come so close! Fought so hard, paid such a horrible price. Why hadn't it even occurred to him that the interface would be ID-coded?!

"Tam!" he croaked. "If the interface's coded, what about voice access?"

"Tried it," Tamman said grimly, never looking away from the tunnel while the surviving Malagoran infantry hastily reloaded and turned to cover the main hatch. "No good. They took out the regular verbal access and set up a series of stored commands when they cut out the interface. We could spend weeks trying to guess what to tell it to control the inner defenses!"

"Oh, God," Sean whispered, his face ashen. "God, what have we *done*? All those people—did we kill them for *nothing*?"

"Stop it, Sean!" Sandy was splashed from head to toe in blood, and her eyes still smoked as she rounded on him. "We don't have time for that! Think! There *has* to be a way in!"

"Why?" Sean demanded bitterly. "Because *we* want there to be one? We fucked up, Sandy. *I* fucked up!"

"No! There has to be—"

She froze, mouth half-open, and her eyes went huge.

"That's it," she whispered. "By all that's holy, that's *it!*"

"*What's* 'it'?" Sean demanded, and she gripped his good arm in fingers of steel.

"*We* can't access without the ID-code, but *you* can—maybe!"

"What are you *talking* about?"

"Sean, it's an *Imperial* computer. A *Fourth Empire* computer."

"So?" He stared at her, trying to comprehend, and she shook him violently.

"Don't you understand? It was set up by an Imperial *governor*. A direct representative of the Emperor!"

Comprehension wavered just beyond his grasp, and his eyes bored into hers, begging her to explain.

"You're the heir to the throne, second only to the Emperor himself in civil matters, *and you've been confirmed by Mother!* That means she buried the ID codes to identify you to any Imperial computer in your implants!"

"But—" Sean stared at her, and his brain lurched back into motion. "We can't be sure they were ever loaded," he argued, already turning to run towards the console. "Even if they were, it's going to take me time to work through them. Ten, fifteen minutes, minimum."

"So? You got anything else to do right now?" she demanded with graveyard humor, and he managed to smile.

"Guess not, at that," he admitted, and stopped beside the console.

"They're reforming on the stairs, Lord Sean!" one of the Malagorans called, and he turned, but Sandy shoved him back towards the console.

"You take care of the computer," she told him grimly. "*We'll* take care of the Guard."

"Sandy, I—" he began helplessly, and she squeezed his arm.

"I know," she said softly, then turned and ran for the hatch. "You, you, and you," she told three of the Malagorans. "Go watch the arch. Tam, over here! We've got company!"

"*Here they come!*" someone shouted, and Crown Prince Sean Horus MacIntyre closed his eyes and inserted his neural feed into the console.

Chapter Forty-One

Ninhursag MacMahan rubbed weary eyes and tried to feel triumphant. A planet was an enormous place to hide something as small as Tsien's super bomb, but there was little traffic to Narhan, and most of it was simple personnel movement, virtually all of which went by mat-trans. Her people had started out by checking the logs for every mat-trans transit, incoming or outgoing, with a microscope and found nothing; now a detailed search from orbit had found the same. She couldn't be absolutely positive, but it certainly appeared the bomb had never been sent to the planet.

Which, unfortunately, made Birhat the most likely target, and Birhat would be far harder to search. There were more people and vastly more traffic, and swarms of botanists, biologists, zoologists, entomologists, and tourists had fanned out across its rejuvenated surface in the last twenty years. *Anyone* could have smuggled the damned thing in, and Maker alone knew where they might have stashed it if they had.

Of course, if it was in one of the wilderness areas, it shouldn't be *too* hard to spot. Even if it was covered by a stealth field, Imperial sensors should pick it up if they looked hard enough. But if Mister X had gotten it into Phoenix, it was a whole different ball game. The capital city's mass of power sources was guaranteed to confuse her sensors. Even a block-by-block or tower-by-tower scan wouldn't find it; her people would have to cover the city literally room by room, and that was going to take weeks or even months.

But at least they'd made progress. Assuming whoever

had the thing didn't intend to blow up Earth herself, they'd reduced the possible targets to one planet. And, she thought with a frown, it was time to point that out.

"No."

"But, Colin—"

"I said no, 'Hursag, and I meant it."

Ninhursag sat back and puffed her lips in frustration. She and Hector sat in the imperial family's personal quarters facing Colin and a Jiltanith whose figure had changed radically over the past few months. Tsien Tao-ling, Amanda, Adrienne Robbins, and Gerald Hatcher attended by hologram, and their expressions mirrored Ninhursag's.

" 'Hursag's right, Colin," Hatcher said. "If the bomb's not on Narhan, it's almost certainly here. It's the only thing that makes sense, given our estimate of Mister X's past actions."

"I agree." Colin nodded, yet his tone didn't yield a centimeter. "But I'm not going to have myself evacuated when millions of other people can't do the same thing."

"I'm only asking you to make a state visit to Earth!" Ninhursag snapped. "For Maker's sake, Colin, what are you trying to prove? Go to Earth and stay there till we find the damned thing!"

"*If* you find it," Colin shot back. "And I'm not going to do it."

"The people would understand, Colin," Tsien said quietly.

"I'm not thinking about public relations here!" Colin's voice was harsh. "I'm talking about abandoning millions of civilians to save my own skin, and I won't do it."

"Colin, you are being foolish," Dahak put in.

"So sue me!"

"If I believed it would change your mind, I would do just that," the computer replied. "As it will not, I can only appeal to the good sense which, upon rare occasion, you have exhibited in the past."

"Not this time," Colin said flatly, and Jiltanith squeezed his hand.

"Colin, there's something neither 'Hursag nor Dahak have pointed out," Amanda said. "If, in fact, Mister X killed the kids, and if he's the one who has the bomb, and *if* he's put it on Birhat, then you and 'Tanni are the reason. If you're not here, there's no point in his setting the thing off. By that standard, your moving to Earth might be the one thing that would keep him from detonating it before we find it."

"Amanda raises a most cogent point," Dahak agreed, and Colin frowned.

"Both Dahak and Amanda are correct," Tsien pressed as he sensed Colin weakening. "You are the Imperium's head of state, responsible for protecting the continuity of government and the succession, and if you and Jiltanith *are* 'Mister X's' targets, you may provoke him into action by remaining on Birhat."

"First," Colin said, "you're assuming he has some means of setting this thing off at will. To do that, he'd have to have someone here to transmit a firing order, which would just happen to kill whoever transmitted it. I'm willing to concede that he might have set up a patsy without telling the sucker what would happen, but Mister X himself certainly won't sit around on ground zero. That means he'd have to get the firing order to his patsy by hypercom, and 'Hursag and Dahak are monitoring all hypercom traffic. It's still possible he could sneak something past us, but, frankly, I doubt he'd risk it. I think the means of detonation are already in place with a specific timetable."

"I could take half of Battle Fleet through the holes in that logic," Adrienne said grimly.

"Maybe. I think it's valid, but you may have a point—which brings me to *my* second point. You're right about protecting the succession and the continuity of government, Tao-ling, but *I* don't have to go to Earth for that."

"Nay, my love!" Jiltanith's voice was sharp. "I like not thy words—nay, nor thy thought, either!"

"Maybe not, but Tao-ling's right, and so am I. One of us has to stay, 'Tanni. We can't just run out on our people. But if we send you to Earth, we protect both the government and the succession."

Jiltanith looked into his face for a moment, pressing a hand against her swollen abdomen, and her eyes were dark.

"Colin," she said very quietly, "already have I lost two babes. Wouldst make these yet unborn the pretext for my loss of thee, as well?"

"No," he said softly. His left hand captured hers, and he cupped her face in his right. "I don't intend to die, 'Tanni. But if there's any chance Mister X will hold his detonation schedule unless he can get both of us, then one of us has got to go. All right, I'm selfish enough to be glad of an excuse to get you out of the danger zone and protect you. I admit that. But you're pregnant, 'Tanni. Even if I *do* die, the succession is safe as long as you're alive. I'm sorry, babe, but it's your duty to go."

" 'Duty.' 'Protect.' " The words were a harsh, ugly curse in her lovely mouth. "Oh, how dearly have those words cost me o'er the centuries!"

"I know." He closed his eyes and drew her close, hugging her fiercely while their friends watched, and one hand stroked her raven's-wing hair. "I know," he whispered. "Neither of us asked for the job, but we've got it, love. Now we've got to do it. Please, 'Tanni. Don't fight me on this."

"Did it offer chance o' victory, then would I fight thee to the end," she said into his shoulder, and her voice was bleak. "Yet thou'rt what thou art, and I—I am *duty's* slave, and for duty's sake and the lives I bear within I will not fight thee. But know this, Colin MacIntyre. The day these babes draw breath do I leave them in Father's care and return hither, and not thou nor all the power of thy crown will stop me then."

"Jiltanith's coming early?" Lawrence Jefferson said. Horus nodded, and the Lieutenant Governor frowned. "Is something going on I should know about?"

"Going on?" Horus raised his eyebrows.

"Look, Horus, I know Jiltanith's planned all along for these children to be born on Earth, but she's not due for another month. Where she goes and what she does is her business, not mine, but I *am* Security Minister as well as Lieutenant Governor, and the Sword of God's still mighty active. Don't forget that bomb they planted right here in our own mat-trans facility! I wish she'd stay on Birhat where it's safe, but if she won't, I'm responsible for backing up her Marine security while she's here. So if there's any reason I should be thinking in terms of additional precautions, I'd like to know it."

"I think her security's more than adequate, Lawrence," Horus said after a moment. "I appreciate your concern, but this is just a daughter visiting her father. She'll be safe enough here inside White Tower."

"If you say so." Jefferson sighed. "Well, in that case, I should get busy. When, exactly, is she arriving?"

"Next Wednesday. You'll have almost a week to make any arrangements you think are necessary."

"That's good, anyway," Jefferson said dryly.

He left, and Horus sat gazing down at his blotter. Damn it, Lawrence was right. He *was* Security Minister, and he *should* be warned, but Ninhursag was adamant on maintaining strict need-to-know security on Mister X, and Colin backed her totally. Horus pursed his lips, then shook his head and made a mental note to buttonhole Colin for one more try to get Lawrence onto the cleared list when the Assembly of Nobles met week after next on Birhat.

Jefferson settled into his old-fashioned swivel chair and clenched his jaw. *Damn* the bitch! He'd gone to all this trouble to get her, Colin, Horus, Hatcher, and Tsien onto the same bull's-eye, and *she* had to decide to visit Daddy! Why couldn't she stay home on Birhat where she was safe from terrorists?

He swore again, then inhaled deeply and made himself relax. All right, it wasn't the end of the world. He couldn't change the timing on the detonation, but as he'd just told Horus, he *was* responsible for backing up her security detachment whenever she visited Earth. It shouldn't be too hard to arrange the right sort of backup. Sloppy, yes, and with the potential risk of pointing a finger at him after she was dead, but the operative point was that she—and the rest of them—would *be* dead by the time anyone started asking questions. He'd already set up an in-depth defense against such questions, and with Ninhursag killed along with the others, Security Minister Lawrence Jefferson would be the one responsible for answering them. Better still, he could probably make it look like a Sword of God operation, and with the Narhani branded with responsibility for the bomb and the Sword with responsibility for Jiltanith's assassination, he'd have all *sorts* of threats to justify whatever "temporary" special powers he chose to assume, now wouldn't he?

He smiled thinly and nodded. *All right, Your Majesty. You just come on home to Earth. I'll arrange a* special *homecoming for you.*

"Got those mat-trans logs you wanted, Ma'am."

Ninhursag looked up as Fleet Commander Steinberg entered her office. The newly promoted commander handed over the massive folio of datachips, but her face wore a thoughtful frown, and Ninhursag cocked an eyebrow at her.

"Something on your mind, Commander?"

"Well. . . ." Steinberg shrugged. "I'm sorry, Ma'am. I know I'm not cleared for everything, but this—" she gestured to the folio "—seems like a pretty peculiar, ah, line of inquiry for the head of ONI to handle personally. I know I'm not supposed to ask questions, but I'm afraid I haven't quite figured out how to turn my curiosity off on cue."

"A serious flaw in an intelligence officer." Ninhursag's voice was severe, but her eyes smiled, and she waved at a chair. "Sit, Commander."

Steinberg sank into the indicated chair and folded her hands in her lap. She looked like a uniformed high school student waiting for a pop quiz, but Ninhursag reminded herself this was the ice-cold interrogator who'd gotten them the break that proved the bomb's existence. Commander Steinberg had been a major asset ever since her transfer to Birhat, and Ninhursag had already added her to her mental list of possible successors to take over at ONI when she stepped down in another century or two. She had no intention of telling *Steinberg* that, but perhaps it was time to bring her up to speed on Mister X and see what her talents could do to push the bomb search here on Birhat.

"You're right, Esther," she said after a moment. "It *is* a peculiar thing to ask for, but I've got a rather peculiar reason for wanting it. And since you can't turn your curiosity off, I think you've just talked yourself into a new job." She flipped the folio back to Steinberg, and smiled at the commander's look of surprise. "You're now in charge of analyzing these for me, Commander, but before you start, let me tell you a little story. You've already played a not so minor part in it yourself, even if you didn't know it."

She tipped her chair back, and though her voice remained whimsical, her expression was anything but.

"Once upon a time," she began, "there was a person named Mister X. He wasn't a very nice person, and . . ."

"Good to see you, 'Tanni. Maker, you look wonderful!"

"Art a poor liar, Father." Jiltanith smiled and returned Horus' hug while Tinker Bell's pups lolled on the rug at their feet. "Say rather that I do most resemble a blimp, and thou wouldst speak but truth!"

"But I always liked blimps," her father said with a grin. "Zeppelins were nicer, though. Did I ever tell you I was aboard the *Hindenburg* for her first transatlantic crossing in 1936? Didn't appear on the manifest, because I was hiding from Anu at the time, but I was there. Won eight hundred dollars at poker during the crossing." He shook his head. "Now *there* was a civilized way to travel! I was always glad I wasn't at Lakehurst in '37."

"Nay, Father, thou didst not tell me, yet now I think upon it, 'twould be the sort of thing thou wouldst like."

"Yes." He sighed and his smile faded. "You know, despite all the terrible things I've seen in my life, I'll always be glad I've seen so *much*. Not many of us get the chance to watch an entire planet discover the universe."

"No," she said, and his eyes darkened and fell at the involuntary bitterness that cored the single, soft word.

" 'Tanni," he said quietly, "I'm sorry. I know—"

"Hush, Father." She pressed her fingers to his mouth. "Forgive me. 'Tis only being sent to 'safety' once more maketh my tongue so bitter." She smiled sadly. "Well do I know thou didst the best thou couldst. 'Twas not our fate to live the lives we longed to live."

"But—"

"Nay, Father. Say it not. Words change naught after so many years." She smiled again, and shook her head. "Now am I weary, and by thy mercy will I seek my bed."

"Of course, 'Tanni." He hugged her again and watched her leave the room, then walked to the window and stared sightlessly out over Shepherd Center. She would never truly forgive him, he thought. She couldn't, any more than he could blame her for it, but she was right. He'd done the best he could.

Tears burned, and he wiped them angrily. All those years. Those millennia while she'd slept in stasis. He and the rest of *Nergal's* crew had rotated themselves in and out of stasis, using it to spin their own lives out beyond mortal imagination in their war against Anu, yet he hadn't been able to let her do the same. He'd *kept* her in stasis, for he'd been unable not to, and his weakness was his deepest shame. Yet he'd lost too much, given too much, to change it. Her mother had never escaped from the original mutiny aboard *Dahak*, and he'd almost lost 'Tanni, as well, when her child's mind broke under the horrors of that blood-soaked day.

No, he told himself bitterly, he *had* lost that child that day. When one of his own Terra-born granddaughters managed to heal her, somehow, she'd been someone else, someone who'd survived only by walling herself off utterly from the broken person she once had been. A person who never again spoke Universal, but only the fifteenth-century English she'd learned. One who never, ever again called him "Poppa," but only "Father."

He'd been unable to risk that person again, unable to bring himself to lose her twice, and so, against her will, he'd sent her back into stasis and kept her there another five hundred years, until *Nergal*'s dwindling manpower forced him to release her from it. He'd turned her into a symbol, his defiant challenge to the universe which had taken all he loved. He . . . would . . . *not* . . . lose . . . her . . . again!

And so he hadn't. He'd kept her safe, and in doing so, he'd robbed her of so much. Of the foster mother who'd saved her mind, of her chance to fight by his side for all those centuries—of her right to live her own life on her own terms. He knew, knew to the depths of his soul, how unspeakably lucky he was that, somehow, she'd learned to love him once more when he finally did release her. It was a reward his selfish cowardice could never deserve, and, oh Maker of Grace and Mercy, he was so *proud* of her. Yet he could never undo what he'd done, and of all the bitter regrets of his endless life, that knowledge was the bitterest of all.

Planetary Duke Horus closed his eyes and inhaled sharply, then shook himself and walked slowly from his daughter's apartment in silence.

Chapter Forty-Two

"Got a second, Ma'am?"

Esther Steinberg stood in the door of Ninhursag's office once more, and Ninhursag's eyebrows rose in surprise. It was the middle of the night, and Steinberg had been off duty for hours. But then she frowned. The commander was in civvies, and from the looks of things she'd dressed in a hurry.

"Of course I do. What's on your mind?"

Steinberg stepped inside the door and waited for it to close behind her before she spoke.

"It's those mat-trans records, Ma'am."

"What about them? I thought you and Dahak cleared all of them."

"We did, Ma'am. We found a couple of small anomalies, but we tracked those down, and aside from that, everything was right on the money."

"So?"

"I guess it's just that curiosity bump again, Ma'am, but I haven't been able to get them out of my mind." Steinberg smiled crookedly. "I've been going back over them on my own time, and, well, I've found a new discrepancy."

"One Dahak missed?" Ninhursag couldn't keep from sounding skeptical.

"No, Ma'am. A *new* discrepancy."

"New?" Ninhursag jerked upright in her chair. "What d'you mean, 'new,' Esther?"

"You know we've been pulling regular updates on the mat-trans logs ever since you put me on the project?" Ninhursag nodded impatiently, and Steinberg shrugged.

"Well, I started playing with the data—more out of frustration at not finding any answers than anything else—and I had my personal computer run a check for anomalies *within* the database. Any sort of conflict between downloads from the mat-trans computers on a generational basis, as well as a pure content one."

"And?"

"I just finished the last one, Ma'am, and one of the log entries in my original download doesn't match the version in the most recent one."

"What?" Ninhursag frowned again. "What do you mean, 'doesn't match'?"

"I mean, Ma'am, that according to the mat-trans facility records, I have two different logs with precisely the same time and date stamp, both completely official by every test I can run, that say two different things. It's only a small variation, but it shouldn't be there."

"Corrupted data?" Ninhursag murmured, and Steinberg shook her head.

"No, Ma'am. *Different* data. That's why I came straight over." Her mouth tightened in a firm line. "I may be paranoid, Admiral, but the only reason I can think of for the difference is that between the time we pulled the first log and the time we got the latest update, someone changed the entry. And under the circumstances, I thought I should tell you. Fast."

"Esther's right," Ninhursag said grimly. She and the commander sat in Colin's Palace office. Steinberg looked acutely uncomfortable at being in such close proximity to her Emperor, but she met Colin's searching look squarely as he rubbed his bristly chin. "I double-checked her work, and so did Dahak. Someone definitely changed the entry, and that, Colin, took someone with a *hell* of a lot of juice."

"Are you telling me," Colin said very carefully, "that the goddamned bomb is sitting directly under the Palace right this instant?"

"I'm telling you *something* is sitting under the Palace."

Ninhursag's voice was flat. "And whatever it is, it isn't the statue that left Narhan. The mass readings matched perfectly in the first log entry, but they're off by over twenty percent in the second one. You have any idea why *else* that might be?"

"But, good God, 'Hursag, how could anyone make a switch? And if they pulled it off in the first place without our catching it, why change the logs so anyone who checked would *know* they had?"

"I don't know that yet, but I think we're going to have to reconsider our theory that Mister X and the Sword of God are two totally separate threats. I find it extremely hard to believe the Sword just *coincidentally* blew up the officer who oversaw the statue's transit here the very night he did it. If Esther hadn't caught the discrepancy in masses, we never would have connected the two events; now it hits me right in the eye."

"Agreed. Agreed." Colin leaned back with a worried frown. "Dahak?"

"My remotes are only now getting into position, Colin," Dahak's mellow voice replied from thin air. "It is most fortunate Commander Steinberg pursued this line of inquiry. It would never have occurred to me—I have what I believe humans call a blind spot in that I assume that data, once entered, will not subsequently metamorphose—and the Palace's security systems would almost certainly have prevented our orbital scans from detecting anything. Even now—"

He broke off so suddenly Colin blinked.

"Dahak?" There was no response, and his voice sharpened. "*Dahak?*"

"Colin, I have made a grave error," the computer said abruptly.

"An error?"

"I should not have inserted my remotes so promptly. I fear my scan systems have just activated the bomb."

"*The bomb?*" Even now Colin hadn't truly believed, not with his emotions, and his face went pale.

"Indeed." The computer's voice seldom showed

emotion, but it was bitter now. "I cannot be certain it is *the* bomb, for I had insufficient time for detailed scans before I was forced to shut down. But there is a device of some sort within the statue—one protected by a Fleet antitampering system."

The humans looked at one another in stunned silence, and then Ninhursag cleared her throat.

"What . . . what sort of system, Dahak?"

"A Mark Ninety, multi-threat remote weapon system sensor," the computer said flatly. "My scan activated it, but it would appear I was able to shut down before it reached second-stage initiation. It is now armed, however. Any attempt to approach with additional scan systems or with anything which its systems might construe as a threat, will, in all probability, result in the device's immediate detonation."

" 'Tanni! 'Tanni, wake up!"

Jiltanith sat up as quickly as her pregnant condition allowed, and the shaking hand released her. She rubbed her eyes and stared at her father, and the ghosts of sleep fled as his expression registered.

"Father? What passeth?"

"They think they've found the bomb," he said grimly. Her eyes flew wide, and his mouth twisted. "It's under the Palace, 'Tanni—hidden inside the Narhani's statue."

"Jesu!" Her eyes narrowed. There'd been a time when she'd personally managed *Nergal*'s Terra-born intelligence net against Anu, and she hadn't lost the habits of thought that had engendered. " 'Tis a ploy most shrewd," she murmured now. "Should it be discovered, as, indeed, 'twould seem it hath, then would all assume 'twas the Narhani concealed it there."

"That's what we think," Horus agreed, but his voice's harshness warned her he hadn't yet told her everything, and her eyes demanded the rest. "It's armed and active," he said sighing, "and it's covered by an antitampering system. We can't get to it to disarm it, or even to destroy it."

"*Colin!*" Jiltanith whispered, and clutched her father's arm.

"He's all right, 'Tanni!" Horus said quickly, covering her hand with his own. "He and Gerald and Adrienne are activating the evacuation plan now. He's fine."

"Nay!" Her fingers tightened like talons. "Father, thou knowest him too well for that, as I! He will not flee so long as any of his folk do stand exposed to such danger!"

"I'm sure—" Horus began, but she shook her head spastically and threw off the covers. She swung her feet to the floor and stood, already reaching for her clothing.

"I must go to him! Mayhap, were I there, I—"

"No, 'Tanni." Her head snapped around, and he shook his head.

"I tell thee I am going." Her voice was chipped ice, but he shook his head, and her tone turned colder still. "Gainsay me in this at thy peril, Father!"

"Not me, 'Tanni," he said softly. "Colin. He's ordered me to keep you here and keep you safe."

Her eyes locked with his, and her fear for her husband struck him like a lash. But he refused to look away, and a dark, terrible sorrow, like a premonition of yet more loss, twisted her face.

"Father, *please*," she whispered, and he closed his eyes, unable to face her pain, and shook his head once more.

"I'm sorry, 'Tanni. It was Colin's decision, and he's right."

"Dahak is correct," Vlad Chernikov said. "We dare not send any additional scanners into the gallery, but I have deployed passive systems from beyond a Mark Ninety's activation threshold and carried out a purely optical scan using the Palace security systems. While I can find no outward visual evidence, our passive systems have detected active emissions from a broad-spectrum sensor array which are entirely consistent with a Mark Ninety's. I fear that any remote—or, for that matter, any human with Imperial equipment—entering the gallery will cause it to detonate."

"God." Colin closed his eyes, propped his elbows on the conference table, and leaned his face into his palms.

"The evacuation will begin in twenty-five minutes," Adrienne Robbins' holo image said. "I'll coordinate embarkation from the Academy; Gerald will handle ship-to-ship movement from Mother, but we don't have enough ships in-system to handle the entire population."

"Some additional transport'll begin arriving in about ninety-three hours," Hatcher's image said. "Mother sent out an all-ships signal as soon as I got the word. We'll have another six planetoids within a hundred and fifty hours; anything after that'll take at least ten days to get here."

"How many can we get aboard the available ships?" Colin asked tautly.

"Not enough," Hatcher said grimly. "Dahak?"

"Assuming *Dahak* is used as well, and that we move as many as possible to existing deep-space life support in-system but beyond lethal radius of the weapon, we will be able to lift approximately eighty-nine percent of the Birhat population from the planet," the computer responded. "More than that will be beyond our resources."

"Mat-trans?" Colin said.

"On our list," Adrienne replied, "but the system's too big an energy hog to move people quickly, Colin. It's going to take at least three weeks to move eleven per-cent of Birhat's population through the facility."

"We don't *have* three weeks!"

"Colin, all we can do is all we can do." Gerald Hatcher didn't look any happier than Colin, but his voice was crisp.

"We've got to take that bomb out," Colin muttered. "Damn it, there *has* to be a way!"

"Unfortunately," Dahak said, "we cannot disarm it. That means we can only attempt to destroy it, which will require a weapon sufficient to guarantee its instant and complete disablement from outside the Mark Ninety's perimeter, and the device is located in the most heavily protected structure on Birhat. While we possess many weapons which could assure its destruction, the Palace's structural strength is such that any weapon of sufficient power would effectively destroy Phoenix, as well. In short, we cannot ourselves 'take out' the device without obliterating the Imperium's capital, and all in it."

"Horus! What the hell is going on?" Lawrence Jefferson had commed from Van Gelder Center, Planetary Security's central facility, not his White Tower office, and like many of the people swarming about behind him, he looked as if he'd dressed in the dark in a hurry. Horus wondered how he'd gotten to Van Gelder so quickly, but he wasn't about to look a gift horse in the mouth.

"Big trouble, Lawrence," he replied. "Get as many of your people as you can to the mat-trans facility. We're going to have thousands of people coming through from Birhat, starting in about—" he checked his chrono "— twelve minutes."

"*Thousands of people?*" Jefferson shook his head like a punch-drunk fighter, and Horus bared his teeth.

"Some lunatic's put a bomb under the Palace, and the damned thing's got an active antitampering system," he said, and watched Lawrence Jefferson go bone-white. The Lieutenant Governor said absolutely nothing for a moment, then shook himself.

"A bomb? What sort of bomb? It sounds like you're evacuating the entire planet!"

"We are," Horus said grimly. "This thing's probably powerful enough to take out all of Birhat—and Mother."

"With a single *bomb*? You're joking!"

"I wish I were. We've been looking for the damned thing for months. Well, now we've found it."

"What about the Emperor?" Jefferson demanded.

"He's hanging in until the last minute, the damned young fool! Says he won't leave until he can get everyone else out."

"And Jiltanith?" Jefferson asked quickly, and Horus smiled more naturally.

"Thanks for asking, but she's safe. She's still in White Tower, and she's staying here, by the Maker, if I have to chain her to the wall!"

Jefferson closed his eyes for a moment, mind racing, then nodded sharply.

"All right, Horus, I'm on it."

"Good man! I'll be down to give you a hand as quick as I can."

"Don't!" Horus raised an eyebrow at the Lieutenant Governor's quick, sharp reply, and Jefferson shook his head angrily. "Sorry. Didn't mean to bark at you. It's just that you can't do anything down here that *I* can't do just as well, and from your tone of voice, Her Majesty isn't too happy at staying here on Earth."

"That," Horus agreed, "is putting it mildly."

"Well, in that case you'd better stay there and keep an eye on her. God knows no one *else* on this planet has the seniority—or the balls!—to tell her no if she orders them out of her way. Besides, it's going to be a madhouse down here when refugees start coming through. I'll feel better with both of you tucked away someplace nice and safe, where whoever's behind this can't get at you in the confusion."

"I—" Horus started to reply, then stopped himself and nodded unwillingly. "You may be being paranoid, but you may also be right. I can't see why anyone would want me dead if they can't get 'Tanni and—please the Maker—Colin, but whoever's behind this has to be a lunatic."

"Exactly." Jefferson gave him a grim smile. "And if he's a lunatic, who knows what he may do if he thinks the wheels are coming off?"

Chapter Forty-Three

Lawrence Jefferson stared at the blank com screen. How? How had they *found* it? Had he come this far, worked this hard, to fail at the last minute?!

A fisted hand pounded his knee under cover of his borrowed desk, and a chill stabbed him as something else Horus had said struck home. If they'd been hunting the bomb "for months," they knew far more than he'd imagined. Ninhursag! It had to be Ninhursag, and that gave ONI's increased activities on Earth a suddenly sinister cast. Obviously they hadn't ID'ed him, but if they'd deduced the bomb's existence, what *else* had they picked up along the way?

He drew a deep breath and closed his eyes. All right. They knew the bomb was there and active, but if they'd known more, Horus would have said so. Which meant they *didn't* know it would detonate twelve hours after the Mark Ninety activated. Would they assume the fact that it hadn't *instantly* detonated meant it wouldn't unless they triggered it somehow?

He bit his lip. The bomb had originally been timed to detonate during the next meeting of the Assembly of Nobles, when Horus would be on Birhat with Colin, Jiltanith, and both the Imperium's senior military commanders. That would have gotten all five of them at once, but now they were spread out in two different star systems and they knew someone was after them, which meant the chance of recreating that opportunity was unlikely ever to come again. Yet Horus said Colin was going to "hang in" to the last possible minute, and Hatcher and Tsien must be up to their necks in the evacuation operation.

Even if they guessed time was short, their efforts to save Birhat's population were almost certain to keep the two officers within the danger zone until too late. But by the same token, both of them would be doing everything they could to convince Colin to leave, and if he gave in, he'd evacuate to *Dahak*. Any other ship would be unthinkable, and if Colin MacIntyre got away from Birhat aboard *Dahak*, very few things in the universe—and certainly nothing Lawrence Jefferson had—could get to him.

The Lieutenant Governor hesitated in an atypical agony of indecision. There was still a chance Colin would die with his senior military commanders. If that happened, and if Jefferson could insure Horus and Jiltanith died as well, his original plan would still work. But if Horus and Jiltanith died and Colin *didn't*, he'd move in with Battle Fleet and the Imperial Marines. He'd take Earth apart stone by stone, and the hell with due process, to find the man who'd destroyed Birhat and murdered his wife, unborn children, and father-in-law, and when he did—

Jefferson shuddered, and the panicked part of his brain gibbered to give it up. They didn't know who he was yet. If he folded his hand and faded away, they might *never* know. In time, if they continued to trust him, he might actually have the chance to try again. But he couldn't count on eluding their net, not when he didn't know how much they'd already learned, and the gambler in his soul shouted to go banco. It was all on the table, everything he had, all he'd hoped and dreamed and worked for. Success or failure, absolute power or death: all of it hinged on whether or not Colin MacIntyre agreed to leave Birhat within the next twelve hours, and Jefferson wanted to scream. He was a chess master who calculated with painstaking precision. How was he supposed to calculate *this*? All he could do was guess, and if he guessed wrong, he died.

He pounded his knee one more time, and then his shoulders relaxed. If he stopped now and they found him out, the crimes he'd already committed would demand his execution, and that meant it was really no choice at all, didn't it?

"—so Adrienne's parasites are embarking their first loads now, and my Marines have taken over at the mat-trans," Hector MacMahan reported. "So far, there seems to be more shock than panic, but I don't expect that to last."

"Do you have enough men to control a panic if it starts?" Hatcher asked. "I can reinforce with Fleet personnel if you need them."

"I'll take you up on that," MacMahan said gratefully.

"Done. And now," Hatcher's holo-image turned to Colin, "will you *please* get aboard a ship and move out beyond the threat zone?"

"No."

"For Maker's sake, Colin!" Ninhursag exploded. "Do you *want* this thing to kill you?"

"No, but if it hasn't gone off yet, maybe it won't unless we *set* it off."

"And maybe the goddamned thing is ticking down right now!" MacMahan snapped. "Colin, if you don't get out of here willingly, then I'll have a battalion of Marines *drag* your ass off this planet!"

"No, you won't!"

"I'm responsible for your safety, and—"

"And I am your goddamned Emperor! I never wanted the fucking job, but I've got it, and I will by God *do* it!"

"Good. Fine! Shoot me at dawn—if we're both still alive!" MacMahan snarled. "Now get your butt in gear, *Sir*, because I'm sending in the troops!"

"Call him off, Gerald," Colin said in a quiet, deadly voice, but Hatcher's holo-image shook its head.

"I can't do that. He's right."

"Call him off, or I'll have Mother do it for you!"

"You can try," Hatcher said grimly, "but only the hardware listens to her. Or are you saying that if Hector drags you aboard a ship with a million civilian evacuees you'll have Mother order its comp cent not to leave orbit?"

Colin's furious eyes locked with those of Hatcher's image, but the admiral refused to look away. A moment of terrible tension hovered in the conference room, and then Colin's shoulders slumped.

"All right," he grated, and his voice was thick with hatred. Hatred that was all the worse because he knew his friends were right. "All right, goddamn it! But I'll go aboard *Dahak*, not another ship."

"Good!" MacMahan snapped, then sighed and looked away. "Colin, I'm sorry. *God*, I'm sorry. But I can't let you stay. I just *can't*."

"I know, Hector." It was Colin's turn to turn away, and his voice was heavy and old, no longer hot. "I know," he repeated quietly.

Brigadier Alex Jourdain sealed his Security tunic and looked around his comfortable apartment. He'd lived well for the last ten years; now the orders he'd just received were likely to take it all away, and more, yet he was in far too deep to back out, and if they pulled it off after all—

He drew a deep breath, checked his grav gun, and headed for the transit shaft.

" 'Tanni, I—" Horus cut himself off as Jiltanith, still in her nightgown, turned from the window and he saw her tears. His face twisted, and he closed his mouth and started to leave, but she held out a hand.

"Nay, Father," she said softly. He turned back to her, then reached out to take her hand, and she smiled and pulled him closer. "Poor Father," she whispered. "How many ways the world hath wounded thee. Forgive my anger."

"There's nothing to forgive," he whispered back, and pressed his cheek to her shining hair. "Oh, 'Tanni! If I could undo my life, make it all different—"

"Then would we be gods, Father, and none of us the people life hath made us. In all I have ever known of thee, thou hast done the best that man might do. 'Twas ever thy fate to fight upon thy knees, yet never didst thou yield. Not to Anu, nor to the Achuultani, nor to Hell itself. How many, thinkest thou, might say as much?"

"But I built my Hell myself," he said quietly. "Brick by brick, and I dragged you into it with me." He closed his eyes and held her tight. "Do . . . do you remember the last thing you ever said to me in Universal, 'Tanni?"

She stiffened in his arms, but she didn't pull away, and after a moment, she shook her head.

"Father, I recall so little of those days." She pressed her face harder into his shoulder. " 'Tis like some dark, horrible dream, one that e'en now haunteth my sleep on unquiet nights, yet when waking—"

"Hush. Hush," he whispered, and pressed his lips into her hair. "I don't want to hurt you. Maker knows I've done too much of that. But I want you to understand, 'Tanni." He drew a deep breath. "The last thing you ever said was 'Why didn't you *come*, Poppa? Why didn't you love us?' " Her shoulders shook under his hands, and his own voice was unsteady. " 'Tanni, I *always* loved you, and your mother, but you were right to hate me." She tried to protest, but he shook his head. "No, listen to me, please. Let me say it." She drew a deep, shuddering breath and nodded, and he closed his eyes.

" 'Tanni, *I* talked your mother into supporting Anu. I didn't realize what a monster he was—then—but I was the one who convinced her. Everything that happened to you—to her—was my fault. It was, and I know it, and I've always known it, and, O Maker, I would sell my very soul never to have done it. But I could never undo it, never find the magic to make it as if it had never happened. A father is supposed to protect his children, to keep them safe, and that—" his voice broke, but he made himself go on "—that was why I put you back into stasis. Because I knew I'd failed. Because I'd proven I couldn't keep you safe any other way. Because . . . I was afraid."

"Father, Father! Dost'a think I knew that not?" She shook her head.

"But I never told you," he said softly. "I cost us both

so much, and I never had the courage to *tell* you I knew what I'd done and ask you to forgive me."

Colin paced the conference room like a caged animal, fists pounding together before him while he awaited his own cutter, and his brain raced. The evacuation Adrienne and Hatcher had planned but never been able to rehearse was going more smoothly than he would have believed possible, but all of them knew they weren't going to get everyone out. Unless they could deactivate the bomb, millions of people would die, yet how in God's name did you deactivate something you couldn't approach with as much as a scanpack, much less the weapons to—

He stopped suddenly, then slammed himself down in his chair and opened his neural feed to Dahak wide.

"Give me everything on the Mark Ninety," he said sharply.

The door chime sounded, and Horus turned from Jiltanith to answer it.

"Yes?"

"Your Grace, it's Captain Chin," an urgent voice said. "Sir, I think you'd better come out here. I just tried to com the mat-trans center, and the links are all down."

"That's impossible," Horus said reasonably. "Did you call Maintenance?"

"I tried to, Your Grace. No luck. And then I tried my fold-com." The captain drew a deep breath. "Your Grace, it didn't work either."

"*What?*" Horus opened the door and stared at the Marine.

"It didn't work, Sir, and I've never seen anything like it. There's no obvious jamming, the coms just don't work, and it'd take a full-scale warp suppressor within four or five hundred meters to lock a Fleet com out of hyperspace." The captain faced Horus squarely. "Your Grace, with all due respect, we'd better get Her Majesty the hell out of here. Right now."

✧   ✧   ✧

"You know, it might just work," Vlad Chernikov murmured.

"Or set the thing the hell off!" Hector MacMahan objected.

"A possibility," Dahak agreed, "yet the likelihood is small, assuming the force of the explosion were sufficient. What Colin suggests is, admittedly, a brute force solution, yet it has a certain conceptual elegance."

"Let me get this straight," MacMahan said. "We can't get near the thing, but you people want to pile explosives on top of it and set them off? *Are you out of your frigging minds?*"

"The operative point, General," Dahak said, "is that a Mark Ninety is programmed to recognize *Imperial* threats."

"So?"

"So we don't use Imperial technology," Colin said. "We use old-fashioned, pre-Imperial, Terran-made HE. A Mark Ninety would no more recognize those as a threat than it would a flint hand-ax."

"HE from where?" MacMahan demanded. "There isn't any on Birhat. For that matter, I doubt there's any on Terra after this long!"

"You are incorrect, General," Dahak said calmly. "Marshal Tsien has the materials we require."

"I do?" Tsien sounded surprised.

"You do, Sir. If you will check your records, you will discover that your ordnance disposal section has seventy-one pre-Siege, megaton-range nuclear warheads confiscated by Imperial authorities in Syria four years ago."

"I—" Tsien paused, and then his holo-image nodded. "As usual, you are correct, Dahak. I had forgotten." He looked at MacMahan. "Lawrence's Security personnel stumbled across them, Hector. We believe they were cached by the previous regime before you disarmed it on Colin's orders before the Siege. Apparently, even the individuals who hid them away had forgotten about them, and they were badly decayed—they used a tritium booster, and it had broken down. They were sent here for disposal, but we never got around to it."

"You want to use *nukes?*" MacMahan yelped.

"No," Dahak said calmly, "but these are *Terran* warheads, which rely on shaped chemical charges to initiate criticality, and each of them contains several kilograms of the compound Octol."

"And how do you get the explosives into position?" MacMahan asked more normally.

"Somebody walks in, sets them, fuses them, and walks back out again," Colin said. MacMahan raised an eyebrow, and Colin shrugged. "It should work, as long as he doesn't have any active Imperial hardware on him."

"Background radioactivity?" Hatcher asked. "If this stuff's been squirreled away inside a nuclear warhead for twenty-odd years, it's bound to have picked up some contamination."

"Not sufficient to cross a Mark Ninety's threshold," Dahak replied.

"You're certain?" Hatcher pressed, then waved a hand. "Forget that. You never make unqualified statements if you *aren't* certain, do you?"

"Such habits imply a certain imprecision of thought," Dahak observed, and despite the tension, Colin smiled, then sobered.

"I think we have to try it. It's a risk, but it's the smallest one I can come up with, and you may be right about a timer, Hector. We don't have time to come up with an ideal, no-risk solution."

"Agreed. How long to strip out the explosives and get them down here, Dahak?"

"I have already initiated the process, General. I estimate that they could be delivered to the Palace within twenty minutes in their present state, but I would prefer to reshape them into a proper configuration for maximum destructive effect, which will require an additional hour."

"Eighty minutes?" MacMahan rubbed his chin, then nodded. "All right, Colin, I'll vote for it."

"Gerald? Tao-ling?" Both officers nodded, and Colin glanced at Chernikov.

"I, too," the Russian said. "In fact, I would prefer to place the charge myself."

"I don't know, Vlad—" Colin began, but MacMahan interrupted crisply.

"If you were thinking about doing it yourself, you can just rethink. Whatever happens down here, you, personally, are going to be aboard *Dahak* and outside the lethal zone when we set it off. And if *you* know anybody better equipped for the job than Vlad, *I* don't." Colin opened his mouth, but MacMahan fixed him with a challenging eye and he closed it again.

"Good," MacMahan said.

"Suppressor's active, Brigadier," the Security tech said, never looking up from his remote panel. "Their coms are blocked."

"Elevators and switchboard?" Brigadier Jourdain asked, and another man looked up.

"Shut down. They've pulled almost all the regular Security people for crowd control, and I've cut the links to the lobby station. We're placing the charges to blow the switchboard when we leave now; it'll look just like a Sword of God hit, Sir."

"All right." Jourdain faced his handpicked traitors. "Remember, these are Imperial Marines. There's only twelve of them, but they're tough, well trained, and if they've tried their coms since the suppressor went online, they're going to be ready. Our coms are out, too, so stick to the plan. Don't improvise unless you have to."

His men nodded grimly.

"All right. Let's do it."

Horus stood outside Jiltanith's bedroom while she jerked on clothes, and his mind raced. It was preposterous. He was in his own HQ building in the middle of Earth's capital city, and he couldn't even place a com call! There could be only one reason for that, but how had

"Mister X" pulled it off? Captain Chin was right. The only thing that could shut down fold coms without active jamming was close proximity to a warp suppressor, but a suppressor powerful enough to do the job was far too large to have been smuggled through White Tower's security . . . which meant someone on his own security staff must have brought it in, and if he'd been penetrated that completely—

He crossed to his desk and touched a button, and the desktop swung smoothly up. The habits of millennia of warfare die hard, and despite his fear, he smiled wolfishly as he lifted the energy gun from its nest. He punched the self-test button, and the ready light glowed just as the bedroom door opened . . . and Captain Chin half-ran into his office.

"Your Grace," the Chinese officer said flatly, "the elevators are out, too."

"Shit!" Horus closed his eyes, then shook himself. "Stairs?"

"We can try them, Sir, but if they've cut the coms and elevators, they're already on their way. And without the elevators—"

"Without the elevators, they're coming up the stairs," Horus grunted. Wonderful. Just fucking wonderful! Head down the stairs and they risked running into the bastards head-on. For a moment, he was tempted anyway, but Imperial weapons were too destructive. If they got caught in a stairwell, a single shot might take out all their men— and 'Tanni. But if they didn't try to break out, they left the initiative to the other side. On the other hand—

Jiltanith stepped out of the bedroom, convoyed by four stocky, black-and-tan rottweilers. Her dagger glittered on her belt, and Horus' mouth tightened as she reached out and took Captain Chin's grav gun from its holster. The Marine didn't protest; he simply shifted his energy gun to his left hand and passed over his ammunition belt with his right, and she gave him a strained smile. The belt wouldn't fit around her pregnancy-swollen waist, so she hung it over her shoulder like a bandolier.

"All right, Captain," Horus said. "We have to let them come to us. The stairs merge into the central core one floor down; have ten of your people set up to cover the landings. Leave the other two here to cover the access to my office. 'Tanni, lock your bedroom door, then go to *my* room and lock yourself in. Hopefully, if anyone gets this far, they'll head for your room first."

"Father, I—" she began, and he shook his head savagely.

"I know, 'Tanni, but you're going to have to leave this to us. We can't risk you, and even if we could—" He waved at her swollen belly, the gesture both tender and oddly apologetic, and she nodded unhappily.

"Art right," she sighed, and looked down at the bioenhanced dogs.

"Go thou wi' Captain Chin," she told them, "and watch thyselves."

"We go, pack lady," Galahad's vocoder said, "but keep Gwynevere with you." She nodded, and Horus looked at Chin as the other three dogs leapt away.

"We're out of communication, and we're going to be spread out. Watch your rears as well as your fronts."

"Yes, Your Grace!" Chin saluted and vanished after the dogs, and Horus turned to the two Marines who'd been left behind.

"Anyone who gets this far will have to come up the last stair. After that, they'll go for 'Tanni's bedroom first. Pick yourselves positions to cover the stairs. If you have to fall back, head *this* way; *don't* head for my room. We want them to keep on thinking she's in her room as long as we can."

"Yes, Sir." The senior Marine jerked his head at his companion, and they ran towards the tower's central access core.

"Go, 'Tanni!" Horus said urgently.

"I go, Father," she said softly, yet she paused just long enough to throw one arm about him and kiss him before she wheeled away. He watched her go, Gwynevere trotting ahead of her like a scout, and turned to survey his office one more time. He'd accomplished a lot from this place. Commanded the Siege of Earth, directed the reconstruction in its wake, coordinated the introduction of an entire planet to Imperial technology. . . . He'd never expected to fight for his daughter's life from it, but if he had to do that too, then, by the Maker, he would.

He walked slowly to the office foyer. It was the only way into his personal quarters, and he upended his receptionist's desk and piled furniture about it. He built a sturdy barricade facing the entry, then stepped away from it to the wall beside the entry and settled his back into a corner.

"The explosives have arrived at the Palace, Colin," Dahak said as Colin entered the command deck of the computer's starship body.

"Good." Officers popped to their feet as their Emperor and Warlord strode across to the captain's couch, but he waved them back to their duties. *Dahak* had moved beyond the weapon's threat radius, and Colin felt a sick surge of guilt as he realized that, whatever happened, he personally was safe. It seemed a betrayal of all his subjects, and knowing Hector and Gerald were right to insist upon it only made his guilt worse.

He settled into the command couch. The display was centered on Birhat, not *Dahak*, and he watched sublight craft streaming from the planetary surface to the waiting planetoids. Like *Dahak*, all those starships were beyond threat range, and thousands more of his subjects were embarking aboard them as he watched, but it was taking time. Too much time they might not have. He drew a deep, deep breath and pressed himself back in his couch.

"Tell them to proceed, Dahak."

Brigadier Jourdain followed his men up the stairs. There were only twelve Marines, one tired old man, and a pregnant woman to stop them, while he had over a hundred men, all fully enhanced courtesy of Earth

Security. It would be more than enough, he told himself yet again. Some were going to get killed, but not enough to stop them, and dead Security men would be convincing proof of how hard Brigadier Jourdain and his men had fought to protect their Empress.

He bared mirthless teeth at the thought as his point man approached the landing. They were one floor below Duke Horus' office and living quarters, and they hadn't seen a soul. Perhaps he'd worried too much. Surely if the Marines *had* figured anything out—

Something rattled. The lead Security man saw the small object skitter past his feet, and his eyes flared. No! His implant scanners hadn't picked up a thing, so how—

Eleven men died in a blast of fury, and the Marine who'd thrown the grenade grinned savagely as he and his partner reactivated their own implants and brought their energy guns to bear on the smoke-streaming door.

Captain Chin's head jerked up as the explosion rattled. *Please, God, let someone* else *have heard it!* he prayed, then settled back down in firing position.

Brigadier Jourdain's ears cringed as thunder filled the stairwell. The screams of the merely wounded were faint and tiny in the explosion's wake, and he swore viciously. So much for surprise!

"Clancey! Get up there!" he barked, and Corporal Clancey settled his automatic grenade launcher into firing position. He jerked his head at the other three members of his section, and the four of them pushed forward through the men above them on the stair.

The waiting Marines had their own implant sensors on-line now, but there was a limit to what the devices could tell them. They knew the stairs were full of men, but they couldn't tell what weapons they carried or precisely what they were doing. The second Marine held a grenade, ready to throw it, but the same suppressor that blocked their coms from hyper-space would smother any hyper grenade's small field, and they'd had only one HE grenade each. He couldn't afford to waste it, and so he gritted his teeth and waited.

Clancey and his team reached the landing and eased forward, boots skidding in what had once been their point men, backs pressed to the walls. They, too, had their sensors on-line, and they didn't like what they were telling them. There were two Marines up there, and only one of them was where their grenades could get at him; the other was further back, sheltering in a cross-connecting corridor to cover his companion, and Clancey swore. God, what he wouldn't give for hyper grenades! But at least the bastards didn't seem to have any more grenades of their own.

He nodded to the two men against the opposite wall. "Go!"

They spun into the doorway, launchers coughing on full auto. The closer Marine's fire ripped both of them apart, but their grenades were already on the way, and a staccato blast rattled teeth as they detonated in sequence, killing him instantly.

Clancey cursed as an energy gun splattered his companions over him, but his implants told him the Marine who'd fired was dead. He went down in a crouch, hosing more grenades to keep the surviving Marine's head down while more Security men charged the door. Explosions shattered walls and furnishings, and the building's fire suppression systems howled to life as flames glared. More men charged up the stairs, white faces locked in death's-head grins, and then Corporal Clancey discovered he'd been wrong about what the Marines had.

The grenade landed 1.3 meters behind him, and he had one instant to feel the terror before it exploded and killed six more men . . . including Corporal William Clancey, Earth Security.

Vlad Chernikov felt blind and maimed. For the first time in twenty-five years, every implant in his body had been shut down lest the Mark Ninety decide they were weapons, and the sudden reversion to the senses Nature had provided was a greater psychic shock than he'd anticipated.

He grimaced the thought aside and hoisted the charge Dahak had designed. The initiator charges of the obsolete warheads had been formed in hundreds of precisely shaped blocks, and Dahak had reassembled a hundred and fifty kilos of them into a single massive shaped-charge. That might be more than they needed, but Dahak believed in redundancy.

He slung the charge on his back—at least his muscular enhancement still worked, since it used no power and hence offered no emissions signature to offend the Mark Ninety's sensibilities—and started down the hall to the gallery on the longest sixty-meter hike of his life.

The scream of alarms filled the stairwell as thermal sensors responded to the fires the explosions had set. Their shrill, atonal wail set Jourdain's teeth on edge, but White Tower's soundproofing was excellent, and his men at the switchboard had cut all lines to its top fifteen floors. None of which meant people wouldn't notice if grenades started blowing out windows.

"Push 'em back!" he shouted, and started up the stairs. His point had stalled amid the carnage of shattered bodies, and he snarled at them. "Come on, you bastards! There's only *twelve* of them!"

He flung himself through the doorway, landing flat on his belly in Clancey's blood. More of his men crouched behind him or threw themselves prone, and at least a dozen energy guns snarled. Walls already torn and pocked by grenade fragments ripped apart under focused beams of gravitic disruption, and the Marine fired back desperately. Another of his men went down, then two more, a fourth, but there was only one Marine left. It was only a matter of time—and not much of it—until one of those energy guns found him.

There were five separate stairs. Captain Chin had placed two Marines to cover each, but Jourdain had

elected to assault only three, and combat roared as his
other assault teams ran into their own defenders. The
Marines had the advantage of position; their attackers
had both numbers and heavier weapons. It was an
unequal equation, and it could have only one solution.

Jourdain's number three assault team lost ten men in
the first exchange, but its commander was a hard-bitten
man, an ex-Marine himself, who knew what he was
about. Once he'd pinpointed the defenders, he sent six
men down one floor. They positioned themselves directly
beneath the Marines, switched their energy guns to maximum power, aimed at the ceiling, and simply held the
triggers back. The Marines never had time to realize what
was happening, and assault team three charged forward
over their mutilated bodies.

Captain Chin heard feet behind him and rolled up on
one knee just as the leading "Security men" appeared
in the hall. His energy gun howled, and three of them
vanished in a gory spray. He flung himself back down,
flat on his belly against the wall, and his single grenade
killed three more attackers.

"Wire the doors and get your ass up here, Matthews!"
he shouted to his teammate. Private Matthews didn't
waste time answering. She yanked the pin from her own
grenade and wedged it against the stairwell door so that
any effort to open it would release the safety handle.
Then she grabbed her energy gun and headed for the
captain's position.

She arrived just in time to help beat off the next
assault, and then Chin swore as the attackers fell back.

"They're not coming up our stair at all," he spat.
"They're going to leave someone to pin us down and get
on with it."

"Only if we let 'em, Cap," Matthews grunted, and
before Chin could stop her, the private lunged to her
feet. She charged down the hall, energy gun on continuous fire, and Chin leapt to his feet and followed. Matthews killed six more men before answering fire blew her

apart, and Chin vaulted her body. The captain landed less than a meter from the remaining three men holding the blocking position, and four energy guns snarled as one.

There were no survivors on either side.

Staff Sergeant Duncan Sellers, Earth Security, swore monotonously as he ran down the hall. He'd gotten separated from the rest of his team, and the entire floor had filled with smoke despite the fire suppression systems. His enhanced lungs handled the smoke easily, but he dreaded what could happen if he blundered into his friends and they mistook him for a Marine.

He turned a corner and gasped in relief as he picked up the implants of his fellows ahead. He opened his mouth to shout his own name, then whirled as some sixth sense warned him. A shape bounded towards him, but his instant spurt of panic eased as he realized it was only one of the Empress' dogs. Big as it was, no dog was a threat to an enhanced human, and he raised his energy gun almost negligently.

Gaheris was four meters away when he left the floor in a prodigious spring. Sergeant Sellers got off one shot—then screamed in terror as bio-enhanced jaws ripped his throat out like tissue.

Alex Jourdain advanced in a crouch, weapon ready, and disbelief filled him. There were only *twelve* of them, damn it!

Perhaps so, but by the time his three assault teams merged at the foot of the single stair leading to the next floor, he'd lost over seventy men. Over *seventy*! Worse, he'd added up the Marine body count from all three teams and come up with only eight. Two more were pinned down at the west stairwell, but the last pair of Marines was still unaccounted for—and ten of his own men were equally pinned down in the stairwell firefight. That left him with only nineteen under his own command, and he didn't like the math. Eight Marines had killed seventy-six of their attackers. That worked out to

almost ten each, and if Horus and the two remaining
Marines did as well . . .

He shook his head. It was the stupid and incautious
who died first, he told himself. The men he had left were
survivors, or they wouldn't have gotten this far. They
could still do it—and they'd damned well *better*, because
none of them could go home and pretend this hadn't
happened!

"Hose it!" he barked to his remaining grenadiers, and
a hurricane of grenades lashed up the stairs and blew
the doors at their head to bits.

"Go!" Jourdain shouted, and his men went forward in
a rush.

Corporal Anna Zhirnovski cringed as another grenade
exploded. The bastards had gotten Steve O'Hennesy with
the last salvo, but Zhirnovski was bellied down behind
a right-angled bend in the corridor. They couldn't get a
direct shot at her, but they were trying to bounce the
damned things around the corner, and they were getting
closer. It was only a matter of time, and she rechecked
her sensors. At least seven of them left, she thought, and
despair stabbed through her. They wouldn't waste this
much time—or this many men—on killing one Marine
unless they had enough other firepower to kill the
Empress without their input, but there wasn't a damned
thing she could do about it. She and Steve had been cut
off from the central core, and even launching a kami-
kaze attack into them would achieve nothing but her own
death.

Her muscles quivered with the need to do just that,
for she was a Marine, handpicked to protect her
Empress' life, but she fought the urge down once more.
She was going to die. She'd accepted that. And if she
couldn't kill the men attacking her (and she couldn't),
she could at least keep them occupied. And, she told herself grimly, she could make them pay cash when they
came after her to finish off the witnesses.

Another string of grenades exploded, and she detected

movement behind them. They were trying a rush under cover of the explosions, and she waited tensely. Now!

The grenadiers stopped firing to let their flankers go in, and Anna Zhirnovski rolled out into the corridor, under the smoke. Men shrieked as her snarling energy gun ripped their feet and legs apart, and Zhirnovski snap-rolled back into her protected position.

Two more, she thought, and then the grenades began to explode once more.

Oscar Sanders unwrapped another stick of gum, shoved it into his mouth, and chewed rhythmically without ever taking his eyes from the HD. Every news service was covering the chaos at the mat-trans facility across the Concourse from Sanders' position in the White Tower lobby, and he shook his head. Virtually every member of White Tower's usual security force was over there trying to sort out the confusion, and they were fighting a losing battle. Sanders had never seen so many people in one place in his life, and the threat that could produce it was enough to make anyone nervous. Evacuating an entire planet because of *one* bomb? What the hell sort of bomb could—

He looked up at a sudden slamming sound. It came again, then again, and he frowned and glanced at his console. Every light glowed a steady green, but the slamming sound echoed yet again, and he stood.

He walked around the end of the counter and followed the sound up the corridor. It was coming from the stairwell door, and he drew his grav gun and reached for the latch. He gripped it firmly and yanked the door open, then relaxed. It was only a dog, one of Empress Jiltanith's.

But Oscar Sanders' relief vanished suddenly, and his gun snapped back up as he realized the dog was covered with blood. He almost squeezed the trigger, but his brain caught up with his instincts first. The dog was not only covered with blood; one of its forelegs was a mangled stub, and the door was slick with blood where the injured animal had tried repeatedly to spring the crash bar latch with its remaining leg.

It took only a fraction of a second for Sanders' stunned brain to put all that together—and then, with a sudden burst of horror, to remember *whose* dog this was. He jerked back, a thousand questions flaring through his mind, and that was when the strangest thing of all happened.

"Help!" Gaheris' vocoder said just before he collapsed. "Men come to kill Jiltanith! *Help her!*"

Vlad Chernikov turned the last corner, and the magnificent statue stood before him. Even now he felt a stir of awe for its beauty, but he hadn't come to admire it, and he advanced cautiously.

The shaped charge on his back seemed to take on weight with every stride. It was silly, of course. He was already well inside a Mark Ninety's interdiction perimeter; if the thing was going to decide the charge was a weapon, it would already have blown up the planet.

That, unfortunately, made him feel no less naked and vulnerable, and he missed his implants' ability to manipulate his adrenaline level as he stepped around the inert scanner remote still lying where it had fallen when Dahak hastily deactivated it.

He moved to within two meters of the sculpture and studied it carefully. The problem was that his weapon was insufficient to reduce the entire statue to gravel, so he had to be certain that whatever bit he chose to blow up contained the bomb. And since neither he nor Dahak could scan the thing, he could only try to estimate where the bomb was.

It would help, he thought irritably, if they knew its dimensions. It was tempting to assume they'd used Tsien's blueprints without alteration, but if that assumption proved inaccurate, the consequences would be extreme.

Well, there were certain constraints Mister X's bombmakers couldn't avoid. The primary emitter, for example, *had* to be at least two meters long and twenty centimeters in diameter, and the focusing coils would each add another thirty centimeters to the emitter's length. That gave him a minimum length of two hundred sixty centimeters, which meant the bomb couldn't be inside the human half of the statue. It would have had to be in his torso, and while the Marine was more than life-sized, he wasn't *that* much larger, so the bomb itself had to be inside the Narhani. Unfortunately, the Narhani was big enough that the thing could be oriented at any of several angles, and he couldn't afford to miss. Of course, the power source for the bomb was a fair-sized target all on its own, and the designers had had to squeeze in the Mark 90, too. They'd undoubtedly put at least part of the hardware inside the Marine, but *which* part?

They'd counted on the bomb's never being detected, Vlad thought, so they *probably* hadn't considered the need to design it to sustain damage and still function, which might mean the power source was inside the Marine and the rest of the hardware was inside the Narhani. That was a seductively attractive supposition, but again, he couldn't afford to guess wrong.

He stepped even closer to the statue, considering the angle of the Narhani's body as it reared against its chains. All right, the bomb *wasn't* inside the human and it *was* the next best thing to three meters long. It couldn't be placed vertically in the Narhani's torso, either, because there wasn't enough length. It could be partly inside the torso and angled down into the body's barrel, though. The arch of the Narhani's spine would make that placement tricky, but it was feasible.

He rocked back on his heels and wiped sweat from his forehead as the unhappy conclusion forced itself upon him. The possible bomb dimensions simply left too many possibilities. To be certain, he had to split the statue cleanly in two, and to be sure the break came within the critical length, he'd have to come up from below.

He sighed, wishing he dared activate his com implant to consult with Dahak, then shrugged. He couldn't, and even if he could have, he already knew what Dahak would say.

He wiped his forehead one more time, took the bomb from his back, and bent cautiously to edge it under the marble Narhani's belly.

The last exchange of fire faded into silence, and Brigadier Jourdain's mouth was a bitter, angry line. Ten more of his men lay dead around the head of the ruined stairs. Two more were down, one so badly mangled only his implants kept him alive, and they wouldn't do that much longer, but at least they'd accounted for the last two Marines.

He glared at the closed door to the foyer of Horus' office and cranked his implant sensors to maximum power. Damn it, he *knew* the Governor was in there somewhere, but the cunning old bastard must have shut his implants down, like the Marines covering that first stairwell. As long as he stayed put without moving, Jourdain couldn't pick him up without implant emissions.

Well, there were drawbacks to that sort of game, the brigadier told himself grimly. If Horus had his implants down, he couldn't see *Jourdain* or his men, either. He was limited to his natural senses. That ought to make him a bit slower off the mark when he opened fire, and even if he'd found an ambush position to let him get the first few men through the door, he'd reveal his position to the others the instant he fired.

"All right," the brigadier said to his seven remaining men. "Here's how we're going to do this."

Franklin Detmore ripped off another burst of grenades and grimaced. Whoever that Marine up there was, he was too damned good for Detmore's taste. The ten men assigned to mop him up had been reduced to five, and Detmore was delighted to be the only remaining grenadier. He vastly preferred laying down covering fire to being the next poor son-of-a-bitch to rush the bastard.

He fed a fresh belt into his launcher and looked up.

Luis Esteben was the senior man, and he looked profoundly unhappy. Their orders were to leave no witnesses; sooner or later, someone was going to have to go in after the last survivor, and Esteben had a sinking suspicion who Brigadier Jourdain was going to pick for the job if he hadn't gotten it done by the time the Brigadier got here.

"All right," he said finally. "We're not going to take this bastard out with a frontal assault." His fellows nodded, and he bared his teeth at their relieved expressions. "What we need to do is get in behind him."

"We can't. That's a blind corridor," someone pointed out.

"Yeah, but it's got walls, and we've got energy guns," Esteben pointed out. "Frank, you keep him busy, and the rest of us'll go back and circle around to get into the conference room next door. We can blow through the wall from there and flank him out."

"Suits me," Detmore agreed, "but—" He broke off and his eyes widened. "What the hell is *that?*" he demanded, staring back up the corridor.

Esteben was still turning when Galahad and Gawain exploded into the Security men's rear.

Vlad settled the charge delicately and sighed in relief. He was still alive; that was the good news. The bad news was that he couldn't be certain this was going to work . . . and there was only one way to find out.

He set the timer, turned, and ran like hell.

Alarms screamed as Oscar Sanders hit every button on his panel. Security personnel and Imperial Marines fighting to control traffic in the mat-trans facility looked up in shock, then turned as one to run for White Tower as Sanders came up on their coms.

The foyer door vanished in a hurricane of fire, and two men slammed through the opening. They saw the piled fortress of furniture facing the door and charged it frantically, firing on the run, desperate to reach it before Horus could pop up and return fire.

He let them get half way to it, and then, without moving from his position in the corner, cut both of them in half.

Jourdain cursed in mingled rage and triumph as his men went down. *Damn* that sneaky old bastard! But his fire had given away his position, and the brigadier and his five remaining Security men knew exactly where to look when *they* came through the door.

Energy guns snarled in a frenzy of destruction at a range of less than five meters. Men went down—screaming or dead—and then it was over. Two more attackers were down, one dead and one dying . . . and the Governor of Earth was down as well. Someone's fire had smashed his energy gun, but it didn't really matter, Jourdain thought as he glared down at him, for Horus was mangled and torn. Only his implants were keeping him alive, and they were failing fast.

Jourdain raised his weapon, only to lower it once more as the old man snarled at him. Horus couldn't last ten more minutes, the brigadier thought coldly, but he could last long enough to know Jourdain had killed his daughter.

"Find the bitch," he said coldly, turning away from the dying Governor. "Kill her."

Vlad rounded the last corner, skidded to a halt, and flung himself flat.

The charge went off just before he landed, and the floor seemed to leap up and hit him in the face. His mouth filled with blood as he bit his tongue, and he yelped in pain.

It was only then that he realized he was still alive . . . which meant it must have worked.

Agony drowned Horus in red, screaming waves—the physical agony his implants couldn't suppress, and the more terrible one of knowing men were hunting his daughter to kill her. He bit back a scream and made his broken body obey his will one last time. Both his legs were gone, and most of his left arm, but he dragged himself—slowly, painfully, centimeter by centimeter—across the carpet in a ribbon of blood. His entire, fading world was focused on the closest corpse's holstered grav gun. He inched towards it, gasping with effort, and his fingers fumbled with the holster. His hand was slow and clumsy, shaking with pain, but the holster came open and he gripped the weapon.

A boot slammed down on his wrist, and he jerked in fresh agony, then rolled his head slowly and stared into the muzzle of an energy gun.

"You just can't wait to die, can you, you old bastard?" Alex Jourdain hissed. "All right—have it your way!"

His finger tightened on the firing stud . . . and then his head blew apart and Horus' eyes flared in astonishment as two bloodsoaked rottweilers and a Marine corporal charged across his body.

"Your Majesty! Your Majesty!"

Jiltanith stiffened, then shuddered in relief as she recognized the voice. It was Anna, and if Corporal Zhirnovski was calling her name and there were no more screams and firing—

She jerked the door open, and Gwynevere shot out it, hackles raised, ready to attack any threat. But there was no threat. Only a smoke-stained, bloodied Marine corporal, one arm hanging useless at her side . . . the sole survivor of Jiltanith's security team.

"Anna!" she cried, reaching out to the wounded woman, but Zhirnovski shook her head.

"Your father!" she gasped. "In the foyer!"

Jiltanith hesitated, and the corporal shook her head again.

"My implants'll hold it, Your Majesty! *Go!*"

Horus drifted deeper into a well of darkness. The world was fading away, dim and insubstantial as the hovering smoke, and he felt Death whispering to him at last. He'd cheated the old thief so long, he thought hazily. So long. But no one cheated him forever, did they? And Death wasn't that bad a fellow, not really. His whisper promised an end to agony, and perhaps, just perhaps, somewhere on the other side of the pain he would find Tanisis, as well. He hoped so. He longed to apologize to her as he had to 'Tanni, and—

His eyes fluttered open as someone touched him. He stared up from the bottom of his well, and his fading eyes brightened. His head was in her lap, and tears soaked her face, but she was alive. Alive, and so beautiful. His beautiful, strong daughter.

" 'Tanni." His remaining arm weighed tons, but he forced it up, touched her cheek, her hair. " 'Tanni . . ."

It came out in a thread, and she caught his hand, pressing it to her breast, and bent over him. Her lips brushed his forehead, and she stroked his hair.

"I love you, Poppa," she whispered to him in perfect Universal, and then the darkness came down forever.

Chapter Forty-Four

Lawrence Jefferson gazed into the mirror and adjusted his appearance with meticulous care, then checked the clock. Ten more minutes, he thought, and turned back to the mirror to smile at himself.

For someone who'd seen almost thirty years of planning collapse with spectacular totality less than two months before, he felt remarkably cheerful. His coup attempt had failed, but the governorship of Earth was a fair consolation prize—and, he reflected, an even better platform from which to plan anew after a few years.

He'd gone to considerable lengths to set Brigadier Jourdain up as the fall guy if his plans miscarried, and the brigadier had helped by getting himself killed, which neatly precluded the possibility of his defending himself against the charges. Lieutenant Governor Jefferson had, of course, been shocked to learn that one of his most senior Security men had formed links to the Sword of God and had, in fact, used Security's own bio-enhancement facilities to enhance his own select band of traitors! The stunning discovery of Jourdain's treason had led to a massive shakeup at Security, in the course of which an Internal Affairs inspector had "stumbled across" the secret journal which chronicled the brigadier's secretly growing disaffection. A disaffection which had blossomed to full life when he was named to head the special team created by newly appointed Security Minister Jefferson to combat the Sword's terrorism following the Van Gelder assassination. Instead of hunting the Sword down to destroy it, he'd used the investigation to make contact with a Sword cell leader and found his true spiritual home.

It was a black mark against Jefferson that he'd failed to spot Jourdain's treason, but the man had been recruited away from the Imperial Marines by Gustav van Gelder (no one—now living, that was—knew it was Jefferson who'd recommended him to Gus), not Jefferson, and he'd passed every security screening. And if his journal rambled here and there, that was only to be expected in the personal maunderings of a megalomaniac who believed God had chosen him to destroy all who trafficked with the Anti-Christ. It detailed his meticulous plan to assassinate Colin, Jiltanith, Horus, their senior military officers, and Lawrence Jefferson, and if it was a bit vague about precisely what was supposed to happen when they were dead, the fact that he'd hidden his bomb inside the Narhani statue suggested his probable intent. By branding the Narhani with responsibility for the destruction of Birhat, he'd undoubtedly hoped to lead humanity into turning on them as arch-traitors and dealing with them precisely as the Sword of God *said* they should be dealt with.

Jefferson was proud of that journal. He'd spent over two years preparing it, just in case, and if there were a few points on which it failed to shed any light, that was actually a point in its favor. By leaving some mysteries, it avoided the classic failing of coverups: an attempt to answer *every* question. Had it tried to do so, someone—like Ninhursag MacMahan—undoubtedly would have found it just a bit too neat. As it was, and coupled with the fact that the dozens of still-living people named in it had, in fact, all been recruited by Jourdain (on Jefferson's orders, perhaps, but none of *them* knew that), it had worked to perfection. The most important members of Jefferson's conspiracy weren't listed in it, and several of his more valuable moles had actually been promoted for their sterling work in helping ONI run down the villains the journal's discovery had unmasked. Best of all, every one of those villains, questioned under Imperial lie detectors, only confirmed that Jourdain had recruited them and that all of their instructions had come from him.

The clock chimed softly, and Jefferson settled his face into properly grave lines before he walked to the door. He opened it and stepped out into the corridor to the Terran Chamber of Delegates with a slow, somber pace that befitted the occasion while his brain rehearsed the oath of office he was about to recite.

He was half way to the Chamber when a voice spoke behind him.

"Lawrence McClintock Jefferson," it said with icy precision, "I arrest you for conspiracy, espionage, murder, and the crime of high treason."

He froze, and his heart seemed to stop, for the voice was that of Colin I, Emperor of Humanity. He stood absolutely motionless for one agonizing moment, then turned slowly, and swallowed as he found himself facing the Emperor, and Hector and Ninhursag MacMahan. The general held a grav gun in one hand, its rock-steady muzzle trained on Jefferson's belly, and his hard, hating eyes begged the Lieutenant Governor to resist arrest.

"What . . . what did you say?" Jefferson whispered.

"You made one mistake," Ninhursag replied coldly. "Only one. When you set up Jourdain's journal, you fingered him for everything except the one crime that actually started us looking for you, 'Mister X.' There wasn't a word in it about Sean's and Harriet's assassination— and the murder of my daughter."

"Assassination?" Jefferson repeated in a numb voice.

"Without that, I might actually have bought it," she went on in a voice like liquid nitrogen, "but the megalomaniac you created in that journal would never have failed to record his greatest triumph. Which, of course, suggested it was a fake, so I started looking for who *else* might have had the combination of clearances necessary to steal the bomb's blueprints, have it built, smuggle it through the mat-trans, alter the mat-trans log so subsequent investigators would know he had, *and* get a batch of assassins into White Tower. And guess who all that pointed to?"

"But I—" He cleared his throat noisily. "But if you

suspect me of such horrible crimes, why wait until now to arrest me?" he demanded harshly.

"We waited because 'Hursag wanted to see who distinguished themselves in your 'investigation' of Jourdain." Colin's voice was as icy as Ninhursag's. "It was one way to figure out who else was working for you. But the timing for your arrest?" He smiled viciously. "That was *my* idea, Jefferson. I wanted you to be able to *taste* the governorship—and I want you to go right on remembering what it tasted like up to the moment the firing squad pulls the trigger."

He stepped aside, and Jefferson saw the grim-faced Marines who'd stood behind the Emperor. Marines who advanced upon him with expressions whose plea to resist mirrored that of their commandant.

"You'll have a fair trial," Colin told him flatly as the Marines took him into custody, "but with any luck at all—" he smiled again, with a cold, cruel pleasure Jefferson had never imagined his homely face could wear "—every member of the firing squad will hit you in the belly. Think about that, Mister Jefferson. Look *forward* to it."

Colin and Jiltanith sat on their favorite Palace balcony, gazing out over the city of Phoenix. Colin held their infant daughter, Anna Zhirnovski MacIntyre, in his lap while her godmother stood guard at the balcony entrance and her younger brother Horus Gaheris MacIntyre nursed at his mother's breast. Amanda and Tsien Taoling stood side by side, leaning on the balcony rail, while Hector and Ninhursag sat beside Colin. Tinker Bell's pups—including Gaheris and his regenerated leg—drowsed on the sun-warmed flagstones, and Gerald and Sharon Hatcher, Brashieel, and Eve completed the gathering.

"I do not fully understand humans even now, Nest Lord." The Narhani leader sighed. "You can be a most complex and confusing species."

"Perhaps, my love," Eve said gently, "yet they are also a stubborn and generous one."

"Truly," Brashieel conceded, "but the thought that Jefferson planned to implicate *us* in our Nest Lord's murder—" He bent his head in the Narhani gesture of perplexity, and his double eyelids flickered with dismay.

"You were just there, Brashieel," Colin said wearily. "Just as the Achuultani computer needed a threat to keep your people enslaved, Jefferson needed a threat to justify the power he intended to seize."

"And the Achuultani history of genocide made us an excellent threat," Eve observed.

"Indeed," Dahak's voice replied. "It was a most complex plot, and Jefferson's association with Francine Hilgemann was a masterful alliance. It not only permitted him to further inflame and sustain the anti-Narhani prejudices the Church of the Armageddon enshrined but gave him direct access to the Sword of God. A classic continuation of Anu's practice of employing terrorist proxies."

"Um." Colin grunted agreement and gazed down into his daughter's small, thoughtful face. She looked perplexed as she tried to focus on the tip of her own nose, and at this moment, that was infinitely more important to him than Lawrence Jefferson or Francine Hilgemann.

Jefferson's interrogation under an Imperial lie detector had led to the arrest of his entire surviving command structure. The last of them had been shot a week before, and it was even possible some good would come of it. The Church of the Armageddon, for example, was in wild disarray. Not only had their spiritual leader been unmasked as a cold, cynical manipulator, but the fact that she and Jefferson had intended to use their anti-Narhani prejudice to whip up a genocidal frenzy to support their coup had shocked the church to its foundation. Colin suspected the hardcore true believers would find some way to blame the Narhani for their own victimization, but those whose brains hadn't entirely ossified might just take a good, hard look at themselves.

Yet none of it seemed very important somehow. No doubt that would change, but for now his wounds, and those of his friends, were too raw and bleeding. Jefferson's execution couldn't bring back their children any more than it could restore Horus or the Marines who'd died defending Jiltanith to life. There was such a thing as vengeance, and Colin was honest enough to admit he'd felt just that as Jefferson died, but it was a cold, iron-tasting thing, and too much of it was a poison more deadly than arsenic.

Anna blew a bubble of drool at him, and he smiled. He looked up at Jiltanith, feeling his bitter melancholy ease, and she smiled back. Darkness and grief still edged that smile, but so did tenderness, and her fingers stroked her son's head as he sucked on her nipple. Colin turned his head and saw the others watching, saw them smiling at his wife and his son, and a deep, gentle wave of warmth eased his heart as he felt their shared happiness for him and 'Tanni. Their love.

Perhaps that, he thought, was the real lesson. The knowledge that life meant growth and change and challenge, and that those were painful things, but that only those who dared to love despite the pain were the true inheritors of humanity's dreams of greatness.

He closed his eyes and pressed his nose into his daughter's fine, downy hair, inhaling the clean skin and baby powder and stale milk sweetness of her, and the peaceful content of this small, quiet moment suffused him.

And then Dahak made the quiet electronic sound he used when a human would have cleared his throat.

"Excuse me, Colin, but I have just received a priority hypercom transmission of which I feel you should be apprised."

"A hypercom message?" Colin raised his head with an expression of mild curiosity. "What sort of message?"

"The transmission," Dahak said, "is from the planet Pardal."

" 'Pardal'?" Colin looked at Hatcher. "Gerald? You have a survey mission to someplace called 'Pardal'?"

"Pardal?" Hatcher shook his head. "Never heard of it."

"You sure you got that name right, Dahak?" Colin asked.

"I am."

"Well where in the blazes is it and how come I never heard of it?"

"I am not yet certain of the answer to either of those questions, Colin. The message, however, is signed 'Acting Governor Midshipman His Imperial Highness Sean Horus MacIntyre,'" Dahak replied calmly, and Jiltanith gasped as Colin jerked upright in his lounger. "It reports the successful reclamation of the populated planet Pardal for the Imperium by the crew of the sublight battleship *Israel*: Midshipwoman Princess Harriet Isia MacIntyre, Midshipman Count Tamman, Midshipwoman Crown Princess Consort Sandra MacMahan MacIntyre, and Mishipman Nest Heir Brashan."

Colin's head snapped around. His incredulous gaze met Jiltanith's equally incredulous—and joyous—eyes, then swept to his friends, the friends who were coming to their feet in joy that matched his own, as Dahak paused for just a moment. Then the computer spoke again, and even Dahak's mellow voice could not hide its vast elation.

"Will there be a reply?"